Praise for

How to Sleep with a Movie Star

"Kristin Harmel dishes with disarming honesty and delivers
a sparkling, delightful story about the push and pull
between being average and being a celebrity."

> —Laura Caldwell,
> author of *The Year of Living Famously*
> and *The Night I Got Lucky*

"A delightful, dishy debut. Kristin Harmel delivers a juicy,
behind-the-scenes peek into the fascinating world of
celebrity journalism."

> —Marianne Mancusi, author of
> *A Connecticut Fashionista in
> King Arthur's Court*

How to Sleep with a Movie Star

Kristin Harmel

NEW YORK BOSTON

5 Spot

Warner Books
Time Warner Book Group
1271 Avenue of the Americas, New York, NY 10020
Visit our Web site at www.twbookmark.com.

5 Spot and the 5 Spot logo are trademarks of Time Warner Book Group Inc.

Printed in the United States of America

First Edition: February 2006

10   9   8   7   6   5   4   3   2   1

Library of Congress Cataloging-in-Publication Data

Harmel, Kristin
  How to sleep with a movie star / Kristin Harmel—1st ed.
    p. cm.
  Summary: "A young magazine reporter having problems with her live-in boyfriend finds herself entangled with a hot Hollywood actor"—Provided by publisher.
  ISBN 0-446-69447-9
  1. Triangles (Interpersonal relations)—Fiction. 2. Motion picture actors and actresses—Fiction. 3. New York (N.Y.)—Fiction.
  4. Women journalists—Fiction. I. Title.
  PS3608.A745H69   2006
  813'.6—dc22   2005017757

Book design and text composition by Nancy Singer Olaguera/ISPN
Cover design by Brigid Pearson

To Mom, whose strength, wisdom, and kindness have always been an inspiration. I can never thank you enough. Everything I am, I owe to you.

Acknowledgments

A giant "Thank you!"

To Mom, to Karen and David, the best sister and brother I could ask for, and to Dad, Grandma, Grandpa, Donna, Pat, Steve, Grandma from Texas, Anne, Fred, Merri, Derek, Jessica, Gregory, and my entire family.

To my literary agents, Elizabeth Pomada and Michael Larsen, my film agent, Andy Cohen, Jim Schiff at Warner Books, and to my fabulous editor, Amy Einhorn, whose patience, kindness, and amazing editorial eye have made this whole experience a wonderful one.

To *People* magazine's wonderful Miami bureau chief Mindy Marques (who is a joy to work with); former bureau chief Joseph Harmes; my University of Florida editor (and the world's best boss) Steve Orlando; and my first editor, Al Martino, all of whom believed in me and taught me so much.

To my wonderful friends, many of whom are guinea pig readers for this book: Kara Brown, Kristen Milan, Lauren Elkin, Ashley Tedder, Megan Combs, Amber Draus, Cris Williams, Josh Henchey, Michael Ghegan, Jessica Cudar, Heather McWilliams, Martin Pachcinski, Gillian Zucker, Courtney Harmel, Stacie Beck, Jen Rainey, my Rock Boat girls (Matie, Amanda, Gail, and Michelle), Lana and Joe Cabrera, Megan McDermott, Samantha Phillips, Lindsay Soll, Amy Tan, Joan and Arde, Kristin Weissman, and Pat Cash.

To all the great people I've worked with, including: Cecilia Gilbride and Jane Chesnutt from *Woman's Day*; Gina Bevinetto from *Organic Style*; Liesl O'Dell and Cinnamon Bair from the UF Foundation; Lori Rozsa, Leslie Marine, Steve Helling, and Linda Trischitta from *People* magazine; Rebecca Webber, Caroline Bollinger, and Sarah Robbins from *Glamour* magazine; Nancy Steadman from *Health* magazine; Kate Kelly, Dorre Fox, Susan Soriano, and Christine Porretta from *American Baby*; Tara Murphy and Kelly Vahaly Long (two of the nicest publicists on the planet); Meghann Foye from *Woman's Day*; Pulitzer Prize-winning photographer John Kaplan; Anne Rach, Troy McGuire, Andrea Jackson, John Brown, Clayton Morris, Mitch English, and Dao Vu from The Daily Buzz; all my editors at *People*; my *Glamour* poll girls, the folks at The Daily Buzz, and all the great people I've worked with over the years.

To Matthew McConaughey, Ben Affleck, John Corbett, Joshua Jackson, Jay Mohr, Andre Benjamin (from OutKast), Ken Block (from Sister Hazel), and John Ondrasik (from Five for Fighting) for being truly nice people—the kind of celebs who make my job so enjoyable.

In memory of Don Sider, a fabulous mentor and one of the greatest journalists—and nicest people—I've ever known, and Jay Cash, the best childhood friend I could have asked for. You'll always be my superhero.

And to all you single gals out there: Value yourselves. *Be* yourselves. Your Mr. Perfect may not be a movie star, but believe me, he's out there. Never settle. And make sure you wind up with a guy who deserves someone as wonderful as *you*.

Cover Stories

10 Reasons to Have a One-Night Stand

Surely nothing good had ever come out of a one-night stand.

Except in a one-night stand, you actually got to have sex. Which was more than I could say for myself right now. It had been twenty-nine-days. *Twenty-nine days.*

Which would be okay if I were single. But I had a boyfriend. A live-in, sleep-in-my-bed boyfriend. That made the twenty-nine-days figure rather pathetic.

It wasn't helping that the headline "10 Reasons to Have a One-Night Stand" was splashed across the top of my computer screen. I stared at the words blankly, wondering if they were purposely taunting me. I didn't necessarily agree that there were ten or even five reasons that anyone should consider such a thing, but that wasn't the biggest problem.

It would be bad enough to be *reading* a self-esteem-stomping, flaky article about going out and getting laid by a random guy. It was worse when I was the one who had to actually *write* the article.

Besides, in my past experience, there was no reason in the world anyone should encourage that kind of thing. You always woke up the next morning with a hangover, dark circles under your eyes, and a strange guy in your bed who was bound to mumble something like, "You were great last night, Candi, baby," when your name was clearly Claire.

I must have been mumbling my protests audibly, for Wendy, *Mod* magazine's assistant features editor, popped up over the wall of my cubicle, an eyebrow arched. The first time I'd laid eyes on her a year and a half ago on my first day at *Mod,* she had looked somewhat nondescript to me. Then she'd smiled at me for the first time, and I was nearly blinded by a seemingly endless display of pearly whites. I'd been powerless to keep from grinning back. If you put Julia Roberts's smile on a younger Kathy Bates's face, you'd come pretty close to approximating Wendy, who had quickly developed into my closest friend.

Since she had dyed her hair red, the latest in a bimonthly series of shades that had little to do with her natural color, she'd looked suspiciously like she was beginning to channel the hamburger queen who shared her name. Today I was momentarily distracted by the neon-green scarf she had tied around her neck, which seemed to have nothing to do with her fitted black tee from Nobu, one of New York's trendiest restaurants, or her pleated red schoolgirl skirt. But I'd long since given up trying to figure out Wendy's style.

"Problem?" she asked wickedly. I couldn't resist responding to her mile-wide smile. I grinned back.

She knew I was having a problem all right. I'd unleashed a flood of complaints this morning about *Mod*'s editor-in-chief, Margaret Weatherbourne, as the elevator whisked us silently up to the forty-sixth floor. Beneath her seemingly flawless Upper East Side exterior, Margaret had been a bit off-kilter since the release of the recent circulation figures that had put our biggest competitor, *Cosmopolitan,* at 3 million while *Mod* stayed steady at 2.6 million. (This was still a notch ahead of *Glamour*'s 2.4 million. Thank goodness, or Margaret probably would have tossed all of us out her forty-sixth-floor wall of windows.) She had been spotted more than once mumbling words that wouldn't befit her classy persona in the general direction of *Cosmo*'s offices eleven blocks up Broadway.

At our weekly editorial meeting on Monday, she had announced that this was war. If it was the last thing she did, we would beat *Cosmopolitan* in circulation next quarter.

So I suppose it shouldn't have completely blindsided me when she called me into her office at 6 p.m. last night to tell me she'd had a brilliant idea and wanted to crash the August issue with a story about how wonderful one-night stands were for a twenty-first-century girl's self-esteem. Apparently this would be a circulation-raising feat that would restore Margaret to the status of Supreme Fashion Goddess of New York.

"But they're *not* good for self-esteem," I said flatly. The magazine was going to press on Monday morning, which meant that I'd have to turn around her latest ridiculous idea in less than forty-eight hours if I had any hope of having a weekend free from work.

Besides, I was just about the last person on the *Mod* staff who should be writing the article. Sure, I'd had my share of wickedly fun one-night stands in college (not that I'd admit it to just anyone) but I'd like to think that at twenty-six, I was past that. Besides, there was the fact that I'd been dating my boyfriend, Tom, for over a year now. (Even if he didn't *technically* appear to be sleeping with me at the moment. I was convinced it was just a fluke, or maybe a phase.)

So what did I know about one-night stands?

It wasn't even my department. As *Mod*'s entertainment editor, I was responsible for all of the magazine's celebrity profiles. I just happened to be the only editor still in the building, and my reputation as the "nice girl" had seemingly convinced Margaret that I would take on impossible projects without putting up a fight.

Note to self: Plan to reconsider reputation as the nice girl.

"Yes they are," Margaret said, of course offering no examples or proof to support her point that one-night stands were suddenly chic and "in." Her green eyes blazed, and for a moment I thought I would see fire shoot from her nostrils.

"One-night stands?" I asked finally.

"One-night stands," she echoed cheerfully. She waved a slender hand in the air with a dramatic flourish. "They're so in. They give the woman the power." I grimaced. Like she'd know. The only thing that had given her "the power" was that her mother's fourth husband (whom she still called "Daddy"—despite the fact that she was in her forties) owned Smith-Baker Media, *Mod*'s parent company.

"Power?" I repeated. I tried to think back to a time when one of my college one-night stands had made me feel powerful, but I was at a bit of a loss. Margaret glared at me over the top of her custom rimless Prada glasses, complete with diamond-studded arms, that had no doubt cost more than I was spending each month on rent.

"Just do it, Claire," she said firmly. "The magazine is closing in four days, and I want this article in there. And you'll write it." Before I could open my mouth to ask the obvious, she said with unmistakable finality, "Because I said so."

That's how I'd landed at my desk on a Thursday morning with a headache and a seemingly impossible task before me. The fact that I seemed to have no recent experience in the field of sex or anything sex *related* was only making matters worse.

"That screen still looks pretty blank to me," Wendy said over the cubicle, winking at me as I slumped over my keyboard and banged my head against my desk. Wendy had wrapped August earlier in the week—we all had—and was already working on September. Other than the layout people, who were rushing at the last minute to include room for the one-night-stand article and splash a teaser for it across the cover, I was the only *Mod* staffer scrambling to finish up for August on such a tight deadline.

"What can you say about a one-night stand?" I moaned, rolling my eyes at Wendy. It was pretty much common knowledge that I was the least sexually advanced of anyone in *Mod*'s offices, due to an inexplicable dating drought B.T. (Before Tom.) Wendy, on the other hand, was to sexual liberation what Manolo Blahnik was to shoes—a fearless leader and trendsetter, not to mention a face for a movement.

"Oh, *I* could say plenty," Wendy said, tossing her red curls over her shoulder and readjusting her Day-Glo scarf. "I mean, *I* could go out and do field research. Think *Mod* would pick up the tab?" She winked again at me. "In fact, I have a hot date tonight. Maybe I can test your theory then."

"A date? With a waiter?" I asked innocently. Wendy nodded excitedly, and I rolled my eyes.

"Pablo," she said, putting her right hand over her heart and doing a little twirl. "From Caffe Linda on Forty-ninth Street. He's *so* sexy."

"You think anyone in an apron who takes your order and brings you food is sexy," I muttered, trying not to smile. Wendy laughed. Around the office, we called her a "serial waiter dater," a title she wore as proudly as Miss America wore her crown. Wendy was an aspiring chef who was convinced that culinary greatness would one day be magically bestowed upon her if she ate out every night at Manhattan's top restaurants, sampling the creations of the city's best chefs.

As a result, she barely had enough money for rent and was in massive credit card debt, but she had an endless supply of waiters whom she somehow managed to seduce somewhere between her salad course and dessert. I still couldn't figure out how she did it. I was thinking of asking her for lessons.

"See, I'd be the perfect one to write this article," Wendy said. Well, I couldn't argue there. "Hey, you can write me off if you want, but my first piece of advice would be to drop Tom and go out and do some field research." Wendy raised an eyebrow at me. "How often do you get to explain a one-night stand to yourself by saying that you just *had* to do it for work?"

"You just want me to drop Tom," I said, wrinkling my nose at her. Wendy had never liked him. I trusted her—she was my best friend—but that didn't mean she was always right. And even if she was getting laid a lot more than I was, I didn't necessarily want to live like her, hopping from one man's bed to the next in a dizzying array that read like a *Zagat*'s guide.

Although on day 29 of my inadvertent reborn-virgin status, I had to admit, there was a certain appeal to her dating philosophy.

My friends back home in suburban Atlanta, where I had spent my entire childhood, were marrying off left and right, and at almost twenty-seven, I was experiencing the first symptoms of feeling like an old maid. With a closetful of useless taffeta in all the colors of the matrimonial rainbow, I was beginning to give new meaning to the saying "Always a bridesmaid, never a bride." Of course by New York standards, I was years too young to worry about marriage. But by the standards of the South I was already over the hill, matrimonially speaking. At friends' weddings (which now seemed to take place on a bimonthly basis), I was already hearing the sad whispers and standing on the receiving end of the pitying glances reserved for the eternally unmarriageable.

I had confided last month to the most recent of my newlywed friends that I thought Tom might be "The One." And I really did feel that way, don't get me wrong. After all, we were both writers, he made me laugh, we had lots of fun together. . . . It seemed so logical.

Of course, this was mere hours after my mother had taken me aside and reminded me, "Claire, you can't be too picky, you know. You're not getting any younger."

Thanks, Mom.

"He doesn't even have a job," Wendy said simply, snapping me out of the beginnings of a daydream about my own nuptials.

"He's writing a novel," I said, shrugging with what I hoped looked like nonchalance. I knew I sounded like a broken record, but I pressed on. "He needs the time to work on it. He's a really great writer, you know. He's always working really hard on it at home."

Wendy sighed.

"And it's totally normal that he doesn't want to sleep with you?" she asked gently. As my best friend, Wendy had, of course, heard the full and unfortunate details of my dry spell.

"It's just a phase," I muttered. Okay, so I didn't entirely believe the words myself, but they sounded good. "Anyhow, I think maybe he has a sleeping disorder or something. I mean, he sleeps all the time. Maybe it has nothing to do with me. Maybe I should suggest that he see a doctor."

"Maybe," Wendy said after a moment. She smiled at me mischievously. "Or maybe you should just go out and test this one-night-stand theory."

I rolled my eyes and turned resignedly back to the computer, trying to ignore her giggles. I gritted my teeth and tried to think about sex, which wasn't too hard, considering it had absorbed just about every one of my waking thoughts for the past few weeks.

⌒

By the end of the day, I had managed to dash off two thousand words I didn't really believe in and that didn't sound much different from any of the nearly identical "How to Please Your Man" articles we pushed on readers each month. Not that I didn't think you could find useful information within the pages of *Mod*—in fact, I'd read it religiously every month even before I worked here—but let's face it: We weren't solving any real problems here. At the end of the day, there would still be tensions in the Middle East, civil strife in Colombia, and kids dying of hunger in Sub-Saharan Africa. But at least our readers were wearing the right shades of lipstick, buying skirts with the right hemlines, and learning things like how one-night stands could raise their self-esteem.

In other words, all the important things.

This isn't *exactly* what I visualized doing when I graduated from college. I'd been the kind of English-lit dork who preferred a night with Joan Didion or Tom Wolfe to a day lounging by the pool with the latest issue of *Vogue*. And despite the crash course in the merits of Michael Kors, Chloe, and Manolo Blahnik that I'd received during my first week at *Mod*, I was, to the chagrin of many of my coworkers, still mostly a Gap girl. With the notable exceptions of the two pairs of Seven jeans I'd fallen in love with and the six Amy Tangerine designer tees I'd developed an obsession for in the last year, most of my clothes were from the sale racks of the Gap, Banana Republic, Macy's juniors department, or the ever-popular cheap chic of Forever 21 or H&M. The fifteen dollars max I usually spent on a T-shirt was a far cry from the $180 some of my coworkers spent on a white tee that could just as easily have come from Fruit of the Loom.

Thankfully, the atmosphere wasn't anything like that of the high fashion magazines where a few of my classmates from college worked. They had all been promptly assimilated and now had matching haircuts, matching Fendi and Louis Vuitton bags for every season, and wardrobes that consisted only of the most expensive and trendy designer clothes. Margaret just asked that we look presentable, polished, and stylish, which I usually didn't have a problem with, even on my admittedly meager salary.

After all, I had to look the part if I was going to inter-
act with the fabulously wealthy A-list set. I'd made the mistake my first year at *People* of dressing professionally but
without much of a stylish edge, and I'd quickly learned my
lesson. Spending a bit more on designer items—even if I
could afford just a scarf to pair with less impressive non-
designer threads—would go a long way. When you were an
actress decked out in tens-of-thousands-of-dollars of dia-
monds, strutting down the red carpet, there was just something about a reporter wearing a Gucci scarf that made you
just a bit more likely to stop and chat. Sad, right? But those
were the rules of the game.

And the articles. Sheesh, the articles. Don't get me
wrong—I love what I do. I love getting inside people's
heads (even if those heads often belong to vacuous celebrities) and finding out what they're thinking, what they're
worrying about, what makes them tick. So the job as senior
celebrity editor of *Mod* fits me with a perfection that might
surprise you, considering I originally had my sights set on
the lofty literary world of *The New Yorker*.

But it's the other articles, the in-between assignments
that a Prada-clad Margaret dumps on my desk at the last
minute, that drive me crazy. I mean, there are only so many
ways you can address your readers' "Most Intimate Sex
Questions" (clue: they're not so intimate anymore when 2.6
million women are reading about them); the truth behind
"How to Drop Those Last Five Pounds" (um, exercise and
eat less—duh); and the ever-popular "How to Know If He
Likes You" (well, men who like a woman usually want to
sleep with that woman—wait, should I be taking notes
here?).

Even the celeb interviews have their moments, when I
wish I could just bury my head in Jane Austen and slink back
to my college English class with my tail between my legs.

I became an editor because I love to write. And I took
this job at *Mod* because I really like one-on-one interviews

and profiles. As a little girl, I loved reading my grandmother's celebrity magazines: *People, The Enquirer, Star.* The lives of the beautiful people in the pictures seemed so glamorous, so exciting. Perhaps that was what had drawn me to celebrity journalism to begin with, although after several years of working in the field, I knew better than to think that everything was as it appeared to be.

At *People,* where I worked before I started at *Mod,* I'd made a name for myself in the business by breaking two major stories in the same year: the biggest celebrity breakup of the decade, the split between movie star Clay Terrell and pop princess Tara Templeton (thanks to the friendly relationship I'd developed after numerous interviews with the down-to-earth Clay); and the story of musical diva Annabel Warren's breast cancer diagnosis. (I had also interviewed her numerous times, so when the cancer rumors broke, mine was the only call she decided to take.) As a result, *Mod* had come looking for me. Margaret dangled a higher salary—and much more important, the chance to work on lengthy honest-to-goodness human interest profiles—and I was sold. And just like that, I became the youngest senior celebrity editor in the business.

I loved the job, but the move had made me some quick enemies. In the ever-gossipy world of magazines, a rumor had circulated (and lingered for six months) that I'd slept with Margaret's boss, Bob Elder, the president of Smith-Baker Media. Of course I hadn't, but professional jealousy tends to rage when someone several years shy of thirty snags a dream job that scores of women a decade older were after. I saw the suspicious looks sometimes, and there were still editors out there who refused to speak to me, but I was over it. I hadn't done anything wrong to get here. I certainly hadn't slept with Bob Elder, who was pushing sixty and was easily three times my weight. I had just done my job. And ironically, this wasn't *my* dream job at all, anyhow.

When I was an English major at the University of
Georgia, analyzing Shakespearean innuendos, I wouldn't
have suspected that four short years later, I'd be enthusiastically asking pop stars whether they wear boxers or briefs.
Or asking actresses whether they feel like Sevens, Diesels,
or Miss Sixtys lift their already-perfect butts better (as if
Gwyneth Paltrow and Julia Roberts *had* butts to lift).

Speaking of perfectly sculpted women poured into
designer clothing, I was snapped out of my reverie by the
approach of a heavy cloud of perfume as Sidra, Sally, and
Samantha all glided by in the hallway, as if on cue, on three
pairs of Jimmy Choos I couldn't have walked in if I tried.

Wendy and I called them "the Triplets." Somehow, mirac-
ulously, the three rulers of the fashion department roost all had
names that began with an *S*, were pencil thin, abnormally tall,
and had painfully pointy noses that seemed to match the
painfully pointy toes of their stilettos. They all looked perpet-
ually polished, as if they visited a beauty salon each morning
before they appeared at the office, which was entirely possible
since they normally didn't grace us with their presence until
after 11 a.m. There was never a hair out of place, never an inch
of face without perfectly applied makeup, never a moment
when their noses weren't fixed permanently in the air.

I caught pieces of their conversation as they passed.

"Oh . . . my . . . God," Sidra DeSimon, *Mod*'s coldly
beautiful fashion and beauty director, said, sounding
remarkably like Chandler's ex-girlfriend Janice, from
Friends. I wondered momentarily just how one managed to
develop a voice that nasal. "She was carrying a Louis
Vuitton bag from *last season*."

Sally and Samantha both gasped at this apparent mor-
tal sin.

"Last season?" Sally asked incredulously, scurrying
after Sidra.

"Ugh." I could see Samantha shudder in horror before
they disappeared around the corner.

I made a face as I choked on the cloud of Chanel No. 5 they left swirling in their wake.

How they managed to afford the latest in designer fashions on editorial salaries was beyond me. I suspected that, like many of the stick-thin, model-tall fashionistas who inhabited the hallways and abused the expense accounts of the country's top women's magazines, all three Triplets were trust-fund babies. It didn't hurt that their penchant for $2,000 pants and the latest Jimmy Choos, Manolo Blahniks, or Prada boots was assisted by their access to the magazine's fashion closet and a ream of eager-to-please designers they probably had on speed-dial.

In fact, just last week when I cruised through the fashion department to pick up some copy Wendy was supposed to edit, I'd heard Sidra cooing into the phone, "But Donatella, *dahling,* I simply *must* have that suede skirt for my trip to Paris next week. . . . Yes, *dahling,* I'd really owe you one if you'd messenger it over right away." The call was followed an hour later by the conspicuous arrival of a carrier case from Versace, which was whisked into the fashion department. The doors slammed shut behind it.

Sidra, the oldest of the Triplets and their fearless leader, was a bit of a legend in the New York editorial world. She claimed to have dated George Clooney for a month or so in the mid-nineties and had used that fact as a sort-of job reference throughout the rest of her career. She was known to frequently drop, "When George and I were dating . . ." into various conversations where the words really didn't belong.

For George's part, he denied that he knew her. That hadn't stopped her from dragging his name through the mud to her advantage—and to the endless delight of the New York gossip scene. Her name was a Page Six staple.

For reasons I still hadn't entirely figured out, Sidra had developed an instant dislike for me the moment I'd set foot through *Mod*'s doors as the magazine's youngest senior editor a year and a half ago. The more I got to know her, the more I suspected it was a case of clear-cut professional jealousy. I was fifteen years her junior, and I was just one step below her on the editorial chain. I'd done some checking up on her, and at my age, twenty-six, she had still been an editorial assistant at *Cosmo*.

My few attempts during the first month to ingratiate myself with a quick chat were met immediately with a cold shoulder, and to date, we'd never even had an actual conversation. Half the time she refused to even acknowledge my existence, and otherwise she badmouthed me around the office. My coworkers, thankfully, knew her well enough that her complaints tended to go in one ear and out the other.

Unfortunately, she also loved badmouthing me to people at other magazines who didn't quite know how catty and bizarre she was. Once, at a Fashion Week celebrity fashion show, I even overheard her telling a senior editor from *In Style* that I was a delusional intern who liked to pretend that I was *Mod*'s celebrity editor, and it was best to just ignore me and play along.

As the director of fashion and beauty for *Mod*, Sidra oversaw Sally and Samantha, who were clearly being groomed to become her clones. So far, it was working out. Sally, the fashion editor, didn't yet understand that dressing models in Gucci and Versace couture didn't quite fly with Margaret, who was—wonder of all wonders—smart enough to realize that most *Mod* readers didn't make enough money in a decade to buy the clothes that Sally would order for one shoot. Not exactly the best way to compete with *Cosmo* in the circulation trenches.

Samantha, the beauty editor, was responsible for the magazine's makeup tips. She was apparently equally confused, failing to realize that not everyone had the high cheekbones, full lips, and flawless complexion that she did. Of course, not everyone had the good fortune to be sleeping with Dr. Stephen McDermott, Manhattan's premier "Dermatologist to the Stars," either.

The only way to tell the Triplets apart, I sometimes thought, was by the fact that Sidra was the only one who had already invested $20,000 in breast implants by Dr. David Aramayo, arguably the best plastic surgeon in Manhattan. I was sure that the others weren't far behind. They were doubtlessly working out payment plans now.

I wished that Wendy hadn't gone home already. I would have loved to end the day by trading one-liners about Sidra. It was a favorite pastime of ours. And it was completely harmless, because Sidra liked to pretend, for whatever reason, that she had no concept Wendy and I even existed, despite the fact that we had attended editorial meetings together for the last eighteen months. If we didn't exist, then I figured our derogatory comments didn't matter much.

I looked back at my computer screen, which still appeared to be taunting me. A one-night stand actually sounded frighteningly good at the moment. Hell, even Sidra, who had all the warmth and sex appeal of the iceberg that took out the Titanic, was probably getting laid more often than I was. Maybe some men—apparently including George Clooney, if you believed Sidra—found that Fran Drescher-esque twang to be a turn-on. Maybe I could try holding my nose and squawking nasally at Tom tonight. Maybe that would unlock his chastity belt.

Was it possible I was grasping at straws here?

On that note, I printed out the two thousand words I'd managed to choke out throughout the day so that I could do a first edit at home that night, then I clicked on Save, closed the program, and shut down the computer. It was 6:30. On the off chance that Margaret was lurking somewhere in the nearly empty office, I knew I'd better get home before she could blindside me with another ridiculous assignment.

How to Live Together Happily Ever After

Okay, day 30. I was getting worried. And this *Mod* assignment was starting to make me just a little desperate.

"Is there something wrong with me?" I whispered to Wendy over the wall of my cubicle the next morning. "I mean, there's obviously something wrong if my boyfriend suddenly stops wanting to sleep with me."

"No way," Wendy said, just like I knew she would. "My question would be, is there something wrong with him? What red-blooded American man doesn't want to have sex?"

Okay, so she had a point.

"Tom," I muttered. But it wasn't exactly like he was *refusing* to sleep with me. It was just that he always seemed to be too busy or asleep when I was ready to go. Our timing was off. That was it.

Last night, day 29 had turned into night 30 with Newly Celibate Tom. That's two-and-a-half-dozen sexless nights for all of you who are keeping track. I'd even pulled out the big guns, slinking into the bedroom in a red teddy and a garter belt, feeling ridiculous.

"You're going to be cold in that," he'd said briefly, glancing up from the television for a millisecond before refocusing his attention on a rerun of *Gilligan's Island*, which, as you can imagine, created quite the conundrum for me. Was he into Mary Ann or Ginger? Pigtails, or evening gowns? You'd think the teddy would trump both.

Apparently not.

"You'd better put something on, sweetie," Tom added a moment later without glancing up. I gulped and tried again, leaning seductively into the doorframe, wobbling a bit in my stilettos.

"Tom," I'd said in my best sexy Ginger voice (he'd probably pick Ginger over Mary Ann). I'd paused, unsure of what to say next. "Uh, I have something I want to show you," I said throatily. I batted my eyelashes at him flirtatiously as he looked up.

"Do you have something in your eye, Claire?" he'd asked before turning his attention back to the Professor's latest ingenious invention, which Mary Ann appeared to be giggling about. "There's some Visine in the medicine cabinet if you need it," he'd added helpfully.

I'd heaved a sigh, stomped back to the bathroom, and changed into a T-shirt and sweatpants while Tom sang along with the *Gilligan's Island* theme song in the other room. He hadn't even looked up when I stormed by him and threw myself into bed, huffing and puffing pointedly.

It hadn't always been this way. Tom and I had chemistry from the beginning, which I suppose led to my willingness to tumble into bed within a week of meeting him at a writers' seminar in the East Village. Okay, I know, I know, you're judging me. I don't usually sleep with guys after knowing them for only a week. But with Tom I felt something instantly, something between an animal and an intellectual attraction, which I didn't know could coexist. He had this gorgeous, kind of tousled floppy hair that seemed to scream "struggling intellectual writer" and the way he kissed always left me breathless.

The seminar, a free program put on by the Eastside Writers' Group, had been about how to write a novel. I was impressed that Tom was already halfway through a draft of what he called "a slice of Americana mixed with a slice of suspense and a slice of intellectualism." All those slices left me a bit woozy, more than a bit awed, and hungry for more. After all, the closest I'd come to writing anything fictional was a short story I had to write for a college lit class. I'd gotten a C+. Here was this Prince Charming who gave great massages, could talk about anything from politics to poultry seasonings, and he was doing the one thing I'd always wanted to do with my life.

I was instantly in love. I stood by him a month later when he decided to quit his job peddling medical supplies in order to write full-time, and I'd been only too happy to let him move into my rent-controlled apartment a month after that so that he wouldn't have to worry about making ends meet while he wrote the Great American Novel. Sure, I was a bit hurt that he still hadn't let me read any of it. And I was a bit surprised that it was taking so long to write, but we were in love. And the sex was great. Or it *had* been, before it started to decrease in frequency a few months ago. Then again, he seemed more and more worried about his book. And I figured it probably bothered him a bit that he had lived with me for almost a year and hadn't been able to contribute to the bills at all. The few times we'd gone out to dinner and he had offered to pay, his credit card had been rejected, and I had to pick up the check. I didn't mind, though. I knew he'd pay me back when he sold the book.

"You deserve better, you know," Wendy said gently, breaking into the slow-motion replay in my head. "I've always said that. But I know you think he's right for you."

"He *is* right for me," I said. He was, really. He was cute, and smart, and nice. He made me laugh. "Maybe he's just going through a rough spot or something. I'm sure it's just our timing, you know? He's always up late working on his novel, and I'm fast asleep by the time he comes to bed. And I'm up hours before he is in the morning."

I paused.

"Unless . . ." I sighed. "You don't think I've put on a lot of weight recently, do you?"

"Are you kidding me?" Wendy asked, rolling her eyes at me and grinning. "You look gorgeous, as usual."

"I don't feel very gorgeous," I mumbled, looking down at my stomach, which wasn't nearly as flat as I remembered it. I shuddered and tried not to picture Tom raptly staring at the television while I tried to gyrate sexily against the doorframe.

"Jeffrey thinks you look just like Christina Aguilera," Wendy said triumphantly. I wrinkled my nose. I didn't quite know how to take the comparison from *Mod*'s art director.

"Pre- or post-'Dirty'?" I asked skeptically.

"Pre-," Wendy reassured me. "Like from her *Mickey Mouse Club* days. You know, when she was cute and thin, and had all that long blond hair."

"So you're saying I look like a sixteen-year-old *Mickey Mouse Club* kid?" Hmm, this was not so good for the whole sex appeal thing.

"First of all, Jeffrey's saying it. Not me."

"But you agree?"

Wendy paused.

"I think you look like Christina from the 'Lady Marmalade' video."

Hmm, this was a bit better. But not totally.

"Just because I have a bit of a frizz problem with my hair?"

"No," Wendy said with a laugh.

"Is it because I wore those slutty boots last time we went out?"

"No." Wendy giggled. "But that *was* kinda funny."

"Glad you were amused." Actually, my one public attempt at sexy in the last few months had ended in disaster, when I got my heel stuck in a subway grate and smashed face-first into the sidewalk.

"Whatever it is with Tom, it's not you," Wendy said firmly. She hesitated for a moment, then added, "Maybe you're right, and it is just bad timing."

I shook my head and sighed.

"I bet Christina Aguilera never has this much trouble getting laid," I muttered.

Note to self: Learn to dance like in that "Dirty" video. And if there's time, start a public feud with Britney Spears.

⁓

Having a live-in boyfriend was a bit like high-stakes poker, I figured. The similarities had begun to dawn on me one insomniac night as I blearily watched three hours of a six-hour *Celebrity Poker Championship* marathon on Bravo.

See, that was the great thing about my job. As *Mod*'s celebrity editor, I was supposed to keep up with what was going on in the kingdom of celebrity, at least to some extent. And I figured that if I couldn't sleep, watching Ben Affleck, Matthew Perry, and Rosario Dawson battle it out in a Vegas casino was *sort of* like working. At least that's what I told myself the next morning, when I hit the snooze button six times in a row and rolled into work an hour late.

Of course, no one noticed. That was the other great thing about my job. People are always late. No one ever notices. If only I didn't guilt-trip myself into arriving at the crack of dawn most mornings.

Anyhow, I figure in high-stakes poker, you're supposed to put everything on the line, do your best, and hope that you win. It's kind of the same situation when you take your relationship to the next level and agree to live with a person. You're giving up your independence and your solitude, putting all of your effort into making it work, and hoping for the best. Also, if you're not dealt exactly the hand you expect, you're not allowed to just get up and move to another table.

So I figured I was in it for the long haul with Tom, even if it wasn't going so well now. I mean, sure, I was being dealt a hand full of low cards at the moment—but in gambling, your luck changes all the time, doesn't it? And sure, I was betting everything I had—my heart, my future—but it had worked out so far. I mean, it had been a great year.

Tom had swept me off my feet (full house!), sent me roses every week (straight!), told me he loved me after just a month and a half of dating (three-of-a-kind!), and moved in a month after that (straight flush!). He was a good guy. He loved me. So what if the sex had dropped off? It was only temporary, I was sure. And any day now, I was sure he'd come up with the royal straight flush: the engagement ring he had hinted at a few times.

Come to think of it, maybe that's why he was acting so strange lately. Maybe he was planning to propose. Maybe he was just nervous, trying to find the right time.

That would explain a lot.

I turned back to the computer and tried to focus. Already, the office was buzzing with activity. Telephones were ringing, editorial assistants were running copy back and forth between editors, and Maite Taveras, the managing editor, was moving from office to office, chatting with senior and assistant editors about the September issue. I'd already told her that we'd have to put off our conversation until Monday.

"You have to turn your full focus to one-night stands, hmm?" she had asked with a laugh, pushing her shining black hair over her shoulder. I knew she shared my low opinion of Margaret and her inexplicable whims.

"Ugh," I'd moaned, rolling my eyes as she winked at me.

Maite held the third-highest editorial position at the magazine, after Margaret and the executive editor, Donna Foley. Fortysomething and beautiful, Maite had ascended the ranks of women's magazines by being a creative editor, a stickler for detail who always stuck with her writers' original tones. I'd liked her from the day we first met, and since then we'd had a comfortable rapport.

I turned back to the computer and tried to concentrate, but I was having trouble shutting out the rest of the office. Two of the copy desk assistants, both clad in Earl Jeans and black Bebe tops so similar I could hardly tell them apart, swapped dating stories over the desk in the office they shared, emitting high-pitched sonar giggles every few moments. Anne Amster, the wiry-haired senior features editor, argued with someone on the phone, and a group of senior editors clustered around a bulletin board, one of them jabbing her finger pointedly at a blown-up mock-up of the August cover, saying something insistent in an annoyed squeaky voice.

Then of course there was Chloe Michael, the television and music editor, who was always blasting the latest in pop music from inside the walls of her cubicle. At least she *claimed* it was the latest in pop music. I swore I'd caught her sneakily listening to New Kids on the Block when she thought she'd turned her stereo down low enough to get away with it.

In fact, come to think of it, a song that sounded suspiciously like "Hangin' Tough" was currently wafting down through *Mod*'s halls. Yes, I know, I should be ashamed that I even know the name. But hey, I was eleven once too. And I *may* have had more than one Donnie Wahlberg poster on the walls of my sixth-grade bedroom. I *may* have taken up playing the drums in middle school simply because Donnie played the drums. And I *may* have been to two NKOTB concerts where I sat in the nosebleed section, miles from the stage, convinced that Donnie was looking at me—and only me. But that's beside the point.

Jeffrey Zevon, the magazine's art director and the sole male on the editorial staff, had been pacing the hallway for the last fifteen minutes, and his nervousness was starting to rub off on me. As always, he was impeccably dressed—a tight black Kenneth Cole ribbed tee with gray Armani slacks that fit his perfect curves like they'd been made for him. "'Buns of Steel,' girl," he'd confided to me once. "I swear by those DVDs." He looked like he belonged at a fashion shoot for GQ. His dark hair was speckled with gray, but on him it was salt-and-pepper that said distinguished and sexy.

Unable to concentrate on the silly one-night-stand article, I watched him as his eyes followed Marla, the fashion department's summer intern. She shuffled down the corridor toward the fashion closet with her eyes downcast and her shoulders slumped. Marla looked like she wanted to disappear. She twirled a finger through her stringy brown curls, her slightly heavy frame covered in a balloon of fabric.

"Poor girl," Jeffrey murmured mid-stride, finally ending his impatient pacing at the entrance to my cubicle. He shook his head from side to side. "Tsk, tsk, tsk. Those princesses in fashion do it every time, don't they?"

"Do what?" I asked, my eyes following the self-conscious Marla, then settling back on Jeffrey. I tried to stop imagining the diamond ring that Tom might be picking out at this very moment. Princess cut? Channel set? One carat, or two?

"Torture those poor young girls," Jeffrey answered, placing a hand on my cubicle wall and leaning forward, apparently oblivious to the admittedly unrealistic visions of Tiffany rings dancing through my head. "They all come to *Mod* with big dreams of being fashion editors and leave thinking they have to weigh ninety pounds and be six feet tall to succeed."

"I know," I said with a sigh. But at *Mod,* they actually *did* have to weigh ninety pounds to make it under Sidra. So poor Marla was completely correct. I wondered if she knew about the last-season designer rule ("Those who recycle last season's fashions aren't worthy to walk the streets of New York," Sidra had once sniffed). Or how to hold her nose to mimic Sidra's nasal tone.

"They're getting worse," Jeffrey said in a stage whisper. "You should see the way Sidra talks to her. And the others, Sally and Samantha. They're just like Sidra. Something's up with them, girl."

"Something's up?" I repeated skeptically. Jeffrey tended to go just a bit overboard sometimes.

"I don't know what it is, but something's not right in their little designer world," Jeffrey said. He leaned forward again and grinned mischievously. "Maybe Sidra finally realized that all the collagen, chemical peels, and silicone in Manhattan can't make her look twenty-five anymore." I laughed.

"About time she realized," I muttered. It had been a long time since Sidra had looked twenty-five, but I had a feeling she didn't know that.

"You know that's why you piss her off so much, don't you?" Jeffrey asked, an eyebrow arched. He grinned at me. "You're everything she wants to be. She's just fifteen years too late."

I laughed and shook my head.

"Nah," I said. "She just hates me because I'm beautiful." I winked.

Jeffrey laughed—a little too heartily, I might add—then wrinkled his brow in concern and looked somberly at me.

"Really, doll, I'd watch your back," he said, suddenly dead serious. "With the executive editor position opening up, she's getting antsy and is bound to start backstabbing anyone she feels threatened by."

I stared at Jeffrey for a moment, sure I had heard him wrong.

"What?" I asked. "The executive editor position?"

"You haven't heard?" Jeffrey asked, his eyes sparkling again. He loved being the one to deliver gossip. "Donna Foley just announced that she's retiring on August fifteenth. The word is that Smith-Baker has decided to let Margaret hand-pick a successor in-house."

I felt my eyebrows shoot up in surprise. More often than not, magazines hired from the outside to fill major vacated positions. Then again, most magazines didn't have a woman like Margaret, with virtually no editorial skills, at the helm. I suppose that put *Mod* into a different category altogether. It was no wonder we were still struggling at sub-*Cosmo* circulation levels.

"Apparently, Margaret has said she's narrowed it down to two people," Jeffrey said, flicking his eyes around again and arching an eyebrow. "It's between Maite and Sidra, and they have the summer to prove themselves to her before she makes a final decision."

I stared at him for a moment, speechless.

"Sidra?" I finally asked, my voice hoarse. It made no sense. Maite Taveras was our managing editor. She'd been in the business for twenty years and was infinitely more qualified for the position. Granted, Sidra had been working in magazines for over a decade, but her experience was all on the fashion side. I wasn't entirely sure she was capable of stringing together an entire sentence that didn't include a condescending fashion reference.

I could just see it now. She'd probably require all *Mod* staffers to get breast implants and liposuction so that we'd weigh in at under a hundred pounds and match her two protégées in the fashion department. I resisted the urge to cast a suspicious gaze down at my own less-than-generous, decidedly A-cup bosom. Then again, I'd probably be out on the street, anyhow. My five-foot frame wouldn't fit with Sidra's supermodel ideal.

On top of that, of course, was Sidra's one-sided feud with me. I was no stranger to people snubbing me out of professional jealousy. It came with the territory of being the youngest senior editor in the competitive and often catty world of women's magazines. But Sidra took it to the extreme. She and the other Triplets were always snickering at my fashion choices, and Sidra had even been quoted on

Page Six once saying that a "certain extremely young celebrity editor" at a "certain women's magazine" had a habit of coming into work "drunk as a skunk." I'd confronted her, of course, and she had innocently batted her eyes at me and claimed that she *obviously* wasn't talking about me.

"Sidra," Jeffrey confirmed with an astonished nod, bringing me back to the present. "I know. I couldn't believe it either. But apparently Margaret is thinking about taking *Mod* in a more fashion-oriented direction. You know, more *Vogue*-ish. It's her latest plan to compete with *Cosmo*."

"Unbelievable," I muttered.

"And can you imagine?" Jeffrey continued, leaning in closer. "Can you just imagine how drunk with power Sidra would be? She would basically be running the whole magazine. It would be a complete nightmare."

"I guess it would be," I murmured, suddenly feeling very uneasy about my job.

"Stranger things have happened," he said. "Get ready for some catfights, doll. Sidra can be vicious when she's after something she really wants."

❧

I finished the one-night-stand piece by 4 p.m., and to be honest, I was pretty proud of it. Not proud of its content, of course—how could I be?—but proud that I'd managed to make it coherent and that I'd managed to come up with a list of ten reasons why one-night stands were actually a pretty good idea. (Hey, you actually got laid in a one-night stand, right? More than I could say for the current state of my relationship.) Wendy, the die-hard food aficionado, had insisted upon including reason number nine: "Because it's a good excuse to order breakfast in." (Mangia, the favorite gourmet breakfast delivery restaurant in Manhattan, probably had *her* number on speed-dial. It was only a matter of time before she ran out of Manhattan waiters and had to switch to Mangia's delivery boys.)

My personal favorite was reason number three: "Because you might really hit it off with the guy and begin to develop a relationship." (Wendy snorted, stifled a laugh, and said something about me living in Never-Neverland.) We'd both agreed that reason number ten was a good kicker: "Because we all know that getting laid feels pretty damned good." (Well, I had foggy memories of it feeling good, anyhow. And Wendy helpfully vouched for the statement's veracity.)

I didn't exactly feel good about myself for writing several pages in support of sleeping around, but the article could have been worse in someone else's hands. Heck, who was I kidding? Maybe I should have taken a stand and refused to do it on moral grounds. But I had better battles to fight.

Or more accurately, better battles to avoid, which seemed to be my latest combat plan.

Besides, our readers were going to go out and have sex whether I told them to or not. Hooray for them. Maybe I should write Tom an article: "Ten Reasons You Should Have Sex with Your Girlfriend Who Sleeps Beside You Every Night."

I knocked lightly on Margaret's door, which was ajar, and let myself into her office.

"Here it is," I announced grandly, plunking a printed-out, pared-down final draft of the article on her desk. She looked up, surprised, her over-tweaked dark brows arching upward. She lifted a corner of the draft with two perfectly manicured fingernails, looked at it from over the top of her perfect diamond-studded glasses, and reached up to brush a speck of invisible lint from the collar of her perfect Chloe shirt.

"Claire, darling," she said with that sappy formality and hint of a British accent she'd somehow adopted after a recent trip to Paris. She'd forgotten, apparently, that we all knew she was born and raised in Ohio. "I must have forgotten to tell you," she said.

"Forgotten to tell me what?" I asked suspiciously. I held my breath as she did what appeared to be a little pirouette behind her desk. Rarely a meeting went by when she didn't remind the *Mod* staff that her mother, Anabella, had been a prima ballerina. Those of us who valued our jobs refrained from adding that Anabella had peaked with the Dayton City Ballet. Nothing to be ashamed of, but it wasn't like she had performed arabesques and pliés around the world with Baryshnikov.

"I won't be needing this for August after all," she said casually, finishing her ballerina turn. My jaw dropped as I contemplated two lost and wasted days of my life. "We'll use it for September, of course, darling. I'm sure it's a great piece." She took the article from me and tossed it into a stack of papers on the corner of her immense desk.

"Um, okay," I said, my eyes following the article to her slush pile and returning to rest uneasily on her.

"But not to worry," she said brightly. "We'll be using the space for a feature on Cole Brannon."

I looked at her in confusion.

"But I haven't done a story on Cole Brannon," I said blankly. He was the hottest young actor in Hollywood at the moment, and had been for the past few months. He had shared the screen with Julia Roberts, Reese Witherspoon, and Gwyneth Paltrow in the last year, and his movies drew millions of excited women—many of them *Mod* readers— like moths to the light. His tall, muscular frame, eternally tousled brown hair, and sparkling blue eyes had launched many a fantasy.

On top of that, he seemed to have quite the social life, too. He was always being linked in the tabloids—not that you could always believe them—to various A-list actresses. And a certain blond pop princess had been overheard by a Page Six reporter telling a friend over lunch how spectacular he was in bed. Accordingly, *People* magazine had just named him their Most Eligible Bachelor for the year.

Margaret had never even suggested an interview with him. And most of our celeb stories were about women. It was an unwritten rule among the Seven Sisters of women's magazine publishing. Women wanted to read about women.

Although I supposed that any woman with a pulse would want to read about the delicious Cole Brannon too.

"Of course you haven't done a story on him . . . yet," Margaret said. "But his publicist has just agreed to let us speak with him, if we put him on the cover of the August issue."

I tilted my head to the side and squinted at her.

"Just think," Margaret said, gazing into space, already off in dreamland. "This could be the major story that helps us pass *Cosmo*. I can see it now. '*Mod* Magazine's Exclusive Interview with Hollywood's Most Eligible Bachelor, Cole Brannon!' The August issue will fly off the newsstands!"

Margaret's eyes were sparkling, and her collagen-injected lips were twisted into a bizarre smile.

"But we're closing the August issue tonight," I said blankly. That meant all the edits and editorial had to be in.

"But it doesn't ship until Monday morning, darling," Margaret said, smiling and ignoring my worried expression. "And your interview with Cole Brannon has been scheduled for tomorrow morning. That gives you two days."

"Tomorrow morning?" I squeaked. Margaret smiled thinly.

"Yes, *tomorrow morning*," Margaret mimicked me. "That will give you two whole days to get it in. I'm sure you'll be able to, darling. After all, I don't want to find out that my decision to make you the youngest senior editor in the business was a mistake. . . ."

Her voice trailed off and she looked at me meaningfully. I knew it was a threat. I didn't even bother to pretend I wasn't rolling my eyes.

"Anyhow, I trust you to get all the details right, so I won't be calling the research department in over the weekend," Margaret said casually. "You've never gotten a detail wrong before."

It was true. My coworkers teased me, but I was so neurotic that I had to quadruple-check every quote, every detail, every line of text. I had never gotten even a minuscule detail wrong in my entire career, a fact I was immensely proud of.

"And besides, did you know we have to pay the researchers overtime if we call them in over the weekend?" Margaret added, sounding astonished. "It cuts into our bottom line."

She looked momentarily perturbed. She was such a cheapskate.

"So I'm going to have Sidra DeSimon look it over instead," Margaret continued breezily. "This will be a good chance for her to try her hand at editing."

I could feel my jaw fall.

"Sidra?" I squeaked, suddenly finding it somewhat difficult to breathe. Margaret ignored me.

"Lots of women would love to be in your shoes, Claire," she said brusquely. "After all, Cole Brannon is the most eligible bachelor in Hollywood at the moment."

Which would probably translate into him being my dullest and most egotistical interview of the year so far. The glow of celebrity had long since worn off for me. I ignored Margaret's smile, which was clearly an attempt to soften me up and convince me that we were indeed comrades.

"But . . ." I began. Margaret cut off my protest with a single raised finger and a shake of her head.

"Brunch at Atelier at ten a.m. tomorrow," she said crisply. I groaned and rolled my eyes. Brunch. Fantastic. It had to be the worst meal of the day to interview people. Visions of celebs nursing hangovers while sipping Bloody Marys or gulping mimosas, barking hoarse orders at waiters about too-crisp toast or too-runny eggs danced through my head.

Besides, I'd been hoping to spend the weekend with Tom. No one—not even I—could deny anymore that our relationship needed some serious work. I did love him, after all, even if he was being a bit odd lately. And now, I would be spending Saturday with Cole Brannon and a looming deadline instead.

I was probably the only woman in America who wouldn't appreciate the trade-off.

"Of course we'll need the copy by Sunday afternoon so that the art department can do layout, Sidra can look it over, and it can be at the printer by Monday morning," Margaret said.

"But Margaret, I . . ." I began. Again, she cut me off with a raised finger and a clucking sound.

"Thank you much, Claire, darling," Margaret said with finality. I opened and closed my mouth without a word, because I knew it would be a waste of breath. "I'll expect that copy by Sunday afternoon. Have a lovely weekend."

"You too," I muttered, defeated, because I couldn't think of anything else to say.

⌒

"COLE BRANNON?" Wendy shrieked. I resisted the urge to cover my ears. "You're having brunch with *Cole Brannon*? At *Atelier*? You are, like, the luckiest girl alive!"

"Hmph," I grunted. I wasn't really in the mood to indulge Wendy, but I was beginning to realize there was really no way to get out of it. I plunked down in my chair and swiveled toward my computer in silence. I typed in my password and logged in to the news clipping service we subscribed to. I tried to ignore Wendy, who was still standing at the entrance to my cubicle, seemingly bubbling over while she waited for me to look at her. I took my time, avoided her glance for as long as I could, and typed "Cole Brannon" into the search box. Three hundred twenty-six entries in the last six months. Yikes. This guy had gotten a lot of press, which meant I would be up late doing my research so that I was fully prepared. I finally gritted my teeth and looked up at Wendy.

"*Well?*" she demanded, her eyes as big as saucers.

"Well, what?" I asked, because I really didn't know what she was asking me.

"*Well,* aren't you going to say something? What do you think? It's *Cole Brannon*!"

"I know," I said. I sighed and tried not to wince. "And it's not that I'm not excited. I mean, I do think it's cool to meet him. And yeah, I liked him in *Goodnight Kiss.*"

Okay, that was a lie. Actually, I'd *loved* him in *Goodnight Kiss*—it was one of my favorite movies—but that was beside the point. I tried to explain.

"It's just that, well, you know—I've told you," I said, well aware that my words weren't penetrating. Wendy had stars in her eyes with Cole Brannon's name on them. "They're never what you expect them to be in person. Sometimes I think I'd rather just see them in their movies or whatever, and not really know what they're like in real life. It kind of ruins it all for me."

Which was especially disappointing this time because I actually *liked* Cole Brannon. No doubt brunch at one of Manhattan's toniest restaurants would change my opinion. Besides, what if all those rumors about him being a ladies' man and a sex addict—which I didn't entirely believe, because the gossip often wasn't true—turned out to be right?

"They're not all bad," Wendy pointed out.

"I know," I admitted, offering a smile as a bit of a truce. "You're right."

"Matthew McConaughey, for instance," Wendy said helpfully.

"He was nice," I graciously agreed.

"And Joshua Jackson," she added.

"But who would expect any less from Pacey?" I smiled, but Wendy simply shook her head. This was serious business to her. There was no time for idle *Dawson's Creek* banter.

"Look, you have a date with Cole Brannon tomorrow morning. Can't you get a *little* excited?"

Unfortunately, I was taking a sip of my coffee as she spoke. I nearly choked.

"A date?" I gurgled, my eyes wide and my cheeks suddenly burning. "It's not a date! I'm interviewing him over brunch!"

"Hmph," Wendy said. She crossed her arms defiantly over her chest and leaned forward conspiratorially. She winked. "If I were you, I would tell people that it's a date."

"Have you been taking cues from Sidra again?" I asked her in mock exasperation. Wendy finally laughed. Sidra DeSimon's involvement with the tabloids was legendary. *Tattletale,* the gossip rag that hit newsstands each Tuesday, always seemed to feature a recollection from her about "a special moment" she had shared with George Clooney. Wendy and I still held to the belief that she'd never dated him at all.

"First stop, gossip columnists." Wendy winked at me. "Really, though, what else did you have to do this weekend? What could *possibly* be more important than having brunch with Cole Brannon? I mean, it's *Cole Brannon.*"

As if we hadn't already established that. I sighed.

"I was hoping to talk to Tom, you know? Maybe spend some time together to straighten things out."

Wendy shook her head at me in what looked a lot like disappointment. Of course, on her face, with her wide eyes and toothy grin, it was often impossible to tell which emotion she was trying to project.

"That's it," she said. "You're insane, clearly. You want to spend your Saturday with an unemployed creep who won't even sleep with you rather than with *Cole Brannon?* You should be committed!"

I refused to laugh. "Really, Wendy, I'm serious. It means a lot to me."

Wendy looked skeptical. I changed the subject before

she could launch into an anti-Tom tirade. Lately, her points were hitting too close to home.

"You're a good friend," I said seriously. I cleared my throat. "And I appreciate it. Now are you just going to give me a hard time or are you going to help me research Cole Brannon?"

Wendy looked at me for a moment, then grinned.

"Research him?" she said with a sly grin. "*Research* him? I'll give him some research!" She arched an eyebrow seductively.

"Okay, mind out of the gutter," I chided with a smile. "That's not even funny." Wendy laughed.

"Seriously, girl, you're on your own," she said. She checked her watch. "You know my rule. Never stay past five o'clock on a Friday unless I absolutely have to."

"It's a good rule," I muttered. At this rate, I'd be here all night. Not that there would be anyone missing me at home, from the look of things.

"Now remember," Wendy said with a mischievous grin, turning off her computer and slipping into her jacket. "According to *Mod* magazine, which of course should be your first stop for *all* questions of advice, it's great for your self-esteem to have a one-night stand. I think you should try that theory out on Cole Brannon." She was already down the hall by the time I'd balled up a piece of scrap paper to throw at her. "Have fun!" Her voice wafted down the hallway as she disappeared around the corner.

I laughed for a moment, then turned back to my computer screen, sighing. I hit Print and heard the printer down the hall whir to life as it started spitting out the 326 articles I had found about Cole Brannon. It was clear I'd be here for a while.

I sighed again, picking up the phone to call Tom.

"I just wanted to let you know that I'll be a bit later than usual tonight," I said after he answered on the third ring.

"Oh?" he said, sounding disappointed. "I'm sorry to hear that. I was going to take you to dinner tonight."

I felt my heart leap in my chest. I couldn't even remember the last time he had suggested going out to dinner with me.

"I'm really sorry," I sighed. "I have to do an interview tomorrow morning, so I'm going to be stuck here for a few more hours doing research."

"That's too bad," Tom said.

"Yeah." I groaned. "It's Friday! I just want to come home!"

"Don't worry," said Tom, sounding more cheerful than I'd heard him sound in weeks. "You'll be home soon enough."

"I guess," I said reluctantly, not feeling much better. Then I thought, maybe his sudden cheerfulness was due to the fact that he had found an engagement ring and knew when he was going to propose. A sudden warmth flooded through me, and I grinned.

"If you won't be home in time to go out, would you mind picking up some Chinese?" Tom asked.

"Sure," I said. My head was suddenly filled with images of Tom seductively feeding me lo mein noodles from perfectly poised chopsticks.

"Okay," he said. "I'll see you when you get home. Give me a call before you leave the office, okay, sweetie?"

"Okay," I agreed. "See you in a few hours. I love you."

"See you then," he said. Then the line went dead.

"Yeah, I love you too, Claire," I said to myself, placing the receiver in its cradle.

Top 10 Hot
Summer Reads

I'm sure you think I'm crazy. Half the women in America would probably kill for a chance to sit down with Cole Brannon.

Well, a few years ago I would have been excited. But that was before I started having to do celebrity interviews every month for *Mod*. They're not as exciting as they sound. It's usually just me sitting across the table from an actor, an actress, or a rock star while they indulge themselves in an empty-headed monologue embodying everything that's wrong with America. I mean, why should I care what Liv Tyler thinks about politics, or how Kylie Dane still struggles with insecurities, or how Winona Ryder really didn't mean it when she slipped some merchandise into her handbag?

The interviews aren't always bad. And the Livs, Kylies, and Winonas of the world all actually seem to be pretty nice people. It's just that after I've gone through a month of back-and-forth tug-of-war with a publicist, rescheduled our interview seven times, listened to briefings about what I can and can't bring up, and finally make it to an interview that has been mysteriously downgraded at the last minute from a two-hour luncheon to a forty-five-minute coffee break, I'm usually on my last nerve. But I paste the smile on any-

how, ask very *Mod* questions, and give our readers a profile of their favorite star.

Then it's back to reality. Sure, we can share a cup of
coffee at a hip, overpriced café, laugh together over rasp-
berry sorbet, commiserate over cappuccino, but then I
return to my world, and they return to theirs—and our
worlds never intersect again. At the end of the day, I shop
at the Gap while they're having their clothes individually
designed by Giorgio Armani himself while lounging pool-
side at his sprawling Lake Como villa. I worry that I won't
find anyone else if I break up with Tom, while they worry
about whether to date Tom Cruise, Leo DiCaprio or Ashton
Kutcher after their current relationship ends. I agonize over
spending $1,000 a month for a rent-controlled apartment
that's practically falling apart while they spend millions of
dollars on their Beverly Hills mansions or Manhattan pent-
houses and don't think twice about it.

Sure, I'm happy with my life. I don't think I'd ever want
to swim in the fishbowl of fame anyhow. But sometimes it
can be a bit demoralizing when I have to have a close-up
glimpse of how my life looks next to theirs.

So, hot or not—okay, grade-A gorgeous or not—Cole
Brannon didn't make the top of my People I Want to Have
Brunch with Tomorrow list. Really. He may have been the
sexiest guy in Hollywood—quite possibly in all of
America—but he was probably just as self-absorbed as the
rest of them. Maybe more so. Ego is usually directly pro-
portional to physical attractiveness, and by those standards, Cole's ego should be roughly the size of Texas.

Besides, I'd prefer breakfast in bed with Tom, preferably post-sex, to a boring breakfast with yet another movie
star.

Unfortunately, I had to remind myself, breakfast in bed
with Tom didn't actually appear to be an option at the
moment, however, as Tom had never technically prepared a
meal for me in his life. Then of course there was the whole

post-sex thing, which seemed equally unlikely. We would actually have to *have* sex at some point in order to be *post-sex*. Details, details.

I finally shut down my computer, grabbed my notes, and called the company car service—the one perk to working late. I could finish my Cole Brannon research at home just as well as I could here.

On the ride downtown, I resisted the workaholic urge to look over my notes and instead looked out the window at the twilit city streaming by me. Manhattan rolled by in waves of yellow taxis, strolling couples, and businesspeople trying to flag down rides home. The hectic glow of Times Square disappeared behind us as we drove, passing the Flatiron Building, then Union Square, where I often bought fresh fruits, vegetables, and bread at the farmer's market on Saturdays. The Virgin Megastore on Fourteenth flashed its bright lights as we drove by, and three-story posters of Madonna, matchbox twenty, Courtney Jaye, and Sister Hazel—all of whom I'd interviewed—kept watch over the city from the windows. As we passed the Strand, I recalled with longing the days when I had time to browse through their endless supply of books for hours, finally settling on a quick read or two to get lost in over coffee in Little Italy. It felt like ages since I'd had that kind of spare time.

Finally, the car turned left on Eighth Street. In a moment, we slowly crossed St. Mark's Place, where NYU students and Village funksters decked out in all the colors of the rainbow perused record stores, scanned the endless rows of silver rings, sunglasses, and scarves, or ducked into cheap sandwich shops. As we turned onto Second Avenue, I asked the driver to drop me at one of my favorite Chinese restaurants in the neighborhood, two blocks up from my apartment. It wasn't until I stepped inside that I remembered I'd promised to call Tom before leaving the office.

"I thought you were going to be a few more hours," Tom said when he answered the phone a couple of minutes later. I grimaced as my stomach growled, triggered by the sweet, spicy smells that now surrounded me. Mr. Wong, the store owner, stared at me patiently.

"I figured I'd just finish up reading all these clips at home," I said, smiling at Mr. Wong. "I wanted to see you."

"Oh," said Tom. He was silent for a moment. "So where are you now?"

"At the Chinese place. What do you want me to get?"

"You're already back?" He cleared his throat. "That was quick."

"I guess so," I said with a shrug. "Do you want the Szechuan chicken?"

"That sounds good," Tom said.

"With lo mein, white rice, and an egg roll?" I asked. Man, I knew him well. Either that, or we ordered Chinese way too much. Looking at Mr. Wong, who was still staring at me patiently, I realized it was probably the latter. I talked to him more frequently than I talked to my own mother—and he barely spoke English.

"Yeah," Tom said again. "Thanks for picking it up. I'll see you in a few minutes."

The line went dead, and my stomach growled again. I ordered quickly and didn't refuse when Mr. Wong, who must have been a mind reader, silently passed me a little bag of crispy noodles to munch on while I waited.

"Dinner has arrived!" I panted, pushing open the door to my apartment and catching my breath after climbing the four flights of stairs. If I hadn't gotten this apartment at a very reduced, rent-controlled price (my dad's cousin Josie had lived here for twenty years before I moved in, and I was lucky enough to share her last name—therefore, somewhat illegally, her rent-control reduction), I definitely would have insisted upon a building with an elevator.

"Hi, Claire." Tom emerged from the bathroom, drying

his hands on a towel. His shirt was half tucked in and looked like he'd been sleeping in it for a week. He looked every bit the part of a stereotypical struggling novelist. "You're home."

"Finally!" I exclaimed, setting the brown bag of Chinese food down on the kitchen table and thinking how cute he looked. The maternal instinct in me wanted to tuck his shirt in and spray it with wrinkle releaser. The sex-starved twenty-six-year-old who had been writing about one-night stands for the last forty-eight hours wanted to jump him. My stomach growled and reminded me to put off both alternatives until after I'd eaten. "What a day!"

Tom crossed the room and kissed me on the top of my head.

"Thanks for getting dinner," he said. He sat down at the table and started unpacking the contents of the bag, which Mr. Wong, who was not only a mind reader but also apparently a mechanical engineer of Chinese food, had assembled perfectly. "Can you grab me a Coke?"

"Sure," I said. I grabbed two Cokes—regular for Tom, diet for me—from the fridge and set them down on the table. "I'm just going to wash up, then I'll be out in a sec."

"Sure," said Tom, his mouth already full of lo mein noodles. "Grab me a napkin too, would'ya?"

"Yeah," I said, reaching under the sink. I grabbed a handful of paper napkins from the cabinet and put them on the table. "I'll be right back."

With Tom hungrily slurping lo mein behind me and the crispy noodles doing very little to fill the growling hole in my stomach, I hurried to the bathroom, flicked the light on, and closed the door behind me.

I washed my hands and looked at myself in the mirror carefully. I'd long stopped cursing the freckles that were splashed across my nose and both cheeks. I used to hate them—they didn't quite seem to go with my wavy, hard-to-tame blond hair—but now I thought they were sort of cute.

Even if Tom said they made me look like a teenager. At twenty-six, I was anything but.

I sighed and went into the bedroom to change into my favorite University of Georgia T-shirt and a pair of jeans. Stripping off the black A-line skirt and H&M boat neck tee I'd worn to work that day, I frowned as I caught a glimpse of my pasty white shape in our full-length mirror. In the past few months it seemed my thighs had started to thicken, and I'd added a few inches around the waist. Sure, I'd probably put on only five pounds or so, but when you're just five feet tall, every pound seems to show in triplicate. Of course, not one ounce had distributed itself to my breasts. Story of my life. I was still holding strong at the A-cup level.

Maybe the added cellulite in my thighs and pounds around my waist, which were really only noticeable with my clothes off, were the culprits for Tom's seemingly waning interest in me. Geez, didn't I know better? "You'll never find a man if you don't keep up your appearance." My mother's voice echoed in my head, as it often did in times of crisis. Easy for her to say. She did an hour of aerobics and an hour of Pilates each day. Of course, she had little else to do. Mortimer, her third husband, was a retired surgeon with one hell of an investment portfolio. He'd insisted she quit her job immediately after she married him, and she had happily agreed.

My stomach growled, reminding me of my original objective. I wriggled into my T-shirt and jeans, smoothed my flyaway blond strands, and, resolving to ignore my reflection for the time being, hurried back into the kitchen to join Tom at the table.

But Tom was already sitting back at his computer, his arms crossed over his chest, staring impassively at the screen. His plate and fork, still covered in remnants of noodles and vegetables, sat in the kitchen sink. His empty can of Coke stood vigil at his spot at the table.

"Thanks for picking up the food, Claire," he said

absently. I stared at the empty box of lo mein noodles that stood in the middle of the table, as if I might have some use for the three or four strands that clung to the inside of the cardboard container. "It was great."

I clenched my teeth and helped myself to the meager portion of chicken and white rice that he apparently hadn't been hungry enough to eat.

I didn't need to eat that much anyhow, I reminded myself. I definitely needed to drop a few pounds. I looked down at my stomach, which growled insistently at me again. So actually, Tom had done me a favor, right? He was inadvertently aiding my diet.

As if to second the motion, he burped complacently, uncrossed his arms, and started typing.

———

I was still poring over pages and pages of Cole Brannon clips hours later, after Tom had turned in for the night.

"I'm just really worn out," he explained. "I'll see you when you come to bed, babe."

I struggled to keep my eyes open as I read by the light of the table lamp. I was starting to feel annoyed at Cole Brannon, not because he didn't sound like a nice guy (on the contrary, he sounded surprisingly great in his interviews), but because he was now single-handedly depriving me of sleep and time with Tom.

Not that anything was guaranteed anymore in my time with Tom. But tonight might have been different. You never know. Maybe day 30 was the charm. I crossed my fingers at the thought, which temporarily made it impossible to turn the pages.

I sighed and returned to reading about Cole Brannon. I was already reading the final interviews, ones he had done just a few weeks ago, and the screen of my laptop was filled with pages of questions for him and notes to myself about topics I hoped to cover the next morning at brunch.

All the papers and magazines seemed to love him. The *Boston Globe* ran a piece by columnist Kara Brown last month that started like this:

> He's larger than life, and in person, Cole Brannon is no less impressive than he is on-screen. He holds doors like his gentlemanly character in *Friends Forever*, laughs at my admittedly poor jokes with the cheerful politeness of his character in *A Night in New York*, and makes intense eye contact with all the skills of his *Goodnight Kiss* charming rogue.
>
> He grins and scribbles his name graciously as giggling teenage autograph seekers approach the table, and he takes more than a few seconds to chat with each approaching fan.
>
> "I wouldn't be where I am without them," says the Boston-born Brannon with a self-effacing shrug. "The day I stop signing autographs will be the day I start worrying about the future of my career. I'm just so grateful that people like my work."

He certainly sounded nice. But, I reminded myself, he was an actor. It was his job to be able to convince you that his personality was whatever he wanted you to believe.

A short item from MSNBC addressed the recent buzz about Cole Brannon's rumored romance with a married actress:

> While rumors of a budding affair with Aussie actress Kylie Dane persist, Cole Brannon denies them.
>
> "She's a lovely woman, and I'm proud to call her my friend," Brannon said. "But it's ludicrous to suggest that there is anything more between us. She's married, and I would simply never cross that line."

He sounded genuine, but he was an *actor*, and rumors get started for a reason. But perhaps it wasn't true—I would give him the benefit of the doubt, as I tried to do for everyone I interviewed. It was only fair. No doubt he would expect a question about Kylie Dane in every interview he did now, anyhow, so he'd be prepared for my nosiness.

This may not seem very journalistically sound, but in a way I regretted that I would have to ask. I was a firm believer that a celebrity's personal life should be, well, personal. That was what I hated most about my job—that I had to ask things that were really none of my business. Personally, *I* didn't care who was dating whom and who was sleeping with whom. But many of our readers did. And as much as I hated having to look at someone over coffee and ask who they were sleeping with, and whether they were cheating on their wives or husbands, I knew it came with the territory. It was part of being famous. And oddly, the more fame someone achieved for his or her personal exploits, the more fame that person seemed to achieve on-screen or on the *Billboard* charts.

I mean, look at J-Lo and the whole "Bennifer" debacle. Or Colin Farrell and how quickly his bed-hopping (okay, and his sexy, lopsided grin) had catapulted him to stardom.

As a reporter, I simply couldn't ignore the hottest gossip concerning an actor. I would ask the question as politely and unobtrusively as possible, eyes downcast, feeling guilty.

The actors, in turn, would act annoyed at my intrusion, but I suspected they were secretly pleased that the buzz around them was so prevalent that it would be part of our interview.

It was all part of the dance I did with every celeb who had graced our cover since I started working for *Mod*.

The last article in the series of clips was a small Page Six item:

Despite rumors of a romance with actress Kylie Dane, Cole Brannon was seen earlier this week canoodling

How to Meet a
Movie Star

I was at the Ritz on Central Park South at quarter to ten,
fifteen minutes before the scheduled brunch with the
hottest guy in Hollywood. I rubbed the sleep out of my eyes
as I waited in the entryway to Atelier, the Ritz's premiere
dining room, and one of the chicest restaurants in New
York. And by chic, I mean ostentatious. Pretentious.
Showy. Froufrou.

I was surprised, in a way, that Cole Brannon would
choose such a place to meet. But who could tell with celebs
these days? Maybe his everyday, middle-class Boston-born
persona had been replaced with that of a wealthy, caviar-
loving Upper East Sider. It figured. I felt embarrassingly out
of my element as I shifted from foot to foot and watched a
parade of Gucci, Prada, and Escada float by.

I always hated meeting celebrities for meals. On the
surface it seemed glamorous. I got to dine out at exclusive
restaurants that I wouldn't, in a million years, be able to
afford on my own. Once the celebrity had glided in, twenty
minutes late and often armed with a makeup artist, a publicist, and a personal assistant, our table would immediately
become the center of attention, the glowing core of our own
solar system. I'd be the object of envy for dozens of other
diners who were no doubt wondering who I was, and why

a plain girl like me was dining with Julia Roberts, Paris Hilton, or Gwen Stefani.

Then it became an exercise in futility. The actor/singer/model in question would nearly forget I was there, even as I asked questions. Instead of making eye contact and truly having a conversation with me, the celeb would multitask like a pro: scanning the room to bask in the adoration of fans, checking pager and cell phone messages, sipping champagne, and whispering to either the personal assistant or publicist, all at once. I always felt like I was somehow intruding on their little private world, despite the fact that *Mod's* corporate card was paying for the meal for this actor/singer/model and her entourage—and often a doggie bag of food which was, quite literally, for her dog.

So you can imagine why brunch with the gorgeous Cole Brannon didn't excite me quite as much as it perhaps should have. I had no doubt that he would a) be late, b) arrive with an impressive entourage and possibly a model or actress he'd shacked up with the night before, c) be either hung over or simply too bored with me to answer my questions, and d) spend the interview trying to catch a glimpse of his perfect features in the backs of spoons, glossy undersides of serving trays, and the spotless silver carafes the busy waiters bustled by with.

I just wasn't in the mood for yet another prima donna star this morning. But I had a job to do, and I had little choice but to do it.

Ten minutes after arriving at Atelier, I decided out of desperation that I would check in for our reservation and Cole Brannon could join me when he arrived. I was dying for a cappuccino, and I didn't think he'd mind if I got a jump-start on my morning caffeine fix. I asked for a table near the door and watched the entrance intently, knowing that I'd see him when he came in.

The tables were spread far apart, and the soaring ceiling gave the room an airy feeling. The dark wood and tan fabric melded together in classy (a little nondescript if you ask me) harmony. A myriad of colorful modern art, clearly as expensive as it was bright, lined the walls. Expressionless waiters bustled back and forth, nearly running, while the wealthy patrons tittered lightly, using precisely the correct silverware from their selections of roughly a dozen utensils. My manners were nowhere near that advanced. After the primary three utensils and the salad fork, I was lost.

Acutely aware that my pale pink Zara shell and black Gap pencil skirt had no more place here than I did, I slunk down in my chair and tried to blend in with the artwork. Unfortunately, it was much more colorful and exciting than I was at the moment.

When Cole Brannon still hadn't arrived at 11:00, my cappuccino was gone, and my good humor was wearing off. Celebrities often strolled in a bit late, but a whole hour? When I'd given up a weekend with Tom to slave over a last-minute interview and profile? I'd been all ready to give Cole Brannon the benefit of the doubt—especially since he'd actually sounded *nice* and down-to-earth in the overwhelming majority of clips that were now emblazoned on my brain— but this was testing my patience. It was becoming increasingly clear he was just another prima donna star, making a reporter wait while he took his sweet time primping, or sleeping off a hangover, or whatever he was doing. I took out my cell phone to dial Cole's publicist, Ivana Donatelli, who had set up this meeting, but I was put through directly to her voice mail. Apparently, she wasn't up either.

Five minutes later, after I'd grumpily waved away yet another attempt by the obsequious waiter to bring me another cappuccino, my cell phone rang. The caller ID said "Unavailable." I was sure it was Ivana calling back.

"Hello?" I snapped, knowing that my voice must have sounded almost as peeved as I was beginning to feel.

"Claire?" The male voice wasn't the one I was expecting, but it sounded vaguely familiar all the same. It was far too deep and husky to belong to Tom. But there was something about the way he softened the *r* sound in "Claire" that rang a bell.

"Yes . . ." I said slowly, still trying to place the somehow familiar intonation.

"It's Cole." He cleared his throat, and I could feel my eyebrows arch upward in surprise. "Um, Cole Brannon," he clarified, as if I might be receiving calls from another man named Cole. Well, this is a first, I thought huffily, squaring my shoulders in annoyance. I'd never actually had a celebrity call me *himself* to cancel, or blow me off, or whatever it was he was about to do.

"Hi," I said. I couldn't think of anything else to say other than *Where the hell are you?* But that wouldn't be appropriate, now would it? So I bit my tongue and waited.

"Are you here? At the restaurant, I mean?" His voice sounded just as sexy as it always did through the Dolby Surround Sound of theaters, but it wasn't softening me up much.

"Yes, at Atelier," I said grumpily. "I'm at a table near the door. *By myself*." I stressed the last part. "Where are *you*?" Just because he was a gorgeous movie star, it didn't mean he could stand me up.

"Oh my God." Cole Brannon started to laugh. Despite myself, the deep, resonating chuckle made me relax a bit. "You've been here for over an hour!"

"Yes, I have," I said rather sternly, hating that I loved his deep voice. I reminded myself that I was supposed to be annoyed at him. Then it hit me. "Wait, how did you know that?"

"Because I've been sitting two tables over from you the whole time!"

To my horror, I suddenly realized that the laughing wasn't coming just from the phone but from a man in a baseball cap, also sitting alone at a table several feet behind me. The cap was pulled low over his eyes, and I hadn't given him a second glance when I'd arrived at the restaurant fifteen minutes early. Celebrities were *never* early, so I was sure I'd beaten Cole that morning. I hadn't given the restaurant more than a cursory glance.

"Hang on, I'm coming over," Cole said quietly, and I heard my cell phone click off. For a second I couldn't move, and I continued to hold my silent phone to my ear, frozen in embarrassment. By now, my cheeks were fully ablaze, and I wondered if I'd ever felt dumber. (The answer was no, in case you were wondering. This was pretty much the height of my stupidity track record.)

I'd kept the hottest star in Hollywood waiting for more than an hour because I hadn't noticed him. This was a new low in brainlessness, even for me. This definitely topped the sexy-heel-caught-in-the-subway-grate fiasco.

"Hello there," Cole Brannon said cheerfully, arriving at my side. I looked up warily. For the first time I noticed his brilliant blue eyes and strands of his legendary tousled brown hair peeking out from under his Red Sox cap. In person, his face looked even more perfect than it did on the big screen or in the magazine spreads he'd been featured in. Corny as it sounds, he truly looked like he'd been chiseled by Michelangelo himself.

There was a deep dimple in his chin, and when he smiled, adorable dimples appeared in his perfectly tanned cheeks, too. I usually hated sideburns, but I suddenly loved the way his zigzagged down his jawline, ending evenly at the bottom of his earlobes, in closely trimmed perfection. He had a small cluster of eight or so freckles across the bridge of his nose, which I'd never noticed on-screen, and there was a small, nearly imperceptible scar on the underside of his jaw. I remembered reading in the clips that it was from a football injury he'd suffered in high school.

He was dressed simply in faded jeans (which looked like anything but designer) and a navy collared shirt that stretched perfectly over his well-defined contours.

But what stood out most of all was how good he actually looked close-up. I'd been around the merry-go-round of the celebrity world long enough to grasp the fact that people didn't always look as good in person as they did on-screen. Male movie stars always seemed to be shorter in person. Their hairlines always seemed to be receding (I'd even spotted cases of hairplugs up close in two of Hollywood's most popular leading men). Their heads, oddly, tended to seem inordinately large for their bodies. And the faces that looked most perfect on the big screen tended to look so Botoxed in person that they appeared to be expressionless masks.

But Cole was perfect. *Perfect.* His face looked like it had never had a blemish in its life, his frame was perfectly proportioned, and his eyes really did sparkle with the same intensity they seemed to have on-screen. I'd always assumed that his bright baby blues were a cinematic trick, but here they were, sparkling right at me. There were laugh lines around his eyes and on his forehead, which gave away his lack of Botox experience, and he smiled a smile that looked very real. He had just a bit of dark stubble on his chin, and his dark hair was blissfully hairplug-free.

Up until this moment, I had always thought I was not so superficial as to be taken in by looks. But this was a new situation altogether. This was, without a doubt, the most attractive human being I'd ever laid eyes on. He was stunning.

Of course, I took all this in through eyes lowered in embarrassment.

"Oh my God," I said, standing up and extending a hand, which I realized was shaking. I was suddenly having a little trouble breathing. "I am so, so sorry. I didn't notice you there." I was fiercely aware of my red cheeks. Then I noticed something as Cole finished shaking my hand and grabbed the chair next to mine. He didn't look angry. Instead, he was grinning at me. And laughing. Was I missing something? He even appeared to be laughing *with* me instead of *at* me. But perhaps my laugh-detecting senses were off.

He gestured for me to sit down, and even pushed my chair in before he took a seat.

"Hey, I guess that's an endorsement for the disguise then, right?" he said. As I stared at him, unsure of what to say, it suddenly occurred to me why people sometimes described eyes as "twinkling." That's what his blues were doing at the moment.

"I'm . . . I mean . . . Um, wow, I am *so* embarrassed," I stammered, finally allowing myself a nervous giggle. "How long have you been here?" Maybe he hadn't been waiting that long after all. Maybe I was less of a jackass than I'd guessed.

"Oh, an hour and a half, or so," Cole said, still grinning.

I reddened further. Yes, I was definitely a full-fledged jackass.

"Oh no," I moaned. "What an idiot I am. I mean, I know what you look like—obviously." Okay, that sounded dumb. "And I still didn't notice you."

Cole laughed again, and I stared in astonishment. He really wasn't mad. I must have been missing something. I half expected his bodyguard to pounce out from behind a potted plant in the corner and kick me out. No celeb I'd ever met would laugh something like this off. But there was something different about Cole Brannon. And there were no bodyguards among the bushes.

Really. I checked.

"Actually, *I* noticed *you,* but I thought to myself, there's no way that's the girl I'm supposed to meet," Cole said. "I mean, Ivana told me you were much older."

Huh? I'd never even met his publicist. Why on earth would she have assumed that? Unless he meant . . .

"I'm not as young as I look," I said, suddenly defensive.

"I mean, I know I look like a teenager. It's hard not to when you're only five feet tall. . . ." I couldn't help but think of Jeffrey's *Mickey Mouse Club* comparison. I realized that Cole was laughing again, so I shut my mouth.

Perhaps I was being a bit overly sensitive.

"I didn't mean that at all!" he exclaimed. My blush deepened. Great, now I was misinterpreting his words. "And for the record, you don't look like a teenager. You look every bit grown woman to me." I could feel the blood rising to my face in a full-fledged blush again. "And wow, five feet tall? That makes me more than a foot taller than you."

One foot and four inches to be exact, I thought abstractedly, recalling the info on his bio sheet.

"Can I call you Shorty? Or maybe Little Lady?" he asked, feigning seriousness. I finally laughed.

"If it will help me get back into your good graces," I said. I felt the breath go out of me as I heaved a sigh of relief and smiled at him.

"Not that you were ever *out* of my good graces," he said. "But I'll keep those nicknames in mind, in case I ever need them."

I laughed again, and I knew that the ice had been broken. In the space of less than five minutes, this had gone from being the worst-begun interview to being the best. I knew it would be a good morning.

Then again, I suppose that any morning spent with the Adonis-next-door should qualify as a good morning.

"Look," said Cole, leaning forward conspiratorially. His blue eyes were wide and his perfectly white teeth gleamed just inches from me. "What do you say we go somewhere else for breakfast?"

"Um, okay," I said, surprised and a bit disappointed. Geez! Celebrities and their demands! Just when I'd started to think he was different, here he was rearranging the schedule. He'd probably want to go to some place even more expensive. Nobu maybe? Or Tavern on the Green? Great.

"I mean, we can stay if you want." Cole paused, looking at me with concern as I shook my head. "But did you look at this menu? I mean, who eats *Eggs en Cocotte with Truffle Jus* for breakfast? What the heck is that, anyhow?"

He looked up from the menu just as a waiter walked by carrying what appeared to be exactly that egg dish (complete with thyme-roasted potatoes and the twenty-five-dollar caviar supplement offered in the menu). We both collapsed in laughter, and my heart mysteriously fluttered as his right arm brushed my left. I shook the feeling off and chided myself. I knew better than to feel giddy about celebrities.

Even if they had gorgeous blue eyes and the most perfect smile I'd ever seen.

"And look at the price!" Cole exclaimed as we finished laughing, looking back at the menu. "That was thirty-six dollars of egg that just walked by! Are you kidding me?"

"It is sort of ridiculous," I admitted. I tilted my head to the side and looked at him intently, trying not to look accusatory. "But why did you want to meet here, then?"

"Me?" he asked. He shook his head and leaned back in his seat. "Ha! My publicist Ivana suggested it. It's her favorite restaurant. She wanted to meet us and sit in on the interview, but I see from the looks of it that she must have overslept." He laughed again, and I realized suddenly that his laugh sounded different in person than it did at the movies. It was richer, fuller, more musical. "So, what do you say we get out of here before Ivana decides to make an appearance? I need some real breakfast. How about bacon, eggs, and the greasiest hash browns in Manhattan?"

I grinned. "Lead the way."

⟋⟍

Ten minutes later, after arguing about who would pay for my ten-dollar cappuccino—I finally won by insisting that it was against *Mod*'s policy to let a source pay for anything—

we were out on the street, strolling east at the bottom of Central Park. Amazingly, no one had recognized Cole yet. Sixty-story buildings soared around us, and the silence of Central Park was fast disappearing behind us, but we hadn't been rushed by a single fan or even given a second glance. Then again, we were in an area of the city so ritzy that its residents were probably too self-absorbed to notice if a seven-foot green alien with three eyes wandered by.

"Are we going to hail a taxi?" I asked, trying to sound casual. I still couldn't figure out why being with Cole Brannon was making me feel so giddy. I had interviewed dozens of A-listers, and I hadn't reacted this way since the first few A-listers I'd talked to. And that had been years ago.

"A taxi?" he said, playfully nudging me. My skin tingled oddly where he'd touched it. "No way, Little Lady. We're taking the subway!"

"The subway?" I looked up at him incredulously. That was impossible. Every movie star I'd ever known had traveled by limo or chauffeured car—or at the very least, in their own luxury SUV. They never took the subway. Only anonymous nobodies like me took the subway.

"Hell, yeah," Cole said cheerfully, oblivious to my confusion. He looped his arm playfully through mine for a moment. "Look at this. No one recognizes me. Isn't this fun?" It was true. I took a quick look around to make sure we were actually surrounded by live, movie-going humans. It looked that way. I was baffled.

"In my defense, you've got that hat pulled so low I can hardly see your face," I said, grinning up at him. From my vantage point, I had a perfect view of his cleft chin and perfect dimples, which grew even deeper every time he cracked a smile—which was a lot.

"Excuses, excuses," he said, grinning down at me. "But hey, you have to hand it to me. Am I the master of disguise or what?"

"That you are," I said. *Not that looks that good should be covered up,* I wanted to say, but I bit my tongue. After all, I was Professional Claire. *Professional.* I tried to forget that I was also Sex-Starved Claire. It was totally beside the point.

"You are aware, aren't you, that you're part of the disguise?" Cole asked conspiratorially.

"Huh?"

"Well, as far as all these passersby are concerned"—he gestured grandly to the people bustling by—"you and I are just a young couple out for a romantic stroll." My cheeks were suddenly on fire. For a moment I forgot that Tom existed, as I realized that indeed I was out on what looked like a romantic amble with Cole Brannon.

Hmm, I could get used to this.

"I mean, all these people are expecting that Cole Brannon would be out with Kylie Dane, not a beautiful young blonde," he continued, smiling at me as we walked. My jaw dropped, and I wasn't sure for a moment whether it was because he himself had broached the topic of Kylie Dane, or because he'd referred to me as a beautiful young blonde. (Did Cole Brannon really think *I* was beautiful?) As a result, my response came out as a wordless gurgle, and he laughed again.

"No worries," he said quickly. He put a hand on my arm and stopped for a minute. I stopped too, and we stood there in the middle of a parting sea of oblivious passersby. He leaned down, his face inches from my right cheek. "I know you have to ask me about Kylie Dane," he whispered. I could feel myself blushing again as his breath tickled my ear. In fact, I was surprised that the sheer heat emanating from my face hadn't burned him by this time. "But it's not true. I swear to God. Really, she's a nice woman, but there's nothing between us. I would never, ever, ever get romantically involved with a married woman. I'm so sick of all the rumors, you know? I mean, this sounds crazy, but it hurts my feelings sometimes."

I scrambled to dig my pen and notepad out of my shoulder bag and jotted down the words he'd just uttered.

"I mean, I hate that anyone would think I have no morals and would just hook up with someone who's married," he continued, sounding pained. "Is she a beautiful woman? Yes. But that doesn't necessarily mean I want to sleep with her. Or that she wants to sleep with me, for that matter. I just don't get how people make this stuff up in the tabloids. And you can quote me on that. All of it. In fact, please do. I hate all this tabloid crap."

He shook his head and made a face that reminded me so much of a lost little boy that I instantly wanted to cup his face in my hands and tell him everything would be okay. Fortunately, I managed to refrain.

"I mean, she's married to a guy I've worked with, you know?" Cole continued, looking slightly pained as I scribbled. "Where do these rumors come from?"

He pulled away from my ear, and before he straightened up to his full six-feet-four, he looked into my eyes. Our noses were a mere few inches apart, and I gulped as I was overcome by a strange tingling sensation. Those lips . . . that I had seen . . . on the big screen . . . were . . . inches . . . from . . . my . . . lips. (I had to catch my breath.)

Then I suddenly remembered Tom and felt guilty that I was having this much . . . fun . . . with a stranger on a Saturday morning when I should have been at home with him instead. I cleared my throat and looked quickly away.

We wound up on Second Avenue and Seventh Street, just five blocks from my apartment, at a twenty-four-hour diner called Over the Moon. I'd been there more than once on my own. The walls had all been painted in bright blues and vibrant whites, and the local artist had added leaping cows in all the colors of the rainbow. In their honor, I had always refrained from ordering a hamburger.

"I love it here," Cole said as he held the door open. "I think they triple-fry everything in vats of grease."

"Ew!" I said, not really meaning it. I loved fried, greasy food too, although I knew that Merri Derekson, the editor of *Mod*'s health section, would probably kick me for saying so. I was sure I was about to consume three days' worth of fat grams. So I kept quiet and insisted my jiggly thighs do the same.

Cole laughed. "Hey, don't knock it till you've tried it, Shorty," he said. He paused for a moment while I made a face at him, amazing myself with how friendly I was suddenly feeling with the incognito major star. "Hey now, you're not allowed to stick your tongue out at me! We agreed I could use those nicknames at my discretion."

"I thought I was already back in your good graces," I egged him on.

"Simply a technicality, my dear," he said seriously.

As a server led us to a corner table by the window, I realized that I kind of liked it when he used the nickname, silly as it was. God, I was ignoring my own cardinal rule of reporting and actually beginning to *like* Cole Brannon. I was giggling at his jokes and feeling slightly woozy in his presence. And I had a boyfriend! What was I thinking?

"Um, excuse me for a moment," I said as soon as we were seated. "I need to go to the bathroom."

"That cappuccino from Atelier got you, huh?" Cole teased.

"Smallest bladder in Manhattan, right here," I admitted, trying not to blush. He laughed and stood up as I pushed my chair out. I looked at him in surprise.

"Sorry," he said with a sheepish smile. "My mom's manners lessons are too ingrained to ignore. I always have to stand when a lady leaves the table, or I'm afraid Mom will jump out and send me to my room."

I laughed at the image of a matronly, more feminine version of Cole emerging from the shadows to discipline her son.

"No, it's actually kinda nice," I admitted. "I don't think anyone's ever done that before."

"What?" Cole feigned horror with perfection only a professional actor could achieve. "For a lady like you? You're kidding. Men must trip all over themselves to charm you."

I suddenly had a mental picture of Tom slurping down the lo mein noodles I'd just brought home before I'd even had a chance to wash up.

"No, not exactly," I said. Cole shook his head in astonishment as I turned to walk toward the back of the restaurant, where I hoped to find a bathroom—and regain my vanishing sanity.

I actually did have to go to the ladies' room, but more than that, I needed a moment away from Cole Brannon. I felt that things were spinning a bit out of control.

I liked him. I wasn't supposed to like him. My insides weren't supposed to tingle when he grinned. I wasn't supposed to be acting like a smitten teenager.

There were two things wrong with that. First, obviously, there was Tom. But that wasn't bothering me too much. I'd never cheated on anyone, nor would I ever. I loved Tom and would never act on my attraction to anyone else.

What concerned me more was that I was letting my professional objectivity slip. It was fine if I found the people I interviewed to be nice and friendly, but this was different. I found myself talking to Cole like I'd known him for years, and I was more comfortable with him than I was with people I saw every day. It was strange. Although I couldn't explain why it was happening, I knew it wasn't supposed to be this way.

Sure, lots of reporters hooked up with the celebs they interviewed—or at least they aspired to. But I had always vowed to myself that I'd never be that kind of reporter. There were plenty of those kinds of reporters out there, believe me. But once they'd made the decision to cross that line, there was no going back. The world of magazines was possibly the most gossipy one in existence. Within five minutes of a reporter's stumbling out of a movie star's hotel suite, editors at *Glamour, Vogue, In Style,* and *People* would be talking. And you'd always be "that reporter who slept with Colin Farrell," or "that reporter who went down on Chad Pennington." You never got promoted, people whispered about you in the halls, and even the celebs themselves seemed to have some kind of sex-tips wire service—meaning that a third of the interviews you showed up for from then on would include a slew of sexual innuendos and come-ons designed to get you into bed. And it was hard to do a serious interview when you were fending off lascivious stares and groping hands.

Eventually you're forced to quit, because the whole sex stigma affects your work from the bottom up. You can no longer score the best interviews because the publicists all know your reputation. They secretly wish they could be in the position to sleep with movie stars every day, so they're pissed off at you and refuse to answer your calls. Your editors frown upon the reputation you're spreading for the magazine. And the movie stars who *don't* want to sleep with you start the interview off hating you because your exploits make their profession look bad.

It had happened to Laura Worthington, the girl I'd roomed with the first year I lived in Manhattan. She was an editorial assistant at *Rolling Stone,* and she was frustrated because, as the newbie, she was never sent out on exciting assignments. Once in a blue moon she got to cover a party, but most of the time she was responsible for editing the *Billboard* charts, fact-checking the feature editor's always-sloppy work, and calling publicists to verify facts and figures. When the features editor was sick one day and Laura was sent out to interview Kirk Bryant, the floppy-haired, tattooed, and not-at-all-good-looking lead singer of an up-and-coming rock band whose single had just broken the

Billboard Top Ten, she was thrilled and just a bit star-struck. Thirty minutes into the interview, which he'd conveniently moved from the Four Seasons lobby to his suite on the sixth floor, she was naked on his bed. Forty minutes into the interview, he was zipping up his pants and showing her the door. By the time she got back to the office, other editorial assistants were glaring at her suspiciously, and she realized that she didn't have *quite* enough information to write an article about Kirk, as they hadn't actually *talked* about anything. So she fudged the quotes and sat by the phone for a week, wondering why Kirk Bryant didn't call. Two weeks later she enthusiastically spread her legs ("To help me forget about Kirk," she told me with a sigh) for Chris Williams, whose band, Mudpile, had just catapulted from obscurity to being the most-requested band on MTV's *Total Request Live*. Of course, she had to make up quotes for that interview too, as there wasn't much time for work-related talk between the sighs and the moans. It was after another year—and eleven rock stars later—that Laura was finally fired. Now she answered phones at a talent agency in L.A. for seven dollars an hour.

I had always vowed that I would keep my emotions completely removed from my job. I wasn't Laura. No crushes allowed. And here I was making googly-eyes at Hollywood's Most Eligible Bachelor. What was wrong with me?

I chided myself for responding like a rookie to Cole Brannon's charms. After all, it was his job to charm me if he wanted to appear to be a good guy in the media. Maybe he was just a friendly guy who wanted to come across well in *Mod* magazine.

I looked in the mirror and rolled my eyes at myself. I knew better. I needed to grow up and start acting like the professional I was and always had been. I'd done my job, I'd put him at ease. Now it was time for me to stop drooling—surely he saw enough of that every day—and get on with the interview. The sooner I got back to the office to transcribe the interview and type up the article, the sooner I'd get home to Tom, which is where I belonged.

Maybe Tom and I could actually have sex today—on day 31 of the famine—if I made it home early enough. After all, it was a weekend. Surely Tom had slept in, so he couldn't claim exhaustion. Yep, tonight would be the night. The night for some serious lovin'. *Voulez-vous coucher avec moi?* as Christina Aguilera would say.

I smiled at myself in the mirror with new resolve, turned away, and headed back through the bathroom door.

Cole was sitting just where I'd left him, and I tried not to admire the broad contour of his shoulders as I approached from behind. After all, the width of his shoulders and the beautifully sculpted way his whole body fit together were really irrelevant. Right?

"Hey there," he said cheerfully, standing as I came up beside him. He waited to sit down until I'd settled into my chair. "I was starting to worry that you'd fallen in."

I resisted the urge to laugh and instead tried to frown—professionally, of course. I imagine my expression must have come out oddly twisted and meaningless, for I could have sworn I noticed a flicker of confusion cross his eyes.

"Um, no," I said. I warned myself to ignore those ridiculously gorgeous blue eyes. I needed to be professional. They were probably contacts anyhow, and what kind of vain guy wears colored contacts to brunch? I cleared my throat. "I've already taken enough of your time. Shall we get on with the interview?"

"Oh no, don't worry about me," Cole said in that perfect, musical baritone. "I love it here. It's my favorite restaurant. And I've got nothing else to do today." He leaned back lazily in his chair and grinned. I resisted the urge to smile back. I was Serious Claire and I would take that role, well, seriously.

"Unfortunately, *I* do," I said with my best attempt at a

frown. "This article on you is due tomorrow, so that means I have to get most of it written today."

"On a Saturday?" he asked incredulously. He leaned forward, his blue eyes wide. "You're kidding me! That's no fun!"

"You're telling me!"

"So there's no escaping the charm of Cole Brannon this weekend, then, is there?" He grinned again. I made another face at him, despite myself.

"No, apparently not."

"Well, let's get to it, then, Little Lady," he said. He gestured for our waitress. "But first we have to order. I can't do an interview on an empty stomach."

I laughed and looked down at the menu as our waitress approached. I couldn't figure out why I thought it was so cute when he called me "Little Lady." There was something in my head that told me his words should offend, but somehow they did anything but. They made me blush.

"Is Marge working today?" Cole asked the waitress who approached our table. I snuck a look up at him as he smiled at her.

"No sir," she said shyly. "Today's her day off."

"That's too bad," Cole said with a grin. "You'll have to tell her Cole says 'hi.'" He turned to me and smiled. "She's my favorite waitress. Reminds me of my mom."

I smiled and nodded. This guy seemed so sweet. But was it all an act?

"Know what you want?" he asked me. As if I had to think about it. I always ordered the same breakfast at every diner I'd eaten in for the past several years.

"I'll have two fried eggs, over easy, with hash browns and bacon, fried extra crispy, please," I said. "Oh, and can you add cheese to those hash browns, too?"

Cole arched an eyebrow at me.

"I like a woman who can eat," he said, smiling. "You know, I'll have the same thing," Cole said finally. "Oh, and a big pot of coffee for both of us. She looks like she needs some caffeine, doesn't she?"

"Hey!" I said, mildly insulted for a split second before Cole flashed me another big smile. I grinned back before remembering my vow to be nothing but professional. "Ahem," I cleared my throat as the waitress walked away. I was vaguely confused that she didn't seem starstruck, like every other server I'd ever seen wait on a celeb seemed to be. But Cole seemed to be a regular here. Was it possible they were simply used to him? "Shall we begin?" I asked.

"Ready when you are, boss," he said, settling his tall frame back into the chair again.

"Mind if I tape this?" I asked, although no one had ever turned me down. "It helps me make sure that I get every one of your quotes accurately when I'm writing the story later on."

"Well heck, I don't want to be misquoted," he said. "Tape away."

How to Talk to Your Dream Man

Two hours later I was on my way to the office, trying to stop glowing. I had managed to remain cool and professional throughout the interview—in which Cole had cheerfully covered everything from memories of learning to cook with his dad, to his first tentative foray into acting at Boston College, to his close relationship with his four-year-old nephew Nicholas, to his upcoming movie *Forever Goodbye*, due out Labor Day Weekend.

It was like no interview I'd ever done before. Normally, the actors I interviewed had already done a thousand interviews just like mine before they ever sat down with me. As hard as I tried to make my questions unique and interesting, I usually got cardboard, cookie-cutter answers that sounded just as rehearsed as they probably were. But with Cole, it was different.

He laughed like he meant it. The corners of his eyes crinkled up when I teased him back. He was humble, and it didn't seem fake. He watched me intently while we talked, whereas most other celebs I'd interviewed tended to scan the room repeatedly, rarely focusing their eyes on me. Cole had even opened up and grumbled to me about how he sometimes got annoyed when fans followed him.

"It's not that I mind the fans," he said sheepishly. "I

really don't. I mean, how cool is it to know there are people out there who've never met you but who like you anyway? But really, I mean, I sign autographs and chat with them for a while, but sometimes there are these girls who follow me, like ten paces behind when I'm at the grocery store or something. It's just awkward, you know? I mean, what do you do? Turn around and ask them to join you? Pretend you don't see them? I never know how to act."

Cole Brannon was just *real*. There was no facade. There were no pretenses. He wasn't *acting*. And that's something I had never expected.

As we parted ways at the top of the steps to the Eighth Street station, Cole had given me a hug before I descended to the R train.

Now I couldn't stop the scene from replaying again and again in my mind.

"I really enjoyed meeting you, Claire," he'd said as we stood there on the sidewalk.

"It was nice to meet you too," I'd said. Then he handed me a piece of paper.

"Here's my cell phone number if you have any more questions," he said, pressing it into my palm. "It will be easier than going through Ivana. She's probably still in bed."

"Um, thanks," I said, my heart fluttering as I clutched Cole Brannon's number. Was he flirting with me? No, I decided. He was simply being kind because he knew I'd be stuck working on the article all weekend. The biggest movie star in Hollywood couldn't possibly be flirting with *me*.

"Okay then, Little Lady," he'd said. "I guess this is where we say good-bye."

"Yeah, I guess so," I said. "Are you going to get back to your hotel all right?"

"I think I can manage without you," Cole said. He grinned. I could feel my cheeks heat up.

"I didn't mean—"

"I know," Cole interrupted. "You're just easy to tease." Then he hugged me. I mean, he actually reached out and hugged me, engulfing my five-foot frame with his muscular arms and chest, pulling me into an embrace that was much gentler than I would have imagined had I put any thought into what it would feel like to hug Cole Brannon.

Which, I was embarrassed to admit, I had. Was that inappropriate? I tried not to think about it.

I could still feel his arms around me as the subway rattled on belowground.

He's a movie star. He dates other movie stars. And you are not *a movie star.* I kept repeating the words in my head, just in case I had forgotten.

I arrived at the Forty-ninth Street stop and reemerged into the daylight, clutching my shoulder bag full of notes and the tape recorder that held my interview with Cole. It had been a wonderful morning, but I was confident that the tape would be all that would remain of it. *Mod* would only do a cover story on an actor once, so I knew the closest I'd ever get to Cole Brannon again was a chance run-in at a movie premiere or a Super Bowl party, where he wouldn't remember my name as I shouted questions at him from behind the ropes of the red carpet.

It was kind of a depressing thought. What a weird world I lived in where sometimes I got to know a person inside and out, only to have them disappear from my life forever. My friends back home envied my access to celebrities. But they never believed me when I told them my job made for the loneliest kind of life.

~

Three hours later, working at breakneck pace, I had managed to transcribe the entire interview, which added up to a whopping twenty single-spaced pages on my computer screen. Now all that was left was to turn the interview into a two-thousand-word profile of Cole Brannon. It wouldn't take me long, I knew. I'd already started mentally formulating the article, trying to avoid being stirred by Cole's deep voice in my headphones.

He had seemed almost too good to be true. Despite the flashy temptations of Hollywood, he truly seemed like he had remained grounded and normal. He was one of the only movie stars I'd interviewed who still shopped for himself rather than have a personal shopper pick out everything from his coats to his socks. He still got excited when he got free clothes in the mail from publicists trying to get him to wear their clients' products.

"It's like Christmas all the time," he had exclaimed, shaking his head in wonder. He loved pulling his Red Sox cap low over his eyes, donning a plain, non-designer T-shirt and jeans, and sneaking out alone to movies, dinners, and malls, unrecognized. He was close with his former costars, including George Clooney, Mark Wahlberg, Brad Pitt, Julia Roberts, Jennifer Anniston, Matt Damon, and Tom Hanks, but his best friends were the guys he'd grown up with and a few pals he'd met in college. He loved reading everything from Shakespeare to James Patterson to Dave Barry, but he hated reading celebrity gossip, because it was so unreliable and silly.

"No offense," he had quickly added. "I promise I'll read your article about me. But I know it won't be gossip or fluff, you know? It's different." He loved cooking, surfing, and tuna fishing. And he was scared of spiders, he shyly admitted.

In short, he sounded absolutely normal, and dare I say it, perfect. The only problem I would have was picking and choosing from the many great details. I couldn't fit them all in the article, although I would have loved to.

My fingers were poised over the keyboard and I was just about to start typing when the phone on my desk jangled loudly, breaking the silence.

"Shit," I cursed under my breath, knocking my mug

over and spilling coffee across my desk for the third time that week. I picked up the receiver.

"Hello?" I answered on the second ring, my heart still thumping from the scare.

"Claire!" It was Wendy, and she sounded accusatory. "You were supposed to call me when you were done interviewing Cole Brannon!"

"Oops," I said, suddenly guilty. "I'm so sorry, I forgot."

"You forgot to call me?" Wendy made a strangled noise. "So? What happened?"

"What do you mean?" I asked, trying to sound innocent. After all, I was innocent, right? I'd just felt a bit attracted to the guy. It wasn't like I had thrown myself at him. Or slept with him. (Although on second thought, perhaps I should have considered it. Talk about ending my sex drought with a bang! But I digress . . .)

"What was he like?" Wendy asked excitedly, talking a mile a minute. "Was he nice? Was he as cute in person as he is in the movies? Did he hit on you?"

"Slow down!" I laughed. "He was very nice. It was a great interview."

"Blah, blah, blah," Wendy said. She giggled. "Interview, schminterview. I don't care. What was he *like*?"

"He was very nice," I repeated, although I knew Wendy would keep pressing until I gave her more.

"He was 'very nice'?" Wendy repeated. "*Very nice?* Girl, you gotta give me something else to work with here."

"Okay," I agreed after a moment of silence. I sighed. "He was gorgeous. You wouldn't believe how his eyes look in person. He talks about his mom and his big sisters like they're his best friends in the world—and I think he really means it. He stood up every time I left the table, he laughs all the time, and when he hugged me, it was more gentle than you could imagine." I was blushing before I finished the sentence. I'd just sounded like a smitten schoolgirl.

Wendy gasped and fell silent for long enough that I started to feel uncomfortable.

"Wendy?" I finally asked gingerly.

"He *hugged* you?" she finally squealed. "He *hugged* you?" I cleared my throat and immediately regretted telling her.

"Well, it was just to say good-bye, you know," I said, trying to backtrack. "It was nothing. Just a professional hug."

"A professional hug?" Wendy repeated flatly. "Claire, c'mon! There's no such thing as a professional hug. He liked you!"

"Yeah, right."

"Are you kidding me?" Wendy said. "How often have you been hugged after you do an interview?" Okay, she was right. Never. "Wake up, honey!"

"No way," I said firmly. I was sure it didn't mean anything. After all, that would be crazy, right? "I think that's just how he is. He's like that with everyone. You should read some of the articles about him that I found in the clip files. He charms everyone."

"He charms the *pants* off everyone," Wendy corrected quickly. "Don't you read *Tattletale*?"

I rolled my eyes and tried to pretend that her words didn't bother me.

"I don't believe that," I said softly. I knew exactly what she was talking about.

Tattletale, was so unreliable that our clipping service didn't even include their articles. But I knew gossip well enough to know that it often contained a grain of truth. And the tabloid rag had reported twice in the last month that Cole Brannon was sleeping around with everyone he could get his hands on—from leading ladies to makeup artists to the nineteen-year-old craft service girl who had worked the buffet line on his last movie set.

I didn't believe it. Okay, or maybe I didn't *want* to

believe it. *Tattletale* was unreliable. (After all, they were the tabloid that constantly published ridiculous claims from Sidra about her "time with George Clooney.") And Cole had seemed so *nice*. It couldn't be true.

Wendy giggled, oblivious to my confusion.

"He's apparently some kind of sex addict," she said brightly. "I mean, he has this reputation for hooking up with anything that walks."

"I don't believe it," I repeated in an unconvincing mumble.

"Believe what you will," Wendy chirped. "But now that he's midway into charming *your* pants off, I thought I'd better warn you." She laughed. I blushed, thankful that Wendy wasn't here to see my giveaway reaction. Which meant nothing.

"He's not charming my pants off," I protested. "And anyhow, it's not true. He's not like that."

"Whatever you say," Wendy said sweetly. I knew she was teasing me, egging me on. She pressed on. "My friend Diane's friend Matty works at *Tattletale,* and she told me this week they're going to report that Cole Brannon's sleeping with his publicist. Some woman named Ivana, I think."

I could feel my heart drop in my chest. For a moment, I was entirely speechless.

Suddenly, it all made sense. Ivana had planned to come to brunch with us. Cole had known that she was still in bed. I tried to ignore the fact that I felt betrayed and hurt. What was the matter with me? Was I actually feeling *jealous* of Ivana Donatelli?

"Um, that can't be true," I stammered. "He didn't seem like that kind of a guy."

"And your judgment about men is so good?"

I knew Wendy was referring to Tom, but I ignored her.

"So . . ." Wendy's voice trailed off suggestively. "I still think you should test your one-night-stand theory on Cole

Brannon. Seeing as how he seemed so willing." She giggled.

"First of all," I said, "it's not *my* theory. Secondly, did you forget about Tom?" I hadn't. I looked at my watch. It was 5 p.m. I told him I wouldn't be home until at least ten o'clock, but I was moving along at a remarkable pace. I had a feeling I'd be done with a first draft by 6:30 if I could just get Wendy off the phone. I'd have to come back tomorrow to fact-check and do some final edits, but I was hours ahead of where I thought I would be today. Cole was just so easy to write about.

"Tell you what," I said finally. "If Cole Brannon is such a sex addict, *you* go and sleep with him. In the meantime, I'm going to finish up my article and go home to my boyfriend."

"You're no fun." Wendy pouted.

"I know," I said. "And because I'm so boring, I have to get going. I'll be here forever if I don't get started writing."

"Okay, okay," Wendy said, sounding resigned. "Suit yourself. It's your loss. 'Claire Brannon' had such a nice ring to it. Or you could hyphenate. 'Claire Reilly-Brannon.' What do you think?" I growled at her and she laughed. We said our good-byes and hung up, and I turned back to the computer screen.

I stared at it blankly for a moment, leaning back in my chair. How had I been so foolish? Of course he was sleeping with Ivana. Why should it bother me, anyhow? I had Tom. And I had a firm rule against being anything but absolutely professional with the people I interviewed. That's what set me apart from the Sidra DeSimons of the world. Okay, that and a significantly smaller cup size, a significantly smaller salary, and a complete lack of designer wardrobe. But still. A girl has to have her standards, even if she can't quite afford Louis Vuitton, Chloe, or Chanel on a regular basis.

Besides, it would be ludicrous to think my affections could ever be returned, if I indeed ever did start developing a

Cole Brannon crush. He was the world's hottest movie star. I was the world's plainest, shortest, most boring magazine journalist. We weren't exactly screaming "compatibility."

Anyhow, I knew better than to actually start developing a crush on an interview subject. I knew better than to believe that his charm was real. And I also knew I had a boyfriend whom I would never even dream of cheating on. Ever. I knew I could never do that to anyone.

I sighed and leaned forward, ready to start writing. Whether he was a sex addict who liked to sleep around or not, I liked what Cole Brannon had said to me during the interview. I was determined that he would come across well in the article, too.

True to my prediction, I'd finished a draft I was happy with by 6:30. Cole Brannon was easy to write about, partially because his quotes fit so well into the flow of the story, and partially because there was so much to say about him. It was rare to find an actor that well-spoken. Plus, he had elaborated on everything—the interview hadn't been like pulling teeth, like it often was with other celebs—so I had plenty of quotes to choose from. By the time I wrapped up, I was happy with the final product.

I picked up the phone to tell Tom I'd be home early, but I replaced the phone in its cradle before dialing. He'd said he'd be in all day. He wouldn't be expecting me until at least 10 p.m. I'd make it home by 7:00 to surprise him. Maybe tonight would be the night we would start working on making things better between us.

And after all, didn't a surprise homecoming sound like something Ginger or Mary Ann would do? (Was there something ridiculous about the fact that I was comparing myself to Tom's favorite '60s TV characters? I tried not to think about it.)

I flipped off the light over my desk and headed for the office door. This was perfect, I thought as I pushed the button for the elevator. I would surprise Tom and take him out to dinner. Maybe this wasn't a lost weekend after all. We could even work on fixing our problems in the bedroom. I could sleep in as late as I wanted tomorrow, as long as I came into the office in the afternoon to polish and fact-check my copy.

Cole Brannon be damned—Tom and I could be the sex addicts tonight.

⌒

I was humming cheerfully by the time I reached the door to our apartment thirty minutes later, after taking the R train downtown to Eighth Street and walking the several blocks over to Second Avenue. I'd thought about making love to Tom the whole way home. Which might account for the strange looks people were giving me as I dreamily walked along, a frighteningly sex-starved look in my eyes.

I had stopped to pick up a bottle of my favorite merlot from the liquor store on St. Mark's Place. I knew exactly how the night would go. We would share a few glasses, then head out to Mary Ann's—no relationship to Gilligan's girl—a great Mexican place up the street where we'd gone frequently during the first few months of our relationship. We would talk and laugh over margaritas like we used to, and we'd split one of their giant burrito platters, stuffing ourselves silly with churros and vanilla bean ice cream for dessert. Later, at home, everything would be the way it used to be. We'd sip wine, talk, and make love. It was going to be a great night.

Things were going to be okay. I could feel it.

When I pushed open the door and stepped into the apartment, it was dark except for a sliver of light peeking out from under the bedroom door. I could hear the stereo on in the bedroom and knew instantly that Tom had fallen

asleep again. I resisted the urge to laugh. This was bordering on ridiculous. He seemed to sleep eighteen hours a day.
No wonder he didn't appear to be making much progress
on his novel.

It would work to my advantage this time, though. I laid
my bag, the wine bottle, and my notes softly down on the
kitchen table and smiled, thinking about what I would do.
I was always so rushed and hassled after work. Maybe if I
crept in and woke him up gently myself, snuggling up
against him, we could make love before we went to dinner,
before we opened the merlot. I felt like a sex addict myself
as I thought about it. Tonight would be the night that
everything would change.

I took out a corkscrew and two wineglasses and put
them on the table beside the wine bottle, careful not to
make any noise. I took a deep breath and readjusted my
Wonderbra to push up my small bosom. In this bra and
shirt I actually looked like I had a bit of cleavage. Hooray
for the Wonderbra! Tonight it would be my secret weapon
in the seduction of Tom.

Cole Brannon was suddenly as far from my mind as he
had been before I'd met him. I mean, who needed some
A-list movie star when you had a great live-in boyfriend
you loved?

I crossed the room and stood by the closed bedroom
door for a moment, smiling. The music was so loud. I never
understood how men seemed to be able to sleep through
nearly deafening sounds. I put my hand on the knob and
envisioned for a moment how it would feel to curl up next
to Tom. The music selection would have to change, though.
Who could make love to "Born in the USA"? I took a deep
breath and turned the knob.

"Hey baby, I'm home," I said quietly as I pushed the
door open. I started to say, "Did you miss me?" but I'm not
sure how many words I got out before I choked on the end
of the sentence.

Tom was in bed, all right, just where I'd expected him to be.

What I hadn't expected was the naked brunette, her hair flying as she moved rhythmically up and down on top of him.

"What the hell?" I yelled over the din of the music. Evidently, Tom hadn't missed me much at all. He looked suddenly up at me, red in the face and mouth agape. The brunette turned and looked at me with flickering eyes.

"What is *she* doing here?" she squealed, her heavily made-up face flushed. She stopped moving and stared at me. For a moment none of us spoke or moved. Through my utter shock, with Bruce Springsteen pumping at full volume through the stereo—*my* stereo—I was acutely aware that the brunette's big breasts (which surely had to have been surgically enhanced) were still moving slightly up and down, an aftershock from their halted lovemaking.

My mouth was trying to shape something to say, but my brain wasn't cooperating. I was vaguely aware that my mouth was hanging wide open, but there was nothing I could do about it.

"You promised she wouldn't be home until later," the brunette finally whined. She gestured angrily at me, turning back around to face Tom. I reached over wordlessly and turned off the stereo, plunging us into complete silence. I noticed the brunette hadn't pulled away. Tom was still inside her. I felt like vomiting. "Well?" the brunette demanded, turning back to glare at me.

"Um, well, er—" Tom stammered, his eyes darting nervously back and forth between us. He paused for what seemed like an eternity, growing redder and redder by the moment.

It suddenly struck me, like a slow-motion revelation, that the brunette looked vaguely familiar. I stared hard at her face for a moment and had a sudden flashback to the *Mod* Christmas party in Margaret Weatherbourne's enormous

Upper East Side penthouse. I'd dragged Tom along against his protests. I remembered feeling relieved when I saw him talking animatedly with a curvaceous brunette I didn't recognize, instead of sulking in the corner as he'd been doing most of the night. It hadn't even crossed my mind to be suspicious or jealous. I had assumed she was someone's girlfriend, sister, or wife who was feeling just as out of place at the party as Tom.

And this was her. I was almost sure of it. In my bed. With my boyfriend. Without their clothes. I finally broke the silence.

"I finished early," I said, surprising myself with my even tone. It took great self-control not to cross the room and begin beating them both to death. "At the office. Who the hell are you?" Instead of answering, she turned back to Tom. Her brown hair glistened with infuriating perfection, spilling over her narrow and deeply tanned shoulders. Why were mistresses always tan? Was it a prerequisite to sleeping with someone else's boyfriend or husband?

"You said she wouldn't be home until ten," she said sharply.

"Surprise," I muttered. I stood stock-still as the brunette rolled off Tom, who was still partially erect. He quickly pulled a sheet over himself, and I gagged on the bile rising in my throat. There were suddenly a million questions racing through my mind as the brunette got up smoothly from the bed and started to get dressed. But all questions were overshadowed by the disgust and shock swirling through my mind. I didn't have the faintest idea how to react.

"How long has this been going on?" I finally asked softly. The brunette, who was much taller and leggier than me, bent down to slip on her shoes. Manolos, I noticed absently. She was wearing $500 shoes and shagging my boyfriend. I wasn't sure why that mattered. Tom greeted my question with silence, his face still the color of tomato sauce.

"Since December," the brunette finally answered, brushing past me on her way to the bedroom door. Her face was still flushed, her hair disheveled. I felt the air vacate my lungs in a swoosh.

"Since December?" I breathed, looking at Tom. He wouldn't meet my eye.

"What a waste of my goddamned time," muttered the brunette. She placed a palm on the door and bent down to adjust her left shoe. She turned to glare at Tom, who looked like he was trying to shrink into the sheets, then she finally turned to look at me.

"He kept telling me he was going to leave you," she said, looking me in the eye, her expression surprisingly calm. "What bullshit. He's great in bed, though." She turned away quickly and didn't look back.

Her words echoed in my ears as she tap-tapped to the front door in her stiletto heels. I stood there in complete silence after she opened and slammed the apartment door behind her. *He's great in bed? He's great in bed?* Hell, not that I would know, lately.

I stared in the general direction of the front door for a moment before slowly turning to look at Tom. He was still wrapped in the disheveled silk bedsheets I'd bought just last month, now curled up against the feather pillows I'd had for years. He stared back at me apprehensively, guilt and fear written all over his face, which suddenly looked ugly and hateful to me. Nothing could have prepared me for walking in and seeing the man I loved deep inside another woman. Another woman with $10,000 breasts, $500 shoes, and silky brown hair that bounced just like the shampoo commercials said it was supposed to.

"Tom . . ." I began finally. The words trailed off into emptiness, because I didn't know what to say. Half of me wanted to leap on top of him and beat him to death, and half of me wanted to break down in tears. My heart pounded rapidly inside my chest, and I could hear the blood rushing inside my head. I wondered for a moment if Tom could hear the pounding, too.

"Claire, I can explain," he said finally. He looked so uncomfortable I almost wanted to laugh. He reached for his boxers, which lay just to the right of my bed, and awkwardly wriggled them on under the sheets.

"I'm not interested," I said finally, my voice icy. I was surprised that I was managing to contain my anger. "I'm not interested in your explanation."

"But, Claire," Tom protested. He had tossed back the covers and was reaching for his jeans, which lay crumpled on the floor. "It didn't mean anything. It's just that you're never around, and . . ."

His voice trailed off—silenced, I suspected, by my icy glare. *Bullshit,* every muscle in my face said. Even caught in the act of cheating on me, he was trying to make it sound like it was my fault.

Suddenly, I felt a cold calm settle over me from out of nowhere, and I smiled at him. He shrank back into the sheets, seeming more alarmed by my smile than by my anger.

"I'm going to leave," I said slowly, calmly. Inside, my stomach churned. I felt like there was an icy fist wrapped around my heart, squeezing as hard as it could. "And when I come back, I want everything that belongs to you gone. Every last shred of your crap."

"Claire, you're overreacting," he squeaked. I realized suddenly, the concern in his eyes wasn't because he was worried about saving his relationship with me. It was because I was the only woman dumb enough to put a rent-free roof over his head, and he had screwed it up. I was furious at myself for ignoring all the signs. I had wanted so badly to be in a functional relationship, I'd let him use me for almost a year while I blindly believed that he loved me, and was just going through a phase or struggling with his novel.

"*I never want to see you again,*" I said finally, my voice hushed and calm. I had never meant anything more in my life. I took one last look at him: his pathetic, beaten expression, his too-hairy, scrawny chest, his brown eyes that were plain, flat, and emotionless. I hated him. In that instant, I truly hated him. I pushed back the lump in my throat, and without another word, turned on my heel and walked to the front door. I grabbed my shoulder bag, my keys, and the bottle of merlot we were supposed to share. As an after-thought, I grabbed the corkscrew and stuffed it into my bag. I could feel his eyes on my back as I opened the door and slammed it behind me. His stare, which I couldn't see but could somehow feel, sent a chill up my spine.

I waited until I was outside on the street to start crying.

How to Do a
Tequila Shot

I didn't know where I was going. Tears ran in hot, salty rivers down my face. I was in a fog as my feet carried me north on Second Avenue and west on Eighth to the N/R subway station. It was quiet this time on a Saturday. As I waited alone for a train, I opened the bottle of merlot with the corkscrew I'd grabbed from the kitchen table on my way out. I struggled with the cork without considering the inappropriateness of opening a wine bottle in the subway. Who the hell cared, anyhow? I was by myself. There was no one there to stop me.

I finally got the bottle open with a satisfying "pop," tilted it back, and took a giant swig, washing the taste of bile out of my mouth. I didn't bother to take the bottle out of the paper bag, and for a moment I was amused that I must have looked like a well-dressed wino. With a $16.95 bottle of merlot. If there had been anyone there to see me, which there wasn't.

I sat down on one of the dirty benches and waited. I took another swig, and then a deep breath. I regretted it immediately, choking on the stench of oil and urine that hung heavy in the station.

Note to self: No more deep breathing in subway stations.

I drowned the smell with another swig from the bottle.

"How could I be so stupid?" I asked myself aloud after I'd taken a few more gulps. I was greeted with silence. I was already feeling the wine. There was no one else in the station, so I voiced my anger a bit more loudly. "How could I be so stupid?!" I yelled at the top of my lungs. This time my question was greeted with the echo of my voice off the cold steel of the subway tracks.

A few seconds later, a middle-aged man in a suit descended into the subway station, looking at me like I was crazy as he passed by. He must have heard me yelling. To prove his suspicions correct about my mental state, I took another giant swig from the bottle. I let the smooth, warming wine slip gently down my throat, embracing the burning in my empty stomach as it settled. When I looked up again, he was staring at me. He looked quickly away when our eyes met.

I laughed. I knew what I looked like.

The subway came after what felt like an eternity, and the man in the suit disappeared into another car. I stepped into the door that pulled up right in front of me and settled into a cold, hard plastic seat. As the doors closed, I stared at the man across from me. He was about thirty, Tom's age, and he was alone. I could smell his cologne from across the car, and it looked like he'd just shaved.

I wondered if he was going on a date. Maybe he was going to see his girlfriend. Did she know that men cheated? Someone should warn her. Someone should tell her not to trust him.

I took another swig without taking my eyes off him. His eyes widened in surprise as I tilted the wine bottle up for a refreshing gulp. I wanted to laugh. In my perfectly tailored black pencil skirt and my pink shell—the same outfit I had worn to interview Cole Brannon—I must have looked the complete opposite of someone who would be swigging wine from a brown bag in a subway car.

Yeah, buddy, we're all full of surprises. Nothing is what it seems.

I got off the subway at Forty-ninth Street (my regular stop, out of habit) and stood aboveground, for a moment, just breathing in and out. I felt invisible. I hardly ever came to midtown during the weekends, and it was strange to see the streets so empty. I was used to rush-hour foot traffic as I made my way over to Broadway for work.

I took one last gulp out of the wine bottle and tossed it in a garbage can. It was almost empty anyhow, and I was getting sick of drinking it. I was lucid enough to know that getting drunk wasn't an answer to my problems—in fact, I'd never tried to solve anything that way before—but I didn't see many alternatives. I couldn't go home. I couldn't face Tom again. I couldn't stand to see his face. I hated him. With all my heart. And yet I loved him. With all my heart. I hadn't realized it was possible to feel both things at once.

"Wendy," I mumbled, suddenly realizing that I could call her. She'd know what to do. I paused for a moment. Would she say, "I told you so"? Maybe. But probably not. She was my best friend. You were supposed to be able to turn to best friends in times like this, right?

Not that I had ever suspected I would have a time like this.

I fumbled in my big bag, pushing past pages I'd written just this afternoon about Cole Brannon, who was evidently a sex addict. He'd tricked me too. He made me believe he was a nice guy, when in reality he was a sex addict who was sleeping with Ivana Donatelli. And probably Kylie Dane too, despite his convincing protests. They were all scum.

Note to self: Men are scum. Lying scum.

I finally found my cell phone. With shaking hands, I pulled it triumphantly out of the bag. I leaned back against the wall of Katzenberg's Deli, just outside the stairs to the Forty-ninth Street stop, to steady myself. Slowly, carefully, I dialed Wendy's number.

It rang and rang, four times. Then her answering machine picked up. Was she out? Damn. She was one of the last people in America who didn't have a cell phone. There was no other way to reach her.

"This is Wendy," her voice chirped cheerfully into my ear. "Leave me a message, and I'll call you back." The machine beeped, and I paused for a moment.

"Wendy, are you there? Wendy?" I realized suddenly that my voice was very slurred. Logic told me that drinking almost an entire bottle of wine on an empty stomach in a thirty-minute period would do that. But hindsight is always 20/20, isn't it? "Wendy, you were right. You were right all along. About Tom. You have to call me, okay? You have to call me. Because I need to talk to you. Please call me, Wendy. On my cell phone. Don't call me at home. Tom's there."

I was still repeating myself and slurring rather unintelligibly into the phone when her machine cut me off. Damned machine. Didn't it know I needed someone to talk to? I held the phone away from my ear for a moment and stared at it, as if it might tell me where Wendy was. When I realized it wasn't about to impart that information, I sighed and jabbed my finger at the End button. I tossed the phone back in my shoulder bag and leaned against the deli window.

The moment I started to relax, images of Tom straddled by the naked, full-breasted brunette from the Christmas party flooded my brain.

"No," I said aloud, shaking my head and forcing my eyes open. I didn't want to think about that. Not here, not now. I couldn't.

Suddenly, I knew what to do. I'd go to Metro, the bar Wendy and I went to after work every so often for happy hour. In fact, I'd had my slutty-boot-in-subway-grate debacle outside Metro. But that felt like eons ago. And they probably wouldn't remember me.

In any case, it would be a familiar place to sit down. And I knew I needed to sit down. I also knew I needed a glass of water and probably a nice cold shower, but it was clear that as soon as I sobered up, I'd start thinking about Tom again. I didn't want to do that tonight. I wouldn't think about him, and I wouldn't cry again. The only way I could avoid that was to have another drink. Metro had drinks.

I started walking in the direction of Broadway.

Metro was nearly empty when I staggered in the door. It was the first time I'd seen it like that. I'd only been there after work, when the happy-hour crowds threatened to overflow onto Eighth Avenue, which was always creeping by in a blur of taxis outside the darkened plate-glass windows.

I surveyed the room as I stood in the doorway. A young couple was huddled together in a corner booth, looking into each other's eyes. Yuck. Three thirtysomething women laughed and talked in another corner, all holding brightly colored martinis. A fiftysomething couple played pool in the back, and sitting at the bar was a man in a black shirt and a baseball cap, his back to me, deep in conversation with the bartender. I sat down at the opposite end of the bar, as far away from the man as I could get. I knew what I would look like. A single girl all by herself on a Saturday night, already drunk by 9 p.m., sidling up next to the bar.

I'd look like I was trying to pick up a date.

But really, if a guy tried to hit on me tonight, I might just turn around and punch him.

It actually seemed like a good idea. I mulled it over for a moment. I could skip all the steps where he courts me, buys me dinner, buys me gifts, moves in with me, and then cheats on me. I could cut a whole year out simply by slugging him the first time we met.

Too bad I hadn't done that with Tom.

The bartender raised an eyebrow at me and took a few steps closer. His friend, the broad-shouldered man in the black shirt, turned to look at me from the shadows at the other end of the bar. I snarled at him and sent him telepathic messages (which, of course, you're able to do when you're drunk).

Don't even think about it, buddy. Unless you want to get hurt. I have a mean right hook.

"I'll have the usual," I said as the bartender approached. He looked at me in confusion, and I giggled. I'd always wanted to say that at a bar. "A Corona," I said when I was done laughing. "And a shot of tequila." If I was going to get drunk—okay, *drunker*—I might as well do it right.

"Can I see some ID?" the bartender asked suspiciously. Damn. I was so sick of looking like I was sixteen. I fumbled in my bag until I found my wallet, which I pulled out triumphantly. It took me another full minute to grasp my driver's license and pull it out from the plastic enclosure.

"Aha!" I exclaimed as the license finally came out. I squinted for a moment until I could read the bartender's name tag. "Here ya' go, Jay," I said with false cheer. I handed him the ID. He looked at it closely for a second, then handed it back with a strange expression on his face that I couldn't quite interpret. Not that I had the energy to care. Maybe he looked strange simply because he was a man. They were all strange.

"Okay," he said. I watched him walk down to the other end of the bar, where he reached into the glass-front fridge and pulled out a Corona. He said something to the man in the baseball cap, who turned and looked at me for a moment from the shadows. I growled another telepathic message in his general direction. *What are you looking at? Haven't you seen a drunk girl before?*

"Here's your drink," Jay the bartender said a minute later, plunking the Corona down in front of me. He reached under the bar for a shot glass and pulled out a bottle of Jose Cuervo.

"Ah, Jose, old friend," I mumbled, prompting another strange look from the bartender.

He filled the shot glass with the smooth, gold liquid, then reached down for two lime slices. He stuck one into the top of my Corona bottle and handed the other to me. "Here," he said. He lifted a glass of soda in a mock toast. "Cheers."

I downed the tequila in one gulp and bit hard into the lime, my taste buds balking at the sour taste.

Three Coronas, two tequila shots, and four bathroom trips later, I could barely keep my eyes open, but at least I wasn't thinking about Tom. Nope. I was thinking about what I wanted to drink next. I knew I'd end up with either a Corona, a tequila shot, or both, so it shouldn't have been a hard decision, but somehow it was. As I strained my eyes to read the labels of the liquor bottles lining the back shelf— impossible, given my drunken stupor—Jay set down a tall, full glass of clear liquid over ice in front of me.

"A drink from the gentleman," he said, winking at me. Or at least, I thought he winked at me. I couldn't see too well anymore. I examined the glass through bleary eyes. Vodka, maybe? Gin? I looked at it closely. I sniffed it. It was water.

"Huh?" I mumbled as he walked away. Gentleman? What gentleman? And wasn't that word an oxymoron? Why had I never thought of that before? Men weren't gentle. They broke your heart. Even the ones who hugged you good-bye. They were probably just sex addicts who wanted to get in your pants.

I looked down the length of the bar. The man in the black shirt and baseball cap was gone. I hadn't noticed him leave. Who had sent me the drink? Was the bartender going crazy? Or was I the only one losing my mind?

"Twice in one day," said a deep voice suddenly in my ear, startling me. I jumped and nearly fell off the bar stool. A strong hand steadied me.

"Twice in one day, what?" I mumbled crossly, swiveling on my stool to see who stood behind me. I almost swiveled right off the stool, but again, a gentle hand on my lower back kept me in place.

"Twice in one day you sit a few feet away from me, and don't even notice me," said the voice in my ear. "I should be insulted." I blinked as the swivel was complete. It was the guy from the other end of the bar, the guy who'd been looking at me from the shadows. What the hell was he talking about? Was this some kind of new pickup line?

Obviously, I needed to get out more. I was used to the generally cheesy "So, were you born this beautiful?" lines that men had been using throughout the '90s and the early years of the new millennium. But perhaps things had changed during my time with Tom.

The man looked good—although blurry—in a black shirt and khakis, with a baseball cap pulled low, casting a shadow over the rest of his face. But, I reminded myself, men are scum. Scum. Maybe I should punch him.

I squinted at him, and suddenly I realized that he looked familiar. Really familiar. It took another second for realization to fully dawn.

When it did, I was mortified.

There, in the familiar Red Sox cap, just inches away from me, was Cole Brannon. The movie star. The gorgeous, polite, perfect movie star. The sex-addicted, lying movie star.

He grinned, waiting for me to say something. Damn those twinkling blue eyes. They'd sucked me in once, but now I knew his secret. I squinted at him. *He's a sex addict!* Wendy's words rang in my head.

"Where's Ivana?" I slurred. Aha! That would teach him. *The jig is up, mister. I'm on to you.*

"Huh?" He looked at me closely for a moment, confusion suddenly etched across his perfect face. "Ivana? My publicist?"

He was playing dumb. How coy. Like I didn't know.

"You know who I mean," I said, trying to sound accusatory, but probably just sounding drunk.

"Ivana, my publicist?" he repeated. He stared at me for a moment. Then he laughed. "You know, Claire, she doesn't go everywhere with me. I'm allowed out alone once in a while without a chaperone."

I tried to make a face at him, but scrunching my eyes up only made me dizzy. I swayed, and he steadied me again.

"Whoa, looks like somebody's had a little too much to drink," he said softly, his hand still on my back. I liked it there, I realized. But only because it meant I wouldn't fall off the bar stool, which seemed like a pretty real possibility at the moment. Why didn't they put backs on these things?

"Not me," I mumbled.

"No, of course not," he said solemnly. He looked suspiciously like he was fighting back a grin. He pulled up the stool next to me, keeping his hand on my back all the while to steady me. "Is this a typical Saturday night for you, then?"

It took me a minute to realize he was kidding.

"No," I said stiffly. "It is not." I tried my best to sound haughty. "Is it a typical Saturday night for *you*? What are you doing at my bar?" What *was* he doing here? Of all the bars in Manhattan, why would he have to wind up at the same bar where I was trying to drink my troubles away?

"No, this is *not* a typical Saturday night for me," Cole said, smiling with what I could have sworn was gentle pity. I was suddenly just lucid enough to feel embarrassed. "And I didn't realize this was *your* bar." I made a face because I was pretty sure he was teasing me.

"Jay Cash, there," he gestured to the bartender, "is an old college buddy of mine. I usually drop in on him when I'm in New York." The bartender waved from the other end of the bar as I looked up. Cole looked at me for a minute. "Your turn."

"My turn what?" I asked grumpily. I'd already forgotten what we were talking about.

"Your turn to tell me what you're doing here by yourself, getting drunk on a Saturday night," he said. "Even if this is *your* bar." His face was inches from mine. I squinted at him and suddenly noticed that his blue eyes were flecked with gold. How cool.

"I'm not drunk," I said. He laughed.

"Oh yeah, I can tell," he said. "Totally sober." He picked up the glass of water and handed it to me. "Here, have a sip."

I was too tired to protest. I took a long drink of the water. It actually felt good going down my throat. Better than the tequila.

"Do you want to talk about it?" Cole asked softly as I drank. I didn't answer for a moment, too busy gulping down the water. Cole gently took the glass out of my hand when I was done, setting it back on the bar. I closed my eyes because I could feel thoughts of Tom rushing in, and I wanted to hide from them. Finally, I opened my eyes and looked at Cole. He had an expression of deep concern on that perfectly formed face that I'd seen so many times in movie theaters.

"When I got home from the office today," I said, speaking slowly because I knew my words were all running together, "I found my boyfriend in my bed. Having sex. With another woman." The mental image of the brunette bobbing up and down on him flooded back into my mind with all the clarity of a television show played on Tom's precious high-definition TV that I'd bought him. But I'd never seen *that* kind of thing on Nick at Nite. If Gilligan had gotten it on with Mary Ann, he had done it off-screen. I swallowed hard.

"Oh, no," Cole breathed. He started rubbing my back with the strong hand he had there to steady me. I closed my eyes for a moment. His touch felt good. "Claire, I'm so sorry."

I shrugged, fighting back the tears that had suddenly welled in my eyes.

"I should have known," I said, sniffing. I felt a single tear escape and roll down my right cheek. "I'm an idiot."

"Don't ever say that," Cole said, gently leaning in. He put an arm around me. I remembered Wendy's words again. *He's a sex addict!* Did he think he was going to have sex with me?

I struggled to pull out of his embrace for a moment, but then I stopped. What the hell. I could use the help staying upright. I leaned in to him.

"Don't ever say you're an idiot, Claire," Cole said as he hugged me. "Your boyfriend, he's the idiot. To cheat on a woman like you . . ." Cole's voice trailed off, and his pity somehow triggered the opening of my floodgates.

"I let him live with me, and he never wanted to have sex with me!" I was rambling now through sniffles and tears. "And he said he was writing a novel, and he never worked or anything, and he was always in bed, and he treated me like I didn't matter, and I don't know what I was thinking." I wasn't making much sense as I continued to blubber unintelligibly. I realized that I was crying, hard. Damn. I'd come into Metro to forget about Tom, not to talk about him. But somehow, it was nice to tell someone. Finally. Someone who didn't seem like he was judging me.

Cole pulled me closer and rubbed my back as I sobbed into his shoulder. It felt good to be held. As his hand moved in small, gentle circles, I forgot that I was supposed to have a totally professional relationship with him. I forgot about Tom. I forgot that Cole Brannon was a sex addict. I forgot that he was a movie star who wasn't supposed to remember who I was. Right now, he was just Cole. A friend. My friend who cared and wanted to listen to me.

Finally, I pulled away and tried to steady myself on the bar stool. But suddenly I didn't feel quite right.

"Cole?" I said quietly. Shit. The room was spinning. When had the room started spinning?

"Yes?" he asked with concern, leaning forward.

"I think I'm going to be sick."

Then I threw up. All over the floor. And Cole Brannon's shoes.

Oops.

"Sorry," I croaked, ashamed and humiliated. It was the last thing I remember saying before I passed out.

Gossip and Vices

Drinking

Somewhere in the distance, I could hear the phone ringing. I wished someone would make it stop. With each shrill jangle, the throbbing in my head seemed to get worse. I started to open my eyes, but even the smallest sliver of invading morning light turned out to be too much for the powerful ache in the back of my skull. Far off, the phone continued to ring.

"Tom," I mumbled. "Tom, can you get that?" There was no reply. Finally, the ringing stopped. I groaned and sank back into the sheets. I wanted nothing more than to drift back to a place where my head didn't throb like I'd been clubbed with a baseball bat.

I pulled the sheets up, still squeezing my eyes tightly shut in a vain effort to block out all the offending sunlight. I shivered, fought back my rising nausea, and reached for my quilted comforter. I pawed around for a moment at the foot of my bed, but I couldn't find it.

"Tom!" I groaned, hating how my stomach swam and my head throbbed with additional force every time I spoke. "Tom, what did you do with the comforter? I'm cold!" I felt like I was yelling, but I was dimly aware that my words were coming out at a decibel just above a whisper. Any louder, and I feared my head would explode.

I knew I'd woken up from a nightmare, which might begin to account for the throbbing in my head. I couldn't remember much of it. Tom was there, and in the dream I was angry with him. Cole Brannon had been there too, in a bar, which was strange. I couldn't understand why I would be dreaming about him. Even if he was the hottest man I'd ever met.

"Tom!" I moaned again, a bit louder this time. He still didn't answer, and I suddenly realized I could hear the shower running. I couldn't remember hearing it from the bedroom in the past. But perhaps my throbbing headache had given me superhuman hearing.

Finally, I realized that if I wanted the comforter, I'd simply have to crawl out of bed and get it myself. Reluctantly, I forced my eyes open and groaned as the sunlight poured in, blinding me momentarily. Slowly, the room started to come into focus.

Then suddenly, time seemed to stop as I realized that I wasn't in my bedroom at all.

Awe mixed with utter confusion as I slowly blinked at my surroundings, still blurry through my sleepy eyes. My drab and pale bureau, which I'd bought four years ago at a garage sale, had been replaced by a glistening black chest of drawers, topped by a massive oval mirror. Instead of my faded blue gingham curtains over tiny windows, thin white gauze did little to block the sunlight streaming in through giant panes that stretched from floor to ceiling. I was awash in white satin sheets, and the bed they covered was at least twice the size of my double. Beneath me was a seemingly endless sea of plush, snow-white carpeting that covered a floor easily bigger than my whole apartment.

I lay back for a moment, the breath knocked out of me. My head continued to throb and my stomach churned threateningly. But both were overshadowed by the mounting horror I was feeling. I had no idea where I was.

Think, Claire, think. A quick assessment of my physical condition told me I'd gotten drunk last night. But where? With whom? I had never been here before. Had I gone home with a stranger?

That triggered a foggy memory. One-night stands. There was something about one-night stands. . . . My God. The article for *Mod*. Had I done it? Had I taken my own misguided advice and had a one-night stand? No, that wouldn't be right. I would never do that to Tom.

Tom. Oh God. Tom.

I closed my eyes, trying to block out the images that suddenly flooded my brain, but it was too late. Tom with the leggy brunette from the Christmas party. Tom *inside* the leggy brunette. That damned Bruce Springsteen singing like nothing was wrong. Me, storming out of the apartment. The bottle of merlot, Metro, the tequila shots, the Coronas.

And Cole Brannon.

Oh no. Cole Brannon.

With rising horror, I remembered seeing him at the bar. Crying on his shoulder about Tom. Letting him hold me and comfort me . . .

Vomiting on his shoes.

Suddenly, I had a very bad feeling about all of this.

As if a director from one of his movies had suddenly yelled, "Action!" the bathroom door far across the massive bedroom swung open dramatically and Cole Brannon stood in the doorway, clad only in a skimpy white towel wrapped around his waist. His darkly tanned upper body, filled with perfectly toned muscles bulging to get out, gleamed with droplets of water. His perfect washboard stomach drew my stunned eyes tantalizingly toward the top of the low-slung towel, which seemed mere inches away from exposing what it was supposed to be hiding. As our eyes met, Cole grinned and quickly adjusted his towel for more coverage.

"Well hello, sunshine," he said cheerfully. "You're awake." I couldn't move. I just stared. I desperately tried to recall the events of the previous evening. It was hard to think with my head pounding like the bass on a bad rap album. Hard as I strained to remember, though, everything after vomiting was blank.

"I threw up on you last night," I moaned finally. I was completely humiliated and dimly aware that I was processing my thoughts very slowly. I had puked on the biggest star in Hollywood. This was not how journalists were supposed to behave. I felt sure I'd read that in the *AP Stylebook*.

But instead of looking at me in righteous fury, he laughed.

"Why yes, you did," he said, the corners of his eyes wrinkling with amusement. He took a few steps closer. "I must say, that's the first time that's happened. I'm used to journalists kissing my feet, not throwing up on them."

"Oh my God," I moaned. I sank back into the pillows and pulled the sheets over my head, wondering if it would be possible to disappear and wake up in my own bed instead.

"I was just kidding," said Cole's voice with sudden concern, muffled by the covers over my head. "I really don't mind. . . ." I groaned and emerged from the covers. Evidently, it was not possible to teleport home from beneath his sheets.

"No, it's not what you said," I said finally. "I just can't believe . . . Oh my God, I have never done anything like this before. Never. And especially not with someone like you."

"Someone like me, eh?" Cole grinned again. "And exactly what do you mean by that?" I would have blushed if all the blood in my body hadn't been coursing in throbbing currents through the back of my skull.

"Someone I've interviewed," I mumbled. "I don't even know what to say. I'm always so careful to be completely professional. And look at me now." I groaned. As I spoke, something nagging at the back of my mind came closer to the surface, and I scrunched up my nose in concentration, trying to remember what it was.

"Claire, no worries," Cole said gently. He crossed the room in a few long strides and sat down beside me on the massive bed. My embarrassment was momentarily overshadowed by the realization that the most attractive man I'd ever seen was mere inches away from me, nearly naked, in a silk-covered bed. Unfortunately, before I had a chance to process that realization, the hyperprofessional-journalist portion of my brain kicked back in.

"I'll lose my job," I moaned.

"Claire," Cole began, his voice gentle and soothing. He put a hand on my shoulder and looked so deeply into my eyes that it set my heart pounding. "I told you. No one has to know. This is between you and me, okay? No one's going to lose their job."

I glanced down at my lap and received another shock I hadn't been prepared for.

Instead of the pencil skirt and pink blouse I had on last night, I was clothed in a massive gray Boston College T-shirt that certainly didn't belong to me. Before I had time to freak out about the fact that I was no longer wearing my own clothes, the thought that had been nagging me suddenly came into full focus. I could hear Wendy's voice replaying in my head.

"Cole Brannon is a sex addict," her disembodied voice chirped, suddenly loud and clear.

I stared at Cole for a moment in horror, my heart pounding. He was still grinning at me, which made me even more afraid. His grin suddenly looked knowing, almost smug and lascivious.

"Oh my God, did we . . . ?" My voice trailed off. I couldn't even complete the sentence. My heart pounded hard and fast.

"What?" asked Cole, tilting his head to the side and looking at me in confusion.

"Did we . . . ?" I still couldn't say the words. I looked down again at my body, wrapped in one of his T-shirts. Surely we had. I would have to quit the magazine. I had slept with someone I'd interviewed.

And I didn't even remember it.

"What's wrong?" asked Cole, concern now mixing with the confusion splashed across his face. "Do you need to throw up again? Are you okay?"

I just stared, the little voice in my head squeaking in horror. *Am I okay? What, did you think that I wanted you just because you were able to drag my unconscious body home?*

I realized suddenly that he was still looking at me in bewilderment. I had to know how it had happened.

"Did we . . . Did we . . ." I couldn't complete the sentence. I looked at him with a mixture of exasperation and shame. "Did we . . . ? You know!" And suddenly, he did. Realization dawned, and he laughed. He actually *laughed* at me. Had it been that bad?

"Are you asking me if we had sex?" he asked incredulously. It hurt to hear the words, but I nodded anyhow, then squeezed my eyes shut. I braced myself for the words I knew would end my career, my whole professional life as I knew it. He paused, then spoke.

"Claire, you were unconscious all night!"

"What?" As much as I'd braced myself, those were not the words I'd been prepared to hear. He had sex with my unconscious body? What kind of a guy was he? I needed to start taking the tabloid rumors more seriously. I shuddered involuntarily.

"So we . . . ?" I began. I just needed to hear him say it. So I knew that my life was over. He squinted at me.

"No, Claire!" he said finally, looking distressed. "Of course not!" I blinked and tried to process what he'd said. "I slept over there," he added, gesturing to a small love seat near the window that still had a blanket, a sheet, and a pillow strewn across it.

"What?" I asked, confused. It wasn't adding up. I looked down at the T-shirt and suspiciously back at him. "But where are my clothes?"

He sighed in exasperation and gave a kind of half laugh.

"You were, um, covered in your own vomit," he said

uncomfortably. I just stared at him. "I didn't know what to do, so I called the front desk, and they had someone from housekeeping come up and help you change."

"And you . . . ?" My voice trailed off as I had a sudden mental image of Cole watching my vomit-encrusted clothes being stripped from my jiggly body.

"I stepped outside," Cole said softly. "I had the woman come get me when she was done."

I looked at him for a moment. He was blushing. A new wave of humiliation coursed through me.

"Oh," I said finally. I didn't know what else to say. "Thank you."

"Hey, no problem," he said breezily. He squinted at me. "Although I haven't yet decided whether I should be offended by your line of questioning." This time I could physically feel the blood rushing to my face, which must have meant my headache was starting to subside.

"I'm so sorry," I said. "I didn't mean . . . It's just that . . . Well, I mean, I'm not dressed, and I'm in your bed, and . . ." Suddenly it dawned on me. He didn't want to sleep with me. Maybe he *was* a sex addict and I was just too repulsive. My heart sank.

"I prefer my partners to be conscious," Cole said, as if reading my mind. He winked. "I try to keep that as at least a minimum standard."

"Oh," I said stupidly.

"I'm kidding, Claire," he said, nudging me gently in the shoulder. "I'm just giving you a hard time."

"Oh," I repeated. I felt like such an idiot. I groaned, closed my eyes, and leaned back into the pillows. I wished I could go back to sleep, wake up, and realize this had all been a bad dream.

"I hope it's okay that I brought you here," said Cole, sounding almost shy. I cracked my eyes open and looked at him. "I didn't know what else to do, and I wanted to make sure you were okay."

"Thank you," I said finally. "I am so embarrassed."

"No need to be," Cole said with a dismissive wave of his hand. But he wasn't making me feel much better.

I shuddered. This was horrible. This was more than just a step over the line of professional ethics. This was a pole vault into the next time zone. What was I doing?

"I have to go," I blurted out suddenly. Cole, still perched on the edge of the bed, looked surprised.

"What?" he asked. "Where?"

"I just have to go," I repeated, trying to sound firm.

"Oh, okay," Cole said. He looked a bit hurt, I thought, but perhaps that was my imagination. "Well, listen. I had your clothes sent out to be dry-cleaned." My jaw dropped. "They should be ready any minute now. Why don't you hop in the shower while I call down to the front desk and see if they can bring them up, okay?"

"I can just shower at home," I protested weakly.

"You have vomit in your hair," Cole pointed out wisely.

"Oh," I said, blushing. That changed things. I looked at Cole for a moment, wrapped in his skimpy towel. A few drops of water still glistened on his body, and his dark hair was damp. I tried to ignore the warm feeling spreading across my abdomen. "Don't you need to get back into the bathroom?"

"Nah," he said. "You go ahead. I'll change out here." He grinned. "No peeking, though."

I smiled, blushing, and tried not to let my eyes wander down across his tanned, hard body.

"No peeking," I agreed, trying not to sound as reluctant as I felt.

❧

Twenty minutes later I had taken a quick shower, swallowed two ibuprofen tablets, dried my hair, washed my face, and used the only makeup I had in my purse—powder, lipstick, and an old tube of mascara—to make myself look somewhat presentable. I was no Gwyneth Paltrow, but I was exponentially more attractive than I'd been when I first stumbled in. Okay, so that was the understatement of the year.

I was still standing with a towel wrapped around me when there was a knock at the bathroom door.

"Your clothes are here," Cole said through the door, his voice muffled.

"Oh," I said, startled. I readjusted my towel and tucked in the end tightly to make sure it stayed put. I did a quick check down below and wished that I wasn't showing so much flabby thigh, but at least all the important areas were covered up. "Um, come in."

Slowly, the door opened. Cole Brannon stood on the other side of the threshold, holding my perfectly pressed shell and pencil skirt, which hung innocently on a hanger as if they hadn't seen me at my very worst just hours earlier. He looked effortlessly sexy in a pair of dark jeans and a black ribbed T-shirt that traced his contours perfectly. As we stood there in silence, I was conscious of Cole's eyes moving slowly up and down my body. I suddenly felt naked, vulnerable.

"Well, you sure do clean up well, Little Lady," Cole said finally, his eyes coming to rest on mine. He looked almost embarrassed. "Here are your clothes, good as new."

"Thank you so much," I said quietly, looking down. I took the hanger.

"Now get dressed and get out here to have some breakfast with me," he said cheerfully.

"Breakfast?" I asked, my eyes widening. "No, I couldn't."

"Well, it's already here," he said with a grin. "And your coffee is just getting cold." I opened my mouth to protest, but Cole cut me off before I even began. "And don't even try to tell me you don't want any coffee. I saw you yesterday morning. I know about your caffeine addiction, Little Lady."

"Guilty as charged," I said weakly, forcing a smile. "I'll be out in a second."

I quickly pulled on the shirt and skirt, then stared at myself in the mirror.

What had I done? In the past I'd never so much as looked at an actor with lusty eyes, or smiled the wrong way at a rock star. And here I was in the bathroom of Cole Brannon's hotel room after puking on him, sleeping in his bed, and letting him see me wrapped in a tiny towel. I just had to go home. I couldn't let this go any further. I already felt like my professional reputation was ruined.

I took a deep breath and opened the bathroom door. Cole Brannon was sitting on the corner of the bed. He grinned at me as I emerged. I quickly forced a frown, but couldn't stop my eyes from darting eagerly around the room.

In front of him a table had been rolled in, and on it were a big pot of coffee, matching crystal pitchers of orange juice and water, and a buffet-sized display of breads, croissants, muffins, Danish, and fruits in every color of the rainbow. The ibuprofen was already kicking in, and my stomach growled, but I ignored it. I had to go. Maybe if I got out of here, we could both eventually forget what had happened. I doubted it, but it was worth a shot.

"Took you long enough," Cole teased, apparently oblivious to my internal conflict. "Your coffee's getting cold." He held out a mug he'd already poured for me. "Cream and one Sweet'N Low," he said. I just stared. "I remembered from breakfast yesterday."

"Oh," I said, taken aback. I shook my head and cleared my throat. "Um, I'm sorry, but I have to go. You were very kind to have helped me out last night." *And to remember what I take in my coffee.* Cole looked confused. I took a deep breath and started for the door.

"Really, thank you," I said as I walked, refusing to meet his eye. I could feel him watching me, but I couldn't bear to look. "But I have to go. I have to go home. Please send me the dry-cleaning bill."

Eyes downcast, I slipped on my shoes and opened the door. I couldn't resist taking one quick look over my shoulder before I shut it behind me. After all, this was Cole Brannon, America's favorite movie star. He was, among other things, the man who had saved me from myself last night. I felt a horrible pang of guilt as I caught a last glimpse of him staring at me from behind the overflowing table of food. I tried to ignore my rapidly beating heart as I hurried into the hallway.

Bingeing

My heart was still pounding as I stood on Park Avenue minutes later, trying to flag down a taxi. But of course in this city of 8 million people, it always seemed that approximately 7.9 million of them wanted a cab at the same time I did. Today was no exception. I desperately waved my arms in the air, beckoning to cab after unresponsive cab.

I had almost given up and resigned myself to the subway when a driver two lanes away pulled a death-defying move, cutting almost horizontally across Park and screeching to a halt in front of me, missing my toes by mere inches. I yanked open the back door.

"Second Avenue and Second Street," I said quickly as I heaved myself onto the slick backseat. "And please hurry." The driver nodded wordlessly, pulling slowly away from the curb into traffic that was now motionless, stopped at a light. I closed my eyes and leaned back in the seat, willing the light to change and the traffic to move.

But clearly the fates weren't taking requests from me this weekend.

Suddenly, there was a loud knock on the window. Given the luck I'd had in the past twenty-four hours, and the fact that a pounding on your cab in the middle of Manhattan was rarely a good thing, my eyes flew open in alarm. My mind started racing through the horrific possibilities of what would be outside. Perhaps a knife-wielding psychopath. Or a ski-masked robber with a 9mm.

Instead, I looked out the window and saw a crazed-looking man fiddling with the door handle. I gasped.

"That's Cole Brannon," said the taxi driver in a thick Indian accent. He turned around to look out the window in astonishment.

"Yes, it is," I agreed slowly. Outside, Cole was mouthing something to me while trying to juggle a mug of coffee, an apple, a banana, a muffin, and a croissant. The driver and I just stared.

Cole gestured to me, a look of desperation on his face as he struggled to rearrange the breakfast items he was carrying. He looked like he was about to start some kind of gourmet circus act.

"Well, open the door for him," said the cab driver, looking like he was ready to start drooling at any second. "He's a big star!"

"Do I have to?" I mumbled reluctantly, starting to feel sorry for Cole despite myself. I stifled a giggle as he dropped a banana and looked positively devastated. Around us, traffic started to move—but the taxi driver stayed put, and so did Cole.

"Yes, yes!" the cab driver responded desperately, oblivious to the scores of honking horns now aimed at him. "You open the door now!" Reluctantly, I reached over and opened the door for Cole, who immediately sighed in relief.

"Claire!" he said, panting from his efforts. "What took you so long?"

"I have to go home, Cole," I said, trying to sound stern. Without a word, he handed me the muffin (which looked like blueberry) and the croissant. Still clutching the coffee and the apple, he slid into the taxi, placed the apple on his lap, and swung the door closed behind him.

"Those are for your breakfast," he said, nodding to the pastries he'd handed me, as if it was the most normal announcement in the world. I looked down at the muffin and the croissant, one in each hand, not sure what to say. "They'll make you feel better. It's good to eat bread products when you're hungover."

"Well, thank you, Mr. Surgeon General," I muttered. Cole ignored me.

"And here's an apple, but I'll hold it until you're ready for it," he pressed on at full speed. "I brought you a banana too, but I dropped it. And a cup of coffee. But be careful not to spill it."

The cab driver was staring at us in the rearview mirror. The honking had temporarily subsided now that the light had turned red, and we were once again mired in traffic.

"Hello, Mr. Cole Brannon." The cab driver had apparently mustered the courage to greet his newest passenger. His face was flushed. "It is an honor to have you in my car."

"Oh," said Cole, looking up at the driver as if surprised to see him there. "Thank you. It's a pleasure to be here." He sounded like he was graciously accepting an Oscar. I suppressed a laugh. He sounded so earnest. He looked back at me like he was expecting me to say something.

"Um, thank you," I said finally, looking down at the croissant and the muffin. They *did* look good. "But Cole—"

"Wait!" Cole interrupted me triumphantly, digging in his pocket. Finally, he pulled out a bottle of water and displayed it for me. "This is for you, too. It will help your hangover." I finally gave in and laughed.

"Cole . . ." I began. I didn't know what to say. "Thank you. But you didn't have to do this." But somewhere inside of me, where Unprofessional Claire was hiding, I was glad that he had.

"Excuse me, Mr. Cole Brannon," the cab driver cut in again, interrupting the little war that was raging in my head between Professional, Ethical Claire and Recently Dumped, Sex-Starved, A-Movie-Star-Is-Feeding-Me Claire. "It would be a great honor to have your autograph."

"Yes, yes, of course," Cole said graciously. The driver handed him a piece of paper, and he quickly scribbled his name.

"Thank you so much, Mr. Cole Brannon," the cab driver said. He took the piece of paper from Cole just as the light changed.

"Anytime," Cole said with a smile. The cab lurched forward into traffic, and I looked at Cole suspiciously.

"You're coming with me?" I asked.

"Yes," he said firmly in a voice that made clear it wasn't open for discussion.

"Why?" I asked, squinting at him in confusion as the car crept downtown. I was aware that my heart was suddenly racing, and I didn't know why. Cole shook his head and changed the subject.

"Why did you leave so quickly?" he asked softly. Before I could answer, he nodded at my muffin. "Eat something," he commanded like a concerned parent. I looked at him for a moment, shrugged, and took a bite of the muffin. Apparently, he was coming along for the ride whether I liked it or not. Okay, and despite myself, I had to admit: I liked it.

I thought for a moment before I answered Cole's question. What would I say? I finally decided upon the truth.

"I didn't know what else to do," I admitted after I'd swallowed my third giant bite of muffin. I was hungrier than I'd realized. Cole looked at me with concern and handed me the bottle of water. I took a big sip and handed it back. "I'm so embarrassed about everything, and I thought maybe if I just left, we could just forget about it, you know? I mean, this isn't me. This isn't the kind of thing I do."

"I know," Cole said gently, looking closely at me. "Do you think I would be doing this now if I thought you did this kind of thing all the time?"

I thought for a second.

"No," I admitted. He had a point. I took a deep breath. "It's just that I try so hard to keep those professional boundaries in place, and now look what I've done."

I sighed and was silent for a moment. The cab inched forward.

"Okay, it's my turn to ask you a question," I said finally. "What are you doing here? Why did you follow me?"

Cole looked defensive for a moment, then his face softened.

"I didn't know if your boyfriend would still be at your apartment," he said finally. He handed me the mug of coffee and steadied my hand as I took a sip. It was perfect— exactly the amount of cream and sweetener I used myself each morning. "I didn't want you to have to face him alone if he was still there."

I stared at Cole for a moment over the rim of the mug.

"You followed me in case I had to deal with Tom?" I asked incredulously.

"Yeah," said Cole with what I could have sworn was a blush. "I didn't want you to have to be alone with him, you know? He doesn't sound like a very good guy."

"He's not," I agreed, smiling at Cole now, despite myself. He was almost too good to be true.

But that was the problem. He *was* the perfect guy—the guy every woman in America probably dreamed of—and I couldn't so much as touch him. It would violate everything I stood for professionally. I suddenly understood the concept of forbidden fruit.

Not to mention that even if I *did* develop a crush on him, it would be totally useless. I knew from the clips I'd read that his last serious girlfriend had been Kris Milan, the glamorous, willowy model-of-the-moment. Her flawless face looked down over Times Square from not only a Calvin Klein billboard, but also a Burberry perfume board, and an Audi ad. Not exactly in my league.

"Thank you," I said, realizing I was relieved that he was here with me. I *had* been worried about seeing Tom. Imagine his surprise if he were still in the apartment and I walked in with Hollywood's most eligible bachelor. "Really, thanks."

Cole lowered his eyes.

"You're welcome," he said softly. He looked back up at me and smiled gently. "Now eat that croissant, okay? I promise you'll feel better."

"Okay," I said, finally smiling at Cole. The cab heaved forward, and Cole sat in silence, watching me eat.

The remainder of the cab ride seemed to take forever, and by the time we reached the corner of Second Avenue and Second Street, I'd polished off all the food Cole had given me, as well as the water and the coffee. As a result, my bladder felt like it was about to burst.

"It was a pleasure to drive you today, Mr. Cole Brannon," said the driver formally as we alighted from the cab. "And I won't tell anyone about you and your lady friend here. You can trust me."

Cole grinned at me. I blushed furiously.

"Thank you," he said seriously to the driver. He handed him the fare plus a twenty-dollar tip. Our starstruck driver simply sat and stared until Cole and I were inside my building.

I dashed for the stairs the moment we pushed past the big entryway. Cole kept pace two stairs behind me. While I huffed and puffed my way up four flights, Cole hardly seemed winded.

"This is me," I panted as I reached my door. I put the key in the lock and turned it quickly.

But then I stopped, frozen in place.

"You okay?" Cole asked, putting a hand on my arm with a look of concern.

"Yeah," I said, not really meaning it. I couldn't seem to will myself to open the door.

"Here, let me go in first," Cole said quietly, putting his right hand over mine. "In case he's there." I nodded. Cole gave my shoulder a quick squeeze, turned the knob, and disappeared inside while I waited on the doorstep.

The seconds ticked by so slowly, it felt like I was standing there for hours. Finally, he was back at the doorway.

"He's gone," he said simply as he pulled the door open for me.

"Oh," I said, still standing on the threshold.

"Come in," Cole urged. I looked up at him briefly and he stepped to the side, holding the door open for me. Gingerly, I stepped over the threshold into the kitchen.

Everything looked the same as it had yesterday and the day before, and the day before that. I half expected Tom to come ambling out of the bedroom, lazily claiming to have just finished a day's worth of work on his novel.

But he wasn't there. He'd never be there again.

Once I had used the bathroom, I stood there for a moment, leaning against the counter. Tom's toothbrush was gone from the toothbrush holder we'd shared. His shaving cream had been taken from the medicine cabinet. His razors no longer sat beside mine. He was gone, and I knew I should have been glad. But somewhere deep inside, in a dark corner that shouldn't have any place in a self-respecting girl's heart, I missed him. I hated him with all the fury that had erupted yesterday when I saw him screwing another girl, but I couldn't ignore the part of me that had spent a year desperately trying to make it work. I couldn't shake the guilty feeling that I'd failed, miserably.

I looked at myself in the mirror. I looked awful. I had dark bags under my eyes, and the makeup I'd slapped on in Cole's bathroom had done little to hide the puffy redness that my eyes were still sporting, thanks to the flood of tears the night before. And to cap it all off, I had the most attractive movie star in America standing outside my bathroom door, no doubt thinking how pathetic (not to mention pathetic-*looking*) I was.

I took a deep breath. Cole Brannon had helped me when

I was at my most vulnerable, and there was nothing I could do about that. But I was okay now. I was going to be okay. And I had to get him out of here before this went any further.

I tried to ignore the fact that my heart rate was up about 50 percent thanks to the fact that Cole Brannon—*the* Cole Brannon—was now sitting in my kitchen. I ignored the little uninvited fantasy creeping in at the back of my mind that involved me, Cole Brannon, the kitchen table, and substantially fewer clothes than either of us were currently wearing. I ignored the fact that I was developing one major crush. It was beside the point, not to mention totally inappropriate. And about as likely to develop into anything as winning the lottery.

I closed my eyes once more and vowed that I would send Cole on his way, as politely as possible, before any more damage could be done. Tom had already taken every last shred of my personal dignity. I wouldn't let the situation he'd initiated last night steal my professional dignity too.

"Would you like a cup of coffee?" I asked breezily, emerging from the bathroom. I tried not to think too hard about the fact that Cole Brannon was actually sitting at my kitchen table. In Tom's chair. Talk about an over-adequate replacement.

"Yeah, sure, thanks," he said. Damn it. He was supposed to say no, and he certainly wasn't supposed to look that sexy when he said it.

"Um, okay," I said. I should have just been rude. "I'll put a pot on, okay? But then I'm afraid I'm going to have to take off. I have to get back to the office to finish the story." There, that was good. I wasn't throwing him out if I actually had somewhere to be, right?

"That story on me, hmm?" Cole asked, leaning back in his chair and grinning. "It had better be a good one. You better work hard on it. Make me sound good."

I smiled and wondered how anyone could possibly make him sound bad. He was perfect. I was suddenly sure that the whole sex-addict thing had to have been a false rumor.

"I'm going to go change out of these clothes," I said. I flipped the switch on the old Black & Decker that had served me well for the past five years. It began gurgling almost immediately, and I could smell the dark-roasted coffee beginning to work its caffeinated magic.

"But the clothes you're wearing are so nicely cleaned and neatly pressed," Cole teased.

"So true," I replied. "But I would love for you to actually realize that I have more than one outfit."

"Oh, do you? Well, let's see!"

I made a face at him, and we both laughed. I could feel him watching me go as I stepped into my bedroom and shut the door behind me.

The smell of coffee wafted in from the kitchen as I surveyed my room slowly, trying not to think about the scene I'd witnessed here last night, trying not to think about what had happened in the bed I'd shared with Tom for nearly a year now. The room looked just as innocent and welcoming as ever, which struck me as somewhat strange, although I'm not sure what I had expected.

I looked in the closet and was immediately shocked to see that most of Tom's clothes still hung there. From the way he'd cleaned out the bathroom, I assumed he was gone for good and had taken all of his things. I stared for a moment as I realized it meant he'd be making at least one return visit. My stomach turned funny circles as I tried to decide how that made me feel.

As I turned around to survey the rest of the room, an unfamiliar object in the corner of the room caught my eye. I took a step closer.

It was a small Louis Vuitton bag, and it wasn't mine. It lay on its side, half obscured by the faded bureau, its thin strap trailing dangerously toward the bed. I stared warily.

I took a few steps across the room and bent down beside the purse, suddenly feeling choked up and uncomfortable. I weighed it for a moment in my hands and turned it over pensively. I knew instantly that it belonged to the woman with the perfect hair, the perfect breasts, and the perfect legs. Did she have to have a perfect handbag too? Of course she did.

Inside, there was surely an answer to who she was. I had to know. But I wasn't sure I was ready to confront her again, even if this time she'd only be a tiny photo and a name on an ID.

"Cole, can you come in here for a second?" I called out weakly. I sat down on the bed.

"Sure." I heard his footsteps. He knocked lightly. "Are you decent?"

"Yeah," I said absently, still fingering the bag. He cracked the door open slowly and slipped inside.

"You okay?" he asked, looking at me with concern as he joined me on the edge of the bed.

"It's hers," I said, without answering his question. He knew instantly what I meant. I held the purse out to him and finally looked up. Concern was etched across his perfect face as he put a strong hand gently on the small of my back.

"What are you going to do?" he asked softly.

"Open it, I guess," I said. I paused for a moment. "Is that wrong?"

"You have every right to know who she is," he said softly. "If you want to."

"I don't know if I want to." But I did. If for no other reason than to put a name with the face that had turned my life upside down. More important, I had to know if she had indeed been the woman at the Christmas party. If so, who had she been with? Had one of my coworkers known about Tom's affair all along?

"Want me to do it?" Cole asked gently.

"Yes." I nodded, relieved that he'd taken over. I was silent as he unzipped the little purse and reached inside. He pulled out a tiny Louis Vuitton wallet.

He opened it, looked at it for a moment, and silently handed it to me. It was her New York State driver's license, and from the tiny photo on the ID, she looked at me defiantly, almost smirking. Her long hair was dark and shiny, as it had appeared in person yesterday, and her lips were perfectly lined and filled in. Her complexion was creamy and flawless. She looked as if she'd had her makeup professionally done before standing in line at the driver's license bureau.

"Estella Marrone," I said softly, reading her name. The name didn't ring a bell right away. "Estella Marrone." I repeated it once, a bit more softly. There was something familiar about her, but I was sure I'd never heard the name.

"You okay?" Cole asked. He started to rub my back slowly as I stared at the ID. Finally, I nodded.

"Yeah," I said. I sighed. "I think I am." We just sat there for a moment, me staring pensively at her ID, not knowing what to think, and Cole gently rubbing my back.

Suddenly, there was a sharp knock on the front door. I jumped, startled. I wasn't expecting anyone. Cole and I exchanged confused looks.

"It must be Wendy," I said finally. She had surely been worried when she got my slurred message. "My best friend," I clarified. "Hang on a second. I'll get it."

I left Cole sitting on the bed while I went to answer the door, suddenly feeling relieved, despite the fact that Cole was still here and the mysterious Estella Marrone's face was dancing around in my head. Wendy was the one person in the world who would know how to take care of this entire situation.

I was actually smiling by the time I reached the door, fully expecting to be blinded by Wendy's toothy smile and amused by today's choice of wacky outfit. I wrestled with the stubborn lock, swung the door open, and smiled into the hallway.

Then I blinked as I realized that it wasn't Wendy on my doorstep at all.

It was Sidra DeSimon.

I stared wordlessly at *Mod*'s fashion director, dressed from head to toe in black leather, despite the fact that it was a warm June day. As usual, her short, dark hair was perfectly slicked back, her eyebrows were perfectly tweezed into sharp lines, and her lipstick was a perfect bloodred. Her perfume filled the hallway.

She stared back at me wordlessly for a moment, looking inexplicably as surprised to see me as I was to see her. My mind began racing.

Oh my God, someone had seen me leave Cole's hotel. Someone had called *Mod*. Margaret had sent the head Triplet here to check and see if the rumor was true. And she would think it was! Cole was in the other room! In my *bedroom*! She would see him, assume the worst, and my life would be over! How had this happened? Finally, she spoke.

"Hello, Claire," she said, staring at me strangely. She glanced past me into the apartment, and I took a quick step to the right to block her view. I was still confused about her appearance on my doorstep, but I hadn't forgotten about Cole Brannon and his potential to ruin my life if Sidra caught a glimpse of him.

"Can I, um, help you with something?" I asked quickly, hoping to expedite this visit. My discomfort was growing. Sooner or later, Cole was bound to emerge from my bedroom, and I'd have no chance of saving my reputation.

"I didn't know you'd be here," said Sidra cryptically. I just stared at her. She paused. Then she continued. "I'm here to pick up my sister's purse."

I simply stared for a moment, then my jaw dropped. It suddenly clicked, and I realized what I should have known all along. The woman Tom had been sleeping with bore a striking resemblance to Sidra DeSimon. The same thick, dark hair, the same pointed nose, the same high cheekbones (though I would have wagered that they were implants—perhaps by the same plastic surgeon), the same fake breasts. Of course.

"Your sister?" I squeaked.

"That's what I said, isn't it?" said Sidra, looking annoyed. "Honestly," she muttered, rolling her eyes and looking at me like I was a half-wit. She reached into her clutch and effortlessly extracted a cigarette, which she proceeded to light, flicking ash on my doorstep and blowing smoke in my face. "Could we hurry things up here? I don't have all day."

"Your sister?" I repeated stupidly. Sidra stared at me with blazing eyes. I couldn't move. I took a deep breath.

"Yes, Claire." She spoke the words slowly, with forced patience, like she was talking to a child. "My sister, Estella. She left her bag at her boyfriend's apartment, and she asked me to pick it up. Is that really so difficult for you to understand?"

"Her boyfriend?" I choked. "He was *my* boyfriend. This is *my* apartment."

"Ah, yes," Sidra said, still looking bored. She took another long drag from her cigarette. "I know. Rather awkward." The corners of her lips twitched, and I suspected she would have been smirking had she not had so much collagen injected recently. Suddenly I wanted to reach out and strangle her. The only thing that stopped me was the realization that it would likely be difficult to get a grip on the slippery leather that covered her body.

"Did they meet . . ." My voice trailed off. I didn't know how to complete the sentence or even why I wanted to know. ". . . at the Christmas party?" I finally finished the thought.

"Yes, Claire," Sidra said slowly. "Now are we going to stand here and play twenty questions all day? Or are you just going to give me her handbag? I have work to do today, you know."

"Oh," I said, my mind still spinning. This was too much.

"Oh?" Sidra mimicked. "Look, I have a car waiting outside. I don't have time for chitchat."

"I'll get the purse," I said finally. I balled my hands into fists and contented myself by imagining a scenario in which I beat Sidra and Estella to a pulp, perhaps using Estella's Louis Vuitton bag as the weapon of choice. Pummeled to death with Louis Vuitton products. A fitting end to their shallow lives.

But I realized suddenly that Sidra wasn't looking at me anymore. She was looking over my shoulder. I knew with horror, before I even turned around, what she was looking at.

"This must be Wendy!" Cole said cheerfully as he emerged, grinning, from the bedroom. He crossed the kitchen in a few steps and was at my side. He placed a gentle, almost protective hand on the small of my back.

"No," I muttered as Sidra stared. I could practically feel my world crashing down around me. "This is Sidra DeSimon, the fashion director at *Mod*."

"Oh," said Cole, looking confused, but still smiling politely. This was worse than I could have imagined. "Nice to meet you," he said, extending his hand. "I'm Cole."

"Yes, I know," said Sidra finally, taking his hand and shaking it slowly. My stomach churned. She turned back to me. "Well, well, well, what have we here?" she asked, arching an eyebrow at me.

"It's not what it looks like," I stammered. "Really, we just got here a few minutes ago, and I barely know him, and . . ." Sidra cut me off, still smiling dangerously.

"Oh, I know what it looks like," she said. She looked at Cole conspiratorially. "I used to date George Clooney, you know. How nice to see little Claire here, following in my footsteps." She tittered lightly. "Not that *you* would actually date *her*." She laughed again.

"Why not?" Cole asked. I turned around to look at him and was surprised—and a bit flattered—to realize that his grin had been replaced with an icy glare. "I think she's wonderful. And it's funny, but I've never heard George mention anything about you."

I could practically see Sidra's claws coming out. Her eyes flashed, and she prepared to cut into Cole. I interrupted quickly.

"Sidra just stopped by to pick up *her sister's purse*," I said to Cole, turning around to look at him. His eyes widened.

"But I see I'm interrupting something," Sidra said mischievously, her mouth twisting as far into a smirk as it was capable of.

"I'll get the purse," Cole said tightly. He left Sidra and me staring at each other while he disappeared momentarily. She continued to smile knowingly while my stomach again threatened to turn. I distracted myself by returning to the beating-Sidra-with-Louis-Vuitton fantasy.

"Here." Cole surprised me by tossing the purse at Sidra rather than handing it to her. She deftly caught it and smiled smugly at me.

"I'm sure the editorial staff at *Mod* will be thrilled to hear about this," she said, a dangerous edge in her voice. She looked back and forth between Cole and me. "This is just *precious*," she squealed. She started to back away from the door, but as an apparent afterthought, she turned back around and smiled icily at me once more.

"Claire, dear, one more thing. That shade of lipstick looks absolutely *hideous* on you," she said, smiling sweetly. "Just a little tip, from me to you." She looked at me coolly for a moment, as if challenging me. She dropped her cigarette on my cheery blue and yellow welcome mat, stubbing it out with the toe of her leather stiletto boot. "Ta-ta, lovebirds," she said. She spun on her heel and started to click-clack down the hallway and down the stairs. "Have a lovely day. I know I will." Her laughter wafted up through the stairwell as she descended and disappeared from view.

Purging

I sat alone in my cubicle, staring vacantly at my illuminated computer screen, my eyes glazing over the words for what must have been the hundredth time. I knew I needed to finish editing the article on Cole Brannon, but I couldn't quite seem to focus. I was worried sick about what Sidra would do with the knowledge that Cole had been in my apartment this morning. It seemed darkly ironic that she was the one who would be responsible for editing my article about him.

I had considered, for a moment, asking that someone else edit the article instead. But then I'd have to reveal the reason why. And how much damage could Sidra truly do to the article itself, anyhow?

The rest of the office was dark. It was almost unheard of in the women's magazine world to be working on a Sunday, but there was little I could do, given Margaret's timing of the article. Besides, given the events of the morning, I had the distinct feeling that I wouldn't be in the women's magazine world much longer. I knew I would be forced to leave in disgrace as soon as Sidra got ahold of Margaret.

I looked at my watch. Wendy would be here any minute. I had finally spoken with her this morning after Cole left. I knew she could tell from my tone that I was in trouble.

I sighed and turned back to my computer screen, which

was still open to the same page. "COLE BRANNON: HOLLY-WOOD'S HOTTEST HUNK OPENS UP ABOUT LOVE, LIFE, AND THE THINGS HE WANTS YOU TO KNOW." The headline screamed at me, and I grimaced back.

After Sidra had disappeared, taking all hope of my escape from this situation with her (along with Estella Marrone's Louis Vuitton bag), I was too distraught to be polite to Cole anymore. It no longer mattered that he was the guy who had cared enough to help me when I needed him. Nor did it matter that he was the most attractive man I'd ever met, or that he was Hollywood's most eligible bachelor. All that mattered was that my life was mere hours away from being ruined.

"None of this is your fault, Claire," Cole said as we walked down the stairs together.

"Yes it is, Cole," I said glumly. "I know better than to do things like this."

"Like what?" Cole asked gently. "It's not your fault that this happened."

"You don't understand," I said quietly, shaking my head. "Once Sidra tells Margaret, our editor in chief, I'll be fired. Then Sidra will tell the tabloids. By tomorrow morning, the whole world is going to think I'm sleeping with you." I blushed as I spoke.

"So?" Cole asked softly. I looked at him desperately.

"So, it will completely ruin my reputation," I said. "Don't you understand how it works? I'll always be 'that girl.' The one who slept with a movie star she was supposed to interview. No one will ever take me seriously again."

"But we didn't sleep together," Cole said, looking confused.

"It doesn't even matter at this point." I sighed. "A few details from Sidra DeSimon, and the rumor mill will get started. It doesn't have to be true. You know that."

Cole lowered his eyes for a moment, then looked up at me. "You can't always believe what you read," he said softly.

"I know," I said, exasperated. "But just having that story circulating around out there . . . It will never be the same for me again. You know how it works."

"Yes, I do," he said slowly. "Listen, I'm really sorry. I didn't mean to cause you any trouble."

"I know, and I appreciate it," I said as we reached the ground floor. "And I'm sorry I'm doing this. It's not your fault. Not at all. I just can't believe Sidra saw us. This whole thing has gotten so out of control." We walked down the long hallway in silence. Before I pushed the heavy door open to Second Avenue, Cole put a hand on my arm.

"Look, Claire," he said softly. "This whole thing, it's going to work out." I listened, but I shook my head at him. He meant well, but he didn't know what he was talking about. His blue eyes were so earnest and piercing, they reminded me suddenly of the sky on a bright summer day. "You can't let some creep like that Tom guy make you feel like you're anything less than a great, beautiful woman."

After an embarrassed pause, blushing furiously, I mumbled, "Thanks." But I knew that wasn't enough. My heart was in my throat.

"You know, guys are idiots sometimes," Cole said. "Really, Claire, it's not you. And you're better off without someone like that."

"Thanks," I said softly. "I appreciate everything you did for me, Cole. I really do." He gave me a quick hug and then a light peck on the top of my head, which, despite myself, made my heart skip a beat.

"Call me if you need anything, Claire," he said. "Anything at all." He looked sad as he pushed open the door and disappeared into the blinding sunlight outside. I let the door swing closed behind him, and I stood there motionless for a full minute, wondering what kind of an idiot I was to have kicked Mr. Perfect out of my apartment.

Now, an hour later, I could still see Cole's blue eyes in my mind as I stared at the article I'd written about him yesterday afternoon, before my world had fallen apart.

Just then I heard the reception door buzz. I turned in time to see Wendy bustle in, her bright purple sundress swirling around her as she rushed toward me. I was so relieved she had arrived, I almost leaped up to throw myself at her.

I just needed a friend to cry to—preferably one who wasn't the biggest movie star in America.

"Are you okay?" she asked across the office, half walking, half jogging to my cubicle. Her face was etched with deep concern. "What happened?"

Without missing a beat, she yanked a rolling chair out of her cubicle and dragged it quickly over to mine. She tossed her Coach bag on the floor and opened her arms.

"Give me a hug," she demanded. I stood up and let her envelop me. She held me tightly for a moment as I hugged back, heaving a sigh into her shoulder. Finally, she pulled away, still looking concerned, and we both sat down. "I'm sorry I didn't get your message until this morning. I was out late. What is it, Claire? It's Tom, isn't it?"

"Among other things," I muttered. Wendy shook her head.

"What did he do this time?" she asked, looking angry. "I'm so sick and tired of him hurting you."

"I caught him cheating on me," I said flatly. Her eyes widened in surprise. Even Wendy, with all her dire predictions, hadn't seen this coming.

"What?"

"Yep, I actually caught him in the act," I said, sounding much more cavalier than I felt. "In my bed, actually having sex with another woman."

"Oh my God," Wendy said. "Claire, I'm so sorry. I knew he was an ass, but I didn't expect . . ."

"Oh, that's not the worst of it," I continued calmly. "The woman was Sidra's sister." Wendy just stared at me for a moment, looking like she was trying to process the information.

"Sidra DeSimon?" she asked finally, her eyes wide. I nodded. "You've got to be kidding me. How?"

"They met at the Christmas party."

"Oh, no."

"Oh, that's not all," I said.

"It's not?" she asked incredulously.

"Nope. I left out the part where Sidra came to the door this morning and saw Cole Brannon in my apartment. Now she thinks I'm sleeping with him, and I'm sure I'll lose my job."

Wendy blinked.

"Cole Brannon was in your apartment?" she finally breathed. I knew she would get stuck on that. "What happened? What was he doing there?"

So I told her the whole story, relaying it to her with a calmness I didn't feel. She just stared, openmouthed, as I described walking in on Tom, seeing Cole at Metro, waking up in his bed, and then encountering Sidra.

"And now here I am, working on an article about a guy whose appearance at Metro last night will probably ruin my entire career," I said as I finished, gesturing to my computer. "And the ironic thing is, this will probably be the last thing I ever write as a journalist."

"That's not true," said Wendy, finally clamping her gaping mouth shut. "You're not going to lose your job. You didn't do anything."

"But I did," I said miserably. "I got drunk and wound up going home with a movie star I'd just interviewed."

"But you didn't do anything with him," she protested.

"Do you think that will really matter?" I asked. "Or that anyone will believe me?" Wendy didn't respond, which was all the answer I needed.

"Look," Wendy said finally, after we sat there in silence for a moment. "I'm going to edit your piece for you, okay? You can sit right there, and I won't change anything without asking you, but you just don't look quite up to it at the moment." She looked at me with a raised eyebrow. I thought about it for a second and then nodded.

"Okay," I agreed. "That would really help me out. If you don't mind."

"Of course I don't," Wendy said dismissively. "Then you're going to come home with me, and stay for a while, okay?" I started to protest, but Wendy held up a hand to silence me. "Yes, I know I live in a tiny apartment with two roommates and no room to sleep. But it's better than you being in your apartment right now. Bad vibes there. Give it a few days. You don't want to go back there yet."

She was right. It would have been horrible to try to sleep there with images of Tom and Estella fresh in my mind.

"Okay," I agreed finally, giving her a grateful smile. "Hey, thanks."

"That's what friends are for," said Wendy, playfully nudging me. "If Cole Brannon can put you up for the night, so can I."

"But do you look as good as he does without a shirt on?" I asked with a weak smile.

❧

Thirty minutes later, Wendy had saved my sanity—not that there was much of it left—by editing the Cole Brannon piece for me while I looked mutely over her shoulder. She made only a few changes and she had me verify a few facts from my notes, but otherwise, the piece was much as I'd written it the day before.

"He sounds really nice," Wendy said softly as she saved the file and closed it.

"He is," I agreed with just a hint of sadness. I wondered for a moment what he thought of me. No doubt I was his humanitarian project of the year. He'd taken an evening off from shagging movie stars to help some crazy lady who puked on him. How valiant.

I knew he would never look at me the same way he looked at Julia Roberts, Katie Holmes, or any of the other beautiful women he'd acted with. Because I would never look like them. I'd never have their grace, their glamour, or their self-confidence. I was five feet of pure average.

Gambling

It was a cruel twist of fate that left Sidra editing my article on Cole Brannon as part of her competition with Maite for the executive editor position. My only comfort was knowing that she couldn't screw it up too badly or she would be damaging her own reputation and compromising her own editorial credentials. I could imagine the war raging in her head: It must have been difficult for her not to intentionally screw me over, but if she did, it would look like her editing had ruined a perfectly good story.

I'd reviewed Sidra's changes to my article—which were, thankfully, relatively minor—by 8 p.m. and signed off on the copy by 9:00, which meant that the story on Cole was free to make its way onto *Mod*'s pages with my approval. At least one thing had turned out right.

After a nearly sleepless night at Wendy's—I had finally drifted off at about 3:30 a.m., and woke up two hours later in a cold sweat from a nightmare about Tom—I went home quickly to pick up a few changes of clothes. I arrived at *Mod*'s offices at 7 a.m., dreading the next few hours. I was sure I would be out on the street, a cardboard box of my belongings in my arms, by noon.

"Morning, Claire," said Maite from across the hall as I settled gingerly into my chair.

"Good morning," I said, sadly waving to her. She smiled, and I smiled back, realizing I was enjoying the last few hours of her respect. Maite had ascended the ladder of women's magazines by being a good writer and a good editor, and by remaining entirely professional—no matter what. Up until today, she'd probably thought the same of me. I knew she would lose all respect for me the moment she found out what had happened.

I turned on my computer and waited silently as it booted up. I sighed loudly enough that Maite poked her head out of her office to look at me.

"Are you okay?" she asked with concern.

"Yes, of course," I lied. I forced a smile. "Sorry to bother you."

"No bother at all," Maite said, shaking her head and smiling back. "You look stressed out. Rough weekend?"

"You might say that."

By 9 a.m., other staffers had started to drift in. Wendy still wasn't here, which didn't surprise me. She'd still been sleeping soundly—snoring, I might add—when I quietly left her apartment. She usually set her alarm for 8:00, but I knew it took her forever to get ready. That face didn't paint itself on every morning, nor did her closet cough up the latest in eccentric outfits without her input.

She would twirl a variety of combinations in front of the mirror for thirty minutes before deciding on something strange and senseless that would somehow look great on her. She'd float into the office by 9:30, long before anyone noticed she was late.

I had a whole pile of work for the September issue on my desk that I should have been working on, but I couldn't bring myself to do it. After all, it would surely be a waste of time. At most, I'd only be here a few more hours before getting fired.

Just then, Maite's phone rang. She chatted for a moment and then turned back around to me.

"That was Margaret," she said slowly, a strange look on her face. My heart dropped. The editor in chief never called this early. "The editorial meeting is canceled this morning. She says she won't be in until eleven." I gulped.

"Um, did she say why?" I asked gingerly. Maite shook her head slowly.

"No," she said. I gulped and tried not to look guilty. Surely Margaret knew. Sidra had told her. She was probably talking to *Mod*'s lawyers right now, asking how she could legally get rid of me as quickly as possible.

Just then, the speaker on my phone buzzed, signaling an interoffice intercom call.

"Claire, are you there?" The nasal voice of Cassie Jenkins, Margaret's assistant, filled my cubicle.

"Yes, Cassie," I said into the speaker.

"Margaret would like to see you in her office first thing at eleven." For a moment I was speechless. This was really it. I was really going to be fired in less than two hours. It was going to be the first thing Margaret did when she walked into the office. She would throw me out with the morning's trash. "Claire? Are you still there, Claire?" I realized I hadn't answered Cassie.

"Um, yeah, Cassie, I'm here," I said, my voice strained. "I'll be there. At eleven."

"I'll let Margaret know," said Cassie coolly.

"I wonder what that's about," Maite said as my intercom buzzed again to signal that Cassie had hung up.

"Um, I don't know," I lied, looking down, trying my hardest not to look guilty.

"Maybe you're getting promoted," Maite said cheerfully. "I keep telling Margaret that you're worth a lot to the magazine. Maybe she finally listened to me." I looked up at Maite with pained appreciation.

"Thanks," I mumbled.

⌒

At 10:45, I couldn't stand it any longer. Wendy had been in for an hour, and I'd whispered to her about my impending appointment. Her pained and pitying expression had only heightened my fears about what would happen in the dreaded eleven o'clock one-on-one.

"Is there anything I can do, Claire?" she asked softly as the clock inched toward 11 a.m.

"Don't worry," I said, trying to look brave. "I'll be fine."

At T-minus-ten-minutes I slowly pushed my chair back and stood up with a sigh.

"I'm going to the bathroom, Wendy," I said slowly. "I'll be back after my meeting with Margaret." My heart was heavy as I looked around at *Mod*'s offices. My coworkers scrambled from office to office with hands full of paperwork. Phones rang, copy machines whirred, and the comforting click-click of fingers on keyboards surrounded us.

"Want me to come with you?" Wendy asked gently.

"No, I'll be okay," I said, not really meaning it. I wouldn't be okay. I loved the bustle of the magazine business, the (mostly) friendly camaraderie of the women on staff, the quiet pace of the office when we weren't working on deadline. I loved that at twenty-six I was on my way up, and I had the respect of my colleagues. In ten minutes, that would be taken away from me forever. Because of Tom. Because I'd been stupid enough to believe him.

"Good luck, Claire," Wendy said. She stood and walked over to my cubicle to give me a hug. "It's going to be okay."

"No," I said, hugging her tightly and pushing back the sudden tears that had welled in my eyes. "I don't think it is."

As I began the long walk toward the bathroom on Margaret's side of the building, I felt like a prisoner being marched down the cell block on death row one last time before her execution. I looked at each coworker's face as I slowly marched toward my doom, trying to memorize them. A few looked up and smiled at me as I passed—a few said hello.

Some just looked at me strangely, which I'm sure was due to the fact that I was actually traipsing toward the executive offices with the look of death on my face.

Death did not become me.

In the bathroom I splashed water on my face, dried off with a harsh brown paper towel, and blinked at myself in the mirror. I looked horrible, which would only add fuel to Margaret's fire. She always insisted that we look as presentable as possible—after all, we were employees of *Mod* magazine, and we were supposed to look as chic and stylish as the name of the magazine implied. I was never sure how Wendy got away with the outfits she assembled, but I knew that Margaret always cast a critical eye on anyone who wasn't properly put together.

This morning the bags under my eyes and the stricken expression that I just couldn't shake didn't exactly scream "mod," if I do say so myself.

I looked at my watch and knew I had to go. It was almost 11:00, and I was on the verge of being late to my own funeral.

⟍⟋

Margaret kept me waiting for fifteen minutes before she had Cassie show me into her office. As I waited, the second hand on the Bulova clock on the wall ticked in super-slow motion. Cassie watched me silently from her desk with what looked like a little smirk on her face. It took all my self-control not to make a face at her but to smile wanly, which I did only on the slim chance that I could accumulate some last-minute good karma for the meeting if I showed a little kindness to Margaret's snotty assistant.

At twenty-two, Cassie was a recent college graduate with a useless degree in Classics from some Ivy League school her parents had paid a fortune for. The fact that she was the daughter of a woman in Margaret's social circle had earned her a place at *Mod*, which meant, of course, that Margaret had to fire Karen, her assistant of two years. Cassie had promptly alienated everyone by announcing that her assistantship was just a stepping-stone to getting one of *our* jobs.

She sneered at Wendy and me one morning in the bathroom, telling us she'd always dreamed of being a features editor, or perhaps a celebrity writer—so we shouldn't get too comfortable in our jobs.

Not that it always worked that way. Most of the women who had ascended past the rank of editorial assistant—up the chain to assistant editor, associate editor, then senior editor—knew what they were doing and had been promoted because they were talented, hardworking, and professional. After all, we had a magazine to put out. We couldn't *all* be morons if we were going to get a salable product to the newsstands each month.

The lower ranks of the magazine world were filled with young women like Cassie. They had never really worked a day in their lives and were in the business because their father's friend knew somebody who knew somebody who ran a magazine. The hardest thing about breaking into the magazine business was getting a foot in the door in the first place. Unfortunately, many of those foot-in-the-door positions at the glammest magazines went to women who were too busy getting those feet pedicured to actually bother doing any work. Eventually, most of them wound up quitting after the novelty of having a job wore off and they snagged a rich husband.

As Cassie smirked at me this morning over her spacious desk, I knew she was already planning how she'd fill my shoes once I was released. Well, at least someone would be happy about me losing my job.

The intercom on Cassie's desk buzzed, snapping her out of her smirk and jolting me out of my dark daydream.

"Cassie, please send Claire in now," Margaret's voice said. Cassie looked up.

"She's ready for you," she singsonged, smiling evilly. I forced a smile back.

"Thank you, Cassie," I said politely. With all the grace and courage I could muster, I rose from my chair and walked slowly across Margaret's outer office to the big oak doors that led to her inner realm. I placed my hand on the knob and closed my eyes for a minute, willing myself to be calm.

"Are you going in, or are you going to just stand there?" Cassie honked. I wondered for a moment just how much my karma would suffer if I hit Cassie over the head with a chair on my way out, World-Wrestling style. Hey, at least I'd leave a legacy at *Mod* beyond the "She slept with Cole Brannon" gossip that would linger.

Finally, deciding a Cassie smackdown wasn't the way to go, I turned the knob and went in.

Margaret was dressed in a cream-colored tailored pantsuit. Her dark hair was slicked back, and her eyes were heavily made-up. She looked like she would be ready to parade down a fashion runway—if she were six inches taller (and if she hadn't been born with her mother's slightly bulbous nose and too-small chin). I had to give her credit, though—she hadn't used plastic surgery to get rid of these imperfections, and she expertly played up the assets she did have (which of course included her actual *monetary* assets), so she almost always looked untouchably glamorous.

She looked tiny behind her enormous desk, an island in the middle of the spacious room, which was easily the size of three editors' offices put together. Her carpet was a plush cream that matched her pantsuit. Her massive desk and two bookshelves were glistening black, polished each night at her insistence by the janitorial staff. Framed *Mod* magazine covers, blown up to 24 x 30, lined her walls and looked somehow elegant. Last year's June cover, featuring my interview with Julia Roberts, and this year's January cover, featuring my Q & A with Reese Witherspoon, had been recent additions to the Great Wall. I looked at Julia and Reese sadly as I realized glumly that I'd never get the chance to interview people like that again—for anyone.

As shallow as the world of celebrity sometimes was, I really did love my job. I loved getting A-listers like Julia and Reese to let their guard down—if only for a few minutes—so that I could catch a glimpse of who and what they really were. There was just something about humanizing the most untouchable stars that made me feel like I was doing something worthwhile. I wanted our readers to know that the larger-than-life Hollywooders were really people just like them.

"Have a seat, Claire," Margaret said without looking up. I gulped, settling into one of the two plush beige chairs that faced her desk. I grimaced as I sank into the cushions.

I braced myself. This was it, the end of the line.

"Claire, thank you for coming on such short notice," Margaret said, finally looking up from her papers and peering at me over her Prada glasses. This was just like her, to begin politely, to suck me in before she dropped the news that I was fired. As if I wasn't expecting it.

"Of course," I mumbled. I took a deep breath.

"As you know, Claire, we have a series of professional standards at *Mod,*" Margaret began diplomatically, gazing down at me from her throne. I gulped. Great, I was in for the speech. I knew I'd been wrong, but it wasn't as bad as Margaret thought. I hadn't actually *done* anything with Cole Brannon, contrary to what Sidra had surely told her. I hadn't slept with him. Heck, I hadn't even kissed him—although I was beginning to wish that I had. If I was about to lose my job anyhow, I might as well have gone out with flying colors. But hindsight's always 20/20, isn't it?

"I'm sure that the other magazines where you worked had similar standards, so you're no doubt familiar with what I'm talking about," Margaret said. I stared at her until she arched an eyebrow. Oh, she was waiting for a response.

"Yes," I mumbled. Could this be any worse?

"In order to remain competitive, in order to maintain integrity, each magazine has to live up to certain standards of excellence," Margaret continued. "I'm sure you'll agree with me."

"Yes," I said meekly. Margaret peered at me for a moment, and I shrank even more—as if that was possible—under the weight of her gaze. She was looking at me so seriously that I knew this was it. I did a mental countdown in my head. Ten more seconds as a *Mod* employee. Nine. Eight. Seven—

"Which is why I'd like to commend you on your great work on the Cole Brannon piece," Margaret said, suddenly beaming as she interrupted my countdown.

"Huh?" My jaw dropped. Perhaps I was going insane or I'd forgotten to Q-tip my ears that morning.

"You clearly went above and beyond your duty to *Mod* to turn in a great piece that will surely help us in the circulation war against *Cosmopolitan*," Margaret continued cheerfully. "August could be the month we surpass them, Claire, thanks to your great work with this piece. I've decided to feature it on the cover. Between your great writing and Sidra's great editing, the piece is an absolute gold mine."

I simply stared, trying to digest what she was saying. This must have meant that Sidra hadn't said anything after all. Margaret obviously didn't know about my weekend with Cole, or I'd already be out the door with a pink slip. I finally sank back so heavily in relief that I almost disappeared into the chair.

"In fact, Claire," Margaret continued, "this will be the first month we feature a man on the cover. We've pushed your Julia Stiles cover back to September. Cole will be our cover face this month." My jaw dropped again. With the exception of *Good Housekeeping,* with their occasional John Travolta or Tom Hanks covers, women's magazines almost *never* featured men on the cover. Certainly magazines like *Mod, Cosmo,* and *Glamour* never swayed from their beautiful-female cover format. I couldn't count the number of times Jennifer Aniston, Courteney Cox, or Gwyneth Paltrow had graced the covers of the magazines in our genre. You'd think that people would get sick of reading about the same people over and over and over again, but somehow they never seemed to.

"Wow," I said finally, because I sensed that Margaret was waiting for a reaction. I was almost too shocked to speak. Not only had I *not* been fired, which I'd been fully braced for, but Margaret had liked my article on Cole so much that she was taking a risky move—making him the first man in history to appear on the cover of *Mod* magazine.

It surprised me even more that Sidra's editing had pleased Margaret to such an extent. She basically hadn't touched my piece at all. Was it possible she possessed journalistic skills after all? I had thought she was just a talentless spawn of Satan.

I was so shocked that it almost didn't cross my mind to wonder why Sidra hadn't told Margaret about finding Cole in my apartment. No way was Sidra that nice. She had something up her sleeve, and it made me uncomfortable to realize I now had no idea what it was. I had almost felt more comfortable when I was sure she would run immediately to Margaret with the news of my involvement with Cole.

"I'm so confident this cover will do well, Claire, and I am so impressed with your originality and appreciation of your duties at *Mod* that I've decided a little reward is in order," Margaret said. She smiled at me, and in response, I forced a confused smile of my own. Again, Margaret seemed to be waiting for me to say something.

"Um, thank you?" I said hesitantly. This was too much to take in at once. My article on Cole had been good, but it hadn't been *that* good. Or so I thought. Maybe my perception of the article had been tainted by what happened afterwards. Maybe I had done a better job than I thought.

"So, I've decided to give you a raise," Margaret said, folding her hands on her desk and leaning forward. "It's long overdue, I'm sure. You've done great work with us, and I'm simply so impressed with your work with Cole Brannon that I feel you're due."

"A raise?" I asked. "Wow. I don't know what to say." It was like I'd woken up from a nightmare and found myself in a sweet dream.

"Ten thousand more a year." Margaret beamed. Ten thousand dollars! That was enough to take a trip this year. Enough to finally pay off those mounting credit card bills I'd been doing my best to ignore. One step closer to not feeling quite so much like an impoverished New Yorker.

"Aren't you going to say anything?" Margaret asked. I realized I'd been sitting in utter silence for over a minute while Margaret waited for a response.

"I appreciate this so much, Margaret," I said finally. "I worked really hard on the piece, but I had no idea you would like it so much. I'm really flattered." There, that was good. My shocked brain had actually managed to string together a few sentences.

"There should always be a reward for those who go above and beyond the call of duty," said Margaret with an odd smile on her face. I stared at her for a moment, finally accepting the praise.

"Thank you," I said, smiling at Margaret.

"I just want you to know that I appreciate your help in the circulation war," said Margaret, looking at me with the fierce pride of a general praising her troops. I stifled a laugh. She really did see this as war against *Cosmo*. Oh well, if my on-field battle skills earned me a raise, so be it. With one last tight smile at me, Margaret turned back to flipping through the stack of paperwork on her desk. "That will be all, Claire," she said briskly. I nodded and stood up.

"Thanks again," I said. "Really."

Margaret nodded without looking up.

"Just keep up the good work," she said, still thumbing. She reached for a yellow highlighter and went over a line on the page, now ignoring me. I guess that was it. I was dismissed, with my job, my life, still intact.

Outside Margaret's office, Cassie stared at me from behind her desk, looking almost confused as I grinned at her. But the smile promptly fell from my face as I turned and saw Sidra sitting in the outer room, waiting to see Margaret.

"Oh, hello there," she said with a smile. "Tom says hello. He'd like to come by and get some of his things later. That is, if you're not *otherwise occupied*." She smiled icily, and I suddenly felt sick to my stomach again.

I knew better than to think the issue was a dead one. I knew she was jealous that Cole Brannon had wound up at my apartment. And I knew that she was the kind of woman who didn't like to be bested—by anyone, in any situation. She would look at Cole's visit with me as a deliberate affront to her. As if I had been trying to top her George Clooney stories.

As I watched Sidra rise from her chair and glide into Margaret's office, I knew with rising certainty she still had something up her sleeve. And somehow, I knew it would be even worse than getting me fired.

Flirting

hat do you think she's going to do?" I asked Wendy over salads at Les Sans Culottes, a French bistro on West Forty-sixth Street. Wendy had insisted on taking me for a "You didn't get fired" and "You got a raise" celebratory lunch.

"Sidra?" Wendy asked absently, her attention temporarily distracted by a waiter whose name tag read Jean Michel. "Cute, isn't he?" she murmured, batting her eyes at him as he looked in our direction. He smiled shyly and turned back to the table he was waiting on.

"Yes, Sidra," I said, trying not to sound exasperated. I should have known that even lunchtime dining was a pick-up opportunity for the waiter-dating Wendy. "I know this isn't over. The way she looked at me made my skin crawl."

"Claire," Wendy began with a sigh, turning her attention back to me. "Maybe you're being too sensitive about this. I mean, none of us like her, but maybe she's not *that* evil. Maybe she's just going to keep saying things about Tom to get under your skin, and that will be it."

"Maybe," I said, unconvinced.

"So I don't think you have anything to worry about," said Wendy earnestly. She watched me with concern as I stabbed halfheartedly at a leaf of lettuce.

"I don't know," I said finally. "The way she was looking at me . . . but what could be worse than getting me fired?"

"See, you're right!" said Wendy triumphantly. "If she wanted to hurt you, she would have just told Margaret, and that would have been the end of it. Why would she want to hurt you, anyhow?"

"Don't be so naive," I said flatly. "You've seen the way she looks at me. You've heard the things she says. She hates me for being successful. And now she's jealous of me for other reasons too."

"What do you mean?" Wendy asked, looking intrigued. She stopped trying to tear off a piece of the crusty baguette that lay between us and finally gave me her undivided attention. After all, Jean Michel had walked back into the kitchen and was nowhere to be seen for the time being.

I shrugged.

"She saw me with Cole Brannon in my apartment," I said slowly. "I mean, she's always going on and on about her supposed relationship with George Clooney, right? And here I am, this coworker she already hates because I'm fifteen years younger than her. I have the biggest movie star in Hollywood in my apartment, and it looks like he's spent the night. It looks like I'm actually living her lie."

Wendy looked at me for a moment, and I could almost see the wheels turning in her head. She looked down at her salad. Then she looked up at me again with a serious expression.

"You might be right," she said, her voice hushed. Concern was etched across her brow. "But what could she do to you if she hasn't gotten you fired?"

"I don't know," I murmured.

We polished off our salads in silence for a few minutes, deep in thought about what Sidra had up her sleeve. Then again, maybe I was just being paranoid and nothing more would happen.

"Enough of this," Wendy said finally. "We're supposed to be celebrating your raise!" She looked around and beckoned for our waiter, who came rushing over officiously.

"Two glasses of champagne, please," she said grandly. She grinned at me.

"Champagne?" I hissed, fighting back a smile. "We shouldn't drink! We have to go back to work in thirty minutes! And you know I'm a lightweight!"

"Yes, well I think you proved that the other night, as I'm sure Cole Brannon would confirm," Wendy teased. I blushed, despite myself. "Anyhow, what the hell, right? You worked all weekend. Who cares if you're a bit off the mark this afternoon? Besides, with all the hell you went through this morning worrying about your job, I think you need something to take the edge off." I started to protest again, but Wendy held up a hand to silence me. "I insist," she said firmly.

"Okay then," I said, smiling back. "If you insist."

The waiter scurried back in a moment with two flutes of bubbly. He set them down on the table and turned to Wendy. "Anything else, ma'am?" he asked.

"Um, yes," said Wendy, batting her eyelashes again. "See that waiter over there?" She gestured to Jean Michel, who was now filling another table's water glasses, his back to us.

"Yes, Jean Michel?" our waiter asked. "Do you need your water glasses filled? I'd be glad to do that for you."

"No, no, no," Wendy said quickly. "But could you send him over?" The waiter looked confused for a moment; then he seemed to realize what Wendy was getting at.

"Ma'am, he speaks very little English. I don't think—" Wendy cut him off.

"*Je parle Français,*" she said in perfect French. I looked at her in surprise.

"Oh," said our waiter, looking surprised and humbled. "*Oui, mademoiselle.* I'll get him for you."

He hurried off in Jean Michel's direction, and I looked at Wendy in amusement.

"Since when do you speak French?" I asked her.

"I don't," she said, eyeing Jean Michel as our waiter whispered something in his ear and his eyebrows shot up in surprise. He smiled shyly at Wendy and started over in our direction. "I just learned enough to pick up French waiters," said Wendy, still smiling at the approaching Jean Michel. She reached up and fluffed her perky red curls. "I love French restaurants, but I was tired of not being able to talk to the guys who had just come over from France. So I learned pick-up French."

I arched an eyebrow at her as Jean Michel arrived shyly at our table, his cheeks flushed with color. I had to admit, Wendy had good taste, as much as I teased her about her dating patterns. Jean Michel was tall with dark hair cascading nearly to his shoulders. His features were sharp, and his eyes were big and green.

"*Bonjour, mademoiselle,*" Jean Michel said to Wendy, his voice deep and husky. Wendy smiled.

"*Bonjour,*" she said, again with a perfect French accent. I shook my head in wonder as I watched her work. "*Comment allez-vous?*"

"*Très bien, merci,*" Jean Michel responded enthusiastically, apparently convinced that Wendy spoke his language. He launched into several other rapidly spoken French sentences, which Wendy nodded and smiled at.

"You understand him?" I whispered when he looked away for a moment to check on his other tables.

"Not one word," she said. She grinned at me. "But do I really have to?" I shook my head and tried not to laugh as Jean Michel turned eagerly back to us.

"So that's pick-up French," I said.

"That's pick-up French," Wendy confirmed with a grin.

An hour later, I was back at work, flipping through clips I'd pulled from our research service. I was supposed to go to a press conference on Thursday for Kylie Dane's new movie, and I wanted to read everything I could about the movie and about her before I showed up for it.

Of course I was, as usual, overpreparing. But I liked to go into every interview—even press conferences—as fully primed as possible. I was particularly apprehensive about this press conference, because, of course, Kylie Dane had been linked in the tabloids and gossip pages to Cole Brannon. But he had insisted it wasn't true, and I supposed she was as much a victim of the gossip as he was. Still, I couldn't help feeling a tiny twinge of jealousy.

As I flipped through article after article, astonished that I still had a job, I marveled at the media's fascination with everything in a celebrity's life. There seemed to be paparazzi hiding behind every bush, waiting to snap photos of A-listers out to lunch, shopping in Beverly Hills, or whispering in corners with unidentified people of the opposite gender. Everything was speculated upon, feeding rumors that had a habit of sticking around.

Then it hit me.

I got up quickly and crossed over to Wendy's adjoining cubicle.

"Wendy?" I said quickly from her doorway. My palms were already sweating, and my heart was pounding rapidly.

"Hey, girl," she said, turning around, her curls flying as she turned her head. She smiled at me, her miles of teeth gleaming, not yet realizing that I was on the verge of full-out panic. "What's up?"

"*Tattletale*," I said. She looked at me in confusion.

"What?"

"*Tattletale*," I repeated. "That's how Sidra is going to get me. With an article in *Tattletale* tomorrow morning. Why just get me fired, when she can embarrass the hell out of me at the same time?"

Wendy simply stared. My heart continued to race, and I felt like I was going to fall over. I put a hand on the wall of Wendy's cubicle to steady myself, waiting for her response.

"You could be right," she said, her voice hushed. She looked as horrified as I felt. Then she cleared her throat and tried to smile encouragingly at me. "But that probably won't happen. I mean, who would believe her?"

"*Tattletale*," I answered quickly. "*Tattletale* would believe her. Enough to print the story anyhow. They don't care if it's true. Just if it sells copies. And that's pretty juicy, right? *Mod* writer sleeps with hottest movie star in Hollywood?"

"No way," Wendy said firmly, her face full of forced confidence. She reached out for my hand, giving it a quick squeeze as she smiled at me bravely again. "The whole magazine world knows Sidra's reputation. You don't really think anyone believes the George Clooney thing, do you?"

"But *Tattletale* still prints it," I said grimly. "Every time. Because it sells magazines. And because Sidra is tight with the editors there. She's always quoted in there talking about her *time with George*."

"You're right," Wendy muttered finally. She looked down at her lap and then looked up at me again, her brow now furrowed with concern. "But there's no reason they'd believe her about you, right?"

"What if there are photos?" I asked.

"Photos?"

"Like from when I left his hotel. When he got in the cab with me."

"But you didn't see any photographers, right?" Wendy asked, looking hopeful. She reached up and pushed her spilling red curls out of her face.

"That doesn't mean they weren't there. Hiding in the bushes or something. You know the paparazzi."

"Oh, geez," Wendy said seriously. I knew she didn't want to say it, but I was potentially screwed. Very screwed.

We were silent for a moment. I listened to the blood rushing through my ears as my heart pounded double-time. Wendy nervously chewed her lip.

"You didn't actually leave the hotel with him, though," she said finally. "So the best they can do is photos of the two of you together in a cab. Which could be totally innocent."

"Until Sidra adds in her narration," I said quickly. "Until she tells them we had just left the hotel together and were on our way to my apartment to have sex again."

Wendy was silent for a moment, her brow furrowed in concentration.

"Maybe we're overreacting," she said finally. "I mean, maybe Sidra isn't out to get you. She didn't get you fired, right?"

"You know she hates me," I said.

"It doesn't make any sense," Wendy said, shaking her head. "Just because you're a few years ahead of where she was at your age?"

"Just because I became a senior editor a decade younger than she did."

"You'd think she'd be ready to call it even at this point," Wendy muttered. "I mean, her sister was screwing your boyfriend, for God's sake."

I felt unexpected tears rush to my eyes, and I tried to sniff them away before Wendy noticed. Too late.

"God, I'm sorry," she said quickly. "I shouldn't have said that. About her sister, I mean."

"No, no," I said, wiping my eyes with my hand. I forced a smile. "I guess it's still fresh, you know?" I didn't want to tell her that part of the problem was the illogical—not to mention embarrassing—feelings I still had for Tom. What was wrong with me? How was it that every ounce of my brain could be telling me one thing and my heart could feel another?

"I know," said Wendy gently. She got up and hugged me tightly. "He's an asshole, Claire. Forget about him. He was never good enough for you."

"I know," I said. But I didn't know. It wasn't like men were lining up in droves, beating down my door for the chance to have a date with me. And appearances aside, it's not like anything had actually *happened* with Cole Brannon.

The phone in my cubicle rang, snapping me out of my dire self-analysis. Wendy was still looking at me with concern, and I realized I'd been standing in the hallway for at least a whole minute, staring off into space as I thought about what a failure I was as dating material.

"You okay?" she asked as my phone rang a second time. "Want me to get that for you?"

"No, I'll get it," I said. I shook my head and snapped myself out of self-pity mode. Fortunately, the cubicles in our office were so small and close together that I could easily navigate from Wendy's office space to mine in time to answer the telephone. I wondered briefly why this morning's raise couldn't have come with an actual office. I made it around the corner after the third ring, diving for the phone.

"Claire Reilly," I answered, breathless from my dive. I'd knocked a pile of papers on the ground, and I started picking them up, balancing the phone between my shoulder and ear. I was greeted by silence. Perhaps I hadn't reached the phone in time. Great, now on top of everything else, I was missing business calls because I was immersed in self-pity. "Hello?" I said into the silence.

"Claire?"

My breath caught in my throat as I recognized the voice.

It was Tom. I stopped shuffling the papers and stood stock-still. I didn't answer.

"Claire?" he asked again. His voice sounded desperate, searching. Or perhaps that was just me hoping that he missed me enough to sound desperate. "Are you there, babe? It's Tom."

I still didn't answer. Wendy was standing up, looking at me quizzically over the cubicle. She knew something was wrong. I didn't know what to do. What did he want? Should I answer him? Would he ask me to forgive him, to take him back? What would I say?

Still staring at Wendy, as if she could provide an answer to the questions I hadn't asked her, I cleared my throat, but that was as far as I got. I wasn't even sure I wanted to talk to him. I hadn't thought about the possibility of him calling me at work.

"Claire? Are you there?" His voice sounded concerned. But I was too screwed up to deal with this now. I slammed the phone back down without saying a word.

"Are you okay?" Wendy asked, looking at me worriedly. I slowly sat down in my chair, forgetting about the avalanche of papers that had spilled around my feet. "Who was that?"

"It was Tom," I said slowly, staring at the phone. I wondered if he'd call back. I realized suddenly that I wanted him to. I wanted him to work at getting back into my life. I wanted him to show me that I was worth that much.

Geez, I was pathetic.

I willed the phone to ring, but it stubbornly stayed silent.

"Good for you," Wendy said warmly over the cubicle, apparently mistaking my grief for resolve. "You stay strong, girl. Good for you, for hanging up on him."

"Yeah," I said softly, still looking at the silent phone. "Good for me."

⌒

I felt sick all afternoon and wound up alone in the bathroom at about four o'clock, finally vomiting in the toilet. I realized I was setting some kind of record. I'd thrown up twice in the last few days, which was strange for me, as I hadn't thrown up since the eleventh grade, when I puked right in the middle of Mr. Dorsett's American History class. Amazingly, I'd made it all the way through college without ever throwing up once—not even after keg parties, when I was surrounded by vomiting friends. And here I was, for the second time in three days. Someone call the *Guinness Book*.

I rinsed my mouth out in the sink and splashed water on my face, thankful that there were no witnesses to my sorry state. Looking down to make sure that I hadn't gotten any vomit on my clothes, I noticed that my stomach was looking flatter than it had in months. Hey, maybe this was the secret to a slender body—have men break your heart and get rid of all the food you've eaten that day. Excellent. Weight Loss for Losers. Bulimia for the Brokenhearted. I could launch my own diet franchise.

I spit a mouthful of water into the sink, took a deep breath, and looked at myself in the mirror. I looked awful. My makeup was all gone, thanks to the water I'd splashed on my face. Without it, the dark circles under my eyes were more pronounced, and even my freckles looked pale and boring on my lifeless skin.

I was still assessing myself in the mirror when Wendy burst into the bathroom, a ball of energy, as usual.

"There you are!" she exclaimed as she bustled through the door. "I've been looking everywhere for you!" Her face darkened as I turned to her. She looked me up and down for a moment. "Are you okay?"

"I'm fine," I said, forcing a smile that I hoped looked cheerful. She looked at me doubtfully, but I knew she could read on my face that I didn't want to talk about it. "What's up?"

She looked at me with concern for another moment, then seemed to decide that the best course of action would be pretending that nothing was wrong. She smiled at me.

"You just had a bouquet of flowers delivered!" she said. "Let's go see who they're from!" I looked at her, puzzled.

"Are you sure they're for me?" I asked. No one had ever sent me flowers. I know, that's pathetic, right? I'm twenty-six years old and have never gotten flowers from a man. Not once.

In contrast, Wendy seemed to get them from various waiters at least once or twice a month.

"Maybe they're for you," I said.

"They say 'Claire Reilly' on the card," Wendy said, smiling. "They are definitely for you!"

I looked at her for a moment, my mind spinning through the possibilities. They had to be from Tom. I'd hung up on him a few hours ago, and he felt so bad that he'd sent me flowers to apologize. The card would say, "I love you more than life itself," or something equally devoted. He'd call later and tell me how sorry he was, how wrong he had been, how much he loved me. It would take me a long time to forget what happened, but I could make it work. I'd never even have to tell my disapproving mother that I hadn't been able to hang on to yet another man.

"Well . . ." Wendy said, her voice trailing off. She opened the bathroom door. "Are you coming? I can't stand the suspense." She winked at me and I smiled.

"Okay," I said finally. I followed her out the door and back through the narrow hallway toward the editorial room.

"Who do you think they're from?" Wendy asked excitedly as we walked side by side.

"I don't know," I said softly. But I did know. I knew they were from Tom. I just didn't want Wendy to know that I was thinking that way or that I cared. She thought that my hanging up on him earlier was a sign of strength, and I preferred that she see me that way. I didn't want her to know I had spent the rest of the day fantasizing about how he'd apologize and beg me to take him back.

I looked at her sideways.

"Maybe they're from Tom," I said hesitantly.

"Are you kidding me?" Wendy asked sharply. "Tom has never sent you flowers. He's a complete jackass. Are you delusional?"

"I don't know," I mumbled. But they were from Tom. I just knew it.

We rounded the corner, and I felt my breath catch in my throat when I saw the display on my desk.

It was the largest arrangement of flowers I'd ever seen. It was easily triple the size of the bouquets that landed on Wendy's desk a few times a month. Three dozen white long-stem roses stood upright and slightly angled in a giant vase, accented with an immense violet ribbon. They were flanked by scores of perfect white lilies. As we approached, I could see a small white envelope on the end of a plastic wand protruding from the field of lilies.

"Wow," I said involuntarily. It was beautiful.

"I know," Wendy said in awe. "It's the prettiest bouquet I've ever seen."

"Wow," I repeated. We stopped at my desk and I plucked the card from the plastic wand. Wendy waited eagerly beside me, bouncing up and down like a toddler about to receive a cookie. I held the card in my hand for a moment, staring at the flowers and imagining what Tom would say in the note. What would I do after I opened it? Should I call him? Or wait for him to call me?

"Open it, open it," Wendy said eagerly. I looked at her in amusement. She looked ten times more excited than I was. I wondered how she'd react when she realized the amazing spread was from Tom.

Amanda and Gail, the two assistants who manned the copy desk, drifted over to look at the flowers as I held the card in my hand, letting my imagination run.

"They're beautiful," Amanda breathed, smiling at me. She reached out to touch one of the roses, then bent down to admire the vase.

"Who are they from?" Gail asked, also smiling as she gently fingered the baby's breath.

"I don't know," I lied with a smile, forgetting that I'd just been sick mere moments before. Suddenly I felt fine, knowing that somewhere out there, Tom cared. "Let me open the card."

Wendy and the two copy assistants waited eagerly as I slit the envelope with my index finger and pulled out the small note card inside. As my eyes scanned the few quick lines on the card, I felt the breath go out of me, my heart dropping in my chest.

"Who are they from? Who are they from?" Wendy asked excitedly. I looked up at the three eager faces clustered around my flowers. I plastered a smile on my face and tried to will my heart to stop racing. I wondered if they noticed the color rising in my cheeks or my suddenly shaky hands stuffing the card back in the envelope.

"They're from my mom," I said quickly.

"Wow," Gail said admiringly. "That's amazing. My mom has never sent me anything like that. You're really lucky."

"Is it your birthday or something?" Amanda asked. Wendy was silently staring at me. She knew I was lying.

"No," I said softly. "It's not my birthday." They were still grinning at me, so I kept the smile plastered across my face.

I shot a quick glance at Wendy, who was still looking at me suspiciously. "I, uh, have to go to the bathroom. I'll be right back."

I stuffed the envelope into my pocket and rushed back down the hallway with Wendy trailing quickly after me. I took a quick look back and saw Gail and Amanda looking at us strangely, but I ignored them. I was sure they'd cluster around the flowers again and in a moment forget I was gone.

"Who are they really from?" Wendy asked, sounding almost accusatory, as we pushed into the bathroom. I silently bent to look under the stalls. Satisfied that we were alone, I took the envelope out of my pocket and handed it to Wendy.

I watched as she opened the envelope and quickly scanned the card. Her jaw dropped, and her eyes widened. She looked up and stared at me in shock. She looked back at the card, up at me, and then back at the card again.

"*Dear Claire,*" she read aloud finally, sounding incredulous. I blushed more as I heard the words read aloud. "*I'm sorry if I caused you any trouble. You're a wonderful woman, and I'm glad to have spent time with you, even if it was under less-than-ideal circumstances. I just wanted to make sure you were okay. Call me if you need anything at all. Best wishes, Cole Brannon.*"

Wendy looked up at me again, shock splashed across her face.

"Cole Brannon?" she squealed. "*Cole Brannon?!* COLE BRANNON sent you flowers?"

"Shhhh . . ." I hushed her quickly. "Please, I don't want anyone to know." Wendy ignored me.

"Cole Brannon sent you flowers," she repeated quietly. This time, it was a statement instead of a question.

"Cole Brannon sent me flowers," I confirmed softly, my heart still beating rapidly in my chest.

"And he thinks you're a wonderful woman," she breathed.

"I guess so." I shrugged, feeling both embarrassed and somewhat elated. I quickly tried to quash the latter feeling, knowing it would do me no good.

"And you didn't even sleep with him," Wendy said. My eyes widened in shock.

"What? No!"

Wendy looked up at me again. She was holding the card in her hands like it was the Holy Grail.

"He likes you, Claire," she said finally.

"No, no," I protested, aware that my cheeks were growing ever redder. "That's silly. He just feels sorry for me." Wendy shook her head.

"Men who feel sorry for people don't send flowers," she said with certainty.

"Maybe men with millions of dollars to blow do," I said quickly. This was ludicrous. This couldn't be happening. At work, no less. What if someone—what if Sidra— saw the note?

"I don't think so, Claire," Wendy said. She finally handed the card and envelope back to me. I stuffed them both in my pocket. She was still looking at me with a strange expression on her face.

"It's nothing," I insisted, not really meaning it. My face was on fire, and I tried not to meet Wendy's eye. "It doesn't mean anything."

"I think it means a lot," Wendy said softly.

I tried not to acknowledge the fact that deep down, I hoped it meant a lot too. But it would be ridiculous and unprofessional to think that anything could ever happen between Cole Brannon and someone like me. Besides, Tom was out there somewhere, and I knew I'd never forgive myself if I didn't at least try again to make it work.

Gossiping

I was up at 5:30 the next morning, the victim of another mostly sleepless night. When I had finally drifted off, I had nightmares about appearing with Cole in the pages of *Tattletale,* where Margaret would see me and instantly fire me, and Tom would refuse to even speak with me again.

My tossing and turning hadn't been helped when Wendy stumbled in, tipsy and mumbling in broken French, just past 2 a.m., after a date with Jean Michel. She must have forgotten that I was sleeping at her place, on a twin air mattress wedged between her full bed and her tiny closet, because she tripped over the edge of the mattress and landed facedown on top of me as she tried to make her way to the laundry hamper in the corner.

After disentangling from her and listening to her soliloquy about the virtues of French men in general, and Jean Michel in particular, I stared at the ceiling and tried not to think about Tom, Cole, or *Tattletale* until dawn began filtering in through Wendy's window.

It wasn't hard to stay awake, despite the fact that I was exhausted. Wendy's snoring was enough to prevent me from drifting off. Besides, every time I closed my eyes I saw Tom and Sidra's sister together in my bed. As I counted down the minutes until daybreak (not nearly as effective as counting sheep, by the way), I grew more and more worried that Sidra's revenge would come in the form of a *Tattletale* article that would forever cost me my reputation. By the time I got up at 5:30, I was sure of it.

I dressed quickly and grabbed my things. *Tattletale* would be on the newsstands already, and I wanted to see it as soon as possible. My heart was pounding as I ran some lipstick quickly across my lips, gave myself one last look in the mirror, and dashed downstairs. There was a newspaper stand two blocks up from Wendy's apartment, and I jogged all the way there, desperately spinning through the possibilities of what I'd find between the covers of the gossip rag.

"One copy of *Tattletale,* please," I panted as I arrived at the newsstand, breathless from my dash. The vendor was still in the process of cutting the plastic cords binding the stacks of magazines and papers that would soon land in organized piles and displays around his cart. I quickly spotted today's *Tattletale* in the corner.

"We're not open yet," he said, without turning around. I took a deep breath.

"Please," I begged. "I'm desperate. I'll give you . . ." I paused while I rifled through my wallet. "I'll give you twelve dollars for it." I quickly counted my change. "And sixty-three cents."

The vendor finally turned and looked me up and down.

"You're going to give me twelve sixty-three for a tabloid that will cost you a dollar when I open in thirty minutes?"

"Yes, please," I said hurriedly, thrusting the money at him. The vendor stared at me for another moment, shrugged, and took the cash from my hand.

"Fine with me," he said. "Why do you need this so badly anyhow?" He looked at me critically, his box cutter poised over the pile of magazines. I forced a smile.

"Just an important article, that's all," I said. He stared at me for another moment. I could no longer stand it. "Please!" I begged. He rolled his eyes.

"Women," he muttered under his breath. He finally slashed through the cords, and they fell limp on the sides of the stack. He slowly lifted up a *Tattletale* and stared at the cover before he handed it to me. I was practically bouncing up and down now, trying to restrain myself from reaching out and snatching it from him. "Harrison Ford and Calista Flockhart Have Lovers' Quarrel?" he asked, reading slowly from the cover. "Is this what's so important?"

"No, no!" I exclaimed. "Please! Just give it to me." The vendor smiled, and I realized that he was enjoying torturing me.

"Clay Terrell Dishes About Tara Templeton's Booty?" he asked slowly, reading another headline. He looked up at me with an arched eyebrow and laughed.

"No!" I exclaimed again. He looked back at the magazine, and I knew he was about to read another headline. I snatched the magazine from his hands before he had the chance to do so. "Thank you!" I said over my shoulder, ignoring his startled expression and walking away. I had paid twelve dollars and sixty-three cents for a copy of a gossip rag I hated. I didn't need to listen to the vendor's commentary too.

I waited until I'd rounded the corner out of the vendor's sight to rip open the magazine. I leaned into the side of a building and flipped quickly to the table of contents. My heart sank as I read the fifth item in the highlighted "Reads of the Week."

"Cole Brannon's Women: Who's That Girl with Hollywood's Hottest Hunk?"

"Shit," I said out loud as I flipped to page 18. "Shit, shit, shit, shit," I mumbled under my breath, desperately flipping, wondering why pages always stuck together when you needed to see something. It must be Murphy's Law of Magazines. "Shit, shit, shit."

I finally flipped past pages 16 and 17 and took a deep breath. This was it. One more flip of the page and my life would be over. There would be pictures of us together and quotes from Sidra. Hell, maybe they'd even found our star-struck cab driver and paid him to tell his story. I took a deep breath and turned the page.

Cole Brannon's now-familiar blue eyes twinkled from a huge photo, splashed in color across the newsprint rag. My heart thumped as I took it all in. His arm was thrown comfortably over the shoulder of a blond woman as they strolled together—she was gazing adoringly up at him as he looked out in the distance.

But the woman wasn't me.

It was Kylie Dane. The married actress.

Who he had sworn to me that he wasn't seeing.

"What?" I mumbled to myself. I was relieved, of course, but I also had a strange and unexpected feeling that felt suspiciously like jealousy.

But that made no sense. What did I care if Cole Brannon wanted to sleep with Kylie Dane? It wasn't any of my business. I was just mad that he'd lied to me. Yes, that was it. I was mad at myself for believing his lie. I took a deep breath and willed myself to be calm.

The discomfort returned in a flash, though, when I saw the words printed at the bottom corner of the page:

"For more of Cole Brannon's women, turn to page 33."

"Shit," I mumbled again. The big photo of Kylie and Cole was just a teaser. She was the biggest star he was sleeping with. On page 33 my cover would be blown, and it would be even worse than I'd originally suspected. I'd be playing second fiddle to one of the sluttiest women in Hollywood. "Shit, shit, shit." I flipped quickly through the pages, getting stuck again as I desperately tried to rush to page 33.

I finally found the continued article and stared desperately at the page. It featured three photos of Cole with different women, each complete with its own caption. I quickly scanned each photo, trying to keep my eyes from glazing over.

None of them were me.

I heaved a huge sigh of relief and tried not to feel jealous as I looked at Cole walking through Central Park with a scantily clad Kylie Dane. Cole at dinner in a fancy restaurant with a dark-haired woman identified as Ivana Donatelli, his publicist. Cole locked in an embrace with a perfectly toned, leather-clad Jessica Gregory, the star of TV's *Spy Chicks*.

I slowly flipped the page, just in case the story was continued, but thankfully, the next page just featured a story about Carnie Wilson's weight loss. I resisted the urge to look down at my thighs for comparison.

I flipped back to page 33 again and stared hard at the photos, my heart pounding quickly in anger.

He had lied. I couldn't believe it. He'd made me think he was different. He'd made me think he was a real gentleman and that the stories about him with other women weren't true. He'd looked me in the eye and told me that he'd never get involved with a married woman, but here he was canoodling in Central Park with a practically naked Kylie Dane. In full color. There was no denying it. I wouldn't necessarily believe a story in the often unreliable *Tattletale,* but there was no mistaking what the photos meant.

And Wendy's reports about Ivana Donatelli had been true, too. In the photo Cole was leaning across the small round table to whisper something in her ear, and she was blushing. A bottle of champagne sat between them, and they each had a full flute of bubbly near their elbow. Ivana's sparkling black hair cascaded alluringly over her bare shoulders, coming to rest at the level of the diamond necklace she wore around her slender neck, surely a gift from Cole.

And his pose with Jessica Gregory looked anything but innocent. The *Spy Chicks* star had her arms thrown around his neck. He was picking her up off the ground, lifting her up so that they were nose-to-nose, gazing into each other's eyes. It looked like they were milliseconds away from locking lips. Her red leather pantsuit clung to the perfect curves of her body, glistening in the light.

I flipped back to pages 18 and 19, where Cole and Kylie were splashed across two full pages, their arms comfortably around each other. A five-year-old would be able to tell they were more than just friends. She was gazing adoringly up at him, snuggled tightly against his body as they walked. He was pulling her against him, his hand resting on her shoulder as her bosom pressed into his side. He was looking in the direction of the camera, although not right at it. I stared for a moment at his blue eyes, which had seemed so innocent and kind on Sunday.

"Liar," I mumbled aloud at his picture.

I suddenly felt furious. At myself, and at Cole. How could I have been so stupid to have been taken in by his charms? To have actually believed, even for a second, that he cared, even remotely? He was an actor. It was his job to make me think what he wanted me to think. And damn it, I'd fallen for it like a rookie, like some silly little reporter who'd never met a celebrity before. Like some silly little lovesick girl. Like someone desperate to be appreciated.

I was such an idiot.

I wouldn't normally have behaved that way. Tom had crushed me, and in a moment of weakness I'd been taken in by a professional con artist's charms. Damn it, he *was* sleeping with half of Hollywood. And I'd been so ready to give him the benefit of the doubt.

I angrily slammed the *Tattletale* closed and stuffed it into my bag. I pulled away from the brick wall I'd been leaning against, brushed my skirt off, and straightened my blouse. I took a deep breath and began walking toward the F train. It was only 6:30 a.m., and I knew I'd be in the office by 7:15 if I left now, but I didn't have much of a choice. There was nowhere else to go, and besides, what better way to run from my problems? When in doubt, bury yourself in work.

"You like him," Wendy whispered bluntly as she stared at me with wide eyes over the wall that divided our cubicles.

"What?" I asked, making a face at her. "That's ridiculous. I don't *like* him."

"Why do you care who he's spotted with in *Tattletale* then?" she asked innocently. Today, her typically outlandish style was toned down a bit with modest, natural makeup colors and slim Diesel jeans. The only clue of Wendy's peculiar fashion sense was the low-plunging neckline of the lime green shirt she wore under a gauzy beige cardigan, and the orange scarf she had tied around her neck.

"It's not that I care who he's in *Tattletale* with," I said, shooting a dirty glance at the gossip rag protruding from the top of my bag. "It's just that he lied to me."

"And made you think he liked you," Wendy said, finishing my thought.

"No," I protested. "I don't care whether he likes me. Why would I care? You know nothing could happen, anyhow. It would be totally unprofessional."

"Hmm," said Wendy, arching an eyebrow at me. "So you don't care? At all?"

"Nope."

"Okay." She winked at me. "Whatever you say." I fixed her with a glare. Why did she think I cared? I didn't care about Cole Brannon.

"It just proves that all men are scum," I said with finality. Wendy arched an eyebrow.

"All men?" she asked. "I'd agree with you that a vast majority are. But all men? I don't think so."

"I do," I muttered. First Tom, now Cole. Lying, cheating scum. I felt angrier at Cole the more I thought about it. Who did he think he was? Just because he was some hotshot movie star.

"Jean Michel isn't scum," Wendy said dreamily, batting her eyes and looking off into space.

"Glad to hear it," I said, trying not to roll my eyes. I wasn't in the mood to hear the virtues of Wendy's waiters today. I didn't know how she did it. *She* dumped *them. She* was always the one to lose interest and move on. As long as I'd known her, she'd never been dumped. She'd never been cheated on. She'd never even been treated as anything less than a princess. Why did I attract guys who liked to screw me over and lie to me?

"C'mon, Claire, you can't believe everything you read," said Wendy gently.

"I don't," I said firmly. "But I believe what I see. And those were not innocent pictures. With any of those women."

"Maybe there's an explanation," Wendy said quietly.

"And maybe there's not," I said, looking up at her. "He lied, Wendy. He lied, and he's a sex addict. He's sleeping around with everyone. Anyhow, I'm sick of talking about this. I really am. I made a mistake by believing what he told me, but that's over now. He'll get the complimentary article he wants in *Mod* magazine, and I'll never have to see him again." Somehow, the words didn't make me feel as good as they should have.

"What about the flowers?" Wendy asked softly. I'd been trying to ignore them all morning, which was pretty difficult considering they were overflowing all over my desk. They still looked perfect, and they smelled beautifully tantalizing. "Aren't you going to thank him?"

I snorted.

"No," I said firmly. "In fact, we're going to pretend this never happened." I opened my desk drawer and pulled out the card that had come with the flowers—the sweet, sensitive card that was obviously a lie. He didn't care about me. I tore it in half and dropped it into the garbage can. Wendy gasped.

"You're throwing the card away?" she asked.

"I just did," I said. "And I don't want to talk about it anymore."

⌒

Margaret called an editorial meeting for eleven o'clock that morning, to replace the one she'd canceled the day before. I was relieved in a way, because it gave me an excuse to focus on something other than Cole Brannon. Besides, I was looking forward to thirty minutes without Wendy's half-pitying, half-accusatory glances.

The only downside to the meeting was that Sidra would be there. I'd have to squirm in discomfort as she looked at me smugly, content with the knowledge that I'd been summarily dismissed in the most embarrassing way by a slimy boyfriend who was now screwing her sister.

As I settled into a chair at the oval table, I smiled at Anne Amster, the senior features editor and the only other person to have arrived for the meeting. She was Wendy's direct superior, a fantastic features editor who did a great job of directing her section of the magazine. Like me, she looked much younger than she was and sometimes had trouble being taken seriously by those who didn't know her. Her wiry black hair framed her face in a pixie cut, and her features were sharp and childlike. She smiled back at me.

I hadn't yet been able to decide whether the weekly editorial meetings were actually useful or not. In theory, the senior members of the staff were supposed to discuss the magazine and the articles we were featuring in the month we were currently working on. We were supposed to give progress reports to help debate and decide what direction the magazine would take.

Instead, we pitifully offered suggestions and had them immediately shot down by Margaret while the executive editor, Donna Foley, who would soon be retiring, tried to give us encouraging looks. She would jot down notes about what we said and discuss them with Margaret later. Eventually, the good ideas would end up becoming a part of that month's issue. But of course Margaret would take full credit for them, saying things like, "I came up with that idea over dinner at Lutèce the other night," even when there were eight witnesses to the fact that the idea had been proposed by one of us at an editorial meeting. We'd long since learned that it was better to keep quiet and simply be thankful that Margaret was running the *Mod* ship with a little help from those of us who actually knew the magazine industry—even if it was completely thankless help.

Sidra glided in five minutes late, swooping into the empty seat beside Anne, who politely said hello, oblivious to the death looks Sidra was already shooting me. Sidra ignored her greeting, and Anne finally shrugged and shook her head. I had never talked to Anne about the Triplets, but I suspected she wasn't a fan any more than I was.

Today Sidra was dressed in skintight beige leather pants that accentuated her slender hips, and a fitted black top that showed off the curves of her fake bosom.

"It's Gucci," she said haughtily in response to the other editors' stares. No matter how many times we all saw Sidra, her outfit choices never failed to astonish any of us. I'd never seen her wear the same thing twice, and her clothes were always striking. "Couture," she added, tittering lightly. "George loved it on me."

I tried not to roll my eyes. We all ignored her. Her George Clooney references were like a broken record we all hated listening to.

Before anyone else had a chance to speak, Margaret bustled into the room and glided to the head of the table.

One might think that in a conference room with an oval table, we would align ourselves equally, like the knights of King Arthur's court. I'd thought that when I showed up for my first editorial meeting a year and a half ago, until I noticed that the arrangement of chairs divided the oval nearly in half. Eight of us sat squished into the half closer to the door, while Margaret reigned supreme from the other half, splaying her papers out in front of her and gazing down the table at us, her loyal subjects. We were all subjected to an hour of bumping elbows and fighting for space while Margaret leaned back and enjoyed the room.

"Happy *Mod* morning," Margaret greeted us with the same silly words she used to open each editorial meeting.

"Happy *Mod* morning," we all grumbled back, because we knew we'd be the subjects of Margaret's wrath that day if we didn't.

"Let's begin," Margaret said, contentedly leaning back in her throne. She nodded in Donna's direction. "Donna?" she said.

Donna sighed. She ran all of *Mod*'s editorial meetings from her seat in the eight-member throng at the lower half of the oval table.

"It looks like we wrapped up August successfully and on time," Donna said, reading from her notes, trying not to bump elbows with Jeffrey on her left and Carol on her right. "As most of you probably know, Margaret made a last-minute decision to sub the Julia Stiles cover with a Cole Brannon cover, which breaks somewhat from *Mod* tradition." Her voice sounded strained. A few pairs of eyebrows shot up in surprise, and a few editors glanced my way. Sidra and Margaret both looked suspiciously smug.

"According to Margaret," Donna continued, glancing at her boss, "Claire's Cole Brannon interview was very intriguing and will have a good chance of increasing our circulation." I tried not to blush as several heads swiveled toward me. A few editors smiled encouragingly from across the table. "I didn't have a chance to see it myself, but I'm sure Margaret knows what she's doing." She didn't sound too sure. My stomach swam uncomfortably.

"The rest of the issue went off without a hitch, just the way we planned it," Donna continued. "I talked to Julia

Stiles's publicist, and she's okay with us using Julia for the September cover. Her movie is coming out Labor Day Weekend anyhow, so it will be better timing for them. I had to promise another of her clients a Q & A in the September issue, though, so she didn't make a big deal out of this whole thing. Can you do that, Claire?"

I nodded and felt relieved. In this business, timing was everything. If Julia's movie had been scheduled for a late July or August release date, her publicist would be screaming bloody murder right now. Most celebs didn't grant interviews out of the goodness of their hearts. A-listers and most B-listers agreed to features only when they had a movie, TV series, or album coming out, because being featured in a top women's mag was a guaranteed way to increase their fan base. When we had originally agreed with Julia's camp six months ago to feature her this summer, her new movie was scheduled for a late July release, which made the August issue perfect. Thankfully, the release date had been moved to Labor Day Weekend last month, so her publicist had likely been more than willing to make the switch to our September issue.

"Okay, the September issue," Donna continued. A few editors took out pads of paper and started to jot down notes as Donna spoke. "According to the ad department, we're going to have four more pages of editorial than we'd counted on, which will be great. I'd like to use one page to expand the fashion section, because Sidra, Sally, and Samantha are shooting on location in Italy this month, and they've promised us a great romantic spread of fall fashions in Venice."

Sidra nodded without looking up and began filing her nails with a diamond-studded nail file.

"As for the remaining three pages, I'm . . . *we're* . . . open to suggestions." Donna glanced quickly at Margaret to see if she'd noticed the slip, but she hadn't. She was busy gazing out the window.

"The clouds look like little sheep in the sky today,"

Margaret said suddenly. We all looked at her strangely. I stifled a laugh. Sometimes she was like a little child. Donna took a deep breath and continued.

"Claire," she said. I turned to look at her. "Margaret and I discussed adding a celebrity Q & A with someone up-and-coming." Out of the corner of my eye, I caught Sidra's glare. She was no doubt furious that I was getting any extra attention. "Would you be interested in that? If it works out, we could try to make it a monthly feature. It wouldn't be too tough, just a straight one-page Q & A with a young newcomer. You know, identify the next Brad Pitt. That kind of thing."

"Sure," I agreed.

"It was my idea," Margaret interjected, turning her attention momentarily back to the group. "Because of Claire's strong work on the Cole Brannon piece." She winked at me, and I forced a smile. Donna sighed again and Margaret's attention drifted back out the window.

"Any ideas for the remaining two pages?" Donna asked. She made a note on her pad and looked up.

"How about a two-page feature on the '20 Sexiest Things Women Can Do in Bed'?" Cathy Joseph, the sixtysomething copy chief, asked in her perfectly clipped voice. I smiled. It was always strange to hear a woman pushing seventy saying anything at all about sex. But just last month she'd been the one to suggest August's sex feature: "10 New Ways to Have an Orgasm." I hoped I was still having orgasms at her age. For that matter, I wished I was having them now.

Donna smiled at Cathy.

"Sounds good to me," she said. Of course it did. Cathy was a forty-year veteran of the magazine business, and it was no coincidence that she was also the fountain of more editorial ideas than anyone else on staff. The funny thing about women's magazines was that once you'd had a subscription to a magazine for five years or so, you would have read every service article ever written. Sure, there were new celebs to feature every month and new spins on old ideas, but women's mags recycled the same hundred or so self-help, sex advice, and to-do articles every few years. For example, there was no doubt in my mind that the "20 Sexiest Things Women Can Do in Bed" wouldn't include a single thing that had never before been mentioned in *Mod*—or in *Cosmo, Glamour,* or *Marie Claire* for that matter. After all, creative as we might be, there were a finite number of things one could actually figure out to do between the sheets. I had a sneaking suspicion that Cathy had a pile of women's magazines dating back to the '60s at home, and before every editorial meeting she simply flipped through the stacks and pulled some ideas from the February '68 issue or the July '75 issue. If that was the case, she was smarter than the rest of us.

"Anne?" Donna asked. "How does the '20 Sexiest Things' idea sound to you?"

As the features editor, Anne would be the one to assign and edit the piece, so she'd have to give her approval.

"Sure," Anne chirped with a smile. "I've just started working with a new freelancer who's a regular at *Maxim.* She'd be perfect to work on this if she's available." Donna nodded and made a note.

"Margaret?" Donna asked, sounding almost timid. Margaret looked up briefly and waved a hand.

"Yes, perfect," she said. "I was just about to suggest a similar article. That idea will do."

"Excellent," said Donna, making another note. She quickly recapped. "So one extra page to fashion, one to celebs, and two to features. Okay with everyone?"

She was answered with a chorus of "fine's" and "okay's." Margaret abstained because she didn't need to give her approval with the masses. Sidra kept quiet because she believed she was too good to speak in unison with anyone.

We spent the rest of the meeting outlining and confirming assignments for the September issue. Most articles were already assigned or in the works. Freelancers across the country were already busy tracking down "10 Ways to Land Your Dream Man," "15 Ways to Know if His Love for You Is Real," and "10 Ways to Earn the Promotion You Deserve." (Although I was confident that the answers to all those questions could be found in *Mod*'s archives many times over.) The Triplets were busy putting the final touches on the wardrobes they'd take for their models to wear in Venice.

In the next month I'd have to have five proposals for November celeb cover stories, update my Julia Stiles story for September, find and interview an up-and-coming star for the new Q & A, and include a teaser for Kylie Dane's new movie, which would come out Labor Day Weekend. Plus, I had to finish a two-page spread with quotes from various celebs about what they'd eaten for dinner the night before (Margaret's idea), and another spread on celeb secrets to finding lasting love.

Sadly, many of our readers would blindly follow the advice of their favorite stars, many of whom were juggling dissolving marriages with steamy affairs. The majority of women didn't think twice about taking making-your-marriage-last tips from a thrice-divorced thirty-two-year-old television actress. Or body-toning tips from the thirty-four-year-old screen goddess whose entire body was an homage to the best plastic surgery the Western world had to offer (never mind that she had never set foot in a gym in her life). Or political advice from an MTV veejay who had once been completely stumped when asked by Jay Leno to name the vice president of the United States.

Talk about the blind leading the blind.

When the meeting adjourned three minutes before noon, I left feeling relieved that I had a whole pile of work to distract me, and glad that in the last hour I'd thought of Cole Brannon just once. Okay, maybe twice. But the second time hadn't counted. Donna had brought him up.

Not that I cared. It would be ridiculous to care.

Movie Stars

The Starlet

Thursday morning's press conference for Kylie Dane's new movie, *Opposites Attract,* was in a conference room at the Ritz. As I passed the entrance to Atelier, a parade of designer clothes too expensive for me to even consider streamed in and out around me. I tried not to think about Saturday's brunch, but trying to ignore the memory of Saturday was like trying to make your way to the Rockefeller Center Christmas Tree in December without getting swallowed in a sea of tourists. Exactly, impossible.

Of course I knew there was no Cole Brannon hiding beneath a Red Sox cap in Atelier today. Heck, he was probably backstage at the press event, making out with the married Kylie Dane. I tried to block out the offending mental image.

The press conference was in the meeting room at the far end of the first floor. I took my seat inside, nodding to the other writers I saw at most similar events. I wondered vaguely, as always, whether any of them realized what an exercise in futility all this was. A quick glance around the room at several eager faces confirmed what I suspected— most of them had long ago been seduced by the glow of Hollywood. I felt a bit left out. Sure, the whole Hollywood thing was fun and glamorous to an extent, but I'd never been all that impressed. I sometimes wondered what was wrong with me.

Today's interview session was a small one, geared
specifically toward magazines with more than two months'
lead time, like ours. Newspapers and weeklies like *People*
would get their first crack at Kylie and her costars two
weeks before the film's Labor Day Weekend release, to whet
moviegoers' appetites at exactly the right time. Reporters
for the major monthlies—*Mod, Glamour, In Style, Maxim,
Cosmo,* and the like—had been invited today so that our
presumably glowing praise for the film's stars would appear
in our September issues (which actually came out mid-
August) at precisely the same time moviegoers were making
Labor Day Weekend plans. Amusingly, we wouldn't actually *see* the movie, which was still being assembled in a studio somewhere in Burbank. Yet we were supposed to
review and recommend it sight unseen. As I often did at
these events, I wondered if a crystal ball had been included
in the press kit.

The whole dance with the press had been carefully cho-
reographed and planned for maximum benefit to the studio. It was a formula that rarely failed: Take one big star,
mix with a fair-to-good movie, limit press access to pique
interest, and provide senseless snippets from the stars. It all
equaled major buzz around movies that, well, weren't even
movies yet.

As I waited for the press conference to begin, I told
Victoria Lim, *Cosmo*'s entertainment editor and a friend of
mine after four years of attending silly press conferences
together, that Tom and I had broken up. As I filled her in
on the details, I couldn't help but feel a bit embarrassed, as
if I'd done something to invite his infidelity. Had I?

I was secretly pleased when Victoria admitted that
she'd never really liked him in the first place. She and her
husband Paul had once double-dated with us, and Tom had
spent the entire meal lecturing Paul about "those damned
capitalist pigs in Washington." They had never gone out
with us again.

"Well, I could have him whacked, you know," Victoria said seriously once I'd finished. "I mean, I know people. I've never heard of anyone who deserved a good whacking more."

"A whacking?" I asked. Victoria grinned.

"Sure," she said. "Mob-speak, you know? Don't you watch *The Sopranos*?"

"Do they actually call them 'whackings'?"

"Well, I don't know. I always fall asleep during *The Sopranos*. But really, I know people. We could have him offed."

"So now it's 'offed'?"

"Offed, whacked, rubbed out, whatever," she said. She shook her head. "Although I think that Lorena Bobbitt had the right idea. One might argue that was better than a whacking. It's like a specialized whacking."

"That I could live with," I said seriously.

"Me too," Victoria agreed.

Before I could get too lost in the fantasy, a bleached blonde in a skintight, knee-length red Prada dress appeared on the stage with a sheaf of papers in her hand. Her hair was slicked back and clipped in a twist at the back of her head, and she wore a small name tag that identified her as a publicist on the production company's staff. The whispers and murmurs in the small group of eleven journalists quieted, and we all looked at her expectantly.

"Ladies and gentlemen," she addressed us formally. I nudged Victoria, who rolled her eyes. She was obviously new. The veteran studio publicists were well accustomed to treating the press like children who needed to be spoon-fed information. They would never address us as ladies and gentlemen, for in their eyes we were *not* ladies and gentle-men—we were gullible children who could and should be manipulated. Hence, the Ritz staffers wandering throughout the room with trays full of canapés, Perrier, and soda—thinly veiled bribes for positive movie reviews. "My name is Destiny Starr. (Beside me, Victoria stifled a giggle.) Welcome to the Ritz. We have a very exciting morning planned for you today. In just a moment, we'll bring Kylie and Wally out to meet you, but first I'd like to tell you a bit about the plot of the film."

I zoned out as Destiny launched into a monologue about *Opposites Attract.* I wasn't sure why publicists always opened press conferences this way since presumably, all of us had received a) press packets in the mail weeks in advance with pages of flashy prose about how this would be the best movie of the year, maybe the decade, b) press packets upon arrival at the press conference that told us in more compressed (yet still flashy) prose about how this would be the best movie of the decade, maybe of all time, and c) several phone calls over the last few weeks from studio publicists, allegedly calling to see if we were planning to attend the conference (despite the fact that we'd already agreed by e-mail, fax, and telephone), who would then launch into glowing monologues about how the movie was sure to sweep the Academy Awards and go down in history as the best movie of all time.

Believe me, we'd heard the Academy Award hype speech at every press conference since the dawn of time— even at the junket for *Gigli,* and we all know how that turned out. As you might imagine, this considerably diminished our faith in the speech.

Indeed, as Destiny described *Opposites Attract,* I could see eyes glazing over around the room as we all slipped into zombie mode, with the exception of a newcomer to our group, a young intern from *Teen People.* She was staring at Destiny with fascination from her seat in the dead center of the second row. She reminded me of myself when I started at *People* four years ago, before I learned that press conferences did little good, except for the opportunity to snag canned quotes from stars—and the free mini quiches, stuffed mushrooms, and chocolate-dipped strawberries that circulated throughout the room. Some press events even offered champagne, but I supposed that 10 a.m. was too early for that sort of thing, even for this Hollywood cast of publicists.

Besides, considering my track record this week, perhaps it would be better to avoid alcohol for a while. At least in the general vicinity of movie stars. Although Kylie Dane's costar in the movie was no Cole Brannon, he did have undeniable sex appeal—and a slightly shady reputation to go along with it. Wally Joiner, a twenty-six-year-old import from Great Britain who was being called the next Hugh Grant, had gotten his share of press over recent exploits involving an affair with a pop star, a threesome with two *Playboy* models, and a night with a roomful of Vegas strippers.

When Destiny finally finished telling us, in fascinated tones and matching canned facial expressions, that the romantic comedy (boy meets girl, boy screws something up—boy must win girl back, boy wins girl back—boy and girl live happily ever after—big surprise) was the early favorite for several categories in this year's Academy Awards, she paused dramatically and announced that the "talent" would be coming out shortly.

There was silence for a moment, and then we all started chatting again, as if Destiny had never stepped onstage. None of us (save the enthusiastic *Teen People* intern) had taken a single note, as Destiny had read almost verbatim from the press release we were all handed upon entering the room.

Destiny was back less than three minutes later, having refreshed her deep red lipstick. "Ladies and gentlemen, I'd like to introduce the two stars of *Opposites Attract,* who of course need no introduction."

"Then why is she introducing them?" I whispered to Victoria, who giggled.

"Ms. Kylie Dane and Mr. Wally Joiner!" Destiny said dramatically. She paused, presumably expecting us to clap, but none of us did. It was bad form. Journalists weren't supposed to show any emotion or enthusiasm whatsoever during press conferences, premieres, sporting events, et cetera. In fact, I don't think we were officially supposed to have any feelings at all.

If only that were true, life—and unexpected sleepovers with movie stars—would be much easier.

"Okay, then," Destiny said, recovering from the apparently unexpected lack of response. She looked back toward the curtain draped across the back of the stage. "Kylie, Wally, could you come on out?"

Kylie Dane stepped out first from behind the curtain, looking stunning, even in blue jeans and a black shirt. Granted, the jeans were distressed Paper Denim & Cloth, and the shirt was a tiny, glittering number that hugged her curves perfectly, dipping low enough to reveal her tantalizing cleavage and ending high enough to show off her perfectly toned cinnamon-tan stomach. She was wearing impossibly high Jimmy Choo stilettos, making her legs look like they went on forever. She was so slender that I feared we'd lose her if she turned sideways. Her mane of blond hair (which sparkled and bounced in a way mine never had) was professionally tousled and filled with random ringlets that somehow looked perfectly playful and flawlessly sexy at the same time. She smiled demurely as she stepped onto the stage.

"Hello," she said softly, smiling at the room without really looking at any of us.

I disliked her instantly and tried to convince myself that it was because she seemed aloof. She did, of course—most of them did—but I knew the real reason was that I couldn't erase the image of her walking arm in arm with Cole, grinning up at him with the promise of sex and seduction, from the pages of *Tattletale*. Didn't she have enough already without adding him to the collection?

After all, she was married to Patrick O'Hara, a striking actor twenty years her senior. Her glittering engagement ring, which was roughly the size of a disco ball, sent tiny rays of light flying around the room as she sat gracefully on the velvet-cushioned chair center stage. I squirmed uncomfortably in my hard-backed folding chair and tried not to hate her as little beams from her ring blinded me temporarily.

He is a liar, I reminded myself. *Cole Brannon lied to you. And he's helping Kylie Dane cheat on her husband. He's no different than Tom.*

I gulped and tried to focus on something other than how beautiful and perfect Kylie Dane looked. Which was not easy.

"And Wally Joiner," Destiny announced. The British actor strode onto the stage, exuding confidence and raw sexiness. His face was unshaven, his gait was purposeful and relaxed, and his faded Levi's and crisp white shirt, with the top three buttons open, worked perfectly together.

"'Ello," he said, sounding so British the accent almost seemed artificial. He slowly laid eyes on each female reporter in the room, smiling devilishly each time he locked eyes with one of us. I heard Victoria next to me emit a little schoolgirl giggle as his burning gaze fell on her, but before he could lock eyes with me, I focused intently on the blank notebook page in front of me.

Sexy as he was, I'd already had my fill of actors for the week, thank you very much.

"We'll just go ahead and take questions, then," Destiny said after a brief pause, allowing Wally to finish visually assaulting each woman in the room. She looked around the room until her eyes alighted on Karen Davidson from *Glamour,* whose pencil was raised in the air. "Yes, you," she said, pointing to Karen.

"Karen Davidson, *Glamour* magazine," said the sleekly bobbed brunette, identifying herself as we were all asked to do at every press conference. As if the stars cared. I was sure the names went in one ear and out the other. Kylie nodded politely, and Wally leaned forward and winked flirtatiously. Karen tittered. "This question is for Wally." She was blushing now. "You play a nuclear physicist in the movie. Was it difficult for you to learn the ways of nuclear physicism in order to play your role convincingly?"

I leaned over to Victoria.

"Nuclear *physicism?*" I whispered. "Is that a word?" Victoria stifled another giggle and shook her head.

"Excellent question, love," Wally said, settling back into his seat, his starched shirt crackling audibly. He appeared to be undressing Karen with his eyes as he talked. And she appeared to be enjoying it. "Nuclear physicism has always been a passion of mine, you know. So I already had the background, of course. I bloody love all that technical shit. So it was easy for me to just read along with the script and get it all right," Wally concluded wisely. "Nuclear physicism is such a vital field."

Karen Davidson nodded and scribbled furiously. I rolled my eyes. I could just see the article in *Glamour* now. WALLY JOINER IS A CLOSET INTELLECTUAL WHO LOVES NUCLEAR PHYSICS. Sure.

"You," Destiny said, pointing to Victoria.

"Victoria Lim, *Cosmopolitan* magazine," Victoria piped up, her voice sounding tiny and childlike. "And my question is for Kylie." Kylie nodded, expressionless. "Kylie, this is the third time you've played a similar role, the helpless female rescued by the strong, intelligent male. Are you worried about being typecast?"

"No," Kylie said without really meeting anyone's eye. She looked down at her perfectly manicured nails and then seemed to drift into her own little world as she admired her engagement ring. Victoria and I exchanged quick looks. It became apparent that she wasn't planning to elaborate as the uncomfortable silence dragged on.

"Uh, okay," Victoria said. Destiny looked uncomfortable. This wasn't going well. "Could you tell me how you feel the roles fit you, then?"

That was good. A nice open-ended question.

Kylie finally looked up, but again, she didn't meet anyone's eye.

"I can fit any role," she said, her voice full of boredom. She flicked a piece of imaginary lint from her jeans, staring at the ceiling. She pushed a stray ringlet behind her ear and went back to examining her nails. "That's what talented actors *do*."

I heard Victoria growl softly next to me, and I felt like laughing. This was such an exercise in futility.

I raised my hand, and Destiny pointed at me.

"Claire Reilly from *Mod*," I said quickly. I looked at Kylie. "How do you feel, then, about the example you're setting for young women?" I asked her. Destiny raised an eyebrow, and Victoria snickered next to me. I knew I sounded snide, but I didn't care. "I mean, are you concerned that they'll think it's okay for women to just be saved rather than saving themselves?"

"It *is* okay," said Kylie. She sighed and rolled her eyes. I raised an eyebrow.

"So you're saying it's okay for women to just sit around and wait for men to come rescue them?" I prodded.

"That's what I said." She sighed again and looked over at Destiny. "This topic is boring me," she said. "Can we move on?"

I sat back in my chair and stared at her in amazement. How could this be the woman Cole liked? Who he'd been linked with? Who he was pulling close to him in the *Tattletale* photo with such obvious adoration? What was wrong with men?

Then again, it was Kylie Dane who was winning the hearts of thousands of men. I, on the other hand, had lost the only one I'd managed to attract. Perhaps I should take her advice and just sit back, waiting to be rescued by some Prince Charming. It seemed to be working for her. However, Kylie Dane had a few more men throwing themselves at her than

I did, which increased her odds of finding that prince among the frogs. I, on the other hand, was just putting together a frog-kissing track record that would make Miss Piggy blush.

The press conference went on like it always did, and I dutifully took notes that suspiciously resembled those of every other movie press conference I'd been to: canned statements galore, zealous praise for the director, demure commentary about how lovely it would be to win an Oscar, and vague references to plot twists the media hadn't been clued in about. I had almost tuned out—it was easy to scribble down quotes without really listening, if you'd been doing this long enough—when a question from the *Teen People* reporter caught my attention.

"Kylie, who is your favorite actor you've ever worked with?" she asked, breathless, young, and excited to be talking to such a big star. She grinned as she waited for an answer, not seeming to realize that Kylie was too aloof to even meet her eye.

I held my breath. *Don't say Cole Brannon. Don't say Cole Brannon.*

"Cole Brannon," Kylie said after a brief pause. Wally looked surprised, and she shot him a look. "And Wally Joiner, of course," she recovered quickly. But the damage was done.

"Not your own husband, Patrick O'Hara?" asked Ashley Tedder from *In Style*.

"Oh, well, of course Patrick," Kylie said, fixing Ashley with a glare. Excellent, she finally realized we were all out here and made eye contact with someone.

"So does that mean the rumors about you and Cole Brannon are true?" I heard myself ask. I immediately reddened. Kylie's glare was now fully focused on me. Why had I said that? My self-control button had obviously been deactivated.

"Cole Brannon," she said through gritted teeth, although I couldn't help but notice she looked secretly pleased, "is a very, very good friend. A close friend. I'll leave the rest up to your imagination." She batted her eyelashes, and a few reporters laughed. I turned red.

Kylie's attention had shifted back to the ceiling, which was good, because I was fixing her with a death stare. She'd leave the rest up to my imagination? What was that supposed to mean?

Obviously, that she was having wild, passionate sex with Cole Brannon.

How could they? What was he thinking?

More important, why did I care? Kylie Dane was beautiful, glamorous, perfect, glowing. I was probably fixed in Cole's mind as short, clunky, pathetic, and covered in tequila-laced vomit.

Not quite the image of loveliness his leading ladies lived up to.

"Kylie Dane and Cole Brannon," Victoria murmured to me after the press conference, as we were gathering up our belongings. I felt numb. I turned to look at her, trying hard to look like I didn't care. "God, he's gorgeous," she bubbled, oblivious to the bizarre expressions surely crossing my face. "What a couple! Figures he'd go for the most beautiful woman in Hollywood."

"Yeah," I said, feeling sick. "It figures."

The Leading Man

When I got back to my office, I checked my voice mail and was relieved to see that my luck appeared to be turning around. Not my luck in love, of course. In that area it seemed I was permanently cursed. But at least things were going well professionally. At this point, I'd take what I could get.

I had gotten a call back from Carol Brown, Julia Stiles's publicist, telling me cheerfully that she'd be in all afternoon if I'd like to call her with any additional questions, which meant I'd be able to knock out the changes to the cover story by the end of the day. There was also a message from Mandy Moore's publicist, pitching me a Q & A with her client (which I would push Margaret to accept—our readers loved the multitalented young star), and a message from the publicist for Taryn Joshua, the first celeb I'd chosen to feature in the new up-and-coming stars Q & A that Maite had suggested at Tuesday's meeting. Taryn would be thrilled to participate, her publicist said. I was to call her tomorrow to schedule a "phoner." My entire celeb section for next month was falling together perfectly. I could hardly believe it.

I spent the next hour making notes on questions to ask Carol. Then I took a quick lunch break alone. I bought a skim latte in our building's lobby on the way back up to my office and spent the next hour transcribing my notes from the morning's press conference, rolling my eyes childishly every time I heard Kylie's bored voice. I took another break at 2 p.m. to walk Cole's flowers down to the Dumpster, despite Wendy's protests—which, to be honest, weren't too adamant. The French waiter Jean Michel had presented her with a dozen roses at lunch that day, and I think she was secretly a bit relieved that my flowers, which so profoundly overshadowed hers, were gone.

Besides, I was able to give her the vase that my flowers had come in. At least the guy who'd brought her flowers hadn't slept with half of Hollywood. I figured his bouquet deserved the vase more than Cole's did on that basis alone.

I'd just gotten off the phone with Carol and was starting to revise my Julia Stiles feature when I heard the closest staffer to the reception door squeal in delight. I looked up in time to see two more editorial assistants leap up in tandem and race around the corner, out of my sight.

Wendy and I exchanged confused looks as Amber, the magazine's fact-checker, sprang from her desk and raced toward the door, clapping her hands with glee. More excited squeals emanated from the hallway, just out of our sight, and then Anne Amster raced by us too.

"You won't believe who's here!" she exclaimed as she dashed past. "Courtney at the front desk just called and told me to get out there! C'mon!"

I looked at Wendy again. She squinted at me.

"What the hell is going on?" Wendy asked with typical bluntness.

"I have no idea," I murmured. "I've never seen anything like this."

Not that the women on our staff didn't act a bit quirky—sometimes downright kooky—on a pretty regular basis. But this display, whatever it was, took the cake.

Staffer after staffer disappeared around the corner with excited squeals. The growing throng, which was now jutting out of the hallway, around the corner, and into the main office, was coming our way. Wendy and I exchanged looks once more and glanced at Maite, who had emerged from her office to watch the frenzy. It was like something from the Discovery Channel. I half expected to see that khakied Australian guy round the corner to tell us about the new *Mod* mating ritual or something.

The crowd slowly moved into view. Two interns, clearly starstruck, dropped back from the crowd and looked at each other in excitement, emitting little shrieks before scurrying away. The music editor, Chloe Michael (usually the very embodiment of the word "cool"), was hopping up and down like a little schoolgirl, thrusting a pen and a sheet of paper toward the center of the throng.

"They've all gone crazy," Wendy confirmed.

Then he rounded the corner.

There, in the hallway of *Mod* magazine—*my* magazine—thronged by a dozen of my coworkers who had never behaved this way in their lives, was the last person I expected to see in the *Mod* office, today or ever.

It was Cole Brannon.

My Cole Brannon.

Okay, well, really Kylie Dane's Cole Brannon. The Cole Brannon I had totally humiliated myself in front of before realizing he had completely lied to me. The Cole Brannon of coffee-and-croissant fame. The Cole Brannon of embarrassing pity flowers. The Cole Brannon who was way too hot to ever date a girl like me.

I stared at him as he scanned the room, simultaneously scribbling his autograph on pieces of paper thrust in his direction by women too old to be screaming like teenagers. Finally, Cole's eyes landed on me, and he grinned over the throng.

I gave him an involuntary, weak smile in return, then quickly wiped the grin from my face. After all, I wasn't happy to see him. He was a liar, remember? Who cared that he was gorgeous? Certainly not me.

"It's Cole Brannon," Wendy whispered rather unnecessarily. "In our office."

"Yes, it is," I confirmed flatly. I tried to remind myself that the deep dimples on his tanned face, the sharply defined broad shoulders I had once seen rippling with water droplets, and the perfectly straight, perfectly white smile were totally irrelevant.

Cole grinned at me again over the heads of the women surrounding him as he inched closer to me. Why did my cheeks feel hot? Was I blushing? That made no sense! I was a professional woman with no feelings for this man. Even if he was heart-stoppingly sexy, it meant nothing. I had no feelings for him whatsoever. I could never feel anything for someone who would lie to me. Someone who would sleep with a married woman. Someone who was that hot and totally unattainable.

After all, it would be completely stupid and self-destructive to think that someone like him would ever want to go out with someone like me.

Cole smiled and conversed politely with each of the *Mod* staffers in the throng. Little by little, the pack thinned as staffers got their autographs and wandered away in stunned excitement. Anne Amster even asked for a hug. Cole smiled and gently acquiesced. It was probably just my imagination that Anne's hug hadn't looked as warm, as tight, or as close as the one he'd bestowed upon me.

"He's my favorite movie star," Anne admitted sheepishly as she flounced gleefully past us on her way back to her desk. Two giggling editorial interns scurried by, signed scraps of paper pressed to their chests.

Finally, Cole had signed his last autograph and was alone—or at least as alone as he could be with an office full of women staring at him. He stood for a moment, looking at me from down the hall. Our eyes locked over the walls of my cubicle. Was it natural for my cheeks to feel like they were melting from sheer heat? And why was my stomach churning, like it wanted to overturn again?

Suddenly, I was very conscious of how bad this would look. To Maite. To Margaret, if she wandered out. To everyone else in the office. Was Cole Brannon here to see me? Why? Didn't he have something he had to do with Kylie Dane? I fought sudden nausea as Kylie's words replayed in my head.

"I'll leave the rest up to your imagination," her disembodied voice sneered. Great, I could imagine plenty.

Finally, Cole was at the edge of my cubicle, leaning against the doorway and looking as sexy as he had on Sunday morning. His dark brown locks were as tousled as ever, his cheeks were flushed, and his tall, perfectly proportioned frame looked great in a pair of Diesel jeans and a black button-up shirt.

But I tried to ignore all that. After all, it was beside the point that he was the hottest guy I'd ever seen in the flesh, and that every time I saw him he looked even sexier than before. Totally beside the point.

"Hi," he said softly, looking down at me with all the energy and emotion he put into meaningful gazes on-screen. I blushed and reminded myself that he wasn't really sexy. Liars couldn't be sexy, could they?

"Hi," I echoed, trying to remember that I was supposed to be annoyed at him. For lying. For helping Kylie to cheat on her husband. For screwing Ivana Donatelli. For making me think, even for an instant, that I could compare with those women. That I wasn't a nobody.

Okay, that was better. I was starting to feel a bit righteously pissed off instead of just turned on.

I snuck another look around the room. Heads peeked out of offices up and down the hall, staring at us. Phones jangled, but no one was answering. I squirmed uncomfortably. I could practically read their minds as they stared, suspecting us of an affair, suspecting me of compromising my ethics. I looked quickly at Wendy, who raised her eyebrows at me.

"Guess I should have worn the baseball cap, right?" Cole teased, winking at me. I tried to frown at him. "You know," he said, apparently thinking I was confused about what he meant. "To stay undercover?"

"I know," I said softly. I looked back down at my keyboard and wished I could disappear. Or at least that when I looked up again, Cole wouldn't look so damned gorgeous and irresistible and, well, nice. Because he wasn't. It was all an illusion. I knew the truth.

"Claire!" Wendy hissed from the cubicle next to me. I looked up helplessly. She was staring at me with wide eyes, making faces that seemed to indicate I was supposed to do something.

"Oh," I said finally. "This is my friend Wendy." Wendy raised her eyebrows at me, which I knew was her way of telling me that wasn't what she was getting at. Of course it wasn't. What she wanted was for me to be polite and flirtatious. But she didn't look like she minded being introduced as a consolation prize.

"Oh, so *you're* Wendy," said Cole enthusiastically. "Nice to finally meet you." He took a step forward and reached out a long arm. Wendy stood and shook his hand, her freckled cheeks flushed with color.

I tried to shrink into my chair, fiercely hoping that when I looked up again, Cole would be gone. I closed my eyes for a moment. *Go away! Go away!*

"Sorry to bother you at work," Cole said, interrupting my thoughts. I opened my eyes. Evidently, he hadn't disappeared.

"What are you doing here?" I asked. For an instant, I could have sworn he looked a bit wounded.

He leaned forward, his voice soft enough not to carry beyond Wendy. The rest of the room strained to hear, but I knew Cole was at least making an attempt to be discreet.

"I didn't have your phone number, and I've gone by your apartment a few times. You weren't there, and I was starting to get worried. I wanted to make sure you were okay," Cole said. He lowered his voice even further. "You know. After . . . everything."

My cheeks were on fire. I couldn't believe what I was hearing. He'd gone by my apartment to look for me? And now he was so concerned that he'd come by my office?

"So you came here?" I whispered. Cole shrugged and looked uncomfortable.

"I was doing a studio shoot in the building for the cover of *Mod,*" he said. "I figured I would stop by and check on you while I was here."

I was flattered for a moment before I remembered the dozens of eyes on us. The warmth inside me quickly turned to humiliation and then anger—illogical as that was—as a sudden image of Cole and Kylie in the pages of *Tattletale* sprang to mind.

"Thanks," I said, knowing my voice sounded cold. "I appreciate your concern. But I'm fine." I willed my heart to stop pounding. I wasn't quite sure why it suddenly felt like I'd gotten an 808 bass system installed in my chest.

"Oh," said Cole. He leaned back and studied my face for a moment. Was it my imagination, or did he look disappointed at the less-than-warm reception? "Well, I'm glad. I was worried. I never heard from you after I sent those flowers, so I was a bit concerned."

"Thanks for the flowers," I said stiffly. He looked hurt, and I instantly softened, despite my best intentions. Okay, he was a liar, but he *had* sent me flowers. Maybe I could be just the teensiest bit nice.

I took a deep breath and exhaled slowly.

"I'm sorry," I said finally. "The flowers were very nice. I'm sorry I didn't call. I'm just . . . dealing with a lot here." *Like trying not to hate you for lying about Kylie Dane,* said the voice in my head. *Like the shame I feel from thinking, even for a moment, that you could be attracted to me. Like the fact that I'm obviously a delusional idiot. Like the real-*

ization that I'm probably never going to find anyone who could love me. How's that?

"I know," said Cole, who couldn't possibly know what was going through my insanely calibrated brain. "I mean, I figured. I just wanted to let you know that if you need any help . . ." He paused and looked at me gently. I could have sworn that his blush had deepened. "Well, I just wanted you to know that you can call me if you need to. Or if you want to talk, or anything."

"Thanks," I said. I snuck a look at Wendy, who looked like she was about to faint. The rest of the room was leaning forward in interest. I suddenly felt exposed, humiliated.

"Are you sure you're okay?" Cole looked concerned.

"Yes," I said sharply, refusing to elaborate. The stares around the room were growing more intense and, I thought, less friendly.

Not that I'd mind if the world thought that Cole Brannon was in love with me. But I couldn't have my coworkers thinking that there was anything unprofessional going on. Because there wasn't. I would never do that.

I knew they'd never guess how pathetic I truly was, how someone like Cole would never look at me that way. After all, if my own boyfriend didn't want to sleep with me, how on earth could the hottest movie star in the world want to?

"Look, we can't talk here," I said suddenly. I could practically see my reputation crumbling before my eyes.

"Oh," said Cole, looking surprised. He glanced quickly around the room, then back at me. "I'm sorry, I didn't mean . . ."

"C'mon." I stood up quickly, grabbed him by the arm, and dragged him down the hallway. We passed cubicles filled with desperately curious eyes, following our every move. I didn't know where I was taking him until I spotted the door to the men's room at the end of the hall. I paused for a moment and pulled Cole inside, knowing we'd be the only ones there. The odds that the one man on our editorial staff of fifty-two people was using the bathroom at this very moment were slim.

Sure enough, the bathroom was empty, and we were finally alone.

"Look," I hissed at Cole as the door swung shut behind us, keeping out the prying eyes. "You can't just come here. What will people think?"

"I'm sorry," Cole said, looking surprised and a bit wounded. For a moment, I felt a bit guilty, despite myself. "I just wanted to make sure you were okay. I didn't think . . ." His voice trailed off. He leaned into the wall and I stepped in front of him, still going.

"It's bad enough that Sidra saw us together and suspected . . . well, you know. But now the whole office has seen us." I realized I was shaking a finger at him, and I stopped for a moment. I was acting like a disappointed mother. I took a deep breath and felt suddenly embarrassed.

"I'm sorry," I said with a sigh. "I just . . . I know you came here because you wanted to help. And I appreciate that. I'm just so afraid of what people will think."

"Why?" Cole asked softly. As he looked at me, I realized he wasn't angry about my outburst, but was instead peering at me with what looked like pity. I felt instantly shamed. I didn't want or need his sympathy. I didn't need him to feel sorry for me, then dash off with the lovely Kylie Dane or the coldly beautiful Ivana Donatelli. "Why does it matter what they think?"

"Because it does," I answered sullenly, knowing very well that I sounded petulantly childish. "And because I care about my job and my reputation, and I don't want to risk ruining all that."

I suddenly felt perilously close to tears as we looked at each other for a moment. He didn't understand. He couldn't possibly understand what it was like to be the youngest person to hold the position of senior entertain-

ment editor at a major million-circulation magazine, to
have to always remain on the up-and-up so that no one
thought you were in the position for the wrong reasons.

He couldn't possibly understand what it felt like to
catch your boyfriend cheating on you when you'd done
everything in your power to make him love you. When
nothing you did was enough. When your coworker's plastic sister was more desirable than you. When you knew that
no one in their right mind would want you.

I felt as pathetic as I knew Cole thought I was. For a
moment, his gentle gaze made me want to hug him, to have
him put his arms around me, pull me into his strong chest, and
tell me everything would be all right. But that was ridiculous.

"Have you heard from him?" he asked softly, gently. I
blinked.

"Who?"

"Your boyfriend," he said, looking a bit uncomfortable. He shifted his weight. "Or your ex-boyfriend or whatever. The guy you walked in on."

"Oh," I said. Imagine that. A year of building a relationship had turned him merely into the "guy I'd walked in
on." Of course I hadn't heard from him. Which would make
me look even more pathetic to Cole. I couldn't stand it.

"Um, yes, actually. He called and we talked for a
while," I lied quickly. I glanced at Cole, who looked surprised. I cleared my throat and dove deeper into the fib. I
didn't know why I didn't just tell him the truth, but I was
already on a roll. "He sent flowers too. Everything's fine. It
was all a misunderstanding."

Cole was silent for a moment. I mentally kicked myself.
Could I have sounded more moronic? A "misunderstanding"? What on earth did I mean by that?

"Oh," Cole said finally. I stared at the floor. "Good. I
mean, it sounds like you're, um, working things out."

"Yep," I said brightly, digging myself in deeper. I elaborated further. "I mean, he realized what he was throwing

away and how much he really loved me and everything," I babbled, still not meeting Cole's eye. "I have to decide whether or not to forgive him, but when someone clearly loves you that much, you know . . ." My voice trailed off, and I snuck a look at Cole. He still looked surprised.

"Oh, well, I'm glad," he said. He looked like he was avoiding my eye. He was silent for a moment. "Just as long as he treats you right."

Well of course he didn't treat me right. He never had.

"It's between me and Tom," I said stiffly. "But I appreciate your concern."

"Of course," Cole said quickly. "I mean, I just wanted to make sure, you know, that you knew you could call me if you needed anything. That I'm here for you. But I guess you're okay."

"I'm great," I said, flashing him a winning grin. "Really. I'm great. Life's great."

"Good."

"Great."

There was a moment of uncomfortable silence as we stood in the bathroom. I avoided looking at him. I was suddenly painfully aware that we were mere inches apart. I was planted firmly in front of him as he leaned against the wall, and I was so close that I could smell his faint cologne and feel his breath ruffling the top layers of my hair. In that moment I had the strange feeling—just for an instant—that I wanted to stay there forever. But that was stupid. He was completely out of my league. And to top it off, he clearly thought I was pathetic. (It was beside the point that I did actually appear to be pretty pathetic, which would make him right.)

I quickly cleared my throat and stepped away.

"Look, I appreciate your concern, but you really need to go," I said brusquely. What was I, crazy? I couldn't let myself feel attracted to him.

Besides, he was having an affair. Just like Tom. It was

right there in *Tattletale*'s black and white. Even if they weren't always reliable. But photos didn't lie.

Scumbag.

"I don't need your help, thank you," I said curtly. "I'll be just fine, and I'm sure you have much more important things to do." *Or people to do. Like Kylie Dane.*

Cole looked at me for a moment, his perfect features twisted into an expression of confusion.

"Thank you for all your help on this story," I continued with forced cheerfulness, trying my best to sound professional and ignore the fact that Cole smelled wonderful, looked wonderful, and sounded wonderful. He *wasn't* wonderful, though. I had to keep reminding myself of that.

He was sleeping with Kylie Dane, which made him scum. Lying scum. Besides, this was just business.

"Um, okay, sure, no problem," he said uncertainly. If I hadn't known better, I would have thought I'd hurt his feelings. But he was an actor, and I was sure he could fake all sorts of emotions. He sure could lie like a pro.

"Fantastic," I said briskly. I reached out and offered him my hand. He looked blankly at it for a moment, then shook it slowly. I tried to ignore the tingle that ran up my arm when he touched me. "I'll call your publicist when the article comes out and send over some copies."

"Okay," Cole said. He still looked confused. "Thanks."

"No problem. Thank *you*."

And with that, I hurried him out of the bathroom, where a small crowd had clustered just feet away, near the water cooler. Hmm. Taking him into the bathroom to avoid prying eyes probably hadn't been such a hot idea.

Apparently, I didn't need anyone's help to destroy my reputation. I was managing to do it single-handedly. How efficient of me.

"Nice meeting with you, Cole," I said brightly, as I walked him to the door. To my chagrin, I could feel an involuntary, furious blush heating my face. "*Mod* magazine really appreciates your cooperation." I was trying to sound as impersonal as possible. We still had quite an audience.

"Nice meeting with you too, Claire," he said. Was it my imagination, or did he look kind of sad? We paused at the door that opened out toward the reception desk. He leaned in and whispered softly in my ear, "You will call if you need me, right?" My heart leaped in my chest, but I fought it down.

"I appreciate the offer," I said firmly. "But I don't think that will be necessary. I'll be in touch when the article comes out."

"Oh," Cole said. "Okay." He took a step backward, through the open doorway, still looking perplexed.

"Okay," I said cheerfully. "Have a nice day. Thanks for coming by."

My face hurt as I smiled a smile I didn't mean. Why did I suddenly have the sneaking feeling I'd made a mistake?

The door swung closed behind him, and I saw him glance over his shoulder and look at me one last time as he disappeared toward the elevator bank.

The Hunk

What the hell were you thinking?" Wendy demanded. It was just past 6 p.m., and I'd decided to go home to my own apartment tonight. I seemed to be on a roll in the screwing-up-my-life department. I figured I might as well take all my bad karma back to the location where it all started.

But Wendy wasn't letting me off the hook that easily. We walked side by side to the N/R station at Forty-ninth and Seventh Avenue, squished in a private bubble amid the sea of people rushing home from work. Beside us, traffic on Broadway inched south, the drivers trying to cross from east to west honking and trying to maneuver through stopped traffic.

"I don't know what I was thinking," I said miserably. I shrugged and looked at her out of the corner of my eye.

"So you just told him that you and Tom were back together? And then you told him to get lost?"

"Not in those exact words," I mumbled.

"Claire! Why?"

"I don't know." I looked up at Wendy and was instantly silenced by the expression on her face. She was staring at me like I was crazy, which I supposed I was.

Really.

"But it was *Cole Brannon*," she said, drawing out each syllable. "Cole Bran-non," she repeated for emphasis, like she was talking to someone with a very small mental capacity. "You know, Cole Brannon, big movie star, hottest guy in America. That Cole Brannon."

"I know," I said softly. Okay, so maybe this hadn't been my brightest move yet.

"And you just told him that you were taken," Wendy recapped. "By a man we all know is a total creep."

"I know," I said again.

"Why?"

"I don't know."

"You don't know?"

"No."

Wendy sighed and looked away for a moment. I cleared my throat and tried to explain.

"He was just there because he felt sorry for me, you know."

"Oh yeah," Wendy said, looking at me sharply. "I get visits at work all the time from movie stars who feel sorry for me."

"You know what I mean."

"No, I don't. Guys like that don't just swing by the office because they feel sorry for you. And you just totally blew him off."

"Whatever," I said, knowing I sounded like an impetuous child. "What would he want with me? He has Kylie Dane. I'm just this crazy reporter who puked on him."

Wendy stopped, looking at me in exasperation. Finally, she shook her head.

"You know, did it ever occur to you that he was telling the truth about Kylie Dane?"

"But she said—"

Wendy cut me off.

"I don't care what she said. She might have motives you don't know about. What actress's career wouldn't be helped by being linked with Cole Brannon?"

"But the pictures—"

"Could have a logical explanation," Wendy completed my sentence. She shook her head again. "You know, they *are* shooting a movie together. Maybe the picture was from the set. While they were shooting a scene."

I looked at her.

"What about the pictures with his publicist Ivana?" I persisted. "Or with Jessica Gregory?"

"The picture with the publicist was probably just dinner," Wendy said. "There was nothing romantic about it, really. And you know that Cole Brannon was shooting a guest spot on *Spy Chicks,* Jessica Gregory's show. I'm sure a photographer just got a shot while they were filming outside. Those tabloids can make anything look bad."

"I guess so," I conceded. "But I don't have a good feeling about this, you know? I mean, the thing is, he can have any of those women if he wants to. There's not a reason in the world he'd want to date me. That's just crazy."

"It's not crazy, Claire," Wendy said firmly. "You're not giving yourself enough credit."

I shook my head, dismissing the compliment. I appreciated her confidence in me, but I knew it was just best-friend blindness. Tom—who, let's face it, was a bit of a loser—didn't even want me. It was ludicrous to think that Cole Brannon would.

"I'm still not ready to write off the tabloid pictures as meaningless," I said, deflecting attention from the real issue, my lack of desirability. "Maybe one picture. But photos of him with all three women? I don't know. I don't think I can believe him when he says that nothing's going on."

"Not all men are liars like Tom, Claire," Wendy said, looking at me sharply. I looked down, refusing to meet her gaze. "You never used to have a problem trusting people."

"Well, maybe I should have," I said. I took a deep breath and changed the subject. "Look, you know how I feel about people thinking I slept my way into my position or something. Do you know how it would look if something happened now between me and Cole? Not that it would even be an option."

Wendy sighed.

"It's not like you're out trying to get laid by every movie star you interview," she said. "That would be kind of suspicious. But one guy? One guy who you have this connection with?"

"We don't have a connection," I snapped. "That's crazy. He's just a guy who I interviewed, and that's it. End of story. I thought he was nice, but obviously he's just like every other man." Wendy looked at me for a moment and took a deep breath.

"Okay," she said finally. "I'm sorry. It's not my business. I just wish someone would look at me the way that man looked at you."

As we parted at the subway station and went our separate ways, I began to feel vaguely uneasy. But that was silly.

Besides, why would Wendy need men to look at her the way Cole Brannon had looked at me? Men looked at her with lust and an unmasked desire to get her into bed. Cole Brannon looked at me with pity.

I couldn't remember the last time someone had looked at me with lust in his eyes. Least of all my live-in boyfriend, who had spent the last several months screwing someone else.

I had apparently become man-repellant.

The phone rang at 6:45 the next morning, forty-five minutes before my alarm was supposed to go off, and I was rudely awakened from a dream about Cole Brannon. I couldn't remember much of it in those first few seconds that consciousness dawned. But it had been a nice dream, and it hadn't exactly been G-rated. That much I remembered. The thought made me vaguely uneasy, given the circumstances. I tried to excuse it by telling myself there were thousands of other American women fantasizing about him too.

They just didn't happen to be as sex-starved as me.

And Cole Brannon probably hadn't taken most of them home at night. Or sent them flowers at work. But I digress.

Disappointed that I was now awake and couldn't escape back into the dream world, I reached for the rudely jangling phone.

"Hello?" I answered sleepily.

"Claire?"

The voice snapped me instantly awake. I sat up quickly.

"Tom," I said, feeling like the breath had been knocked out of me.

"Hi, baby," he said.

I couldn't speak for a minute. What did he want? Why was he calling? Had he realized that he missed me? That he needed me? That he wanted to come back?

"Hi," I answered finally. I looked at the clock. "Tom, it's six forty-five. What are you doing calling me at this time of morning?" I urged myself to sound casual. Casual Claire. Cool, calm, collected Claire. That was me. I took a breath.

"I wanted to make sure to catch you in," Tom said calmly. "I've been trying you for a few days, but you haven't been there. Where have you been?"

I opened my mouth to tell him I'd been staying with Wendy; then I reconsidered.

"None of your business," I snapped. There. Let him wonder. Maybe I was out on dates with men who actually had jobs. Maybe I was out partying until the wee hours of the morning. Heck, maybe I was sleeping with a movie star. Yeah, sure.

"Sorry, you're right," he said softly. Of course I was right. Even if I wasn't *actually* sleeping with said movie star. I was silent while I waited for him to speak. "Look, I'm sorry about what happened, Claire. I had no right to . . . You didn't deserve that."

His voice was soft and slow, and he sounded genuinely remorseful. I was speechless for a minute.

"You're right," I snapped finally. He wasn't going to get off the hook that easily. "I didn't deserve that. Not after everything I've done for you." Anger welled up inside me.

"I know, Claire, I know," Tom said softly. "There's no excuse."

"No, there's not." The anger bubbled to the surface. "Do you have any idea what that was like? Walking in on you like that? Seeing you in my bed with . . . with . . . that woman?"

I realized I was squeezing the comforter so tightly with my hand that my circulation was nearly cut off. I slowly unclenched and took a deep breath.

"I know," Tom said sadly. "I know, and I am so sorry." He breathed slowly into the phone, and I felt myself soften a bit in the silence between us. "Look, can I take you to dinner tonight, Claire?" His question caught me even more off guard. Dinner? Me and Tom? I didn't answer immediately, and he pushed forward. "I know I'm being really presumptuous here, but I miss you, and I feel like if I can see you in person, maybe I can explain things better." I still didn't answer. I didn't know what to say. "I just want to see you, Claire," he pressed on. "I miss you so much."

No way. I knew I shouldn't go. It would just be plain stupid to agree to see him so soon.

"Okay," I heard myself say. Wait a minute. Had I just agreed to dinner? What was I thinking?

"Great," Tom said, sounding relieved. I was starting to feel very uncomfortable. Not just because I'd agreed, but also because I'd actually felt my spirits rise when Tom said he missed me. Because I was actually looking forward to the dinner.

Clearly there was something wrong with me. Very wrong.

"Meet me at the Friday's in Times Square at six-thirty,"

I said tersely. I knew he hated Friday's. Sure, it was a petty way to punish him, but I'd take what I could get.

"Fine," said Tom agreeably. "I'll meet you out front at six-thirty."

"Okay," I said again. My stomach was doing flips, and my heart was doing somersaults. I had a whole acrobatic team using my internal organs for practice. I certainly didn't feel okay.

"Okay, see you then. And Claire?" Tom paused for a moment.

"Yes?" I said finally.

"I love you," he said softly. My jaw dropped. Then he hung up the phone before I had a chance to answer. I slowly placed the phone back in its cradle and stared at it for a moment.

"You've got a funny way of showing it," I finally murmured, after Tom was long gone.

⌒

"You are not seriously going to go," Wendy said at lunch as she stared at me over her turkey sandwich. We were sitting in the corner at Cosi, and I'd finally worked up the courage to tell her about Tom's call and the fact that I'd agreed to meet him. I knew she would think I was crazy, and to be honest, I wasn't so sure she was wrong.

As Wendy stared at me incredulously, little drops of lettuce and mustard falling from her freeze-framed sandwich, even more of my confidence slipped away.

"Yes I am," I said finally.

"Claire," said Wendy slowly. She put down the sandwich and leaned across the table to take my right hand in hers. "Why? What could you possibly have to gain?"

"I don't know," I said slowly. "But what do I have to lose?"

"A lot," Wendy said quickly. No way. Wendy was being too harsh, right? "He's just trying to use you again."

"No, you're wrong," I said too quickly. "He sounded like he was really sorry."

"Yeah, he's sorry that his source of income has dried up," Wendy muttered.

"Besides, what else could he want from me?" I said, ignoring her. "I think he really just wants to talk this time."

Wendy leaned back in her chair. She studied me for a moment. I wanted her approval. I wanted her to tell me it was okay to meet with him. It was just dinner. I hadn't agreed to marry him or bear his children. Yet.

Not that he'd asked. Not that *anyone* had asked.

"I just think you're going to get hurt," Wendy finally said. "But if that's what you want to do, you know I'm here for you."

I sighed.

"Thank you," I said softly.

She tilted her head to the side and studied me for a moment.

"You should really call Cole Brannon, you know," Wendy said softly. I just stared at her.

"I thought we were talking about Tom," I said finally. Wendy looked down at her sandwich, then back at me again.

"We were. Now we're talking about Cole Brannon."

"I can't just call him!" I said. That would be nuts. Was she crazy?

"Yes, you can," Wendy insisted. "He gave you his cell number. Why can't you?"

"Because," I said stubbornly. Wendy looked at me, waiting for me to say more, so I did. "Because he's a movie star. Because he feels sorry for me, and I don't need his pity. Because he's obviously sleeping with Kylie Dane. And his publicist, Ivana. What would he want with me?"

"I don't think that stuff about those women is true," Wendy said calmly. "I really don't."

I shook my head.

"Look," I said, trying not to sound harsh. "I'm not

going to call him, okay? It would be totally unprofessional.
He gave me his number for work purposes. And besides,
I'm not going to hear from him again. I think he got the
point." I tried to feel smug, but instead, I felt just a bit idi-
otic. Had I really just summarily dismissed Cole Brannon?
But my reasons for doing it were right. Weren't they?

Wendy shrugged. I pretended to ignore her.

"Whatever you say," she said mysteriously, like she knew
something I didn't. I made a face at her and changed the
subject.

"How's it going with that French waiter?" I asked.

"Jean Michel," Wendy filled in dreamily.

"Yeah, Jean Michel," I said. "How's that going?"

"Great," said Wendy, smiling and putting her turkey
sandwich back down. "He's really great, you know. He's
not as young as he looks. He's only a year younger than I
am, and he's really smart. His English is really coming
along well. And I took French in high school, so it's kind of
starting to come back to me a bit, you know?"

"That's good," I said, studying Wendy's freckled face.
She was glowing. It had been a long time since I'd seen her
like this. She normally liked to hop from waiter to waiter—
with an occasional stray investment banker or attorney
thrown into the mix—but she'd already been out four times
with Jean Michel and was seeing him again tonight.

Had the world turned upside down? Waiter-dating
Wendy, finally settling down?

"It's been a long time since I've felt like this," she said,
as if reading my mind. "I really like him, Claire."

"I'm happy for you," I said, and I meant it. "That
sounds great."

"It *is* great," Wendy said, flashing me her wide grin. "He's
great. I went out to dinner at Azafran last night while Jean
Michel was at work, and you know what? I didn't even look at
any of the waiters. It didn't even occur to me. Isn't that weird?"

I reached across the table and squeezed her hand.

"Wow," I murmured, looking at her closely. "You didn't even look?"

"No," said Wendy, looking as surprised as I was. "I don't think I've *ever* not looked. What do you think that means?"

"Maybe you're in love," I said.

"Maybe I am," Wendy agreed softly. She smiled and winked at me. "Stranger things have happened."

I don't know exactly what kind of reception I expected at work, but I had expected there would be at least some kind of fallout after Cole's visit. I'd expected to be greeted with the same suspicion that Sidra had looked at me with. Instead, I had a steady stream of coworkers coming by my desk to squeal about how cool it was that Cole Brannon had dropped in to see me.

It didn't seem to occur to any of them that there was anything romantic going on between us. I didn't know whether to be insulted by that or flattered that my coworkers knew I'd never overstep the bounds of professionalism. I finally decided on the latter, and I allowed myself to breathe a huge sigh of relief. I even basked a bit in their jealousy over the fact that "*the* Cole Brannon" had sought me out in the office.

"What was he doing here?" Chloe Michael had squealed the moment I walked in.

"Uh, dropping by to confirm a few details of the interview," I stammered before I had a chance to think.

Chloe had accepted the explanation and it spread like wildfire. A few editorial assistants even dropped by to *thank* me for bringing him by—they'd been thrilled to get his autograph. No one brought up the fact that I had dragged him into the bathroom, which obviously didn't gel with the rest of my explanation.

Details, details.

My relief was cut short, though, when Sidra glided into the doorway of my cubicle at 4:45 that afternoon, on her way out of the building. Her hair had been blown out, and she was dressed in a skintight black designer dress and pointy black Jimmy Choos. In fact, she looked just a bit like the devil himself would look if he were a fashion editor. But maybe that was just me projecting.

"So now we're bringing our lovers by the office, are we?" she singsonged at me. "I heard about your little encounter with Cole Brannon." My breath caught in my throat. Yes, she was definitely Satan. Beelzebub in the flesh.

"No," I sputtered. "Nothing happened. He was dropping by to answer some questions."

"Is that what the kids are calling it these days?" Sidra laughed. "Are your interviews always conducted in the men's room? No *wonder* you got to be a senior editor so fast."

I blushed furiously and started to protest. Sidra cut me off, batting her long eyelashes at me in faux innocence.

"Oh, and do the movie stars you interview—and refuse to sleep with, according to you—always send you flowers, too?" she asked sweetly.

I was still formulating an answer as she glided away, a smirk plastered across her face. I felt shaken. Obviously, Sidra wasn't done with me yet. I suddenly felt uneasy.

Then it hit me. The flowers. How did she know about the flowers? Wendy was the only one I'd told. Oh no.

"Wendy?" I asked over the cubicle, standing up slowly. I felt a bit sick. "You didn't tell Sidra about the flowers I got the other day, did you?" I already knew the answer, but it was my last resort before I gave in to believing the worst.

"No, of course not," she said quickly. She looked at me for a moment, and then her face blanched. "Why?"

"She knows they were from Cole," I said flatly. This was not good.

"Oh, no," Wendy said. "What did you do with the note?"

"I threw it away," I said softly.

"Here? In the office?"

I nodded. How could I have been so stupid? We looked at each other for a moment. I closed my eyes, then opened them to stare at Wendy in horror.

"She has the note," Wendy said finally. I nodded again. "What do you think she's going to do?"

"I don't know," I said. "But it can't be good."

The Schmuck

Tom was late.

As I stood in the entrance to the TGI Friday's in Times Square at 6:45, I tried not to feel annoyed. After all, he had probably been delayed by traffic or something. He'd be here.

I sank onto a sticky vinyl bench that stretched from the front door to the hostess stand. Around me, tourists with Texas drawls, Southern twangs, and Midwestern inflections crowded in through the big door, between candy-cane-striped pillars. Tray-toting waiters and waitresses with cheerful grins rushed by, their chests lined with buttons that screamed at me to *Give Peace a Chance, Tip Your Waiter,* and remember, *Love Makes the World Go 'Round.* I didn't quite believe that last one.

Stupid saying.

As I sat and waited, I tried to be patient. How would it feel to see Tom for the first time since last Saturday night? Would I hate him the moment I saw him?

But at 6:55, when he walked through the front door, I didn't hate him. I loved how he looked in a crisp white button-down shirt, a pair of khakis, and the Kenneth Cole loafers I'd bought for his birthday. I loved how he smiled, his whole face lighting up when he saw me. I loved his stupid crooked grin. And I hated that I didn't hate him.

"Hey, babe!" he said as I stood up beside him. He

pulled me into his arms and surprised me with a warm hug. Simply out of habit I hugged back, before I realized what I was doing and stiffened. "You're early."

"Early?" I looked at him incredulously. He looked back, wide-eyed and innocent. "I'm not early. You're twenty-five minutes late!" He looked shocked.

"What? What are you talking about? We said seven!"

"We said six-thirty," I said, trying to sound calm.

"No, no, I'm positive we said seven," he said.

"No," I insisted. I was sure we'd said 6:30. Right? I thought so. But suddenly I wasn't a hundred percent sure. "Maybe," I amended. Tom looked satisfied.

"Great," he said. He put an arm around me. I thought about resisting, but I didn't. He pulled me close, and despite the fact that I knew it shouldn't, it felt good. "Let's get a table."

A hostess whose chest told us to *Knock on Wood, Save the Whales,* and *Vote for Kennedy* led us to a table in the middle of the room, afloat in a sea of tourists.

"It's nice to see you, Claire," Tom said formally after our hostess walked away. I looked at him over the top of my menu for a moment.

"You too," I mumbled. I returned my attention to the menu, buying myself some time. My emotions were suddenly a mess. I blinked a few times and tried to focus. I was not supposed to be unraveling this early in the evening. I took a deep breath and vowed to get ahold of myself.

While Tom ordered us an appetizer and drinks, I squirmed. A lock of his hair curled across his forehead, falling lightly across his left eyebrow. A week ago I would have reached across the table and tenderly brushed it away, but today I wasn't sure I wanted to touch him.

I wasn't supposed to feel something when I studied his eyes. I wasn't supposed to love the way his mouth curled up at the left corner. I wasn't supposed to love the tiny, nearly imperceptible scar on his right cheek that he'd gotten falling off his bike at the age of eleven. I wasn't supposed to feel my heartbeat pick up when his eyes met mine.

Yet I felt all those things. And that made me an idiot, didn't it?

I looked at him sadly out of the corner of my eye. How had we gotten here? A year ago, when he first moved into my apartment and we were spending every available second together, basking in each other's glow, I thought it would be perfect forever. I thought we'd be together forever. It had never even occurred to me to worry that he would cheat on me one day.

I wondered what he was thinking, what he would say. I wanted him to say magic words that would make everything okay, that would allow us to go back to living our lives as we had before Saturday.

I didn't know what those magic words would be, though, or if they even existed.

And I felt ashamed that any part of me wanted that to happen. I knew deep down that I should have had enough self-respect to walk away, to move on. But he was like an addiction, and I couldn't stop myself.

I was snapped out of my convoluted thought process by the reappearance of our waitress, whose brown curls were tied up in perky pigtails. She set down a Bud Light for Tom and a Coke for me and smiled at us.

"Are you ready to order?" she asked. She turned to me, and I started to open my mouth, but Tom spoke instead. He asked, of course, for the Jack Daniel's steak and shrimp dinner, one of the most expensive items on the menu. I ordered a chicken Caesar salad.

After the waitress took our order, Tom reached across the table for my hand. He squeezed it and held it gently.

"Look, Claire," he began. He paused and sighed. He squeezed my hand again and looked up at me with soulful eyes. "I don't even know where to begin," he said softly. "I was so wrong. I was so stupid to throw away what we had. I know you can never forgive me, and I don't expect you to, but . . ." His voice trailed off and he gazed at me imploringly. I looked back. I had no idea what to say.

He looked so genuinely pathetic and remorseful that I felt sorry for him. Part of me wanted to squeeze his hand back, smile warmly, and tell him it was okay, that I forgave him. But I didn't forgive him. And it wasn't okay. Maybe someday, but not today.

"Tom," I began slowly. I didn't pull my hand away, and he continued to hold it gently. I had to admit, I liked the way it felt. I liked his quiet strength and the gentle way he folded his big hand around my little one. I cleared my throat and looked up to meet his eye. "Why?" I asked finally. I felt suddenly weary. "Just tell me why."

He looked at me for a moment, and the uncomfortable silence seemed to drag on forever. My heart was pounding as I waited for his response.

"Why what?" he asked finally, in the same gentle tone of voice. I looked at him sharply. What did he think I was talking about?

"Why would you cheat on me?" I asked in a small voice. He looked away for a moment, then looked back at me with mournful eyes.

"I'm sorry," he said softly. "I was totally wrong. I know that. I guess I was just feeling like, I don't know, like you were too busy for me. And I wasn't dealing with that well." It was true. I knew I was a workaholic sometimes. Maybe I shouldn't have poured so much energy into my career. I felt instantly guilty.

"I'm not saying it was your fault," he said quickly. "I'm sure I was being too sensitive, honey." Was he still allowed to call me *honey*? Why did I still like the sound of the word rolling off his tongue? "I made a huge mistake because I felt like I wasn't sure that you loved me anymore."

I gasped.

"I never stopped loving you," I said. My eyes filled with sudden tears. I blinked quickly.

"I know that now," he said, squeezing my hand. "And I know I've gone and screwed it all up. I'm so sorry."

Our waitress interrupted us by setting down the enormous Friday's Three-for-All that Tom had ordered.

"Enjoy, you two!" She grinned encouragingly at us, as if we were two teenagers on a first date.

We busied ourselves with our food for a minute, avoiding each other's eyes. I pushed a potato skin around on my plate, but I couldn't bring myself to eat it.

"Did you meet her at *Mod*'s Christmas party?" I asked finally. I really wasn't hungry. Tom looked up, surprised, his mouth full. "Estella," I clarified. "Estella Marrone. Did you meet her at the Christmas party?" He looked down and then back at me. He chewed thoughtfully, swallowing loudly.

"Yes," he said simply, not sounding nearly as guilty as he should have. "How do you know her name?"

"She left her purse in the apartment," I said. "And her sister came to get it." Anger welled inside me. "Her sister is Sidra DeSimon, you know. The fashion director at *Mod*. You were sleeping with the sister of one of my coworkers." I expected his eyebrows to shoot up in surprise, but he nodded and looked guilty.

"I know," he said. "I'm so sorry."

"You knew?" I was incredulous. "You knew I worked with her sister?"

"Not right away," he said quickly. "But yeah, I knew. Not at the beginning, though. I didn't do it on purpose. What a coincidence, right?" He laughed uneasily.

"How is it a coincidence if you met her at *my* Christmas party?" I asked.

He shrugged.

"Well, there were lots of people there you didn't know," he said sheepishly. "How was I supposed to know you knew her sister?"

I looked miserably around the table. I was no longer hungry. I swallowed again.

"I am so, so sorry," Tom said again. "If I could change things, I would."

"You'd change that I caught you?" I asked bitterly.

"No," Tom said solemnly. "I deserved that. I'd change the fact that it happened in the first place. I had no right. Look what I've thrown away." He looked as miserable as I felt.

"Oh," I said finally, because I sensed he was waiting for a response. I didn't have anything else to say. We sat in silence for another moment, but this time there were no menus to distract us. We had only each other and the uncomfortable wall that stood between us.

The waitress came and cleared away our appetizer. I'd barely touched it. A moment later, a server whisked in with our entrees. I avoided Tom's eye as I started to pick listlessly at my salad.

"Can I ask you something?" Tom said finally. I looked up, surprised.

"Okay." Was he going to ask me to take him back? Ask me to forgive him?

"Are you . . ." He paused and his eyes flicked down at the table and back to me. "Are you sleeping with Cole Brannon?"

I just looked at him for a minute.

"No!" I answered, appalled. "Did Estella," I spat her name, "tell you that?" He paused again and nodded.

"She said her sister Sidra caught you in our apartment," he said finally.

"*My* apartment," I amended, just to be difficult.

I didn't know what to say. I certainly couldn't explain to Tom how pathetic I'd been that night, getting drunk and vomiting on a movie star—all because of him. He didn't need to know he had that kind of power over me. I fixed him with a glare.

"Nothing happened," I said stiffly. "It was a work thing." Tom looked at me for a moment and nodded, seeming to accept the explanation.

"Okay," he said. "I believe you." I simmered silently for a minute, then changed the subject.

"So are you still with her?" I demanded. Tom looked surprised and shook his head.

"No," he said solemnly. "No, Claire, I'm not. You're the only one in my heart. You always have been. I just didn't know how to appreciate it before."

It scared me that the words didn't repulse me. They sent a flush of warmth shooting through my body. I tried to fight it.

"You still have some things in the apartment," I said icily.

"Do you really want me to move my things out?" he asked softly. I held my breath. Was he asking me to say he could stay? My response was put on hold as our waitress came to refill my Coke and deliver another beer to Tom. She set down our check, and Tom handed her his credit card.

"Claire," Tom began after the waitress was gone. He again reached for my hand. "I love you so much. I've never loved anyone as much as I love you. And I can never express to you how sorry I am for what I've done."

My eyes filled with tears, and again, I blinked them back. My heart pounded as we looked into each other's eyes. This was one of those moments you see in Hugh Grant movies. I could practically hear the violin-laced soundtrack. "I don't expect you to forgive me right away. Maybe you'll never be able to. But I want to try, Claire. I want to try." I was about to speak when our waitress interrupted us, wrenching my tear-filled eyes away from Tom and his heartfelt message.

"Excuse me," she said, shifting from foot to foot. "I'm sorry to interrupt. But, sir, your card didn't go through. Do you have another one?" Tom reached into his pocket and pulled out his wallet. He rifled quickly through and looked up at the waitress.

"Gosh, how embarrassing. No, I don't." He looked at

me. "Claire? I'm so sorry. Can you get this meal? I'll get the next one?" I swallowed the lump of resentment that had risen suddenly in my throat and nodded. I reached for my wallet and gave the waitress my Visa. She smiled tightly and walked away.

"I'm so sorry, Claire," Tom said, reaching for my hand again. "I thought I had paid the balance off, but it must not have been processed yet. I feel like such a jerk."

"Don't worry about it," I said tightly, telling myself that he couldn't possibly have done it on purpose. Not when he was about to ask me to take him back. Not while he was in the middle of declaring his love for me. I brushed the thought away and reached for his hand. "You were saying?"

"Right," said Tom. He squeezed my hand and cleared his throat. "Claire, I love you more than anything in the world, and I want to work things out with you. I really do."

"Me too," I said softly. I hadn't intended to admit that to him or even to myself. I hadn't known for sure that I'd felt that way until the words were out of my mouth. Had I gone too far? But my heart was pounding, and I knew as I looked at him that I could forgive him. Things could change between us. I still loved him. And now I knew he still loved me. I should have hated him, but I couldn't. I didn't.

"But I know it will take some time," Tom said slowly. "I don't expect things to be back to normal right away."

"Right," I said softly, astonished that he realized on his own that things couldn't go back to being the way they had been. Just then the waitress returned with my credit card, two copies of the receipt, and a full glass of Coke for me. I signed the receipt, put my card away, and took a small sip. Tom took my hand again.

"So I was wondering . . ." Tom paused and tilted his head to the side imploringly. I leaned forward eagerly. This was it. He was going to beg me to take him back. "I was wondering if maybe you could loan me some money for a while. Since you threw me out and all. Then we can have some time apart and maybe try to work things out, you know?"

Everything inside me went cold, and I drew my hand away. I stared at him. He was still looking at me imploringly, an innocent expression on his face.

Suddenly I wanted to reach out and strangle him. Surely it would be justifiable homicide. Any jury would understand.

"You want to borrow money from me?" I asked very slowly, staring at him. Tom shrugged.

"Just a few thousand. To get on my feet, you know."

"Just a few thousand," I repeated flatly. Everything inside me had turned to ice.

I looked down at the receipt for the meal I'd just paid for. I couldn't believe it. I'd been so stupid. I'd bought everything he'd said. I'd fallen for it hook, line, and sinker.

Again.

"Yeah," he said. I glared at him with the most intense anger I'd ever felt. "You know," he said, smiling at me with a sappiness that was so obviously fake. "I heard you got a raise at work. I don't think we should move back in together right away. That might put too much pressure on us. I want you back, and I want to do it right. And since you threw me out and all . . ." He paused and gave an encouraging smile.

"So you want a few thousand dollars," I said flatly.

He shrugged.

"Give or take," he said casually.

He winked at me, and suddenly I detested him. I had come here prepared to listen to his explanation and maybe even to reconcile. He had come to try and trick me into giving him a check. I felt physically ill. He pressed on.

"I just want to make things right between us," he said with a half smile.

I stared at him for a long time, then I smiled at him slowly.

"You know what?" I said. I suddenly felt calm. "I've been thinking about it. And I want to make things right between us too."

"Really?" he asked hopefully.

"Oh, yes." I stood up from the table. In one smooth motion, I picked up my full glass of Coke and flung it into Tom's face, drenching him in a shower of sticky coldness.

He jumped up, his chair clattering to the floor behind him. Around us, people stopped eating and stared, but I hardly noticed.

"What the hell?" Tom demanded furiously, holding his arms out to his side and shaking the soda off. His face dripped with beads of brown liquid, and his hair was drenched. He looked like a drowned rat. A pathetic, hairy, repulsive drowned rat. I smiled.

"I thought you wanted to make things right between us," I calmly repeated. I shrugged and grinned as he glared at me. "Well, that was a start."

Still smiling, I turned on my heel and marched out of the restaurant, my head held high. I'd been foolish to think anything good could ever happen between us again. I knew that now, and I knew I wouldn't turn back.

"You go, girl!" a woman murmured to me as I stormed out of the dining room.

"Thanks," I said as I kept walking. "I will."

The Sexy Siren

Wendy took me out that weekend, and for the first time since last Saturday—maybe even for the first time in a year—I finally felt like things were okay. I didn't need Tom. I didn't need anyone who would treat me like that. And as Wendy's blossoming romance with Jean Michel proved, you never knew when you were going to run into Mr. Right.

Or at least *Mr. Right Now.* Heck, at this point, I would have settled for Mr. Maybe, or even Mr. Slim Chance if he actually showed me some attention. But no such luck.

On Sunday, Wendy came over and helped me clean out the closet. Everything that belonged to Tom was thrown in big green garbage bags. Then, on second thought, we went through the bags and pulled out all the items I'd purchased for Tom the times we'd gone shopping and his credit card hadn't gone through. All the shirts I'd bought to surprise him, the ties I'd bought because I was thinking of him, the stain-resistant Van Heusen khakis I'd bought because I was sick of scrubbing ink stains out of his pants before trudging them off to the laundromat. By the time we extracted the clothes I'd bought for him, mounds of shirts, socks, boxers, pants, and ties lay strewn across my living room floor.

Wendy grinned.

"What do you want to do with them?" she asked. I smiled. It wasn't like they belonged to him. He'd gotten them under false pretenses, while pretending to be a faithful, sensitive boyfriend. Which he obviously was not.

"I can think of a few things," I muttered. We settled on hacking a few of the ties into satisfying little pieces with a pair of scissors, then we bagged up the rest of the clothing to take to Goodwill. As for the clothes Tom had actually purchased for himself, we put them in a heap outside my apartment, and Wendy called to leave a message on his cell phone.

"Your clothes are on Claire's doorstep, and they'll be there only until ten o'clock tonight," she chirped. "If you want them, you'll have to come get them before then." After she hung up the phone, she turned to me. "You don't need to sit around waiting, wondering when he'll show up. If he doesn't come tonight, those clothes go in the incinerator."

Wendy called a locksmith who came quickly and changed my locks. He gave me new keys, and Wendy pressed my old key into my palm.

"Throw it in a fountain or something," she said. "Maybe it'll bring you good luck." It couldn't hurt, I had to admit. It would be hard for my luck to get much worse.

We set off for Goodwill, each of us hauling a plastic bag full of things I'd bought for Tom. After we dropped them off, Wendy insisted on treating me to dinner, to celebrate getting rid of Tom once and for all. We took the subway uptown and made a quick trip to Rockefeller Center, so I could throw my old key into the fountain. There it settled, alongside mounds of pennies carrying wishes from their previous owners.

"What did you wish for?" Wendy asked me as we walked away.

"I can't tell you, or it won't come true," I said playfully. But I had wished that I would never again settle for someone who didn't treat me like I deserved to be treated.

Oh, and I added a wish to have sex again sometime before I hit thirty. After all, a key is bigger than a penny. I figure I was owed at least two wishes.

Over dinner (which Wendy paid for on a credit card that didn't bounce), we laughed and talked, and toasted freedom and self-respect. Cute waiters smiled at me, and I noticed. They smiled at Wendy, and she seemed genuinely oblivious.

How the tables had turned.

Back at my apartment, the doorstep was bare. Tom had come to get his things. Relief swept through me. I didn't owe him another phone call, another encounter, another smidgen of contact in any form.

"To Tom being gone forever," Wendy said triumphantly, popping the cork in a bottle of champagne we had picked up on the way home.

"I'll toast to that!" I said, raising my glass. "And to my apartment being *my* apartment again."

"Well, I was meaning to talk to you about that," Wendy said, cocking her head to the side and smiling at me. "Now that Jean Michel and I are officially dating, I won't be eating out quite as much, and I have the feeling I'll have a bit more money for rent. I was wondering if you might be interested in a new roommate?"

"Oh my gosh, yes!" I exclaimed, setting my champagne flute down and hugging her. She hugged me back, and we both laughed and jumped up and down with excitement. "Really? I would love for you to move in! I can't believe it! Do you mean it? We can turn the office into your bedroom."

"Really? You sure you want a roommate?"

"Yes! Yes! Yes!" We toasted again.

After Wendy had gone home for the night, I drifted happily into a dreamless sleep.

~⌒~

The phone rang on Tuesday morning at 6:45, jarring me out of the first pleasant sleep I'd had in months. My first thought was that if it was Tom again, I'd kill him. What was with this new trend of shaking me out of bed at the crack of dawn? I was *not* a morning person.

I grumpily answered the phone and was surprised to hear not Tom's voice, but my mother's.

"How dare you?" she demanded, without even a hello. I sat up in confusion and rubbed my eyes. I looked at the clock again, just to make sure I hadn't imagined the time. Nope, it was now 6:46 a.m. I cleared my throat.

"Um, good morning," I said sleepily.

"I can't believe you'd embarrass me like this, young lady," my mother said immediately. "I am just stunned at your behavior."

I pulled the phone away from my ear and stared at it for a moment. Then I put it back to my ear. I couldn't imagine what was going on.

"What are you talking about?" I asked finally.

"Don't play innocent with me," my mother said angrily. I took a deep breath, scanning my brain for any offending activities I might have taken part in, but I came up blank.

"I really don't know what you're talking about," I said finally.

"Your aunt Cecilia just called me," my mother said slowly, her voice icy. "She was on her way to work when she saw a copy of that horrible tabloid *Tattletale*. How dare you embarrass me that way?"

My heart was suddenly pounding although I still had no idea what she was talking about. But I had a sinking feeling in the pit of my stomach. I closed my eyes, and all I could see was a vision of a smug, smirking Sidra DeSimon.

"What was in *Tattletale*?" I asked slowly. This couldn't be good.

"Oh, I think you know," my mother said coldly. "If you want to shack up with a movie star, that's just fine with me. But when you tarnish our good family name by being splashed across the cover of a tabloid magazine as Cole

Brannon's *sex toy*, that is unforgivable. I did not raise you to be a slut."

Suddenly, I couldn't breathe.

A sex toy?

Cole Brannon's sex toy?

"Mom, I never did anything with him," I finally squeaked through a closed throat. My palms were sweaty, my mouth dry. "I swear. Are you sure it was me? Was Cecilia sure?"

"She's sure," my mother said, her voice icy. "You're right on the cover, Claire. How am I supposed to live that down? What am I supposed to say when your eighty-five-year-old grandmother sees you on the cover of a tabloid, looking like a cheap hooker?"

"Oh my God," I murmured, too stunned to respond to the fact that my own mother was accusing me of looking like a hooker. My heart was racing. I finally spoke. "This is all a big mix-up, Mom, I swear. I interviewed Cole Brannon, but that's it. *Tattletale* is a tabloid, Mom. It's not real news. You can't believe everything they print."

"I don't know what to say to you, Claire," my mother said after a moment's pause. "You're clearly not the same young lady I raised."

Her words stung. I took a deep breath and tried again. "Mom, none of this is true," I said. "You have to believe me."

"I am so disappointed in you," she said coldly. Then she hung up without waiting for a response. I sat there stunned for a moment, holding the phone to my ear until the dial tone snapped me into action.

"Shit, shit, shit," I mumbled, jumping out of bed and rushing into the closet. I threw on a pair of jeans and a faded sweatshirt, the first clothes I could find.

I barreled quickly down the four flights of stairs, jogged down the hallway, and burst out onto the street, which hadn't yet begun to bustle with people. I pushed my way inside the convenience store on Second Avenue and Fourth Street, scanned the media rack, and snatched *Tattletale* from its place on the shelf.

I froze as I looked at the cover.

On the upper left corner of the tabloid, there was a black-and-white photo of Cole and me, emerging from the men's room at *Mod*. It looked like a still taken from one of the magazine's security cameras, which meant that someone at *Mod*—no doubt Sidra—had to have sent it in to *Tattletale*. Cole had his arm around me as we emerged from the doorway, and I was looking up at him. It looked damning. But far worse was the headline with it that screamed: MOD EDITOR IS COLE BRANNON'S NEW SEX TOY.

"Ohhhh shit!" I cursed, loud enough for the man behind the counter to look up in surprise.

"Everything okay, miss?" he asked. I grimaced.

"No," I muttered. With shaky hands, I put a copy of *Tattletale* down on the counter and gave him a dollar for it. "Everything is *not* okay."

I stormed out of the store, flipping through the pages as I did. I stopped dead in my tracks as I reached page 32, where there was a whole two-page spread about our "illicit affair." Standing there in the middle of the sidewalk, I stared, feeling my chest tighten as I took it all in.

Photos were splashed across the page, along with a small story. There was a picture of the amazing bouquet Cole had sent, and a close-up reproduction of the taped-together card that had come with it—courtesy of Sidra, I'm sure. There was a paparazzi shot of Cole getting into the taxi with me. There was even a photo of me leaving my apartment building alone.

"Cole Brannon Finds New Sex Toy," the print clearly said. Beneath it, the copy read, "*Mod* senior entertainment editor Claire Reilly is the movie star's latest fling—a *Tattletale* exclusive!"

I was feeling sick as I scanned the snarky text.

Tattletale spies have learned that Hollywood's hottest hunk, Cole Brannon, is getting busy with Claire Reilly, twenty-six, a senior editor at *Mod* magazine, which will be running a cover story about Brannon in their August issue.

"They met when she interviewed him for the August cover story," says a *Mod* insider. "She talks about him all the time. She says he's great in bed."

Ms. Reilly has worked at *Rolling Stone* and *People* as a celebrity writer. She brought her talents to *Mod* eighteen months ago when she joined their staff as the senior entertainment editor. She is the youngest senior editor at a top-thirty magazine.

Tattletale has learned that Mr. Brannon and Ms. Reilly were spotted leaving his hotel together, leaving her apartment together, and ducking into the men's room at *Mod* magazine's New York offices together.

Quickie, anyone?

"They looked quite cozy together," says cab driver Omar Sirpal, who drove Ms. Reilly and Mr. Brannon from his hotel to her apartment last week. "He even fed her breakfast in my taxi."

Ms. Reilly was recently estranged from her live-in boyfriend, so the romance with Mr. Brannon sounds a bit like a rebound to us here at *Tattletale*. As for Mr. Brannon, it looks like he's fallen head-over-heels for his new sex kitten, who joins the ranks of Kylie Dane and publicist Ivana Donatelli in his cast of lovers.

"He sent her flowers last week," says our *Mod* source. "She told everyone in the office who they were from and why he'd sent them. Apparently, he appreciated all the attention she'd been giving him, if you know what I mean."

What kind of attention might that be? We don't know, but we can guess. Ms. Reilly and Mr. Brannon were seen heading into the men's room at *Mod* together last Thursday and emerging together fifteen minutes later, looking embarrassed and satisfied, according to our spy.

"We all knew what was going on in there," says the *Mod* insider. "If it wasn't obvious enough, we could hear them going at it."

Who will be the next flame for Hollywood's hottest, busiest bachelor? Check out next week's *Tattletale* to find out.

I stared at the text in horror for a long time after I finished reading it. I read it once more, as if it might have changed to something less damning by the second go-round.

No such luck.

"Oh . . . my . . . God." I was frozen in the middle of the sidewalk and had no idea what to do next. It would be my word against that of *Tattletale*'s source, who was surely Sidra DeSimon. Everything damning in the text had come directly from her. I was sure of it.

After all, why wouldn't she have run to *Tattletale* once she had damning evidence. They'd pay her big money for a story like this. It would increase her status with them. It would likely thrill her sister Estella. And it would take me down a notch or two. I knew she hated that I was already a senior editor at twenty-six. She had always taken my success as a personal affront.

Basically, I was screwed. Obviously, Sidra hadn't told Margaret about Cole yet, but no doubt Margaret would have been alerted to the *Tattletale* article by the time she got into the office today. After all, the name of her magazine—

not to mention my face—was splashed across the cover of one of the country's most prominent tabloids. And although Margaret pretended to be aloof and high-class, we all knew she secretly loved everything from *Star* to the *National Enquirer*. *Tattletale* was always spread across her desk on Tuesday mornings. How could she miss it?

I gulped back the lump in my throat as I realized that I would be fired today. Tears sprang to my eyes at the unfairness of it all.

Even worse, what would Cole think? He'd surely think I had something to do with this. I was suddenly stiff with embarrassment and disappointment. Sure, he was a liar, but now it would look like I had lied too—and to a trashy tabloid. I was sure he would think I was behind the horrid story of our alleged affair.

I looked up, realizing I was standing in the middle of the sidewalk and that passersby were looking at me like I was crazy. Maybe I was. I quickly snapped the tabloid shut and hurried back down the street to my apartment, still in panic mode.

Forty minutes later, after a tortuously long subway ride to Brooklyn—during which I'd memorized the entire article with a rising sense of panic—I was pounding on Wendy's front door. It seemed to take her forever to answer, but she finally did, dressed in a T-shirt and flannel pants, rubbing sleep out of her eyes.

"Claire!" She yawned, her eyes finally opening all the way. She reached up and smoothed down her frizzy red hair, which had developed into a cross between a halo and an Afro as she slept. "What are you doing here?"

Without a word, I thrust my copy of *Tattletale* at her. She took one look at the cover, and when she looked back at me, she was wide-awake.

"Oh no," she said softly. "Is it as bad as it looks?"

I nodded slowly.

Wendy quickly flipped the magazine open. She gasped

as she saw the two-page spread. Her eyes scanned the short article; then she looked up at me in horror.

"This is awful," she said softly.

"I know," I said. She took one last look at the magazine and handed it back to me. "What am I going to do?"

"I don't know," she said. We just looked at each other for a moment; then she straightened up, gesturing for me to follow her inside. I felt like I was in a trance.

"At least it'll piss Tom off," Wendy said helpfully as I followed her down the hall to the kitchen. I tried a weak smile.

"At least there's that," I agreed. I sighed and looked back down at the tabloid in my hands. "This is Sidra's work." Wendy and I sat down at her kitchen table. When she looked up at me, her face was hard.

"It has to be," she agreed.

"Why is that woman out to get me? It isn't enough that her sister stole my boyfriend?"

"Actually," Wendy clarified, "her sister did you a service, if you think about it."

"True," I said sourly. My hands felt icy, and I could hear the blood rushing through my ears. My body was suddenly tense.

"I have to do something," I said. Wendy looked at me and nodded. I looked down at *Tattletale,* then back at her. "But what? What am I supposed to do?"

"I don't know," Wendy said quietly.

<hr>

We weren't any closer to reaching a solution when we boarded the subway to work thirty minutes later, but at least I felt better knowing that I wasn't alone. I knew I'd have to brace myself for stares and whispers as I walked into the office, but Wendy had promised to walk in beside me and shoot deadly looks at anyone who said anything inappropriate.

"I'll probably get fired today, you know," I said miserably as the subway rattled on belowground. Wendy and I were wedged together between a portly woman in an oversized suit from the '80s and a tall man who had a pointy nose and suspenders pulling his pants up above his waist. All around us, newspapers flipped open and closed as New Yorkers prepared themselves for a day at work. I tried to look down and hide my face as I noticed a few copies of *Tattletale* open in the car. Who knew so many people read that trash?

"You don't know that," Wendy said firmly. But her words weren't much comfort.

When we entered the office at just past 9 a.m., all eyes were indeed on me, as I'd expected them to be. I was totally mortified. Wendy squeezed my arm gently as we began the long walk down the corridor to our adjoining cubicles.

"It's going to be okay," she whispered as copies of *Tattletale* lined our way. Dozens of pairs of eyes peered at me from over the top of the tabloid.

It was like walking into that dream where you show up at your office naked. But somehow it was worse—and I was wide-awake.

I wanted to run, screaming down the hallway that it wasn't true, that it was all a lie. But as Wendy had reminded me, protesting too much would only make it look like I had something to hide. So instead, I settled for holding my head high and pretending I didn't notice the stares, the whispers, the eyes burning holes in my back. Wendy kept a gentle hand on my arm until we reached my cubicle.

"Just ignore them and try to get your work done, okay?" she said softly as I sat down. I nodded. Easier said than done.

As I picked up my phone to play my voice mail, I was surprised to hear that I already had twelve messages. It was only just past nine in the morning. I blanched as I listened to the first one.

"Hello, Ms. Reilly," the voice began. "This is Sal Martino, a producer at *Access Hollywood*. We're very interested in your story. As you of course know, Cole Brannon is huge news right now. Call me back at 212-555-5678 as soon as you can."

The second message was from *Hollywood Tonight*.

"This is Jen Sutton from *Hollywood Tonight*," she began in a high, chirpy voice. "Like, what a great story. We love it. Young, high-powered editor swept off her feet by Hollywood's hottest hunk. We'd love to get Robb Robertson out there to interview you right away. You're hot news right now, girl! Call me at 212-555-3232."

The remaining ten messages were along the same lines. Sal Martino had called back twice. The *National Enquirer* was offering to pay me for my story. *Access Hollywood* wanted to send Billy Bush out to interview me. Page Six wanted something exclusive. Even the city's NBC affiliate wanted in on the action, requesting that I let them send a camera crew to my apartment that night to do a live shot for the eleven o'clock news. I groaned as I hung up the phone in horror. I could practically feel my world crumbling beneath my feet.

I was about to stand up and walk over to Wendy's cubicle when my phone rang. I grabbed it quickly.

"*Mod* magazine, Claire Reilly speaking," I answered.

"Oh, Claire, I cannot believe I caught you in," chirped a voice that I instantly recognized from my voice mail. "This is Jen Sutton, from *Hollywood Tonight*." She paused, waiting for me to respond.

"Hello," I said finally.

"Hey, girl!" Jen continued cheerfully. "I am, like, so jealous of you. This is so cool! You're, like, one of us. A journalist, breaking all the rules to sleep with the hottest guy in Hollywood. That's so awesome!"

"But I didn't—" I started to protest, but Jen rambled on like she hadn't heard me.

"Robb Robertson is so excited about this story," she chirped. "You know Robb, right? He's, like, our most well-known reporter, and he is so all over this story. You are so hot right now, girl."

"But I didn't—" Again, my protest was cut off. Did she ever stop for air?

"Everyone wants your story," she went on, her voice climbing an octave—perhaps from lack of oxygen. "We can promise you star treatment. We'll make you up, send you through wardrobe, the whole nine yards. It'll be so glam." Finally, she stopped and waited for a response. I drew in a breath.

"No," I said. "I didn't sleep with him. I didn't sleep with Cole Brannon. Nothing happened, I swear." Jen was silent for a minute.

"We'll even let you see the questions ahead of time," she bubbled on like she hadn't heard what I'd said. "I know Robb seems kind of tough on TV and all, but we'll let you see the question list, and I'll make him promise not to spring anything on you, okay?"

"No," I said firmly. Was she deaf? "Not okay. There's no story! I didn't sleep with Cole Brannon." Jen was silent for another moment.

"Whatever you say," she said, her voice suddenly icy. "But we're going with the story whether you cooperate or not."

"But how? There's nothing to support it!"

"We're a professional news organization," Jen snapped back. "We'll find something. Give me a call if you change your mind before four p.m." Then she hung up. I was left stunned, holding the handset.

"What was that?" Wendy asked over the cubicle, looking concerned.

"*Hollywood Tonight,*" I said, looking at her in horror. "They're going to report the story whether I cooperate or not. And I have messages from just about everyone else on my voice mail."

"Oh no," said Wendy softly.

"Oh yes."

⁓

My heart nearly stopped when my intercom buzzed at ten o'clock. It was Cassie, snarling at me that Margaret wanted to see me immediately. Apparently my boss didn't want to waste any time putting me in my place.

"Want me to come?" Wendy asked.

"No." I sighed. "This is something I have to deal with myself."

I stood up slowly from my chair and started down the hallway to meet my fate.

The Cold-Hearted Snake

My walk to Margaret's office was somewhat anticlimactic, as I'd made a similar trek just last week, when I'd also been convinced I was about to be fired. Today, I felt a grim certainty that this really would be the end of the line for me.

I'd probably never work in magazines again.

Instead of keeping me waiting, Margaret had Cassie usher me in immediately.

As I sat down in one of the huge chairs facing her desk, shrinking down to the size of a child, the fear that I'd managed to push away started to return. Margaret looked down at me, perfect in a rose tailored suit, her dark hair blown out. We sat in silence for a moment. By the time she finally opened her mouth to speak to me, my heart was beating so hard I was afraid she could hear it. To my own ears, it sounded like the pounding of a battle drum, although I kept reminding myself that I wasn't actually going to battle. It sure felt like I was.

"So I assume you've guessed by this point that I've seen this morning's *Tattletale*," Margaret said flatly, opening our meeting without any ado.

"Um, yes." Boy, I was articulate this morning.

"And I assume that you, too, have seen it," she added

unnecessarily. This time, I just nodded, unable to speak, thanks to the lump that had risen in my throat.

"Uh-huh," I finally gurgled, because she seemed like she was waiting for a verbal response before going on. She looked me carefully up and down as my heart pounded more quickly. My palms felt sweaty, and I could feel droplets of nervous sweat cropping up along my hairline. The hair on my arms was standing up, and I was trying hard not to squirm. I felt like crawling under my chair and hiding from what was to come.

"You've been working for me eighteen months now," Margaret said slowly, as my heart continued to pound. "So I'm quite sure you know that when I assign a story for *Mod* magazine, I expect my writers and editors to conform to certain standards." I nodded again.

"Uh-huh," I gurgled again. She was silent for another moment. I could feel rivulets of sweat starting to drip down my back.

"This article in *Tattletale* would not have been my idea of how my writers and editors should be behaving, however," she said slowly, her dark eyes boring into me. I squirmed uncomfortably.

"I know," I said. "I'm so sorry. But I swear I didn't sleep with Cole Brannon."

Margaret waved her slender hand dismissively. She looked like she hadn't heard me.

"In any case, I've given this a lot of thought," she said. She held up a copy of *Tattletale,* and I looked away. I closed my eyes and braced myself to be fired.

"Claire, this is pure genius," Margaret said from somewhere off in the distance. I sat there confused for a moment, my eyes still scrunched closed. I felt sure I had become delusional or, at best, that I'd heard her wrong. But when I finally opened my eyes, blinking twice, I was greeted by a big grin splashed across Margaret's face.

"Huh?" I asked, dumbfounded. Margaret's smile just

widened. Had she gone crazy? Maybe it was that Mad Cow disease I'd heard about.

"This is the best publicity we could have asked for, Claire!" the mad cow enthused. She tapped the cover of *Tattletale* for emphasis. "This is wonderful! When the magazine comes out next month, everyone will rush out to buy it and get the story behind your romance with Cole Brannon! It's not what I would have expected from you, Claire, but I love it."

I couldn't grin back. I was flabbergasted.

"But I didn't do anything," I said finally. This was too bizarre to take in. I wrinkled my brow and studied her in consternation.

"Oh, Claire, no need to be modest with me," Margaret pushed on, steamrolling right over my words. "I must admit, I am a bit disappointed at being scooped by a tabloid, but what a great way to get the *Mod* name out there. I've already gotten calls from some of the company's biggest investors, and they're all terribly intrigued."

"Great," I said weakly. I was baffled. I forced a wan smile.

"Do you know what this means, Claire?" Margaret asked, leaning forward hungrily. I shook my head slowly. She licked her lips and grinned at me. "It means we're going to pass *Cosmopolitan,* Claire. For the first time in *Mod*'s history. We're going to pass *Cosmopolitan* in circulation for our August issue. Thanks to your fling with Cole Brannon, Claire, *Mod* will fly off the newsstands."

"But . . ." I tried to formulate a response, but my brain didn't seem able to connect with my mouth.

"Because of your hard work, Claire, I've decided to give you another raise," Margaret said, beaming. I started to protest, but Margaret interrupted me. "I wish more of my editors would take your kind of initiative, Claire. Well done."

I opened and closed my mouth wordlessly a few times,

like a fish. Then I just kept it closed as Margaret chattered on about circulation figures, flings with celebrities, and her own crush on Robert Redford that she always wished she'd pursued. I sat stunned until she was finished. I valiantly issued one last denial, then sat back mutely as she rolled over that one too, dismissing it with a tinkling laugh. I was completely flabbergasted by the time she ushered me enthusiastically out of her office, asking me to keep up the good work.

"Oh my gosh, are you okay?" Wendy rushed out of her cubicle to embrace me in the hallway as I walked back to my desk like a zombie. I didn't respond right away, because I was still in shock. Wendy took my silence and my battle-weary demeanor to mean the worst. "Oh my gosh, she fired you, didn't she? God, Claire, I am so pissed off. I'm going in there right now to quit myself." She looked angry and defensive, and she reached down to give me another tight hug.

"No," I finally said. I felt like I was walking in a fog.

"No what?" asked Wendy confused. "Hey, are you okay?" I didn't answer. I looked down and then back at Wendy.

"No, I didn't get fired," I said finally. I watched her eyebrows shoot up in surprise.

"What happened, then?" she asked. The answer to this still confused me.

"I got another raise," I said slowly. "I don't know what just happened."

By noon I'd stopped answering my phone, because every single call I had taken was from a reporter or a producer looking for the "real" scoop on my love affair with Cole Brannon.

I realized by lunchtime that the calls were much more than just an annoyance. None of the dozens of people I'd heard from today took me seriously. In the space of a few hours, I'd somehow gone from being a reporter worthy of respect—even if you didn't believe *Mod* was a bastion of great journalism—to a common tramp who was bent on climbing the ladder of celebrity, who'd gotten lucky by landing Cole Brannon on the first rung.

It was my biggest fear come true. I had always worried, being the youngest senior editor at the magazine, that people would think I was sleeping my way to the top. It was certainly a pattern that had repeated itself on other rungs of the ladder at our magazine and other women's and entertainment magazines, many times over. In other areas of the corporate world, women sometimes made their way to the top by sleeping with their bosses. In the magazine world, it was just as effective to sleep with someone powerful or prominent outside the company—an actor, a politician, a rock star—and let them pull the strings for you.

And now, the world was sure it was true in my case. I had been so careful to always be and appear appropriate. And now it looked like I'd just climbed the ladder with the help of Cole Brannon—instead of my own hard work.

During lunch, which I took alone at my desk after silencing the ringer on my office phone and turning off my cell phone, I thought about Cole Brannon and wondered whether he'd seen today's *Tattletale* yet.

He was probably furious at me. I chewed nervously on the nail of my index finger. He would be mortified. He didn't date women like me. He certainly didn't sleep with women like me. And now he probably thought that I'd lured him into the bathroom just to get a good shot for the cover of *Tattletale.*

I shouldn't have cared, of course. He had lied to me and was probably off somewhere sleeping with a married actress. But I couldn't let it go.

Breathing hard, I pulled open my desk and rummaged through until I found the notebook I had used as a backup when I interviewed Cole last Saturday. I flipped through until I found the cell phone number he'd given me. The one I swore to myself I'd never use. But this was an emergency. I had to tell him the *Tattletale* story wasn't my doing.

Nervously, I dialed the number, noticing abstractly that he still had a 617 area code—from Boston—instead of a 323 from L.A., or a 646 from Manhattan, as I would have expected.

As the phone rang twice, time seemed to slow down. I could feel my heart pounding, my palms sweating, my mouth going dry. Maybe I shouldn't be calling him. Maybe I should hang up.

"Hello?" a sleepy female voice answered midway through the third ring. I was too surprised to say anything for a moment. I looked down at the phone to see if I'd dialed correctly. Indeed, I had. "Hello?" said the voice again, sounding a bit perturbed.

"Uh, hello," I finally said. "I'm looking for Cole." Why was a woman answering his phone? More important, why was it making me feel so jealous?

"Who's calling?" snapped the woman on the other end.

"This is Claire Reilly," I said timidly. There was silence on the other end. Finally, the woman laughed, low and deep in her throat.

"Well, if it isn't Claire Reilly," the woman said with what sounded like an edge of anger. "Claire, this is Ivana Donatelli. Cole's publicist. I'm sure you know who I am."

I gulped and started to sweat. What was she doing there? Why was she answering his cell phone? Maybe I was right, and the *Tattletale* photos of her and Cole together *had* meant something. Now I felt like an idiot. It would look like I was calling him because I was infatuated or something.

"Hi, Ivana," I said, trying to sound as friendly and innocuous as possible. "I was just calling about—"

"*Tattletale.*" Ivana completed my sentence for me.

"Yes, I—"

She cut me off.

"I was going to call you about that too," she said smoothly. "But I see you've beat me to it." I couldn't read her tone of voice. It was very even, not hinting at what she was thinking.

"I was just calling to apologize to Cole," I stammered. "I swear, I had nothing to do with this. Nothing happened with me and Cole, and I wanted him to know that—"

She cut me off sharply again.

"Cole and I just got out of bed, Claire," Ivana said smoothly. My heart dropped in my chest. "He's in the shower, so I'm afraid he can't take your call at the moment. Besides, I think you've had quite enough to do with Cole Brannon."

"But . . ." I started to protest weakly. My God, they *were* sleeping together.

"I believe he'll draw whatever conclusions he will about you and your moral character," she continued smoothly. "As for me, I'd appreciate it if you'd refrain from contacting either one of us in the future."

"No, Ivana, you don't understand," I said quickly. "I swear, I had nothing to do with this. Let me explain . . ."

"No, let *me* explain," she said, her voice suddenly taking on a menacing tone. "I am disgusted with you. I am disgusted at your willingness to take such blatant advantage of my generosity in granting you an interview with Cole. You'd better hope to God that your little story in *Mod* is perfect, or I'll have my lawyers on your ass faster than you can imagine."

"But—"

"Now you listen to me," she said, cutting me off, her voice slow and deliberate. "Never call me again. Never contact Cole again. I can't imagine a reporter behaving more unprofessionally, and I am disgusted by you. If you ever contact either of us, I will make it my mission to make your life miserable, understood?"

"But . . ."

"Cole Brannon would never look twice at a woman like you," she hissed. "Good day, Ms. Reilly." She hung up the phone before I could say another word. I sat stunned for a good few minutes. I had no idea what else to do.

Cole Brannon hated me. I was sure of it. And he *was* sleeping with Ivana Donatelli after all. I could hardly believe it. I had just started to believe that it was possible he was telling the truth. But I should have known better.

I fought back the tears that welled in my eyes. But eventually, they overflowed. There's only so much one person can take in a single morning.

At just past 4 p.m., after a dozen more voice mails from various reporters and producers had pushed me beyond the limits of my patience, I did what I should have done a week before. I stood up with all the fury I had accumulated over the course of the day, and, without saying anything to Wendy or anyone else, I marched directly to the fashion department to find Sidra.

"Well, look who's here," she purred as I turned the corner into her office. She was wearing a black pantsuit and five-inch heels—she had her long legs stretched out, her feet propped up on her desk, when I stormed in.

"What the hell do you think you're doing?" I demanded without any pretense. My voice didn't sound like my own, but then again, I wasn't feeling much like myself.

Sidra looked me slowly up and down, then a slow smile spread across her lips (which looked like they'd been injected with another shot of collagen in the past few days). She slowly swung her legs down to the floor. I clenched and unclenched my fists.

"I can't imagine what you're talking about," she said, batting her eyes innocently. She lazily reached over with one long, perfectly manicured finger and pressed a button on her intercom. "Sally, Samantha," she said, still looking at me with a little smile. "Come into my office. You'll never believe who's here. It's *Tattletale*'s new 'It' girl!" She removed her finger from the intercom and looked me pensively up and down. "You certainly don't *look* like an 'It' girl," she said with a sly smile.

"Screw you," I said. I was so angry, it was hard to breathe. Sidra raised an eyebrow in mock surprise.

"What?" she asked innocently. "Profanity from the mouth of Cole Brannon's new love interest? How inappropriate!"

Just then, Samantha and Sally appeared in the doorway, standing so close together they looked like Siamese twins. Like their fearless leader, they were both decked out from head to toe in fashionable black—Sally in Prada, Samantha in Escada. I wondered for a moment if Sidra called them each morning to issue a Triplet Dress Code for the day. That would explain why they all arrived at the office late, nearly always looking like they'd come off the couture assembly line.

"Claire!" Samantha purred. "We just couldn't believe it . . ."

". . . when we saw you in *Tattletale*." Sally finished the sentence that had apparently initiated in the brain they shared.

"I know," Sidra joined in with a smirk. "It was quite a shock to all of us. I never would have expected such a thing."

"Just stop it!" I barked, feeling my face heat up with anger. "Do I look stupid? I know you did this!"

"What?" Sidra feigned shock. "*Moi?* Why on earth would you think such a thing?"

By this time, Samantha had walked over to Sidra's left

side, and Sally flanked her right side. For a moment, as I stared at them in their matching black designer uniforms, they reminded me eerily of old pictures of Saddam Hussein and his two evil sons.

"I don't know," I responded. "I don't know why you would do it. Jealousy maybe?"

"*Me?* Jealous of *you?*" Sidra's laugh was cold and heartless. She was immediately joined by lifeless chuckles from her two disciples.

"Why are you out to get me?" I demanded. I was starting to feel outnumbered again. It reminded me slightly of elementary school, and I had sudden vague memories of being ganged up on and excluded from kickball games by the "cool" kids. Sidra laughed again.

"My, my, my, this is going to your head, I think," she said coolly. "The universe doesn't revolve around you, Claire, dear. Just because something happens, it doesn't mean anyone's out to get you."

"Why, then?"

"You're playing with fire," Sidra said, leaning forward, her voice low and menacing. "And you're going to keep getting burned until you learn to walk away." Sally and Samantha nodded their agreement as Sidra leaned back, looking satisfied with herself.

"What are you talking about?" I asked. I could hear my voice rise an octave to soprano. "I'm not playing with anything. I never was. If I remember correctly, your sister was screwing my boyfriend. You know as well as I do that I didn't sleep with Cole Brannon."

"Oh, it didn't look like that to me," Sidra said, smiling knowingly at me. Samantha and Sally tittered in unison. I clenched my fists by my sides.

"This had better be the end of this," I said finally. I exhaled and felt suddenly weary. "Fine, you've gotten me back for whatever offense you've imagined. But now we're even, okay? Whatever I've done to you has surely been canceled out by this."

"I still don't know what you're talking about," Sidra singsonged slyly. I ignored her.

"Just stop this now," I said wearily. "I'm serious. You've gotten what you wanted. I'm mortified. Pat yourself on the back. Mission accomplished." As Sidra and I stared at each other, our eyes locked in some kind of juvenile staring contest, I felt some of the anger go out of me. This was ridiculous. We were grown women, and we were acting like schoolchildren at war on the playground. "Just leave me alone, Sidra," I said finally. "I'll stay out of your way if you stay out of mine."

"Deal," she said icily. As I turned and started to walk away, she called after me.

"Oh, Claire? Would you like me to give your regards to Tom?"

I froze in my tracks but didn't turn around.

"He's having dinner at my parents' house tonight," she continued. "My sister thought it was time she brought him home to meet the family."

The words hit me like a cold slap across the face.

"Yes, give him my regards," I said softly without turning around. I couldn't. I wouldn't.

I walked away, leaving Sidra and her designer henchmen behind in their weird little world that I wanted no part of.

The Ingenue

The night the *Tattletale* story appeared had to have been the worst night of my life. Wendy was nice enough to stay with me, but even her comfort didn't help much when I saw my face splashed across *Access Hollywood, Entertainment Tonight,* and two editions of the local news. Friends I'd gone to high school with in Georgia called, drawling in excited tones about how they couldn't believe "Little Clairey Reilly" had hooked up with Cole Brannon. My mother called to chastise me yet again, just in case I hadn't gotten the point that morning, and even my little sister Carolyn called to tell me, "Everybody knows, Claire. It's just soooo embarrassing for me."

Life eventually started returning to a semi-normal state. I never heard from *Access Hollywood* or *Entertainment Tonight* again, and although I kept a close eye on Page Six and *Tattletale* for the next few weeks, there wasn't another mention of me. I started to breathe more easily.

Although my mother hadn't apologized, she was at least starting to act more normal. Well, normal for her, which might not necessarily qualify as normal in anyone else's world. Still, she was back to her old ways, nagging me about finding a husband before I hit thirty (geez, I still had four years to go!), picking at me for being so career-oriented, and criticizing me for putting on a few pounds.

The next few weeks of work, however, were hellish.

There was a sudden chill in the air when it came to me securing celeb interviews for *Mod*. Publicists who had always called right back were suddenly no longer available; interviews that had been set in stone were mysteriously canceled; and I caught coworkers gossiping about me in the break room three times.

On top of that, it was pretty rotten to have everyone believe I'd gotten laid by the hottest guy in America when in reality, I hadn't had sex in so long I probably wouldn't remember how to anymore.

Each week I struggled to meet deadlines I'd never had a problem with before. I spent hours waiting by the fax machine for responses to interview requests—sometimes for *faxed* interview answers from celebs who were suddenly "too busy" to talk to me—and I worked late most days to overcompensate for the fact that my career seemed to be going steadily downhill.

Perhaps the worst work-related fallout from the whole Cole incident was that Margaret still seemed to believe the *Tattletale* story and treated me as though she expected my behavior to mirror that which the tabloid had attributed to me.

When I told her I was having trouble securing an interview with Orlando Bloom, who really shouldn't have been a problem, she had winked at me and said, "I'm sure *you* can come up with a way to convince him." When Jerry O'Connell canceled an interview with me, Margaret suggested wearing sexier lingerie. With Hugh Grant, her suggestion was to show a bit more cleavage.

It had been the same story for every male star I'd failed to snag in the past six weeks, and my continued denials that anything had happened between Cole and me seemed to always fall on deaf ears. Margaret had even referred to me twice in staff meetings as "our little *Mod* vixen." I had turned a decidedly un-vixen-like shade of red.

June and the first half of July were good months—outside of work, at least. Wendy moved in a week after the

Tattletale article, like she'd promised, and I quickly discovered she was the best roommate I'd ever had. When she got home from work before I did—which was most nights, thanks to the increasing difficulty of my job—she often cooked dinner for us, and Jean Michel usually joined us when he had the night off. Her meals were always delicious, and she swore that all of her recipes were from scratch.

"I want to open my own restaurant someday," she told me shyly. It always amazed me when I walked into my apartment and was greeted by the steamy smells of spices, meats, and baking bread.

The summer was a hot one. Wendy and I spent weekend days sunning and sipping lemonade in the Sheep Meadow in Central Park, riding the subway out to the ridiculous attractions of Coney Island, or wading into the water at Sea Bright or Highlands along the Jersey Shore.

As the weeks dragged on, I couldn't seem to shake being bothered by the fact I hadn't heard from Cole. Not once since the *Tattletale* article. I knew he thought it was my fault, which broke my heart. But he was obviously sleeping with Ivana. I knew I shouldn't care. But I did care. Too much.

He'd been nothing but nice with me, taking care of me when I got drunk, comforting me about Tom, and even coming by my office to make sure I was okay. And now he thought I'd paid him back by telling the tabloids that we had slept together. I'd probably embarrassed him beyond words. For a Hollywood star, it was probably mortifying to have everyone think you slept with some frumpy Plain Jane with a low-paying job, A-cup breasts, and clothes bought on sale at the Gap. I was definitely not normal Hollywood fare. He was used to sleeping with women like Kylie Dane—tall, curvaceous, flawlessly complexioned, perfectly dressed—or women like Ivana—coldly beautiful, oozing wealth, with flashing eyes and a throaty, sexy voice. It was stupid to think he'd even looked twice at me. The realization made me feel even more plain and boring than I already did.

It didn't help that everywhere I turned, I seemed to see him. He was on billboards all over the city. His face was on the sides of buses, and early trailers for his movie were on TV. Some nights I'd be flipping through the channels and see a rerun of the night he was on *Saturday Night Live,* or a romantic comedy in which he played the lead. It was like having salt rubbed in my wounds, and each time, I remembered with guilt how I'd left things with him. I'd practically told him I never wanted to see him again. After he'd gone out of his way to make sure I was okay.

I'd started dreaming about him sometimes, which scared me. I was sure it was because he seemed to surround me and because guilt over how things had ended still weighed on my unconscious. I finally talked myself into believing that when *Mod*'s August issue came out in a few days with my cover story about him, that would be it. I would send him several copies of the magazine along with a polite and formal note via his publicist, as I always did each month for the celeb featured on the cover. Then I could forget him once and for all. The article would be out. The *Tattletale* rumor was old news. I would no longer have any kind of connection to Cole Brannon.

The thought should have made me feel relieved, but it didn't.

And that scared me.

Journalism 101

Cover Stories

The second Wednesday in July started out like any other day, except perhaps a bit better. Two publicists called in the morning to confirm interviews with the actresses they represented, I'd already secured commitments from Molly Sims and Kirsten Dunst for the covers of the November and December issues, and I was almost done with the latest silly article Margaret had assigned me: "How to Make Him Fall for You in Less Than a Week."

I was feeling so good, I was barely worrying about the fact that the August issue would be released that day.

After all, it would almost be a relief to have my decidedly unsexual Cole Brannon article hit newsstands so I could be done with him once and for all. Maybe once the article was out, he would stop haunting my thoughts. I was still acutely aware that I hadn't heard from him. I knew he hated me.

The first copies, which would arrive bound in stacks of twenty-five, hadn't arrived by 12:30. I ducked out to lunch without worrying too much about it.

I had already paid for my Styrofoam container of salad and was sitting at an uncomfortably small table—wedged in the back of the Paris Cafe on Broadway and Forty-fifth Street—when Wendy called me on my cell phone.

"You'd better get back here," she said as soon as I picked up. Her tone sounded nervous, and I sensed something ominous behind her words.

"What's wrong?" I asked, wondering if something had happened between her and Jean Michel. I had been afraid it was too good to last.

"Where are you now?" she asked instead of answering my question.

"At the Paris Cafe. Do you need me to come back?"

"Meet me in the courtyard outside our building as soon as you can," she said tersely. "I'll be right down." She hung up before I could say another word. My heart pounding, I quickly threw out the remainder of my salad, grabbed my purse, and pushed my way out of the restaurant onto Broadway. As I waited to cross the street, I could see Wendy standing outside the building, her carrot hair blowing in the wind. In her hands, she held a magazine, which I guessed was the August issue of *Mod*. She was looking around nervously and hadn't spotted me yet.

"Hey," I said, coming up behind Wendy and startling her. She jumped and turned quickly around, her eyes wide. I tried a smile. "What's the big emergency?"

Wendy didn't smile back, which had to have been a first. A strange gnawing began in the pit of my stomach as I took in her nervous posture, her wide eyes, her serious expression. I strained to see the magazine in her hands, sensing that it was central to whatever was wrong, but she held the cover just out of my view.

This couldn't be good.

"Let's sit down," she said finally, taking my arm and leading me to one of the cement planters in front of the building. I obediently sat and waited for Wendy to speak.

"Are you okay?" I finally asked. She looked at me for a moment, and without saying a word, thrust the magazine into my hands, a look of grim resignation on her face.

Sometimes in the movies, when something terrible is about to happen, the characters suddenly see everything in slow motion. A bullet inches toward a person's head, and he's able to watch it come, contemplating his life before it strikes him dead. A train is about to run over a young family in their car, but they're frozen in place, watching the barreling steam engine come toward them so slowly it feels like they could get out and run a mile before it hits. A woman is pushed off a bridge, and as she falls there's time to see the whitecaps, the rolling sea, the fish beneath the surface, before she crashes into the water.

In the first moment that I looked at the cover of the August issue of *Mod,* it felt like time had suddenly slowed for me too. In the mere seconds it took for me to scan the cover, the world seemed to suddenly stop moving. The sudden and intense rushing in my ears blocked out all the sounds I'd normally hear on a summer day: chattering theatergoers streaming into a matinee at the Winter Garden Theater across Broadway, honking traffic inching impatiently and loudly southward. Instead of noise, there was just emptiness.

"Claire? Claire?" I could hear Wendy's concerned voice, but it sounded very far away. My eyes were locked on the cover of *Mod,* which I kept reading and rereading, just to make sure I wasn't seeing things. Each time I squeezed my eyes closed and opened them again, I hoped against hope that the words would have vanished. But they didn't. They were still there, in vivid, unmistakably permanent bright blue ink.

"Claire? Are you okay? Say something!" Wendy finally reached over and gently shook me. I looked up at her in a daze.

"There's been some mistake," I said softly, my voice barely above a whisper. I couldn't think of anything else to say. I couldn't have imagined this.

I looked at the cover once again, taking in the beautiful curves of Cole Brannon's shoulders, the suggestive gleam in his eyes, the arch of his eyebrows, the moistness of his lips, which were parted in just the faintest smile. It was one of the best pictures I'd ever seen of him. For one crazy moment, I was sure that if I just focused on his picture and nothing else, everything would be okay.

Then inevitably, my eyes were drawn back to the glaring blue headline splashed just beneath the level of his shoulders. The right margin was filled with the usual *Mod* fare: "35 Ways to Lose Weight," "20 Sex Tricks to Try This Month," "50 Fashion Finds for Fall." But I barely saw them. Beneath Cole Brannon, who looked perfect and just slightly mischievous beneath the graceful *Mod* logo, a horrible headline screamed out in block letters. I knew it would make the magazine fly off shelves across the country.

HOW TO SLEEP WITH A MOVIE STAR: OUR WRITER'S
ONE-NIGHT STAND WITH COLE BRANNON—A *Mod* exclusive
by Claire Reilly

"Oh my God," I whispered finally. I looked up at Wendy in horror. Her eyes were wide with concern, and her forehead was creased with pity. "How . . . ? What . . . ?"

"I don't know," she said seriously. "Claire, I don't know."

I just stared at her.

I couldn't think. I couldn't move. I couldn't breathe.

"And inside?" I choked on the words. "Is it just as bad?"

Wendy hesitated for a moment, then nodded solemnly.

Numbly, I flipped the magazine open, turned to the table of contents, and quickly found the article. Right in the middle of the page was a huge, blown-up, grainy picture of Cole hugging me good-bye at the doorway to my apartment building. It didn't look familiar, but it had to have been from the morning that Sidra had caught us. It was the only time Cole and I had been together visibly, as he was leaving my apartment. It wasn't a professional shot—clearly, from the slightly out-of-focus blur and nearly imperceptible tilt to the left, it hadn't been taken by a member of the paparazzi. At least their photos came out straight and clear.

Sidra must have come back with a camera after she'd left my apartment that day.

The text was even more damaging than the photo. I began to read, my heart racing.

> For years, men have been the ones to spring one-night stands on unsuspecting women, taking them in their arms and murmuring sweet nothings, making them believe in love at first sight and all the other things that come true in fairy tales.

I realized in horror it was the hastily written lead to the last-minute "10 Reasons to Have a One-Night Stand" article Margaret had assigned just days before the Cole Brannon interview. My breath came in ragged gasps as I read on.

> Because we believe in their promises, we've had our hearts broken and our feelings trampled. But who's to say we can't turn the tables on the men and take control? Ladies, you have the power to go after a one-night stand yourself and to turn the tables by breaking *his* heart.

"Oh no," I murmured as I read on, feeling ill. Suddenly, the one-night-stand article transitioned into the third paragraph of the Cole Brannon cover story I'd written.

> One glance at Cole Brannon, and it was immediately clear how he'd managed to charm his leading ladies on-screen and off. His smile lit up the room, his laugh was kind and genuine, and his handshake firm and gentle.

Then the article deviated horrifyingly into something written by someone else.

I knew I had to have him from the moment I first saw him.

I gasped. The article rapidly switched tracks again, back to the lead of my one-night-stand article. I was amazed at how seamlessly it all seemed to flow together, making it sound like I'd really written about a one-night stand with Cole.

Why have a one-night stand? For one thing, it's a great way to stroke your own ego, especially when the one-night stand is with a guy you've had your eye on.

I recognized the first reason on my hastily assembled top-ten list—which I'd written tongue-in-cheek—cringing at my own words. Now they'd been turned against me, and I was horrified by the next line, the implication of which was obvious.

Like most women in America, I'd had my eye on Cole Brannon for quite a while, making him the perfect person to share a one-night stand with.

I moaned in horror.

It's been rumored that Brannon has been having an affair with his *On Eagle's Wing* costar Kylie Dane, a report he flatly denies.
"I'd never do that," he told *Mod*. "She's a nice woman and I enjoy working with her, but there's nothing between us. I would never, ever, ever get romantically involved with a married woman."

I recognized the quote he'd given me on the street after we left Atelier. The next line, not my own, made me cringe again.

So he sounded single, and with the arch of his eyebrow and the smile he shot me, I began to understand that he was getting at something else. Like he
was available. To me.

"Oh my God!" I moaned to Wendy, who was sitting
quietly at my side with a frozen look on her face. "I
would never have written this! I would never have even
thought it!"
"I know," she said softly. I read on, horrified.

One of the top reasons for a one-night stand:
Because we all know that getting laid feels pretty
damned good.

I blanched, recognizing my tongue-in-cheek reason
number ten from the original article, which Wendy and I
had expected Margaret would primly edit out. No such
luck, apparently.

And who better to get laid by than the hottest star
in Hollywood?

"No!" I wailed to Wendy, finally looking up from the
article. "I can't believe this!"
"I know," she said miserably. "Me neither. It's horrible."
I read on. Altogether, there were four whole pages,
blending my one-night-stand article with the Cole Brannon
feature, tied seamlessly together with damning words I'd
never written. It ended just as badly as it had begun.

As we parted ways in the doorway to my apartment,
I looked at him tenderly and remembered the best
thing about a one-night stand: You might really hit it
off with the guy and begin to develop a relationship.

"No!" I moaned, looking at Wendy. It was the third reason on my original list, the one she'd teased me about.

Time will tell with Cole Brannon. He's the kind of man any woman would fall in love with. I'm sad to say, I'm one of those women. But no matter what happens down the road, I'll always have the memory of our one-night stand.

I closed the magazine as soon as I'd read the last line, handing it immediately back to Wendy. Maybe if I got rid of it, it would be like it had never happened. I couldn't handle having it in front of me anymore. This made the *Tattletale* disaster look like child's play. This was the worst thing I could have imagined.

"What do I do?" I finally whispered to Wendy.

"I don't know," she said, for once at a loss for words.

"It was Sidra, wasn't it?" I asked flatly. I was suddenly beyond furious.

"It had to have been," Wendy agreed. She hesitated and then added, "She's the one who did the editing."

"But I *saw* her edited version," I whispered.

"She must have come back and changed it later that night, after you signed off on it," Wendy said. "This is perfect for her. She gets back at you for supposedly sleeping with a *real* movie star and wins the executive editor position over Maite with her genius editing debut."

"Oh my God," I said softly, looking at Wendy in horror. Of course she was right. I was an idiot for not realizing it on my own. "This is going to increase our circulation, and it's going to look like it was Sidra's editing that did the trick."

Wendy looked at me gravely.

"I have to do something," I said finally. Wendy nodded.

"You could sue, you know," she said softly. I looked at her in surprise. The thought of legal action against *Mod* had never occurred to me. Wendy read the reluctance in my eyes. "You know, this is the kind of thing you're *supposed* to sue for. It wouldn't be a frivolous suit. You almost have to, or it will be like you're agreeing that it all happened and that you wrote this."

"You really think so?"

"Enough is enough," said Wendy firmly. "This is definitely defamation of character, or libel, or slander, or one of those things. I'm sure of it."

I looked at her for a moment. My mind was spinning.

"Okay," I said finally. "I'll do it." I was quiet for another moment as I realized what else I had to do. I stood up and looked sadly at Wendy. "Now I have to go quit."

"Me too," said Wendy. She threw an arm around me. "At least we can be unemployed together."

"You don't have to quit!" I exclaimed.

"But I want to," she replied instantly. "This was a really terrible thing for them to do, and I can't work there anymore knowing they'd treat you like this."

We were silent during the elevator ride up to the forty-sixth floor. I don't know what was going through Wendy's mind. I was trying to keep mine on the task at hand, but it kept drifting dangerously back to Cole, and I realized with a sinking feeling that if he didn't hate me already after the *Tattletale* mess, this *Mod* article would certainly seal the deal.

What was worse, he would never know. He'd probably always think I had set out to hurt him. It looked like I had used him to get ahead. He had trusted me, for whatever reason, and taken care of me in a way that no man had before or since. And look what had happened to him because of it.

"I'll let you go first," Wendy said softly as we stepped off the elevator and through the reception doors. "Good luck," she added as we rounded the corner. She handed the rolled copy of *Mod* to me.

"Thanks," I said under my breath. We turned another

corner and came to Margaret's outer office, where Margaret's assistant Cassie sat smirking at me, a copy of the August issue in her hand.

"Well, this is embarrassing," she said coolly. I ignored her.

"Is Margaret in?" I asked.

"Yes, but she's on the phone," Cassie said, but I was already blowing past her on the way to Margaret's pretentious oak doors. "Hey, wait, you can't go in there like that . . ." Cassie yelled behind me as I yanked Margaret's doors open and stepped inside.

"Claire!" Margaret exclaimed as I slammed the doors behind me, tense with anger. She said something quickly into the phone and hung up. "Well, this is an unexpected surprise," she said. She sounded a bit nervous, and I didn't blame her. "Have a seat," she added, gesturing graciously to the chairs in front of her desk.

"I think I'll stand," I said slowly, clenching my left fist and squeezing the copy of *Mod* hard with my right hand. Margaret looked from the magazine to me. She opened and shut her mouth wordlessly. Silence hung thick and heavy over us while she squirmed.

"Um, good news!" she said brightly, trying to break the uncomfortable stillness that had descended. "That was the president of the company. Circulation is already shooting through the roof. The issue is creating major buzz. We've already gotten calls from CNN, Fox News, the *New York Times,* the *Los Angeles Times*, and Reuters. This is huge. Congratulations, Claire!"

She looked at me hopefully, awaiting a response. It was clear from her expression that she wanted me to be as excited as she was, to spring forward and congratulate her. But as I continued to glare, she started to squirm again. It seemed to dawn on her that I wouldn't be popping any bottles of celebratory bubbly with her today.

"Why?" I asked finally. I'd had it. She looked at me in confusion for a moment.

"Why did circulation go up?" she asked, tittering nervously. "Well, Claire, your article was just wonderful, and it's the talk of the town, and—" I cut her off.

"No," I said slowly. "I'm asking why you did this to me." She looked worried again.

"Why did I do what?" she asked, sounding confused.

"This," I said. I held up the magazine and jabbed my finger at the screaming headline below Cole's picture. "Why did you do this to me?"

"Why, Claire," Margaret said innocently. "I thought you'd be pleased." I simmered in silence for a moment, formulating my next words carefully.

"You thought I'd be *pleased*?" I asked, nearly choking on the last word. "Margaret, this is a *lie*. You've libeled me. You've libeled Cole Brannon. There's no excuse for this."

"What are you talking about?" asked Margaret weakly. Concern appeared to be creeping onto her face. "Sidra told me you'd be a little upset, but she assured me it was true."

"But I didn't sleep with Cole Brannon," I barked.

Margaret laughed. She actually laughed.

"Claire, dear," she said patronizingly. Her artificially light tone wasn't doing enough to mask the nervous expression she still wore on her face. "Is that what this is about? I know you've slept with Cole Brannon. You don't have to lie to me about *that,* dear. There's nothing to be ashamed of."

"I didn't sleep with Cole Brannon," I said, drawing each word slowly out. "I didn't shack up with him. I didn't kiss him. I didn't even bat my damned eyes at him. Do you understand that? I can sue *Mod* for millions. Do you understand that you can't do this to someone?"

The moment I said the word "sue," all the color had drained from Margaret's face. She suddenly looked terrified and uncertain.

"Claire, you can't be serious," she said uneasily. She had started to tremble, and the false British accent had slipped away. "Sidra told me she caught you with Cole

Brannon in your apartment. That you'd slept with him."

"I've told you, time and time again, that I haven't," I said firmly.

"Yes, I know," said Margaret quickly. "But I thought . . . well, I assumed . . . that you were just being modest, or that you were worried about your job. Besides, by the time it came up, because of that *Tattletale* thing, the magazine was already at the printer." She tilted her head and looked at me in nervous confusion. "Are you really telling me you didn't sleep with him?"

She looked genuinely surprised. For a moment, I felt almost sorry for her. She was way out of her league. It hadn't even occurred to her that the article could be a lie. She had known I'd be mortified, but she hadn't cared.

But now that she knew she was in potential legal hot water—very hot water—she looked like a frightened child.

"I'm really telling you I didn't sleep with him," I said softly. She looked shocked and scared. "Which I would have told you again that day if you'd bothered to ask," I added.

"But Sidra said . . ." she protested weakly, looking sick.

"Sidra wants the executive editor position—not to mention the salary bump and the power that go with it—more than anything in the world," I said quietly. "This was how she planned to get it. Look, circulation is through the roof. And it looks like it's because of a story she edited."

"But . . ." Margaret's voice trailed off and she stared at me. "But you wrote this article."

"No," I said firmly. "I wrote a profile of Cole Brannon. Sidra completely rewrote it by combining it with that stupid one-night-stand article you assigned." It was the rudest I'd ever been to Margaret. I had always longed for the day that I could tell her how ridiculous she and her assignments were. I just never thought it would happen like this.

"No, that can't be," Margaret whispered, looking horrified. I stared her down.

"I've got the original—the version that I signed off

on—saved on my computer and printed out in my files," I said icily. "I'll get it for you if you need to see it."

"No," Margaret said finally. Her shoulders slumped in defeat. "I believe you. But why would she do this to you?"

"Sidra has hated me since the day you hired me as a senior editor," I said, giving her the short version. "On top of that, Sidra's sister was sleeping with my boyfriend. Sidra came by to pick up her sister's things one morning, in time to see Cole Brannon in my apartment. He was there because he knew I'd caught my boyfriend cheating on me, and he was making sure I was okay. He's a nice guy. I've never slept with him. I've never even kissed him. Sidra knows that.

"But it gave her the perfect idea for how to get promoted," I continued. "After all, she's been lying about sleeping with George Clooney for years. It wasn't a major leap for her to come up with this and pull all the right strings to make the lie sound real."

I paused, and Margaret stared.

"But why would she do this to *me*?" she asked in a very small voice. I could tell that she believed my explanation about Cole, at long last, and was now scrambling to save her own hide. But it was too little too late. I shrugged and thought about it for a moment.

"She doesn't care about you or anyone else," I said slowly. "She wants to be the executive editor, and she'll do whatever it takes to get there."

"No, that can't be possible," Margaret whispered, looking frightened and pathetic. But I knew from her expression that she didn't believe her own words. It was, in fact, very possible.

"I'm suing the company," I said, ignoring the horrified expression that crossed Margaret's face. I suddenly felt calm. "And I'm going to sue Sidra directly, too." The plan was crystallizing as I said the words. Margaret's flat eyes flickered a bit. "You're going to have to testify against her, because it needs to be clear that this was her doing," I said firmly. "Otherwise, you're going to be the only one who's in trouble for this."

"Yes, yes, of course," Margaret mumbled. I felt very weary.

"I'm going home now," I said finally. I dropped the magazine on her desk. It was over. Just like that. Everything I'd worked for.

"Claire, I don't know what to say," Margaret said hastily, trying to smooth things over. Her eyes shone with pathetic desperation. I knew she was terrified of losing her job, which was probably Sidra's plan all along. "I can make it up to you. I swear. How about a promotion? Managing editor, maybe?"

I shook my head slowly.

"I quit, Margaret," I said slowly. "There's no way in the world I'd work with this magazine again."

I walked calmly through the big oak doors and found Wendy standing there.

"Did you do it?" she whispered. "Did you quit?"

I nodded. Wendy stuck her head inside the office, where Margaret still stood, shell-shocked.

"I quit too!" she singsonged. Margaret just looked at her with eyes that had already glazed over, and Wendy pulled the doors closed behind her. Cassie stared at us with an open mouth.

"Oh, and you?" Wendy addressed Cassie like she was an afterthought. She grinned at me and looked back at the slack-jawed assistant. "When Margaret loses her job, which is a pretty sure thing once Claire files a lawsuit against the magazine, you're going to be out of a job, too. Everyone here knows you're a worthless suck-up. All those times you've deliberately misplaced copy that we've sent to Margaret, all those times you've conveniently forgotten to pass important messages along to assistant editors, all those times you've smirked at editorial assistants and told them it

didn't matter how hard they worked because you'd be promoted before they were . . . Well, don't think any of us will
forget about that. I give you three weeks before you're
crawling back to your daddy."

I laughed as Cassie's eyes widened.

"But it was quite a pleasure working with you, Cassie,"
Wendy added brightly. I laughed again.

"All right, that does it," Wendy said cheerfully, turning
back to me. She patted me on the back. "Let's clear out our
desks and go get a drink."

I smiled at Wendy. I may have lost my boyfriend, my
job, and my reputation, but at least I still had the greatest
friend in the world.

Actual Malice

My whole world had just come crashing down, and I didn't have the faintest idea of how to rebuild it.

I felt numb as I sat alone in the backseat of a taxi headed down Broadway. Wendy had stayed behind in midtown to meet Jean Michel, but after a few drinks, all I wanted was to go home.

I closed my eyes and let the world swim around me as I pressed my forehead against the cool window.

As the cab rolled on, I suddenly knew what I had to do. I had to call Cole Brannon and apologize. For everything. For all the things I'd said and done. I needed to tell him that I hadn't written the article in *Mod*. That I hadn't had anything to do with the article in *Tattletale*. That I'd made a horrible mistake by pretending he didn't mean anything to me. That my sense of professional ethics had been useless and misguided. That I was basically the biggest fool on the planet.

As soon as I walked into the privacy of my apartment, I dialed Cole's cell number with trembling fingers and held the phone up to my ear.

It rang once, then an automated message told me that the number was no longer in service, blaring in my ear.

My eyes filled with tears. I didn't know why he had disconnected his cell number. Had it been because of me? Because he hated me so much after the *Tattletale* and *Mod* stories that he never wanted to hear my voice again? That was ludicrous. But I had no idea how else to reach him.

I sat there for a second and considered what to do. The only connection I had to Cole was through Ivana, his publicist. But the last time I called, I'd caught them in bed together. The thought made me sick, but I knew I didn't have a choice. I *had* to get word to Cole that the *Mod* thing hadn't been my responsibility.

I flipped through the notepad from Cole's interview to find Ivana's cell number, which she had given to Margaret when she set up the interview between me and Cole.

She answered the phone after the first ring.

"Ivana?" I said timidly. There was silence on the other end. "It's Claire Reilly, from *Mod*."

The silence, almost stifling, dragged on.

"Claire Reilly?" she asked finally. Her voice sounded cold and shaken. "I thought I told you never to contact me again."

"I know," I said softly, trying not to react to her words. I had to reach Cole. Even if it meant swallowing my pride. Come to think of it, I didn't have much pride left anymore, did I? "I was calling because—"

She cut me off.

"You bitch," she said flatly. My eyes widened, and I sucked in a deep breath as she continued. "I hope you don't think you can get away with this. Cole Brannon would never sleep with a woman like you."

"I know," I said miserably. Boy, did I know. "I didn't . . ."

"Fuck off," she said coldly. Then she hung up, and I was left staring at the phone.

I slowly set down the handset and sat there numbly for a moment. Okay. That had gone a bit worse than expected. I didn't know what else to do, only that I had to get to Cole.

I rummaged through the box of papers I'd grabbed from my desk at *Mod* until I came across the press release for *Forever Goodbye,* his upcoming movie due out Labor Day Weekend, which had the name and number of the film's press rep at the bottom. Thankfully, it was an L.A. number. It would only be 3:30 there.

I dialed and asked for the publicist, Leeza Smith. I was connected immediately.

"Leeza? This is Claire Reilly, from *Mod* magazine," I said, realizing only after the words were out of my mouth that I actually was no longer from *Mod* magazine. That was a strange thought.

My introduction was greeted by a long silence.

"I saw the magazine today," Leeza finally said, stiffly. "The August issue," she added, as if I hadn't understood that the first time. I cleared my throat.

"Then you'll understand why I need to get in touch with Cole Brannon," I said. I felt stupid the moment the words were out. I opened my mouth to issue a denial, to tell Leeza that I hadn't written the article, that I'd never slept with Cole Brannon or even claimed to, but she was already laughing.

Her peals of laughter were high-pitched and squeaky, and she sounded almost hysterical. I could feel myself turning red as I waited for her to finish. When her laughter finally died down, I started to protest, but she cut me off.

"Are you delusional?" she asked sharply. She laughed again. "Do you really think anyone is going to allow you near Cole Brannon again?" She was still laughing as she hung up.

I fought back tears as I put the handset back in its cradle. I tore the press release into little pieces and angrily shoved them into the trash can next to my desk. It was worse than I thought. I shook my head and forced myself to think. I had to get to Cole. I had to tell him that the *Mod* story wasn't my doing.

"Think, Claire, think," I mumbled to myself. Then it hit me. Jay, the bartender. Cole's friend from college who worked at Metro. He'd know where to find Cole. Better yet, he knew who I was, and he knew what had happened that night at his bar. He had to have realized that I hadn't slept with Cole. I hadn't even been conscious.

I hailed a taxi outside, asking the driver to hurry. Still, it took us twenty-five minutes to fight through traffic to Eighth Avenue and Forty-eighth, where I immediately rushed inside Metro.

It was much more crowded than it had been the last time I'd been there. It was, after all, the middle of the week, and 7:30 meant the end of happy hour crowds. I pushed my way to the bar and quickly looked for Cole's friend. I didn't see him.

"What can I get you?" asked a tall, lanky bartender as I looked desperately around.

"I'm looking for Jay!" I said quickly, trying not to sound too desperate.

"Jay who?"

"Jay." I paused. I knew Cole had mentioned his last name. I racked my brain. "Jay Cash, I think. He's a bartender here."

"Oh," he said. "I don't know. I'm new, hang on." The lanky bartender went and whispered something to a short blonde, who came over once she'd finished pouring a martini.

"You're looking for Jay?" she asked.

"Yes," I said. "Please, do you know where I can find him?" I knew I sounded desperate and probably looked crazy. The girl hesitated before shaking her head.

"I'm sorry, but he quit about a month ago. I don't know where he went."

"Do you know where he lives? Or how to find him? Or anything?"

"'Fraid not." The bartender shrugged. "I think he's opening his own bar or something."

I thanked her and rushed home, where I flipped open the white pages and dialed every Jay Cash in the phone book. None of them was Cole's friend Jay.

So this was it. I had exhausted my options. I had no other way to reach Cole Brannon.

The next day I visited Dean Ryan, a media lawyer, and was encouraged to see his eyes widen when I told him the whole story about the *Mod* article. He said this sounded like an airtight libel case, because Sidra's work met the definition— a false statement of fact about a person that is printed or otherwise broadcast to others—without a shadow of doubt.

"If Mr. Brannon wants to sue, he shouldn't have a problem either," Dean told me as he looked over his notes. "Public figures, such as government officials or, in Mr. Brannon's case, celebrities, have to prove actual malice— that is, that the defendant knew the statement was false, or recklessly disregarded the truth. If he can prove that Ms. DeSimon knew she was lying, which shouldn't be too difficult, then he, too, should have an airtight case against both her and the publishing company.

"Your case will be even easier," Dean said, his eyes gleaming. "In general, private individuals such as yourself must show only that the defendant was negligent in order to prove libel. Ms. DeSimon was not only negligent, but she obviously acted with malice and complete disregard for the truth. There isn't an attorney in the world who could successfully defend against a case like this. If you'll excuse the expression, Ms. Reilly, you've got both Ms. DeSimon and *Mod* magazine by the balls."

Dean looked up at me and smiled, his bleached teeth sparkling in the fluorescence of his office.

"You're going to be a very rich woman," he said.

As I left Dean Ryan's office, I felt a bit better—but not as much as I had expected to. While I felt I was doing *something,* it didn't help me out that much. I didn't care much about the money. I'd already lost my job and my reputation. No amount of cash would bring that back. But I supposed that a successful lawsuit would probably mean the end of Sidra's career too—and that, at least, gave me a bit of satisfaction.

In the next few weeks, I tried to forget Cole Brannon. I really did. It seemed like I would have enough on my mind that there wouldn't be room to worry about him, but of course that wasn't true. The fact that my entire life had seemed to crumble before my eyes did little to assuage the guilt I felt about embarrassing Cole.

Wendy got a job as an assistant chef at a new upscale restaurant called Swank that was opening in the East Village, and I knew she was thrilled.

"I don't miss working in magazines at all," she told me after her first week. "I can't believe I stuck it out there as long as I did."

"I thought you liked the job," I said.

"I did," she said. "But I didn't love it. This, I love."

I had less luck as I hit the job trail, which was starting to worry me. I had enough money to cover August's rent, and having Wendy as a roommate certainly lessened the financial burden, but I wouldn't be able to pay September's rent if I didn't find something soon.

I spent hours each day perusing the job listings on mediabistro.com, scanning the classified ads in the *New York Times,* and calling the major publishers, asking about openings. I sent out several résumés every day and followed up with phone calls.

Everywhere I turned, everyone seemed to know who I was. Did anyone *not* read *Mod*? The answer was always embarrassingly the same.

"We prefer to hire people with better reputations," I would sometimes hear. Or, "The name Claire Reilly might carry a connotation we don't want our magazine to have." And those were the people who bothered to explain. I had a few people hang up when I called and gave my name. A few simply laughed me off the phone. One human resources director actually did return my call—but only to ask for the real lowdown about how Cole Brannon was in bed. I was humiliated.

Then the editor in chief of *Chic,* the newest entry into the crowded women's magazine field, called and asked me to come by her office the next day. I arrived ten minutes early and was shown in thirty minutes late.

"So you're Claire Reilly," announced Maude Beauvais as her assistant shut the door behind me. She was in her late fifties and looked like she should have been wearing a housecoat and slippers rather than the tailored suit (two sizes too small) she was squeezed into. Her hair was bleached an unnatural shade of blond, and her makeup was caked on so thick that I wondered how she could move her face beneath it. She wasn't at all what I'd expected as the figurehead of a trendy new magazine. But she said she might have an opportunity for me, so I was determined to listen with an open mind.

"Nice to meet you, Ms. Beauvais," I said, stepping forward and shaking her hand.

"And you," she said with a nod. She gestured for me to sit down, and she did the same. "Call me Maude." I nodded, waiting for her to begin.

"Because you've had several years of experience covering celebrity events, I thought we'd give you a try here at *Chic,*" Maude said as soon as we were both sitting down. "That is, if you're interested."

"Yes, yes, of course I am," I said. I probably sounded too eager. But I couldn't help it. I was. Impending poverty will do that to you.

"I understand you're having difficulty getting hired elsewhere," she said bluntly.

"Yes, ma'am," I admitted. Great. The whole journalism world knew I was a loser.

"That's why I'm hoping you'll be open to my offer. I don't have the budget to hire another staffer right now, but I need someone experienced who can cover celebrity events.

You know, press conferences here and there, charity events, things like the Grammys and the MTV Movie Awards."

I gulped back my disappointment and nodded.

"I'd like to hire you as a stringer, to do just that," she said. "We'll pay you twenty-five dollars an hour, and I can promise you at least ten hours of work per week. Most weeks, it will be closer to fifteen or twenty hours."

"Okay," I said timidly. I'd never been a stringer. I'd always had a salaried job, and I knew from dealing with the freelancers I'd overseen at *Mod* that the life of a stringer was often difficult and the pay was spotty. But spotty pay was better than no pay. "I'll do it," I said. It wouldn't be work that I loved. I liked to write insightful pieces about public figures, not silly red-carpet fluff.

But a job was a job. And I needed one.

"Fantastic," Maude said. Then she leaned forward. "We need to have a little discussion before we sign anything, though."

"Um, okay."

"I don't know what things were like at *Mod*," she began. "And of course, *Chic* looks at *Mod* as a big sister in the business, a magazine that sets a lot of standards for us. But the thing is, we actually do have our own set of standards here at *Chic*, and those standards don't include sleeping with celebrities."

I reddened. I'd heard the words often enough not to be surprised, but I couldn't help feeling disappointed.

"I didn't sleep with Cole Brannon," I mumbled. "That's why I quit *Mod*. It was something they made up." Maude smiled pityingly at me. I knew she didn't believe me.

"Yes," she said dismissively, waving her hand in the air. "In any case, that won't be acceptable behavior here at *Chic*. I assume you'll understand this."

"Yes, yes of course," I mumbled.

"Fine, then," she said. "I've already alerted human resources that you'll be coming up. They're on the thirtieth floor. Just take the elevator up and ask for Lauren Elkin. She'll walk you through all the paperwork. Give me a call tomorrow morning, and we'll talk about your first assignment."

We shook hands, and I left Maude Beauvais's office feeling shamed. The Cole Brannon story was going to follow me everywhere and haunt me for the rest of my life. I was no longer Claire Reilly, celebrity writer. I was Claire Reilly, the girl who shagged a movie star.

After two weeks at *Chic,* I absolutely hated it. I didn't have a choice, though. I continued to send out my résumé, and I continued to get rejected. Twenty-five dollars an hour from Maude Beauvais was the best I could do.

I was sent out a few nights a week to wait patiently behind the ropes at the opening of a new restaurant, a Broadway play that Anthony Hopkins was supposed to be attending that night, a charity concert for homeless kids in Indonesia at which Angelina Jolie was supposed to make an appearance. Night after night, I shot ridiculous *Chic* questions at B-list stars I hardly recognized. I asked former members of boy bands whether they preferred boxers or briefs. (It was boxers, hands down.) I asked aging actors whom I recognized vaguely from the '80s about the most romantic thing they'd ever done for someone. ("I let my girlfriend lick chocolate off my naked body," was one particularly repulsive answer.) I asked soap actresses what their favorite books were and why. (One even responded, "I read a book once . . ." before her voice trailed off and she wandered away with a dreamy expression on her face.)

I discovered completely useless information, like that Debbie Gibson could hula hoop for hours, or that Chris Kirkpatrick from *NSYNC was terrified of heights, or that Sugar Ray's Mark McGrath loved to juggle, or that Susan Lucci looked like she'd break in half if she was hit by a strong gust of wind.

Not exactly life-changing, earth-shattering, hard-hitting news.

I felt completely debased professionally, but at least I was getting paid. Most weeks, I worked fifteen to twenty hours, so while the paychecks that rolled in weren't excessive, they were enough to scrape by on while I decided what to do with my life.

The whole experience with Cole Brannon and *Mod* had changed everything. I loved to write, but I knew I could no longer work in a world ruled by flaky celebrity gossip as unreliable as the shallow sources who reported it. Sure, I'd always prided myself on my open, honest, ungossipy profiles of people our readers were interested in. But in the end, I was just a part of the same feeding frenzy, the same cult of celebrity worship, that had driven my own life and career into the ground. As my days with *Chic* dragged on from ridiculous celebrity interview to ridiculous celebrity interview, the truth became more and more clear. This wasn't my world. It never had been.

It was a strange feeling to wake up at age twenty-six and realize that the career I'd been working on night and day, using all my time and energy for the last four years, wasn't the one for me. That the career I'd dreamed of since I was a little girl was no more than an illusion. I had somehow talked myself into believing that I was above the whole celebrity gossip scene, even that I helped counteract it by providing a *real* glimpse into the lives of the oft-gossiped-about A-listers whose careers millions of us followed. But it wasn't true. I was just perpetuating the cycle. I felt an immense sense of sadness, loss, and shame. It was like the last four years of my life meant nothing.

And suddenly, I had no idea what I wanted to do with my life. In one fell swoop, the life I had thought I knew— great boyfriend, great job, great sense of self-worth—had vanished. And to make it even worse, it was like the rose-colored glasses I hadn't even known I was wearing had shattered, leaving me to realize that everything I'd believed was never true in the first place. I'd never had the life I thought I had.

I had never felt so alone or so confused.

⁓

On the third Friday in August I was home alone, sitting in front of the TV, stuffing my face with Chunky Monkey ice cream, and trying to figure out how many spoonfuls it would take to add a pound of fat to my already-heavier tummy. Some people lost their appetite when they were stressed out and as a result, shed unwanted pounds. I, on the other hand, found comfort in massive quantities of ice cream and Doritos.

Wendy had tried to set me up on some blind dates, but I just wasn't interested. Who needed a man when I had Ben & Jerry? I was convinced that my relationship with those two was far more fulfilling than any other relationship could be.

Work had to be my focus, despite the frivolity of my job and the fact that I was dreading the breast cancer benefit I had to cover for *Chic* the next night. What a lousy way it would be to spend a Saturday night, standing on the red carpet outside the Puck Building in SoHo, waiting in the August heat for an unimpressive parade of B-listers to show up and respond to my stupid questions. I'd be once again reminded of my station in life when the doors to the theater shut, leaving me on the outside looking in.

Yep, I was pathetic. This was a far cry from the heady days of editing one of the most prestigious entertainment sections in women's magazines.

The eleven o'clock news had just ended and I was in the middle of trying to decide whether to sulk while watching David Letterman or Jay Leno (yes, my life has come to this), when the voice-over for the *Late Show with David Letterman* came on, announcing that Cole Brannon would be one of tonight's guests.

I choked on a particularly chunky bite of Chunky Monkey. I slowly put down the remote and stared at the screen.

I watched, glued to the television, an unfamiliar pain stabbing at my heart, as Cole strode onto the *Late Show* stage twenty-five minutes later. His brown hair was tousled, as usual, and the dark Diesel jeans and tight Rolling Stones shirt he wore clung perfectly to the contours of his body. Women in the audience continued to scream for a long time after he sat down, and he grinned and politely said, "Thank you, thank you."

Why had my throat closed up? This wasn't normal.

"They seem to like you," David Letterman said, smiling at Cole after the last scream had finally died out. Cole laughed, and his face crinkled up in the same way it had for me at Over the Moon months before. I felt sick. What was it about Cole Brannon and instant nausea?

"Well, I like them too," Cole said with a charming smile. The audience erupted in screams and squeals again, and Cole and Letterman laughed.

"So I haven't had you on the show for months. What have you been keeping busy with?" asked Letterman. I held my breath and prayed he wouldn't mention the *Mod* article.

"Just shooting some films, getting ready to promote the movie I have coming out in two weeks," Cole said calmly. Sure. He probably hadn't thought about me once. Why would he?

"*Forever Goodbye*," Letterman added.

"That's the one," Cole said with a dimpled grin.

"So it opens Labor Day Weekend?" Letterman asked.

"Yeah," Cole said. "The New York premiere is next weekend, but it'll be in wide release the following week."

"Great!" Letterman said. "Can you tell us a bit about it?"

As Cole described the plot of the film—a wartime romance in which his character's letters home to his young wife provide a backdrop to tragedy—I watched as his lips moved. The sound of his voice did something to me. His smiles reminded me of the ones he'd given me. His tender sadness as he described the movie's plot reminded me of the gentle way he'd looked at me that Sunday morning in my apartment, when he knew my heart was breaking over Tom. I felt terrible as I thought about how I'd repaid his kindness. With coldness. With forced nonchalance. And with a horrible article in *Mod*.

The show went to commercial break, and I stared at the screen with eyes that had glazed over. I felt like a zombie. It wasn't that I had forgotten about Cole in the previous month, but I'd been so good at forcing myself to ignore all reminders of him. And now here he was, impossible to ignore.

Suddenly, I knew I had to get away from him. I was confused enough about my life already without trying to decipher why I felt so attracted to this man who was off-limits and who obviously detested me—for good reason. I flicked off the TV, stuck the Chunky Monkey back in the freezer (where it would be attacked again shortly), grabbed my purse, and headed out the front door before I could think about where I was going.

I just knew I couldn't stay in the apartment where Cole had once looked at me with those gentle eyes and that kind smile I'd been too stupid to appreciate.

$\sim$

I didn't know where I was going as I walked north on Second Avenue, but I wound up at Over the Moon for the first time since I'd eaten there with Cole. In a strange twist of irony, apparently intended to make me even more miserable, the restaurant now sat in the shadow of a giant *Forever Goodbye* billboard. As I sipped decaf coffee and waited for my eggs, my well-done bacon, and hash browns with cheese, a thirty-foot Cole Brannon looked down on me from high above Second Avenue.

"He's a cutie, isn't he?" asked my waitress. She was a plump, gray-haired woman with deep laugh lines, friendly eyes, and a name tag that read "Marge." She nodded out the window at the billboard as she refilled my coffee.

"Yes, he is." I sighed miserably. It felt like so long ago that we'd sat here together.

"He's a sweet boy, too," Marge said. I looked up sharply. "He comes in here a lot, you know. Can you believe it? To our restaurant?"

"He does?" My breath caught in my throat.

"Sure," she said. "Especially in the last few months. Although I haven't seen him in about three weeks now."

"He comes here?" I asked, my voice high as I still tried to process it. The waitress smiled gently, apparently convinced that she'd come across his biggest fan.

If only she knew.

"He sure does," she said, leaning forward conspiratorially. I noticed she had a Boston accent, an endearing removal of the letter *r* from the ends of her words. "Whenever he's in New York. And he always asks for me. Every time." She looked at me proudly. I just stared.

"Does he . . . say anything . . . about, um . . ." I stammered, not sure what I was hoping for. The waitress winked at me.

"I wish I could tell you he seems available, honey, but he's been pining away over some girl who lives in the neighborhood."

My eyebrows shot up and I suddenly felt breathless.

"What?" I croaked.

"Some girl who lives just down the street," Marge continued, oblivious to my reaction. "Now, can you believe that? The biggest star in Hollywood pining away over some girl who lives in the East Village." She shook her head and smiled.

"Where did he meet her?" I squeaked. Marge shrugged.

"Some magazine thing, I think," she said. I gulped. She couldn't mean me. It was impossible.

"But what about Kylie Dane?" I asked quickly. "I thought he was dating her. I mean, I read it somewhere." I cleared my throat. I didn't want to sound too eager. But the waitress seemed more than happy to gossip. I was her only customer at this late hour, and she was probably trying for a bigger tip. Believe me, I'd give her one.

"He was so frustrated about that," she said. She gestured to the empty seat across from me. "Do you mind?"

I shook my head mutely and she sat down, setting the pot of coffee on the table.

"He never dated that Kylie Dane woman," Marge said, wrinkling her nose. "He thought they were friends, until he realized her publicist was selling paparazzi shots of the two of them together, telling the press they were an item. And it was all that Kylie Dane's idea! Can you imagine?"

"Are you sure?" I asked.

"Of course I'm sure," Marge said proudly, puffing out her chest. "He says I remind him of his mother. He talks to me all the time. The same thing happened with his publicist, you know. People kept shooting pictures of them together, and the rumors got started."

"Really?" I squeaked. "But he really is dating his publicist, isn't he?" I cleared my throat and backtracked a bit. "I mean, that's what I've read. In the newspaper."

"You really know a lot about Cole Brannon, don't you?" Marge looked amused. She smiled at me. "Big fan, huh?" I paused, then nodded. Maybe she'd continue if she thought I was just a crazy Cole Brannon aficionado. "Nah, he was never dating her. It bothered him, you know. That publicist of his is a strange bird, if you ask me. She was in here once and kept stroking his arm, and he looked so uncomfortable. She didn't even want him to talk to me."

"Really?" I said again, because I didn't know what else to say. But I wanted her to go on.

"The next time he was in, I told him he should fire her," the waitress continued. "She gave me the creeps. But he said something about her being the sister of someone he'd known in college. He felt loyal to her for some reason. He's too damned nice for his own good, you know. But she seemed crazy, and I know crazy when I see it, honey."

"Sounds like it," I murmured. My heart was pounding. Could Marge be right? Could Cole have been telling the truth about Kylie and Ivana after all?

"The worst thing is, the same thing happened with that magazine girl in the Village too," Marge continued. I blanched, and my heart sank. "He really liked her. He thought she was different. But she wrote some article in her magazine about sleeping with him. And he never slept with her. He's a real gentleman, you know."

"Maybe it was a misunderstanding," I said so quietly, it was barely audible. I could feel the blood rushing to my cheeks in a furious blush. Marge laughed, and I blinked back my embarrassment.

"Yeah, that's real likely," she said with a snort. "Anyhow, he was real upset after that. I haven't seen him since. Poor boy. He thought he'd finally found someone who he really connected with. Someone who didn't want to use him. He should have known better, I guess." I felt the blood drain from my face. I looked at her miserably.

"Thanks," I said finally.

"Always happy to gossip, sweetheart," she said with a wink. "I'll go see if your food's up. And hey, cheer up, honey. Whatever's bothering you can't be that bad."

"You'd be surprised," I murmured as she walked cheerfully away.

I sat at Over the Moon through two shift changes, drinking coffee and looking out the window at a Cole Brannon I could never have.

I thought about my life and what I was doing with it. I thought about Tom and thanked God he was gone. I thought about my job and considered switching career tracks altogether. I wondered for a long time how I'd managed to screw things up so badly.

But most of all, I thought about Cole—which wasn't hard to do as he silently kept watch over the city, right outside the window.

The Red Carpet

I was exhausted. I stood along the ropes of the red carpet outside the Puck Building Saturday evening after a sleepless night, thrusting my tape recorder toward a seemingly endless parade of the same faces I saw every week at these events. Tonight's was a black-tie benefit to raise funds for breast cancer research, and I'd dutifully pinned my pink ribbon on the collar of my white blouse. My legs were sweating in my gray boot-cut pants, and I was contemplating taking off my ridiculously uncomfortable heels to stand barefoot on the sidewalk. The only thing that stopped me was a huge wad of recently chewed gum about six inches from my left foot. Who knew what else lined the streets of New York?

As was the case with most minor events, the breast cancer benefit had attracted only a few members of the media. Several paparazzi photographers with big flashbulbs lined the carpet—they were ubiquitous in New York—but there were only three reporters other than me. One was from the *New York Post*—they covered everything that might potentially involve even a minor celebrity. Another was from *Stuff* magazine, as there was a rumor Brittany Murphy might show up, and she was, well, hot stuff. The third was Victoria Lim, my old friend from *Cosmo*, who had spent the first half hour apologizing profusely for not having called. She'd been busy with a freelance project she was doing for *Vanity Fair,* and work at *Cosmo* had her swamped.

She was sympathetic about the Cole Brannon story in *Mod* and assured me that she didn't believe it. She had avoided the question when I asked her if it was a source of gossip at *Cosmo*. Then she quickly changed the subject to tell me about a fashion show she'd been to the week before, where the models had actually paraded down the runway in trash bags and stilettos.

"I thought that whole grunge look went out in, like, 1995," she said.

"Is that even grunge?" I asked skeptically.

"I don't know," she admitted. "What else do you call models in trash bags? Seemed pretty grungy to me."

The breast cancer benefit dinner was being organized by Maddox-Wylin, a small book publisher, so I didn't expect much of a celebrity turnout for the $1,000-a-head meal, catered by the four-star Luigi Vernace restaurant. But Susan Lucci was there. Katie Holmes had a table. Breast cancer survivor Kate Jackson (one of Charlie's original Angels) came with a friend, followed by Olivia Newton-John moments later.

As the celebrities made their way gracefully down the red carpet, I held out my tape recorder and asked *Chic* questions that made me feel silly. They all answered them politely and moved on. I was starting to feel better, knowing that Maude Beauvais would be pleased with tonight's unexpected treasure trove of celeb quotes.

And then I saw him, getting out of a limousine.

It was Cole Brannon.

He was coming toward me on the red carpet, and for a moment I thought I was hallucinating.

But he wasn't a mirage.

There he was, larger than life, striding from his limousine toward the theater. Flashbulbs went off all around us, and there was an excited buzz to the media crowd. He was the biggest star to arrive that night.

I was suddenly breathless and moderately woozy,

which I couldn't entirely attribute to the sleepless night and lack of energy I'd suffered from in the last twenty-four hours. I suddenly understood the expression "He took my breath away."

He was stunning in a tuxedo, his broad shoulders filling it out perfectly. He smiled for the cameras and made his way down the red carpet. The reporter from *Stuff* asked him a few soft questions and giggled at his answers. The girl from the *Post* asked him something and he shook his head, then said something softly to her, flashing her his gorgeous smile. A photographer shouted at him, asking why he was at the benefit. He answered in a low voice that his mother was a breast cancer survivor.

Then he turned and saw me.

I froze as our eyes met, and he seemed to freeze, too. I hadn't expected this. I wasn't prepared for it. A sudden stillness fell over the media crowd as Cole and I stood staring at each other for what felt like a small eternity. My face was on fire, and I could hear the whispers around me as photographers and reporters reminded each other that I was the girl who'd slept with Cole Brannon and written about it for *Mod* magazine.

Finally I spoke, breaking the silence between us. My heart beat so quickly, I feared it would jump out of my chest.

"Hi," I said softly.

"Hi," he said uncertainly, a guarded look on his face as he continued to stare at me. I took a deep breath and tried to slow my pounding heart.

"Cole, I am so sorry about the article in *Mod*," I said, my words tumbling out quickly, almost on top of each other. I knew my face was bright red, and I could feel myself shaking. Cole was silent. He just looked at me. I couldn't read his expression. "I swear to you, Cole, I had no idea. I didn't write that article. One of the other editors there wrote it, I swear to you."

Still looking at me, he was frozen in place, and he hadn't said a word. I wanted him to say something, to tell me he believed me, to tell me he forgave me, but he didn't. I took a deep breath and glanced around. Flashbulbs were going off all around us, but suddenly I didn't care. Photos of us would probably land on tomorrow's nighttime entertainment shows—and in Tuesday's *Tattletale*—and rumors would crop up that something was going on between us again. But I ignored all of that. I needed him to know that I would never have hurt him intentionally. This was my one chance.

"You have to believe me, Cole," I pleaded, probably sounding as desperate and pathetic as I felt. "I had nothing to do with the *Tattletale* thing either. I swear to God. I am so sorry that all of this happened." I looked at him desperately, miserably hoping he'd say something. He was silent for another moment.

"I knew the *Tattletale* thing wasn't you," he said finally. "Usually their stories aren't true."

I sighed with relief, then realized he hadn't said anything about the *Mod* article. He looked cold and distant, and I longed to reach across the rope and hug him, like we'd hugged that day that felt like years ago. But I knew I couldn't. It was like a huge valley had opened up between us, and I didn't have what it took to cross it.

"I tried to call you," I said slowly. He looked surprised.

"You did? When?" It occurred to me, just for a moment, that it had to be a good sign he was still standing there.

"After the *Tattletale* thing," I said desperately. "And after the *Mod* article came out. I tried your cell, but it had been disconnected. I tried the studio publicist, I tried finding your friend Jay, the bartender. I even tried calling Ivana." He studied me for a moment. I knew I was being judged. My knees felt weak.

"She never told me," he said softly, looking at me curiously. My heart was pounding. He looked like he was going to say something. My palms were sweaty, and I suddenly felt very hot and a bit dizzy. I blinked a few times and was again aware of the crowd around us, watching our every move and straining to hear our words. Cole leaned in closer, his breath whispering past my ear and sending a tingle through my whole body.

"Ivana told me I wasn't the first actor you'd done this kind of thing with," he said gently. "She told me you had a reputation for things like this. I didn't know what to think." He pulled away, looking at me with sad eyes. I gasped.

"What?" I sputtered. "Cole, I swear to you that's not true. I've never done anything like that, I swear. This whole story has ruined my life. You have to believe me."

He looked at me skeptically.

"Cole," I said desperately. "I quit *Mod* the moment the story came out. I swear to you I had nothing to do with it."

"You quit?" he asked, looking genuinely surprised. For the first time since he'd seen me, his face had started to relax a bit. But before I could answer, Ivana was at his elbow. I hadn't even seen her coming. Her long, dark hair was tied back in a slick, glamorous ponytail, and she was dressed in a tight red gown. A huge diamond sparkled around her neck.

"It's time to go now, Cole," she said, coldly taking his elbow and steering him away from me. "You stay away from him," she hissed under her breath at me. She was shooting daggers at me with her eyes, which were icy and dangerous. Cole gave me one last confused look over his shoulder and allowed himself to be led away.

I had a sick feeling as I watched him go that it would be the last I would see of him. His appearance at the benefit had caught me off guard, and I hadn't said all the things I'd wanted to say. I hadn't been able to convince him that I was telling the truth. He hadn't believed me.

"You okay?" asked Victoria gently, snapping me back

to reality. She squeezed my elbow lightly, and I looked up to see a dozen pairs of eyes staring at me. The reporter from the *Post* was furiously scribbling something in her notebook. I willed myself not to cry in front of the cameras.

"I'm fine," I lied. I took a deep, ragged breath. Then I realized something. "I can't do this anymore," I said softly. It suddenly seemed so clear. Had I been living in a fog for the last few years?

"Do what?" asked Victoria.

"This," I said gesturing around me. "This whole stupid celebrity thing. It's not real."

None of it was what it seemed. None of it was real. And none of it mattered. Who cared who Nicholas Cage was sleeping with, who Nicole Kidman had been spotted with, or where Ben Affleck had been seen out on the town? Why did it matter? What was I doing here, in the middle of this useless circus?

"What am I doing?" I murmured aloud to myself.

Just then, Chris Noth, whom I adored as Mr. Big on *Sex and the City* and as Mike Logan on *Law & Order* before that, stepped from a limousine that had pulled to the curb. The cameras swung toward him, and even Victoria turned away to try catching the latest star to arrive. For a moment I looked at him, debonair and polished in a slick gray suit, smiling that crooked smile that had always seemed so seductive. Suddenly, I didn't care anymore. The feeding frenzy he'd created with his mere arrival seemed so ridiculous, even though I'd been one of those hungry feeders for the past five years.

There was nothing here for me anymore.

Without regret, I turned and walked away.

⟿

Wendy was working the late shift that night, so the apartment was dark when I got home. I poured myself a glass of pinot grigio and changed into sweatpants, a Bulldogs T-shirt, and my ridiculous-looking-but-comfortable Cookie Monster slippers. I sat down on the couch with my laptop, rewound the cancer benefit interview tape, and put on a pair of headphones.

An hour and a half and two glasses of wine later, I had finished transcribing all the celebrity quotes. I e-mailed them to Lauren Elkin, who edited *Chic*'s celeb section, and to Megan Combs, who handled celebrity fashion for *Chic*. I knew they'd both be able to use a lot of the quotes.

For the next hour, I worked on composing a carefully worded e-mail to Maude Beauvais, thanking her for her kindness in giving me a job as a stringer, but telling her that I could no longer work for her. When I hit Send a few minutes past midnight, I felt like a weight had been lifted from my shoulders. I didn't know what I was going to do for work, but I promised myself it would be something self-respecting where my existence didn't depend on gossip, celebrity, and the whims of publicists.

I turned the computer off, kicked off my slippers, put my feet up on the couch, and turned on the TV. I flipped aimlessly through the channels until I found *The Blind Man,* starring Cole Brannon, just starting on TNT. Thanks to my sleeplessness the night before, I drifted off before the second commercial break.

I dreamed of Cole Brannon.

⌒

I woke up to a series of knocks on our front door the next morning. I groaned and opened one eye, squinting at the clock on the wall. It was only 7:30. In the morning. On a Sunday. I rolled back over on my stomach, pulled the blanket over my head, and hoped that whoever it was would go away.

But the knocking continued.

"Wendy!" I mumbled halfheartedly. But I was already awake. There was no use in waking her up too.

The knocking had turned to an insistent pounding by the time I dragged my protesting body off the couch.

"Hang on!" I yelled at whoever was on the other side of the door. "It's seven-thirty on a Sunday morning, for God's sake!"

I slipped into my Cookie Monster slippers and shuffled hostilely toward the door. Whoever it was had some nerve beating down our door at the crack of dawn. Didn't they know there was a depressed, unemployed woman here who needed her beauty sleep?

Mumbling under my breath, I shuffled across the kitchen, not bothering to stop and fix my hair or straighten my T-shirt. Whoever was at the door would be greeted by Nightmare Claire, complete with morning breath. It wouldn't be a pretty sight.

I unlatched the several locks, swung open the door, and blinked into the hallway as my eyes adjusted to the light. Then I gasped.

It was Cole Brannon.

I froze. I couldn't move. I just stared for a moment, my jaw hanging slack, my hand frozen to the doorknob.

"Oh my God," I mumbled finally. I reached a horrified hand up to my head and realized the worst was true. I was sporting the worst bedhead known to mankind. My shirt was wrinkled and falling off one shoulder, and I was wearing Cookie Monster slippers. I probably had a string of drool dried across my face too. I reached up to touch the corner of my mouth, and sure enough, I did. I groaned.

"Good morning," said Cole softly. He wasn't smiling. He was wearing old jeans and a wrinkled T-shirt, and his blue eyes were bloodshot. He looked shaken.

"Oh my God," I said again. Could this be any worse? I looked like I'd been run over by a train—or at least by a bunch of head-hunting Muppets who had left their conquests behind on my feet. I reached up again and smoothed my hair down as well as I could, but I knew it hadn't helped much.

I took a deep breath in, then exhaled deeply. I needed to get ahold of myself.

"Would you like to come in?" I asked. I cast a furtive glance over my shoulder, trying to make sure that the apartment wasn't too messy and that I hadn't unconsciously scribbled "I love Cole Brannon," or something equally mortifying.

The coast appeared to be clear.

"Um, no," Cole said, surprising me. He took a breath. "I just need to know if you meant what you said last night." He hesitated. "About not having anything to do with that *Mod* article."

I exhaled and closed my eyes for a moment. When I opened them again, Cole was looking at me nervously. I looked him right in the eye.

"I swear to God, Cole," I said. "I'd swear on the *Bible* if I had one in front of me. I swear on . . ." I looked around quickly for something to swear on. "I swear on Cookie Monster," I said, pointing to my slippers, cringing the moment I'd said it. I sounded like an idiot.

Cole looked at me for a moment, and I could feel a blush creeping up my cheeks. Why did I always seem to say and do the stupidest things around him? There was a moment of silence. Then he surprised me by laughing.

"It's a pretty serious thing to swear on Cookie Monster," he said gravely.

"I know," I said, trying to match his serious expression with one of my own. "That's how you know I mean it."

Cole looked at me for a moment and sighed. We were still in the doorway, and I felt awkward and strange. I knew he was trying to decide whether or not to believe me, and there was nothing I could do but stand there and wait for his judgment.

"Look," said Cole finally. "You know Ivana, my publicist?"

I nodded reluctantly, biting my tongue before I could tell Cole exactly what I thought of Ivana. It wouldn't be pretty.

Cole took a deep breath and looked at me nervously.

"I want to believe you, Claire, I really do," he said seriously. "But Ivana is friends with one of your coworkers. A woman named Sandra or Sidra or something, I think." I gasped. "The thing is, this woman told Ivana that you told your whole office you'd slept with me. That was after the *Tattletale* thing, and I didn't really believe it at the time. Then when I saw the article in *Mod*, Claire, I thought maybe it was true."

I sighed. I could feel my eyes filling with tears at the unfairness of it all.

"Sidra is the woman who came to the door," I explained softly. I could hardly believe she'd taken her baseless vendetta against me this far.

"The door?" Cole asked, looking confused.

"The morning you were here, and we'd just found the purse," I explained softly. "The woman whose sister was sleeping with Tom."

Realization dawned on his face slowly.

"Oh," said Cole softly. He looked stunned. I nodded.

"She's the one who rewrote the article for *Mod*," I said. Cole just stared at me. I pressed on. "She's up for the position of executive editor, and she was assigned to edit my piece on you. It never even occurred to me that she would do something like this. But this is how she planned to get promoted. And she hated me, because I was more successful at twenty-six than she was by thirty-six. She couldn't stand it."

Cole continued to stare at me, a mixture of doubt and horror on his face.

"I've already filed a lawsuit against Sidra," I said, surprising myself by delivering my monologue so calmly. "And I've tried to call you, Cole. But Ivana called me names and hung up on me."

"She did?" Cole asked, looking genuinely startled. "You told her you weren't responsible for the *Mod* article?"

"Or the *Tattletale* one." I paused. "She told me to . . ."

I paused and took a breath. "She told me to *fuck off* and hung up."

Cole looked embarrassed. I was quiet for a moment. I took a deep breath. I had to tell him how I felt. I had to come clean.

"Cole, I just need you to know that I didn't do this. I'm so sorry that all of it has happened, and I'm sorry for any embarrassment it's caused you. And I'm so sorry that I blew you off like I did. You were so kind to me, and I didn't appreciate it at the time. Then I believed all the stuff in *Tattletale* about you sleeping with all of those women, and then I thought you'd lied about Kylie Dane. Then this happened. . . ."

My voice trailed off. I didn't know where my rambling was going. I had tears in my eyes again, and Cole looked pained.

"But I didn't," Cole said sadly. "I didn't lie to you, Claire."

"I know," I said. I took another deep breath. "I know that. But then I called you to apologize for the *Tattletale* thing, and Ivana answered early in the morning and said you were in the shower, and that the two of you were sleeping together—but then the waitress at the Over the Moon told me that wasn't true, but I didn't know what to believe, and it was too late anyhow."

I paused for a breath. Cole was just staring at me. I plunged back into my monologue.

"You were so nice, and I didn't know what to think," I rambled, quickly, feeling a blush heating my face. "I mean, you're Cole Brannon. And I'm, like, nothing. I'm just this plain, boring girl who worked for a magazine you probably hate. And if anything had happened between me and you, it would be so unprofessional, and I've never done anything unprofessional in my whole life—and I never wanted anyone to think that I slept with the people I interviewed or anything, because I've worked so hard to get where I am—and I never did it by doing anything inappropriate."

He continued to stare at me in impassive silence.

I sucked in a deep breath and continued. The words were pouring out of my mouth like they had a life of their own.

"I liked you so much, but I knew nothing could ever happen, because that would be crazy—because, I mean, someone like you could never like someone like me, but I couldn't help myself from having these totally inappropriate feelings for you—even though I knew it was impossible. And I know it's just silly to think you'd ever be able to feel anything for me when you have women like Kylie Dane and Ivana Donatelli around you all the time. I knew you just felt sorry for me, and that's why you sent flowers, and that's why you came by—and it made me feel even worse to know that not only could you never possibly fall for me, but you realized exactly how pathetic I was."

He stared at me for another moment, and suddenly, the silence felt oppressive. I didn't know what was going on in his mind, but his face betrayed a storm of emotions.

"You're not pathetic," he said finally, looking troubled. "I never thought you were. You're not plain, and you're not boring. I thought you were really something special. Something different." His voice trailed off, and he looked confused. I felt tears well up in my eyes.

"I'm just really sorry," I finally whispered.

"I have to go," he mumbled suddenly. Before I could say another word, he had turned away and was hurrying down the stairs, his eyes downcast. I watched him until he disappeared, listening in the hallway until I heard the front door of the building open and slam closed. I knew he was gone.

I slid down the doorframe and started to cry.

Celebrity Sightings

The next six days passed without another word from Cole. I stayed home a lot, pathetic as that was, just in case he decided to come back. I felt like a preteen waiting by the phone, convinced that her big crush was going to call. But my big crush, or whatever he was, never called and never dropped by. By Saturday, I was sure he wouldn't again. I'd done everything I could to convince him. I'd finally had the chance to tell him everything I wanted to tell him, and he'd made his decision. He had decided to stay away. I wouldn't forget the look of disappointment on his face as he backed away from me into the hallway.

I'd decided midweek that if I couldn't get Cole to forgive me, the least I could do was set the other aspects of my life right. So I'd applied for a job as an associate features editor at *Woman's Day,* where Jen, a friend of mine from college, worked. There, I'd be about as far away from celebrity writing as possible, and it actually sounded good to me to edit and write about "15 Ways to Spring-Clean" and "20 Family Vacations You Can Take on a Budget." There was nothing demoralizing about that. Maybe I'd even be *helping* people. I'd been called in for an interview the following Monday, and I was elated.

I dropped by my attorney's office on Wednesday to check on the progress of my lawsuit, and Dean Ryan sounded hopeful. He had looked over the case and had come up with a dollar figure that he thought I could reasonably sue *Mod* for.

It was over a million dollars.

But that wouldn't bring Cole Brannon back to my door. It was too late for that.

On Saturday morning, Wendy had gotten up early and disappeared before I woke up, leaving a note saying she'd be gone all day. She had comforted me all week, telling me she was sure that the Cole Brannon thing would somehow work out, but I suspected she was probably drained from playing counselor and needed some time away. I felt sorry for burdening her.

I went shopping for the first time in months and splurged on a new pair of Seven jeans and two new Amy Tangerine tees I'd had my eye on. After all, if Dean Ryan was right, I'd be a millionaire soon. However, even the shopping spree and the dollar signs dancing in front of my eyes did nothing to cheer me up. I grabbed a soft pretzel from a street vendor on the way home.

I was watching *Pretty Woman* on DVD, alone—in sweatpants, on the sofa, with a Healthy Choice frozen dinner on my lap—when there was a knock at the door. It was 6:45. I froze for a moment, hoping against illogical hope that it was finally Cole Brannon.

But that was ridiculous. Tonight was the New York premiere of *Forever Goodbye,* his new movie, and of course Cole would be there. If I hadn't quit *Chic* last week, I would have been there too, standing along the ropes of the red carpet—because a star like Cole would draw an A-list crowd eager to be photographed and interviewed. I could have returned to *Chic* with pages of celebrity quotes in reply to their silly questions. But instead of having a chance to see Cole Brannon again, I was snuggled up on my sofa in sweatpants and a Braves T-shirt, feeling pathetic.

Nonetheless, the knock at the door made me hope against hope that maybe Cole Brannon had swung by on his way to the Loews Lincoln Square Theater to tell me he believed me after all.

Yes, I was bordering on delusional. But who else would be at my door? None of my friends just dropped by unannounced.

There was another knock. I could feel the color rise to my cheeks, and suddenly, I was having trouble breathing. I looked in the mirror, smoothed my flyaway hair, and thanked myself for putting on makeup that morning. But when I opened the front door with a pounding heart, half expecting to see Cole's tall frame filling the doorway, I was once again disappointed. More than you can imagine.

Instead of Cole, it was Tom. Talk about a letdown.

"Hi, Claire," he said quietly. His clothes were rumpled, and he looked like he badly needed a haircut. He looked pathetic and beaten, but I wasn't moved by his appearance.

"What are you doing here?" I snapped.

"Estella and I broke up," he announced.

"I thought you'd broken up months ago, like you told me that day at Friday's," I said. I'd known for a long time that he'd been lying about that, but I pushed him anyhow. He reddened.

"Um, no," he said.

"So, you lied," I said.

"Yeah," he admitted. He nervously tugged at the bottom of his T-shirt. "Can I come in?"

"No," I said, moving to block the doorway as he looked hopefully inside. "I don't think you can. Why don't you just tell me what you want. You'd better not be asking me for money, because, so help me God, Tom—I'll kill you."

Tom looked scared for a minute. I felt a rush of satisfaction.

"Um, no," he stammered. "Actually, no, I wasn't going to ask you for money. I, uh, remember what happened last time."

I had a mental image of Tom standing in the middle of Friday's, drenched in twenty ounces of ice-cold soda. It was a good memory.

"Well, what then?" I demanded. I was quickly losing my patience.

"Look, Claire, I wanted you to know that I'm sorry about everything. I was a real jerk."

"No kidding."

"No, really, let me finish." Tom took a deep breath and drew himself up to his full height, which wasn't that impressive. As I looked at him, I wondered vaguely how I'd ever found him attractive. His nose was too big, his eyes were too small, his hair was stringy, and his teeth were crooked. I could no longer imagine what I'd ever seen in him. "I know I treated you really badly, and you didn't deserve that at all. I just want to make it up to you."

I stared at him in disbelief for a moment and finally shook my head.

"Are you kidding me?" I asked, incredulous. "How are *you* going to make any of this up to *me*?"

He played nervously with the hem of his shirt again for a moment, tugging at a thread that had come loose. Then he looked at me again.

"I heard you were going to sue Sidra," he said. "Apparently your lawyer sent her a summons to appear in court."

"So?" I said petulantly.

"So I thought that if I offered to testify, it might help."

I gazed at him coolly for a moment.

"What could you possibly have to say that would help me?" I asked finally. He seemed to consider the question for a moment.

"I overheard Sidra and Estella talking about how to ruin your career," Tom said finally. I raised an eyebrow. Part of me wanted to reach out and wring his neck for doing nothing to prevent my downfall, but I was too interested in what he had to say.

"Go on," I said. Tom sighed and looked at his feet.

"Estella was pissed that I was so upset about your

walking in on us. She thought I was still in love with you or something."

"Were you?"

Tom's hesitation was all the answer I needed.

"Um, yes?" he said finally.

"Don't bullshit me," I snapped. Tom sighed again.

"Anyhow, she knew her sister worked with you, and after Sidra saw you with Cole Brannon that morning, she suggested to Sidra that she spread a rumor that you'd slept together. Just to other people at work, you know, to make you so embarrassed that you would quit."

I frowned. This wasn't news to me.

"And the *Tattletale* thing?" I asked. "Was that her too?"

Tom nodded.

"Why?" I demanded.

"That was just because she was jealous of you," Tom said with a knowing smile. "I don't think she really dated George Clooney, you know."

"Yeah, no kidding," I said dryly. "And how is it that you know all of this?"

"She can't keep her damned mouth shut," he said sourly. "She was always over at Estella's, bragging about what she did."

He paused.

"So would that information help you?" he asked finally, arching an eyebrow at me.

"I believe it would," I said, remaining expressionless. I knew him well enough to know what would come next. "So you're just going to get up there and testify or give a deposition or whatever, just out of the goodness of your heart?"

"Yeah," Tom said, smiling at me. He hesitated for a moment, then leaned in closer. "Well, I mean, it would certainly help if you could give me a little bit of money to help me out right now. Estella threw me out, and I could kind of use a little bit of cash, just for the short term."

"No," I said instantly, without even thinking about it. Tom looked angry.

"I don't have to testify, you know," he said, looking surprised. Evidently he'd expected I'd shower him with cash once I heard what he had to say.

"Actually," I said brightly, "you do have to testify."

"No, I don't."

"Um, yes, actually you do," I said slowly. "See, it's called a subpoena. It will be delivered to you by my lawyer, and it's going to say that you have to testify or get thrown in jail."

Tom blanched. I smiled.

"Now see, the problem with getting thrown in jail is that you appear to have no money. And I'm not coming to bail you out. But look on the bright side," I continued innocently. "Of course, it would be great inspiration for your next novel. You *are* writing a book, right?"

Tom coughed.

"You'd really subpoena me?" he asked.

"I sure would," I said, smiling at him. "You got me into this, now you're going to help get me out of it."

Tom stood on the doorstep and glared at me for a moment.

"Fine," he muttered finally. "See you around." He turned and walked away, and I smiled as I watched him go.

Moments later, I was feeling better than I had in a while, curling back up on the couch with my Healthy Choice dinner and the remote control. I'd rented *Pretty Woman* and *Ghost,* and pathetic as it was, I was looking forward to a night alone with two of my favorite flicks.

I tried not to think about how miserably I had screwed things up with Cole. I knew that one day I'd get over it. For the first time I could remember, everything else in my life had finally fallen into place.

I knew that Tom's information would help my case

against Sidra, because it would actually be solid testimony from a witness. She'd never work in magazines again.

As for Tom, he was clearly just as scummy and shameless as ever—but in a way, that was comforting. It reinforced the reasons why I was no longer with him, and it made me feel like the world had some order to it.

I had just gotten up to throw out the plastic TV dinner tray and pop some popcorn when there was another knock at the door. Damn it. What did Tom want *now*?

"What is it?" I yelled toward the door as I turned away from the microwave. "Haven't you done enough?"

I padded to the door in my beloved Cookie Monster slippers, my hands balled in fists at my side. Couldn't he just leave me alone? He'd taken a year of my life from me. He didn't deserve another millisecond of my time. As I pulled the door open angrily, my eyes flashing, I was fully prepared to tell Tom off once and for all.

But the man at the door wasn't Tom.

It was Cole Brannon.

In my doorway.

Larger than life, in a gray Armani suit and a black tie.

I almost fell over.

"Hey," he said simply. I just stood there and stared. I had completely given up hope that I'd ever hear from him again.

I opened and closed my mouth, but my voice didn't seem to be working. Actually, nothing seemed to be working. I knew I should step aside and let him in, but I couldn't quite move. I didn't know what to say.

"You okay?" he finally asked, looking at me with concern. I nodded slowly.

His presence filled the doorway and the whole hallway. I noticed dully that he was holding a dozen red roses in his hand. The pieces of this puzzle weren't falling together.

"Here," he said as he watched my eyes dart back and forth between the roses and his perfect face. "These are for you."

Silently, I took the roses from him, staring blankly back and forth between the flowers and Cole. I felt numb.

"Thank you," I said finally. I was tongue-tied and frozen on the spot, vaguely aware that I was processing everything slowly.

"You're welcome," he said politely, as if this wasn't the strangest exchange in the world. There was a moment of awkward silence as I wondered what I was supposed to say.

"Um, can I come in?" Cole finally asked.

"Oh," I said dully. "Yes." I moved aside to let him past me, painfully aware of my dusty apartment and my disheveled appearance.

I shut the door behind him and then just stood there. I couldn't seem to think of what to say or do. I didn't know what he wanted.

Cole took a deep breath and turned to me. He looked like he was about to say something important. I waited, my heart beating faster.

"Aren't you going to put those in water?" he asked finally, gesturing to the roses.

"Oh," I said, caught off guard. I'd expected some sort of important revelation or something, not a handy household reminder about what to do with flowers. "Yes. Hang on." I bent down and rummaged around under my sink, pushing past plastic bottles of Mr. Clean, Windex, and Fantastik until I found a vase. I pulled the vase out and filled it with water, putting the roses gently inside. I turned around. "Um, thank you."

"You're welcome," said Cole again. He paused and looked at me closely. He took a deep breath. "I, um . . ." His voice trailed off and he looked nervous. He was still standing in the entryway, near the kitchen, but I couldn't quite bring myself to move and offer Cole a seat inside. I was too baffled. "I came by on Wednesday, and you weren't here."

My mind raced for a moment. Wednesday? Where had I been Wednesday? That was the day I'd gone to see my lawyer. But Wendy had promised she'd stay in while I was gone, just in case Cole Brannon came by. Had she gone out for a few minutes?

I made a mental note to strangle her later.

"You did?" I asked finally.

"Yeah," he said. "Your friend Wendy—well, your roommate Wendy, I guess—was here. She told me you'd gone to see your lawyer."

"Wait," I said, sure I'd heard him wrong. "You talked to Wendy?" He nodded. How could she not have told me? I'd spent the week thinking that Cole Brannon hated me, and I'd spent hours moaning about it to Wendy. "She never told me," I said, slightly dazed.

"I know," said Cole. I looked at him with confusion. "I asked her not to."

"Oh," I said stupidly, completely lost.

"She told me that you quit *Chic* and don't want to do celebrity reporting anymore," he said. I nodded wordlessly, wondering if this was going anywhere other than pointing out my current state of unemployment.

"So I figured that if you're not working with celebrities anymore, we wouldn't be violating any of your professional standards if I, um"—Cole paused for a moment and looked at me shyly—"if I asked you on a date tonight."

I just stared. I must have heard him wrong.

"What?" I asked. I hadn't meant to be quite that abrupt. I was just having trouble getting my tongue to cooperate with my brain to form more than one syllable at a time.

"To my movie premiere," Cole added, looking vaguely uneasy. "Would you come with me?"

I fought the urge to look around for hidden cameras. Maybe CBS was debuting yet another reality show in the fall, *Who Wants to Trick a Pathetic, Unemployed Journalist.* Yippee, I'd be the star.

"What?" I said again, simply because I couldn't think

of anything else to say. I snuck a look around for the secret cameras.

"I was hoping you'd be my date," Cole repeated, looking a bit nervous. Clearly this wasn't going as well as he'd hoped.

I blurted out the first words I could think of. "But I don't have a nice dress."

Cole laughed and a bit of the concern fell from his face.

"Well, I got you one, if that's okay," he said. I stared at him. He paused for a moment and went on. "I mean, no pressure or anything, but I do have a dress if you want to go," he said quickly. "But only if you want to. I know I was kind of a jerk to walk away like I did on Sunday morning, so if you don't want to go, that's okay."

"No," I said slowly. "You weren't a jerk. I just thought you hated me."

Cole looked wounded.

"No," he said. "I've never felt like that about you. I just didn't know how to react after that whole *Mod* thing and after the things Ivana had said. . . ." His voice trailed off. "I, um, I fired her. I should have believed you from the beginning."

"Really?" I asked.

"Really," Cole confirmed. He took a deep breath and smiled at me. "Now are you going to go out with me? Or am I going to have to grovel and beg?"

I stared and then finally smiled.

"I'd love to go," I said softly.

"Good," Cole said. "I'm not very good at the groveling and begging. But I can work on it." He flashed me a wide smile, stood up, and took his cell phone out of his pocket. I stared up at him. This was like some kind of a dream.

Wait, maybe it *was* a dream. I *had* been dreaming of him an awful lot. Just in case, I pinched myself. "Ow!" I said. Cole looked startled.

"What?" he asked, sounding alarmed.

"Nothing," I said slowly. This was real. This was really *real*. I felt like I might faint.

Cole flipped his phone open and started scrolling through his digital phone book.

"Hi there. Can you bring the dress up now?" he said into his cell. He listened for a moment, then grinned. "Yeah, she said yes." He smiled at me and listened for another moment. "I know. It *did* take her a long time. See you in a second, okay?" Then he hung up.

"Who was that?" I asked.

"Your dress," he said with a grin. "It will be arriving shortly."

I looked at him, puzzled.

"Who was that on the phone?" I asked.

"You'll see," he said mysteriously.

I was startled a moment later to hear a key turn in the lock. Cole winked at me and walked to the door to help open it. I stood up just in time to see Wendy's freckled face and wild hair emerge through the doorway, nearly hidden behind an immense mound of gold silk.

I barely saw her. My eyes were glued to the dress, which was one of the most beautiful things I'd ever seen.

As Cole held it up, the silky fabric reflected the light, making it appear to glow with a life of its own in the middle of my fluorescent kitchen. It was sleeveless and elegant, and the neckline plunged low, but not too low, in the shape of an upside-down teardrop. The top was fitted and slender, and the bottom of the dress billowed out gently while a few thin layers of tulle underneath gave it shape. It was a deep color of gold that I knew immediately would look perfect on me.

"It's beautiful," I breathed, nearly hypnotized by the glowing dress, knowing that my words didn't come close to doing it justice.

"I know," said Wendy, beaming. She was still breathing quickly, trying to regain her composure after carrying the dress up the stairs. I finally focused on her in disbelief. "I picked it out," she said. Cole laughed.

"*We* picked it out," he corrected. Wendy rolled her eyes.

"Yeah, yeah, okay," she said. She winked at me. "Actually, Cole picked it out. I just okayed it."

"Unbelievable," I said, still in awe.

"We'll have to do it again sometime," said Cole. He smiled at Wendy, who laughed. Then he turned to me. "Well? Aren't you going to try it on?"

He gently handed me the dress, and in a daze, I let Wendy lead me into my bedroom.

"I can't wait to see it on you!" she squealed.

A hurried five minutes later, Wendy finished buttoning the back of my dress and turned me around to face the mirror.

"Oh my God," I breathed.

"You're gorgeous," she said. The dress fit every curve of my body perfectly, hugging my waist to make it look suddenly slender, cinching perfectly across my chest to lift my bosom, plunging perfectly at the neckline to give the illusion of more cleavage than I really had. My skin, faintly tan thanks to the weekends Wendy and I had spent at the beach, looked dark and smooth against the rich gold color.

"It's perfect," I murmured.

"Oh, I almost forgot," Wendy said, bending to rummage through her bag. She emerged triumphantly a moment later with two gold strappy sandals that matched the dress exactly. She handed them to me with a grin.

"I picked these out for you," she said. "Cole loved 'em."

"They're Manolo Blahniks," I said softly, looking back and forth between the shoes and Wendy's face.

"I know," she said with a grin. "If Sidra DeSimon could only see you now. And those are yours to keep."

"Oh my God," I said. I was in a daze as I bent to put the stilettos on my feet. For a moment I wished my pedicure was more up to date. But it didn't seem to matter much in the grand scheme of things.

"You are one hot mama," said Wendy cheerfully as I straightened back up. I looked in the mirror. The shoes completed the outfit perfectly. "That movie star in our living room won't be able to take his eyes off you." She winked at me, and I grinned back at her reflection in the mirror.

Twenty minutes later, Wendy had expertly applied my makeup and put my hair up, leaving a few curly tendrils tumbling down to frame my face. She led me to the door and gave me a quick hug before she opened it.

"You deserve this, sweetie," she said into my ear as she opened the door.

"You look amazing," Cole said, his eyes wide, as Wendy and I came out of the bedroom. He stood up from the sofa. "I don't even know what to say."

"Thank you," I said, smiling back at him. It was finally dawning on me that this was all happening, that I wasn't hallucinating or imagining things. Cole was very real as he crossed the room and put his arms gently on my elbows, admiring me at arm's length.

"You are so beautiful," he said, staring at me like he was seeing me for the first time. I blushed.

He stood there for a moment, just looking at me, and my heart pounded in anticipation. Then he leaned down and kissed me gently on the lips. I moaned softly without meaning to as my lips parted and his tongue gently searched my mouth for the first time. I forgot for a moment that Wendy was standing there, and I put one hand on Cole's back and the other on the back of his head as he folded me tightly into his arms. I felt the softness of his hair and the stiffness of his jacket with my hands, and I felt like I was drowning in him. In a moment, he pulled away, leaving me wanting more. Slowly, I opened my eyes.

This was better than all those dreams I'd had about Cole Brannon.

And it was real.

"I've been wanting to do that for a while," he said, his voice husky as his blue eyes bore into mine.

"Me too," I agreed.

The Velvet Ropes

The premiere seemed to go by in a blur. The moment our limo pulled up in front of the Loews Lincoln Square Theater, flashbulbs began exploding around us in a seemingly endless galaxy of light. I blinked and tried to adjust my eyes to the constant pop-pop of the cameras.

"Are you okay?" Cole asked, squeezing my hand, as we stepped out of the car. I thought about it for a second.

"Yes," I said finally. "Yes, I am." And I was. The flashbulbs were nearly blinding me, and for a moment, it occurred to me to be worried about being caught with Cole. After all, photos of us together would be everywhere tomorrow morning. But for once, I didn't care what the pictures looked like or what the tabloids and gossip columns would say. I wasn't doing anything wrong, nothing that should have embarrassed me. I was just a girl out on a date with a guy.

It seemed almost superfluous that the guy happened to be the center of the Hollywood universe.

It was almost surreal to be on the *other* side of the red carpet—across the ominous velvet ropes from the snapping flashbulbs, the jutting tape recorders, and the jabbering reporters as they elbowed each other out of the way, following each star's progress down the carpet with wide eyes and eager looks on their faces. It had never occurred to me what we must have looked like from the celebrities' perspective.

But now that I was in their shoes—Manolos, to be exact—I suddenly understood how annoying we, the media, must seem. I suddenly felt like a caged animal in a zoo with a throng of overeager, impolite children fighting to get my attention, to distract me or freak me out in some way.

"Weird, isn't it?" Cole murmured in my ear. "You never quite get used to it."

"Wow." It was all I could think of to say.

"It's okay," Cole said softly. "Just be yourself. It gets easier."

So I stopped and smiled for the cameras while Cole squeezed my hand tightly. I blushed when he leaned over to give me a quick peck on the lips, clearly not caring that it had been captured on a dozen rolls of film.

I glowed when he stopped to tell a reporter from the *New York Times* that yes, my name was Claire Reilly, and yes, this was an actual date. I smiled when he told a reporter from *Tattletale* that their magazine was trash and they'd been wrong about us months ago, but could print whatever they wanted today. I flat out laughed (demurely, of course) when he told a reporter from the *Los Angeles Times* that they might want to have their legal reporter call him if they wanted an interesting story about *Mod* magazine and a certain fashion director.

Then I saw her, and I couldn't stop myself from laughing. It was Sidra DeSimon.

She was standing along the ropes of the red carpet, flanked by Sally and Samantha, trying to get a better view of the stars walking toward the theater. She was dressed in a black gown and chunky silver jewelry, her hair piled on top of her head. She had a notepad in her hand and was evidently reporting for *Mod*—which was quite strange, as I'd never actually seen Sidra on a reporting assignment, of all things. Stranger yet was the fact that she was the only reporter on the line dressed like a wannabe star. She looked like she thought she was going to the premiere herself, or at the very least, like she was hoping she'd be plucked from the crowd by an actor who had somehow neglected to bring a date. Fat chance.

When she saw me, it was almost cartoonish the way her face fell and her eyes widened in shock. Cole was holding my hand tightly, and I couldn't erase the grin from my face. Even when I saw Sidra. She would never ruin an evening for me again.

"What are *you* doing here?" she hissed at me as Cole stopped to talk to a reporter from *Entertainment Weekly.*

"Oh, I'm on a date," I said breezily, loving every second of it.

"With . . ." Her voice trailed off and she looked like she was about to choke. "With Cole Brannon?" Her voice rose an octave as she squeaked out his name.

"Well, yes," I said, calmly raising an eyebrow at her. "Does that surprise you?"

"I just thought . . . I thought . . ." she stammered. "You and Cole Brannon aren't *dating!*"

I smiled at her.

"But, Sidra," I said innocently. "Wasn't it you who told *Tattletale* I was sleeping with him? And then printed it in *Mod?*"

"But we both know it wasn't true," she sputtered. "You never slept with Cole Brannon. You know I made that up."

"Really?" I asked calmly. I turned to the reporter from *Entertainment Weekly,* who had stopped chatting with Cole and was now listening intently to our conversation. "Is that still on, by any chance?" I asked him calmly, gesturing to his mini recorder, which was pointed our way.

"It sure is," he said, grinning at me. "And I just heard every word of that. Want a copy?" I smiled and nodded. Cole quickly scribbled my address and phone number down for the reporter, promising him a phone interview this week. Sidra's face had suddenly turned as red as the carpet.

"But, I didn't mean . . ." Sidra stammered. "I mean, I think you know that—"

I cut her off. Cole was now back at my side, his arm protectively around my waist, pulling me gently toward him. I could feel his body stiffen as he looked at Sidra.

"It was so lovely to see you, Sidra," I said calmly. I winked at Sally and Samantha, who glowered back at me. "But I really must run. I have a premiere to attend."

"But . . ." Sidra sputtered.

"Oh, don't worry," I said cheerfully. "I'll be in touch. Through my lawyer. Oh, and give my regards to George next time you see him. Wait, where is he tonight?"

"He's busy," Sidra muttered, her voice barely audible.

"What a shame," I said. Cole pulled me closer, his arm still protectively around me. I knew that Sidra couldn't hurt me anymore. Ever again. "Have a lovely evening," I said to all three Triplets, who were looking back at me with matching expressions of hatred and awe.

Then Cole and I turned away, without looking back. Once we'd walked through the doors, Cole turned to me.

"You okay?"

"I'm better than okay." I grinned.

"I have the feeling that woman is going to regret the day she crossed you," Cole said, pulling me closer.

"You know, I think so too," I said with a smile.

The movie was wonderful. The war scenes were breathtakingly vivid, the script was beautifully written, and the acting was heart-wrenchingly on target. The movie was an early favorite for the Oscars, and after seeing it, I could see why.

But even better than the movie itself was the way Cole slipped his arm gently around my shoulder midway through the second scene, and the way he squeezed me comfortingly, pulling me closer to him each time there was a sad moment in the film. I loved how he looked at me for my reaction after each major moment. I could hardly believe it when he reached over almost unconsciously and softly kissed the top of my head during a romantic scene.

After the premiere, we went back to my place. Wendy had conveniently disappeared to spend the night at Jean Michel's, and she appeared to have cleaned the apartment for the first time in history. I couldn't have asked for a better friend.

Cole and I opened a bottle of chianti and sat on the couch, talking and laughing for hours, away from the paparazzi, away from the prying eyes of curious onlookers. By the end of the evening, I'd forgotten that I was supposed to be intimidated by him, that I was supposed to feel out of my element being on a date with a movie star.

When the bottle was empty and I was full of liquid courage, I asked Cole if he wanted to stay.

He said yes.

We moved into my bedroom, where the ghost of Tom no longer haunted me. We spent what felt like an eternity exploring each other's bodies. Beneath the tux, beneath the movie star image, beneath all the layers of professionalism that had existed between us, he was the gentlest man I'd ever known.

That night, in the privacy of my own bedroom, far away from the prying eyes of the paparazzi, Sidra DeSimon, and *Mod* magazine, I fulfilled the tabloid prophecy.

I finally *did* sleep with a movie star.

When I woke up the next morning, sunlight streaming in the windows, Cole was already awake, watching me. He smiled and kissed my eyelids, then the tip of my nose, then my mouth. We made love again, slowly, languidly, and I knew I'd never let him walk out the door again.

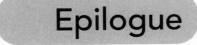

Epilogue

Nine Months Later

I stepped out of my attorney's office with a very nice check in my hand and some very good news dancing through my head. Sidra had just been fired from *Mod*. The *New York Post* would be running the story the next day—she had been ordered by the court to pay me $100,000 in punitive damages, which I figured would put quite a dent in her designer clothing budget.

The victory against Sidra made me feel the most triumphant, but as I clutched the check in my hand, I couldn't help but feel pretty good about my victory over *Mod* too. My attorney had already taken his percentage of the award, but he'd left me with a sizable check. I already knew what I was going to do with it. I opened the envelope and snuck another look at the mind-blowing figure.

$2,400,000.

$2.4 million. It was my portion of the settlement that *Mod* magazine had offered to avoid being dragged through court.

Margaret had, of course, been fired, too. It made me feel a bit bad, because I knew she had believed Sidra's lies and hadn't intentionally libeled me. But now the former managing editor Maite Taveras was running the magazine, and it had finally undergone the jump in circulation that Margaret had obsessively pursued for years.

The day Maite got her promotion, she'd called to offer

me my job back, but I politely declined. I loved writing for
Woman's Day, where there was no catty competition, no
backstabbing, and no gossip. The staff worked nine to five
and went home at the end of the day with smiles on their
faces. I could never go back to *Mod,* regardless of who was
running the show.

I was humming as I turned into the HSBC Bank branch
in Union Square to complete a transaction I'd set in motion
a month ago, when my attorney had called to tell me the
amount of the settlement. My first thought had been, *What
am I going to do with $2.4 million?* I couldn't imagine
spending all that money over the course of a lifetime. But I
knew someone who would benefit from a percentage of it,
and there was no one who deserved it more.

By the time I emerged from the bank an hour later, I had
deposited the check into my account and used a portion of
it to complete a real estate transaction. My real estate agent
Elizabeth met me at the title agency next door. Together, we
reviewed the documents and put a 50 percent down pay-
ment on The Space, a restaurant in the East Village whose
owner was retiring. Wendy had commented more than once
how it was the perfect location for the little French bistro
that she'd always dreamed of owning. Now her dream
would come true. She'd been the only one to stand by me
throughout the tabloid nightmares of the previous summer,
and this was the best way I knew to pay her back.

I would give it to her as a wedding present when she
married Jean Michel next month in a small ceremony at Les
Sans Culottes.

After I left the bank I walked through Union Square,
breathing in the sweet aroma of banana bread and carrot
cake from one of the stalls set up in the farmers' market.
Apple cider simmered at the next stall over—tempting, even
in the early May heat.

I stopped into the Starbucks on the east side of the
square for a Mocha Frappuccino. While I waited in line, I

flipped absently through the *New York Post* and fantasized about Wendy getting a stellar restaurant review in the paper. The words "Next please" from behind the counter snapped me back to the present, and I lowered the paper to look at the guy in the green hat and apron behind the Starbucks counter.

But instead of ordering my Mocha Frappuccino, I started to laugh. Hysterically. The guy behind the counter turned beet red.

"What can I get you?" he asked stiffly.

"Oh my God," I managed to choke out. People around me were looking at me like I was crazy, but I didn't care.

The guy behind the counter was Tom.

"It's not that funny," he said angrily, his face on fire.

"Actually, it is," I said between giggles. "So I'm guessing the novel didn't quite work out?"

"No," Tom mumbled. He looked terrible. He'd put on at least twenty pounds, and most of it had settled in a potbelly that poked out beneath the apron. His hair was so long that it skimmed his shoulders in stringy waves, and his skin was pale and washed out.

"*Was* there even a novel, Tom?" I asked. He paused for a moment and looked down at his feet.

"No," he mumbled, almost inaudibly. I laughed again and realized how far I'd come in the year since I'd been with him. I could hardly imagine that he'd ever been a part of my life.

"I'll have a tall Mocha Frappuccino, please," I said finally.

"Fine," he said glumly. He turned away to put the order in, then turned back to me. "That'll be three dollars and sixteen cents."

I silently handed him a five-dollar bill, stifling another giggle. As he handed me back a dollar and change, he suddenly froze. Instead of giving me my change, he grabbed my left hand and turned it over.

"You're wearing an engagement ring," he said slowly, an odd expression in his eyes. I smiled.

"Yes," I said. "Yes, I am." He turned my hand over to get a closer look. The two-carat stone, princess cut and flawless, set in Tiffany platinum, sparkled alluringly on my ring finger.

"Who is he?" he asked glumly. I turned my hand back over and took my change.

"No one you know," I said brightly with a smile on my face. "Nice to see you again." Then, leaving him staring at me with an open mouth, I made my way to the end of the counter where I picked up my Frappuccino. I left Starbucks without looking back.

As I walked down Broadway a few minutes later, slurping the last few sips of my drink and still giggling to myself about Tom, my cell phone jangled in my purse. I dug for it and pulled it out. I checked the Caller ID, smiled, then flipped it open.

"Hey, sweetie," I said as I answered the phone.

"Hey, honey," said Cole. "Did you get the check?"

"Yep," I said brightly.

"And did you buy the restaurant?" he asked.

"Yeah," I said. "Wendy is going to be so surprised."

Cole laughed, and I marveled for a moment at how the sound of his voice always made me feel warm and tingly inside. Since the night of his premiere, he'd been spending as much time as possible in New York, and he was no longer staying at the hotel where I'd woken up, mortified, nearly a year ago. On his New York visits now, he squeezed into my double bed with me, and I always woke up with his strong arms wrapped protectively around me. He'd flown me out to L.A. on the few weekends he was stuck on movie sets, and in December, I'd taken him home to Atlanta to meet my mother and sister. We had spent Christmas in Boston with his mother, father, his two sisters, and his nephew. I loved them all instantly, and I'd left feeling like I was already a member of the family.

Cole had proposed to me just three weeks ago on bended knee at Over the Moon. His favorite waitress, Marge—who I supposed was somewhat responsible for salvaging the chance of a relationship between us—delivered the ring, which I found baked into a slice of strawberry cheesecake, my favorite dessert. We had celebrated quietly that night over champagne at my apartment with Wendy, Jean Michel, and Cole's bartender friend, Jay. We even invited Marge, who showed up with a giant takeout box full of crispy bacon, eggs, and hash browns with cheese . . . the meal that had started it all between me and Cole.

No one had leaked the engagement to the media yet, although there was a tabloid rumor that I had been spotted wearing an engagement ring. I felt like Jennifer Garner to Cole's Ben Affleck, which was absolutely ludicrous. Who would have thought that the media would one day be interested in what I was wearing on my left hand?

"I have a surprise for you too," said Cole mysteriously as I cradled the phone on my ear and sipped my Frappuccino. "Go pick up a *Tattletale* and turn to page fifteen, okay?"

I groaned.

"*Tattletale?*" I said. "You know I don't read that trash."

"No, trust me, you'll like this," he said, still sounding cryptic. "It's kind of an engagement present from a friend of mine. Call me back once you've seen it."

"If you insist," I agreed with a shrug.

I ducked into the next convenience store I came across and paid a dollar for the last copy of *Tattletale* on the rack. I took it outside with me and flipped to page 15.

As soon as I got there, the hysterics that had started moments ago at Starbucks returned. Once again, I looked like a lunatic to passersby, laughing so hard that tears were falling from the corners of my eyes.

Cole's "friend" was George Clooney, and he had taken out a full-page ad in *Tattletale*. In it, he'd included a terrible picture of Sidra DeSimon, who appeared to be snarling at the camera. Underneath it, in block letters, were the words:

I DID NOT DATE THIS WOMAN.
EVER.
THIS AD WAS PAID FOR BY GEORGE CLOONEY.

I was still laughing hysterically when I called Cole back.

"That is the funniest thing I've ever seen!" I choked out through giggles.

"I know," said Cole, who was laughing too. "When I ran into him last week and told him about our engagement, I told him all about what had happened with Sidra, and he said it was the last straw. He was sick of her using his name to get attention. He swears up and down he's never even met her."

"This is too funny!" I gasped through my laughter.

"Okay, gorgeous, I have to run," Cole said softly as his laughter finally subsided. "I'll be in by nine, okay?"

"I can't wait to see you," I said softly.

"Dinner at Swank, then?"

"Yes," I said. "I'll call Wendy and make sure we have a reservation. Have a safe flight, okay?"

"You bet," Cole said. He paused for a moment. "Oh, and are those reporters still following you, honey?"

"Yes." I laughed. "Every day." You had to admit, it was funny. When I was working as a celebrity editor, I never dreamed that one day I'd have a throng of tabloid journalists camping out on *my* front doorstep, demanding to know whether the diamond ring on my finger meant that Cole Brannon was finally off the market.

"You should tell them," Cole said after a pause. "I want them to know. I want the world to know."

"Me too," I said softly.

"I can't believe we're getting married," Cole said. "I don't think I've ever been happier."

"Me neither."

"Claire?" Cole said after a pause. "I love you. I really do."

"I know," I said. "I love you too." We said our good-byes, and I snapped the phone shut.

As I walked the rest of the way home, the sun shone down on the city, bathing the streets with soft light. Around me, taxis whizzed by, stores overflowed with customers, and people brushed by me up and down the street, hurrying to their destinations. I walked along slowly with a smile on my face, knowing it no longer mattered what any of them thought of me. My life had become more perfect than I could have imagined.

As I turned the corner from Third Street onto Second Avenue, the crowd of paparazzi (who had been clustered on my doorstep since rumors of the diamond ring on my left hand had leaked out) fumbled with their cameras. There were several cries of "It's her! It's her!" Flashbulbs exploded around me in a blinding array, and I was suddenly at the center of the media storm that had been following me for weeks.

"Claire, is it true you're engaged to Cole Brannon?" shouted one reporter as I made my way to the front door of my building.

"Did he really propose, Claire?" yelled another as I pushed through the throng.

I paused for a moment, like I always did, still somewhat taken aback by the attention. Then I did something I'd never done before.

I stood there and smiled. With a tabloid clutched in one hand and my handbag dangling from the other, I stood and faced the press that had first haunted me almost a year before. And for the first time in my life, I didn't care what any of them thought or what their publications printed about me.

"Yes," I said finally. The throng immediately hushed into silence. "Cole Brannon and I are getting married. He proposed three weeks ago."

There was a moment of silence, and then the questions came in an avalanche of noise and the flashbulbs clicked away like a swarm of psychotic fireflies. I soaked it all in for a moment, realizing how liberating it was to simply tell the truth. To simply be me. To have nothing to hide, nothing to be ashamed of.

I gestured for quiet, and the throng immediately hushed again.

"We love each other very much," I said, knowing I was no longer afraid of what they thought of me, what they printed about me. I knew who I was, and I had everything I'd ever needed. "And I've never been happier in my life."

As the bulbs exploded again in what looked like a fireworks display just for me, I smiled at the cameras and knew that everything in my world was finally the way it was supposed to be.

About the Author

I used to think I'd be a famous rock star. I had big plans. My stage name would be Mystica, I'd start a pop rock group called the Popsicles, and fans across the world would know my hit song "Why Did You Leave Me?" Of course I was eight years old, practicing for my big gigs on a Star Stage and a Fisher-Price tape recorder, and my "hit song" was a three-chord little number I'd written on the piano. Then it dawned on me: I can't sing. I mean, I really, really can't sing. As in, I scare people away. So as you may guess, singing stardom was not in the cards for me.

But from the ashes of my Mystica dream (which is revived from time to time in drunken karaoke sessions that everyone regrets) came the beginnings of a writing career that I would fall in love with. Now I contribute regularly to a variety of magazines, including *People,* which has been an incredible experience. I've interviewed Holocaust survivors, civil rights activists, people who have shaped the history of the 20th and 21st centuries, and, of course, the people you would expect me to talk to for *People* magazine: movie stars, rock stars, and celebrities from all walks of life.

I'll admit to developing little harmless crushes on some of the people I've interviewed: Matthew McConaughey, Joshua Jackson, Mark McGrath, and Jerry O'Connell, among others. But unlike the title of the book suggests, I've never slept with any of them! I swear! Not even close. But

How to Sleep with a Movie Star sprang from the thought of "What if?" What if I crossed the line and threw professionalism out the window (something I'd never do)? Or worse, what if someone *thought* I had acted inappropriately with someone I'd interviewed and started a rumor saying that I had slept with a source for a story? My career would be over! In this book, Claire Reilly, a twenty-six-year-old magazine editor a lot like me, has to face just that type of issue.

In addition to *People,* I contribute regularly to *Glamour* and *Health* and am "The Lit Chick" on the nationally syndicated morning show *The Daily Buzz.* Check out my Web site at www.KristinHarmel.com, and please write in and say hello! If I don't write back right away, I'm probably out shoe-shopping!

The amount of money the movie *Titanic* has made in the United States: more than $600 million.

The gross national income of the entire country of Liberia each year: $460 million.

The circulation of *The National Enquirer*: 1.46 million.

The circulation of *The New York Review of Books*: 125,000.

Cost of a beach tote from Old Navy: $16.50.

Cost of a beach tote from celeb fave Prada: $825.00.

Dinner for two at Atelier at the Ritz-Carlton Central Park: $170.

Dinner for two at TGI Friday's: $30.

The amount of money the President of the United States is paid each year: $400,000.

The amount of money Ben Affleck was paid to star in the box office flop *Gigli*: $12,500,000.